Dead Star

The Triple Stars, Volume 1

SIMON KEWIN

Dead Star - The Triple Stars, Volume 1

Copyright © Simon Kewin 2020

STORM
CROW
BOOKS

ISBN: 978-1-9993395-5-5

CONTENTS

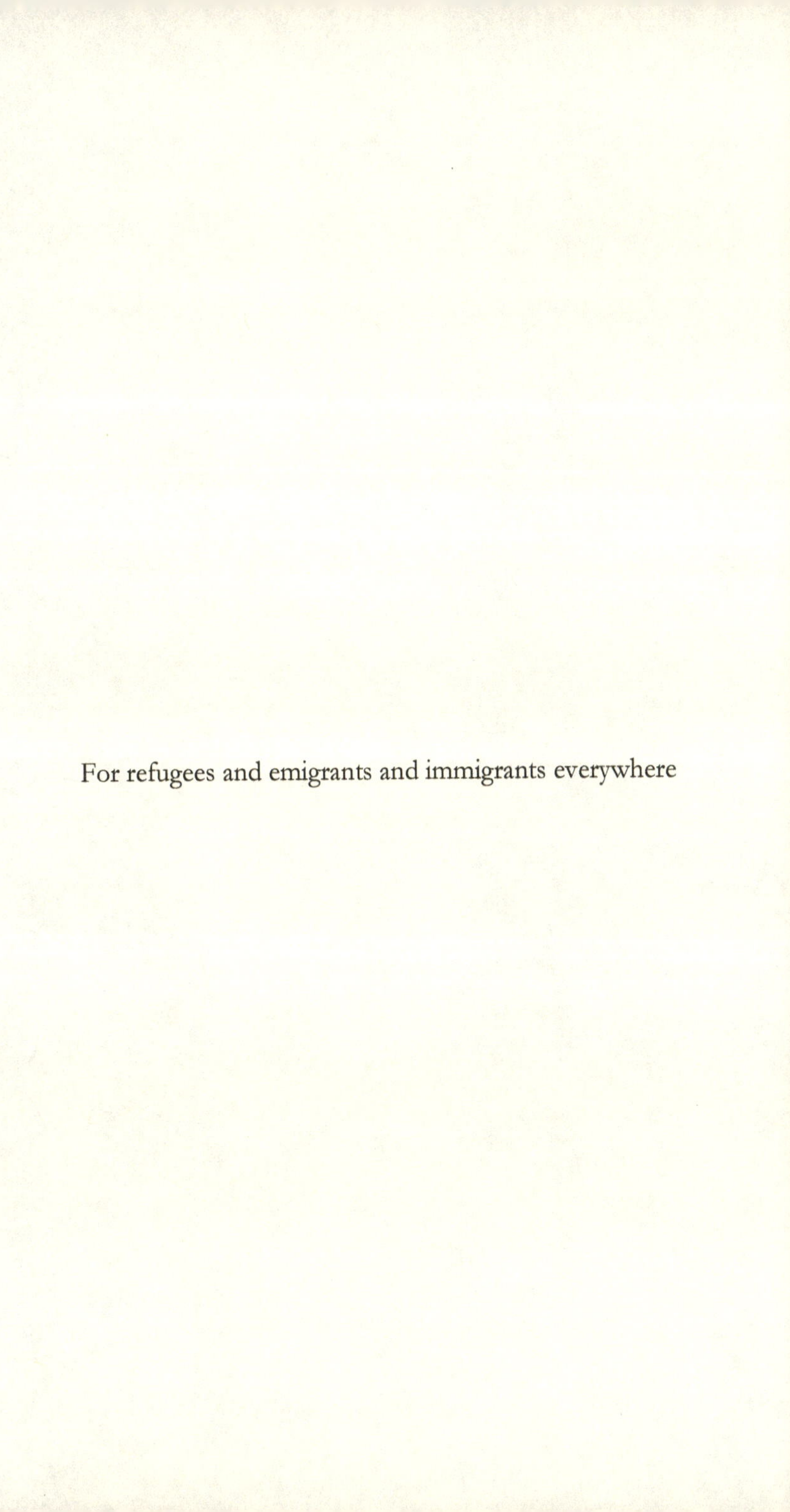
For refugees and emigrants and immigrants everywhere

PROLOGUE

THE MAGELLANIC HERESIES

Fragments recovered from the journal of Semion Achybe, astrophysicist of the deep space exploratory vessel *Magellanic Cloud*, as reassembled and translated by Ondo Ynwa Lagan from discoveries made on the (now extinct) planet Maes Far.

Warning: These fragments form part of the *Magellanic Heresies* as proscribed by Concordance. Ownership or propagation of these documents is considered an act of extreme heresy against Omn. Read or distribute at your own risk.

...and while triple sun systems aren't rare in the galaxy, this one was intriguing given the regularity of the three stars' movements around each other. The patterns of their orbits are complex — but there definitely are patterns. In most ternary systems, the motions of the stellar bodies are so unpredictable over time that they are essentially chaotic. It was the curiously clock-like regularity of the

stellar trajectories we observed in this system that persuaded us to divert the Magellanic Cloud from its itinerary to visit the system in the first place…

…while the highly regular movements of the suns are intriguing, it is the rocky bodies in the system — both the planets and their satellites — that have proved to be more fascinating. At this point in time, we have no good explanations for the orbital movements observed. The planetary moons, in particular, do not conform to any of the predictions made by our computational models; their orbits simply should not be stable or regular. Each moon should have spiralled down onto a planetary collision trajectory long ago in galactic history.

Setting aside some of the wilder speculations among the crew, it is clear that our models must be wrong. Something is going on in this system that we do not understand…

PART 1 - PLANETARY

1. Twenty-three Deaths

Selene Ada died twenty-three times from her injuries – one death, by grim coincidence, for every year of her life.

She had only scattered recollections of her escape from her dying homeworld: the sickening moments of terror as her battered craft crumpled around her, each beam-weapon blast sending her ship lurching from its trajectory; the hard lines of the lander blurring with every hit inflicted upon it; her own screams ragged in her ears; her brain rattling around within her skull. It felt as though some god had reached down from the sky and seized her ship to shake it to pieces. There was nothing she could do but endure, the acceleration and the shuttle's restraints pinning her to the seat of her disintegrating craft.

There was also a moment, high in the atmosphere, the limbs of the planet curving away beneath her, when she thought she'd escaped unscathed. She'd climbed out of range of the ground-based planetary defence batteries. The unfamiliar lander upon which her life suddenly depended had suffered massive structural damage, alarms screaming at her from every display, but its drives continued to power her skywards and her suit's life-support systems remained viable. Against all the odds, she was going to escape the end of her world. A candle-flame of hope flickered in her mind.

Telemetry gave her a glimpse of the Cathedral ship in high orbit, ordnance blazing from its fuselage. She had never seen it so clearly before; it had been a bright light in the sky on summer evenings, moving across the sky with unnatural rapidity. Concordance had kept its form and capabilities deliberately obscure. It had been a constant presence in her life, always up there, always watching, but now she saw its true shape. It was a ship of vast and curious beauty, its twisting, sinuous lines like some coral outgrowth. It was hard to believe an object of such organic pearlescence could have been constructed from mere components. Its angles and forms were like no building, no object she'd ever seen.

Then its first salvo lanced into her. The blast sheared off the aft section of her craft, sending it spinning through the air like a maddened fly, exposing Selene to the atmosphere. She was shaken so violently that she bit a chunk from her tongue. She vomited into her helmet. Suit fans screamed to clear her airways and keep her breathing. Ground, sky, ground flashed repeatedly into view as the craft corkscrewed.

The damaged ship's random trajectory was probably what saved her. More beam-weapon fire lanced down from space, but always just behind, or just ahead of the lurching shuttle, the AI Mind of the attacking ship repeatedly miscalculating.

Then it caught up or got lucky. A solid shaft of coherent energy, one metre wide, hit her. She knew nothing about it. Ondo, later, told her how it must have been. It punched through the shuttle's thin hull, punched through Selene's body as she clung to her seat. The shot destroyed all remaining systems on the lander, evaporating them to mangled scraps. It was just fortunate that Ondo, hanging in low orbit aboard the *Radiant Dragon*, was close enough to capture the ruined shuttle and arc out of the planet's gravity well before the larger Concordance ship, its orbit too high, was able to intervene. Two Void Walker attack vessels pursued from the Cathedral ship but couldn't accelerate rapidly enough to reach the *Dragon*'s velocity.

The direct hit on the lander also destroyed the biological systems of Selene's body. Beam-weaponry fire was designed to cut through the voidhulls of starships, not the soft flesh of people. Most of the left hemisphere of Selene's brain, along with one third of her skull, were burned instantly away. Ondo speculated that the intense heat, cauterizing her blood vessels, may have helped to preserve her surviving tissues for a vital few minutes. Nevertheless, death was instantaneous. Her left shoulder, her left arm, a third of her chest cavity and abdomen, half of her pelvis and her left leg were also obliterated in the same moment. Her right leg and the tissues around the centre-line of her body suffered major damage from the searing heat.

Her bones burned.

That was the first of her deaths, alone in the ruined craft, with the orbital bombardment from the Cathedral ship lancing around her, and with Ondo swooping in aboard the *Dragon* to rescue her and flee before any pursuing Concordance craft could catch them.

Her twenty-two other deaths she endured in Ondo's operating theatre, her body succumbing again and again to the traumas of her repair; the straightenings, the reconstructions, the graftings of flesh and nerves and bone. And often, between each end, there came moments of clarity: sensations of light and pain, glimpses of unexpected, disorientating detail. Those moments were confused, their timeline unclear: reality, nightmare and drug-induced hallucination impossible to tell apart.

She recalled one such moment early on: a sudden emergence from a horror-filled replaying of her last day on Maes Far, of farewells hugged against distant screams and explosions. The backwash from the lander's thrusters flattened a wide circle of red blooms in the flower meadow. Her home was far enough from the town to avoid the mob, but they'd seen the ship descending, and they'd be coming. Her mother's arms around her, the whispered final message. Then her father. His lips moved as he looked at her, grief-stricken, horrified, eyes liquid with tears, but he hadn't been able to find words to say to her. Then the object he handed her as she climbed into the lander, and the simple, inadequate message he finally uttered.

Her wakening was, no doubt, chemically induced, as Ondo battled to stabilize her shattered biology. For once, mercifully, there was no agony. Specks of grit clogged her mouth, fragments of reconstructed tooth or bone. Her body tingled, the long muscles of her limbs spasming. She was aware of dull aches in her left arm, but when she tried to move it, nothing happened. Exploring with her right hand she discovered that her left arm and that whole side of her body simply weren't there. Their absence seemed almost comical, like some magician's trick. Instead of flesh and muscle, there was only an emptiness beside her on the bed, ducts and tubes and cables leading off into a battery of machinery.

She was an incomplete thing, misshapen, half not-there. Half alive.

"The planet?" she said. Her voice came out as a hoarse grunt, her severed lips and mouth and mandible unable to form the words.

The face of the man who had plucked her from the sky – it could only be Ondo Lagan, although she had never seen him before – smeared into view. His hair was wild, his appearance unkempt. As she found out later, he'd been alone for so long he'd stopped giving thought to his appearance. His eyes were bulbous through the complex lenses of his multiglasses as he studied her. Again, as he often repeated later, he could have operated on his own eyes, fixed their age-related defects, enhanced them so that he didn't need external devices to correct them. But he could never find the time, his studies and researches consuming him.

He seemed to grasp what she was trying to say. "I'm sorry, Selene. Only you have survived. Those few who remain on the surface will not be alive for very much longer. The situation was deteriorating rapidly when we left."

"No." The fact of it was too huge to grasp; it was an ocean of dark water engulfing her, consuming her. She'd been chosen by her family as the one to be rescued. Her parents, her aunts and uncles, they'd all been insistent: she had her life ahead of her, she deserved the chance. There was an unborn sister, a surprise and unplanned late pregnancy, her mother barely showing, and perhaps two lives might have been saved aboard the tiny lander, but the risks were greater, and the decision had been made. At the end, there'd suddenly been no time to argue further. The simple calculation of it was brutal.

She'd left behind others, too: colleagues, acquaintances, friends, among whom was Falden, becoming a lover at the time of the appearance of the shroud. She felt the ghost of his grip in her left hand as he led her through the flower meadows that lawned the slopes around their home, a day of perfect, golden light and whispered promises.

"I'm sorry," Ondo said again from beside her, as if he were to blame, as if the solar shroud had been his doing.

The moment of bright clarity faded. Perhaps Ondo had granted her drug-induced oblivion. She slipped back into the welcome fog of unconsciousness, the faces of her dead family, her father's tears and Falden's grasp going with her into the darkness.

It was only Ondo – patient, quiet Ondo – that kept tally of her deaths as he battled again and again to pull her through, bring her back to some semblance of life. Two years later, when she'd physically recovered, he would repeat it to her often, wonder and horror in his voice. *You died twenty-three times: once in the lander, then a further twenty-two times under my hand.* The haunted look in his eyes as he repeated the mantra gave her some clue of the toll those days had taken on him.

At the time, she had no thought for him: no gratitude, no empathy, no insight. He was an unknown figure, her rescuer, her tormentor. There were days when she clung to him as a sick child would to a parent, sobbing from the pain, desperate for reassurance. There were days when she begged for release, all dignity gone, her useless, supine flesh bringing her only suffering. He could anaesthetize her, of course, but always there was the time when arm or leg or chest or skull had to be used, muscles flexed, bone structures tested. The pain of it became her life as she learned to repossess her own body, discovered how to wield limb and sinew.

The original and the new.

One day, nine months into her recreation, she emerged back into consciousness from the latest procedure. Spiky agonies tore through her chest cavity with each breath, as if the wrong tissues had been sutured together. The familiar quiet of the medsuite that was her permanent room lay around her. The subdued glow from the sensors that Ondo kept her hooked up to gave the room an incongruous feeling of the early evening gloaming, some late-summer day on Maes Far. A bitter, chemical taste filled her mouth.

This time he'd reconstructed her chest cavity, implanting the left lung he'd grown from her stem cells, filling in the lost fragments of her rib cage with carbon-fibre bone analogue, attaching intercostal muscles and the malleable mass of her left breast, connecting the artificial to the natural with his customary microscopic artistry and covering everything with the shimmering black dermal substrate upon which, eventually, her own skin could take root.

Ondo's face entered the frame of her vision. Her brain was still adjusting to the exotic sensory inputs her left eye now gave her, so that his features warped for a moment, multiple-wavelength representations overlaying. But of course, it could only be him. There were only the two of them there.

His voice was quiet, full of regret at what she was going through. "How does it feel?"

She had no secrets from him, no defences. He knew the workings and pumpings of her body better she did, knew her more intimately than any lover ever could, knew her from the inside out. She resented it. The pain was muffled by analgesia, but she could tell it would be huge soon enough. It would have its day, a beast that could not be contained. She wished she could stop breathing altogether and let her racked muscles rest, but she refused to show it.

"It's okay." Her voice was a whisper, her lips cracked dry. "How long was I out this time?"

He missed a beat before replying. "There were complications that I hadn't foreseen. Integrating the bioelectronics into your nervous system is always difficult, as you know. It is a difficult procedure to carry out while rebuilding muscle tissues and blood flows. Weaving the neurons from your artificial limbs through your spinal column proved to be rather more difficult than I'd anticipated."

"Tell me how long."

"Twenty-seven hours. Your heart stopped twice. The second time I thought I'd lost you. You were gone for a full minute."

She could see the weariness in his lined face. He had

saved her life one more time. She couldn't stop herself saying it. She didn't want to stop herself saying it. "How many times now?"

"I don't understand."

"How many times have I died?"

"Including the lander, twenty-two times."

"You should have left me. I don't want this. I don't want any of this."

"I couldn't do that, Selene."

In her mind she was screaming, although it came out as a rough whisper. "I've had enough! I don't care what you promised my family. Let me go, Ondo. You have no fucking right to do this. It's my choice to make, not yours."

A part of her could see the effect her words had upon him. She didn't care. She *had* been through too much.

"I'm not doing this because of my friendship with your father, Selene. Nor for your family, nor for all the dead of Maes Far. I'm doing it for you. When I pulled you from the wreckage of your shuttle, resuscitated you that first time, I vowed I would save you, give you a chance at life as best I could. Too many others have died."

"This is no fucking life. I don't want it! Let me go, I'm begging you. I'm ordering you. You do not have the right to know what's best for me. You're controlling me just as much as Concordance did."

That stung him. He hesitated, perhaps debating with himself whether he was doing the right thing. He reached off to one side to touch a control on one of the devices. The fog of anaesthetic filled her brain and she couldn't fight it. He wasn't giving her final oblivion; he was sending her back into unconsciousness from where she couldn't object.

"No, Ondo, don't you fucking dare. Don't you…"

Then the fog rolled through her brain and there was nothing she could do to fight it.

Ondo sat unmoving for an hour, watching over the young woman he'd rescued, his gaze flicking between the monitor readouts and her face. Even deeply sedated, she occasionally winced with pain, her brow furrowing and her mouth half-forming a silent scream. Was he doing the right thing, keeping her alive, putting her through all this?

It was possible he was being selfish. He'd lived a lonely life – a life he'd accepted, sought out – but he'd paid the price. He'd envied Seben, Selene's father, envied the relative normality of his life, the love and family and home he'd enjoyed. Seben was dead now, of course, and he, Ondo, was alive, pursuing Concordance, following his trail. But if it led nowhere, to defeat or a dead-end, he knew he'd regret what he'd done with his time. He sometimes wondered who he might have been if he'd lived in a different age. Occasionally, he dreamt dreams of a life that had never existed: spending his days on research and on building his devices, his family and friends around him, a life peaceful and contented.

He let out a long sigh. Still. He couldn't change the past. The faces of the people in his dreams were always a blur, but now there was this young woman, viscerally real, terribly injured, alone apart from him in the whole universe. He would do what he could for her, despite the rigours of all she would have to go through. If he could, he would save her, let her try and find the sort of life he'd turned his back on. He had no idea who she really was, what she wanted to be, and perhaps she didn't either, but he could give her the chance to find out.

If she survived that long.

2. A Slow Cruelty

She had no idea how much time had elapsed when she came round. The memories of her conversation with Ondo seemed years distant, but it might only have been a few hours, a few days. The tugging pain in her chest was gone, a warmth filling her whole body. Chemically induced, no doubt. She licked her cracked lips, tried to flex the distant reaches of her body: her fingers and her toes. Dimly, they answered. The reconstructed half of her felt different, somehow; her left hand responded immediately when she galloped her fingers, but it also felt like an … emulation of how it should feel. Still, the integration of Ondo's additions had advanced apace. How long had she been out?

As if he could read her thoughts, Ondo spoke from his customary position of the chair beside her. "It's ten days since our last conversation. I needed to keep you in a coma while your natural and artificial neural networks intertwined, but the process is sufficiently advanced now. You should be able to breathe normally, and you will start to gain fine motor control of your new limbs. You should know that in normal use your left arm and leg will behave just as your right ones do, but you must learn to control them. Both are capable of far greater feats of strength and speed: so much so that you could shatter what remains of your natural skeleton if you aren't careful."

She twisted her creaking neck to find him. "I told you to stop. I told you to let me go."

"I know. And truly, if that is what you wish, I will respect it. But I also know the way we think about things can change. A different perspective, a little time, and what once seemed intolerable is suddenly small, a minor annoyance. Forgive me, but there are things I would like you to see before you decide you've had enough."

She had the impression it was a prepared speech, something he'd run through again and again as he watched over her. "Right. This is where you show me a mirror to persuade me I'm not the ruined freak I think I am."

She saw that wasn't it from the brief look of puzzlement on his face. Maybe the idea hadn't occurred to him. She didn't really know anything about this man. She knew the name, of course. Ondo the heretic, the outlaw, pursued for years across the galaxy by Concordance, always evading capture aboard his ship known simply as the *Refuge*. She barely understood why he was even with her, what connection there was between them, how it was that Ondo Lagan had been a friend of her father.

"We can do that," he said, "if it would help."

She considered. No, not yet, she wasn't ready for that. Her body was mostly reconstructed, although her artificial skin hadn't been implanted yet, her left half still gleaming black substrate. She wasn't ready yet to see what he'd done with her face.

"What is it you want me to see?"

"I'd like you to come up to one of the observation domes. You haven't left this room since the day you arrived, and now I think it's time. This chair will carry you anywhere you wish to go on the *Refuge*, until your limbs and body are strong enough to bear you."

"I'll walk, thanks."

He stood to manoeuvre the hovering chair so that it

was beside her bed. "You're not ready for that. Let me help you."

"I said, I'll walk!" Her anger flared into life from nowhere. The room lurched around her as she sat upright. She ignored it and forced herself to stand.

Her left leg buckled beneath her immediately, a useless column of flesh that could never support her weight. She flopped to the smooth floor, bashing her forehead before she could persuade her left hand to move and protect her.

She lay there for a moment, cursing Ondo, cursing everything. "What have you done to me? These new limbs don't work. My body doesn't work."

He knelt to offer her a hand. "You will get stronger. Your tissues are still combining, learning to work together. It will take months, but you will be better, I promise you."

After a moment, she took his hand and allowed herself to be hauled up and deposited in the chair. Her fury had already burned itself out. She hated to be so weak. She didn't even have the energy to remain angry.

When her breathing had calmed, she looked up at the man standing over her.

"Why did they do it?" she rasped. "Why did they build their shroud and blot out our sun? Why this atrocity? Why such a slow cruelty?"

Her nightmares had been full of the scenes she'd witnessed as the light faded from her planet and it fell into savagery. They could have destroyed intelligent life on Maes Far in a few moments, but they'd chosen to draw out the agony. Loss overwhelmed her, and she felt tears brimming in her right eye. The right, but not the left. The vision of her artificial eye remained unclouded.

Ondo took his time to respond, a troubled expression crossing his features. He sat on the bed so that their heads were on the same level. "There has long been a catastrophist tradition within Concordance, these days led by Secundus Godel. Maes Far may be down to her."

"I have no idea what that means."

He seemed content to sit and talk to her at length. He probably didn't get the chance very often. "It's the 'end of days' approach to religious conversion. From what little I know of the founding sect, they believed that the soul flies through a sacred wormhole when a person dies, passing into either a paradise universe or a hellish one, depending upon the individual's actions in life. Omn sits in judgement at the gateway to the wormhole, deflecting each approaching soul into one reality or the other. One tradition within the faith devotes itself to encouraging people to live good lives, and by doing so attain their eternity in the paradise universe. It's a familiar-enough theme in religious belief. But another school – that of Vulpis and now Godel – teaches that people fundamentally can't change, and therefore that their judgement day should be hastened along by all means available. Put simply, Godel wants to wipe out all intelligent life in the galaxy and let Omn decide who is worthy and who isn't. The good get to go to paradise and the bad to their eternal torment. You have to admire its simplicity; it's a convenient way of short-circuiting a whole range of ethical dilemmas."

Of course, she was familiar with Concordance theology from her upbringing on Maes Far, their teachings and strictures, but she'd never heard their ideas set out so plainly. "You don't seriously believe they could do that?"

"No, I don't, but that doesn't mean they aren't going to try. Partly, also, I think the shroud above your planet was a statement to the rest of the galaxy. A warning. Leave the path and this will be the outcome. Pictures of what is taking place upon the surface of Maes Far are being transmitted to every planet controlled by Concordance. The whole galaxy has watched your people tear themselves to pieces, watched them fight for dwindling supplies of food and water. They've watched, fascinated and horrified, as your civilisation unwinds into barbarity."

"Maes Far was hardly some wild, rebellious world. It

was peaceful. It was *dull*."

Ondo nodded. He was trying to work out the best way to tell her something. There was too much she didn't know – about him and about the wider galaxy. Why did she get the feeling he was keeping secrets from her?

"It goes without saying that the people of Maes Far have done nothing to warrant such a terrible fate," he said. "The shroud wouldn't be justified whatever your people had done. It is a weapon of the cruellest genocide."

"You're suggesting the planet was chosen at random from all the inhabited planets in the galaxy?"

"No, no, I don't think that either."

"Then what?"

"Tell me, how much did you know of your father's researches?"

What did that have to do with anything? "Not much. He spent his spare time digging around in the ruins of the crashed starship in the mountains. It was what he did. I resented him not being around when I was younger, begrudged the time he spent with his *work*, but later I stopped paying it much attention. Sometimes I hiked up there to help him, dig alongside him. We never seemed to unearth anything of great interest."

"Which I think was exactly as he wanted. I think he probably did everything he could to protect you from what he was really doing on Maes Far."

What did that mean? "He was living his life, raising his family. Existing. You make it sound like he wasn't even from the planet."

"He never told you? Perhaps that was for the best."

"Told me what?"

Ondo considered her for a moment, still debating with himself what he could tell her. "I suppose the secret doesn't matter anymore. The truth is, your father wasn't from Maes Far. Your mother was, but both your father and I grew up on a planet called Sintorus, a long way from your homeworld. He and I, and that starship ruin he spent his time excavating, we're all a part of the reason Concordance put their shroud into orbit around your world to blot out your star. Partly, we are to blame."

"That makes no sense."

"I will explain as best I can, I promise. You deserve to know everything that I do. But first, can I show you the things I wanted you to see? It isn't far. There will be plenty of time to talk further."

"I can control the chair without your help?"

"I've taken the liberty of embedding control flecks into your skull. A little practice and you should find you can control the chair with your thoughts."

"You put wiring in my brain?"

"Some were essential, to control the additions I've made to your body. Some are useful but non-essential. Forgive me, I should have asked your permission for all the alterations I've made, but without many of them you wouldn't have survived to be asked. When you have recovered, we can discuss which, if any, you'd like me to remove."

She wanted to object but found she didn't have the strength. "Show me the way, and I'll follow as best I can."

It took several frustrating minutes of jerking backwards and forwards, steering into walls and machinery, before she got the hang of directing the chair. Ondo, always, watched patiently, telling her that she nearly had it each time, saying *try again* until she wanted to scream. Eventually, she managed to make it through the doorway without snagging the sides. It seemed like a major achievement. The walls of the passageway she found herself in surprised her. When she crashed into them, trying and utterly failing to move in a straight line, she discovered they were hard stone. "We're on a planet? I assumed the Refuge was a ship. The *Radiant Dragon*'s mother ship."

"That's a story I've fostered, but we're actually in a hollowed-out lone-wolf asteroid."

"Then, where are we?"

"Again, it's probably best I show you."

A spiral ramp, the chair gliding up it once she got the right degree of turn, brought them to a round, domed room, the walls and ceiling of which had an opaque greyness. Selene juddered her way around the room. "It's not very impressive. You think this will give me a cause to cling to life?" Her voice echoed with stone hollowness in the enclosed space.

"Before I show you," said Ondo, "I want to be sure you understand the truth about superluminal travel."

His words made her suspicious. There were things she and her family had talked about in the safety of their own house that no one ever said in public, and certainly not to a stranger. Maes Far had been a liberal world compared to many, but still the risks of being overheard and having their words relayed to Concordance, watching from orbit, were great.

"What truth?"

Ondo, used to his solitude, was unconcerned about the risks. "I'm talking about the true nature of the universe and the lies people live their lives by. You know what I mean, I think. The notion that moving faster than the light barrier rips your soul from your body is a small lie in the grand scheme of things, perhaps, but it is insidious. These days we have alternative lies, equivalent scientific stories. You've heard them. Moving through metaspace degrades the synapses, causing the brain to malfunction. The different physical constants of the metaspace domain are inimical to our biologies, causing cancers and premature senescence. They're the same lies, so very useful to Concordance, keeping people in their place, keeping them apart, preventing them from learning the truth or combining their ships into fleets. Most people in the galaxy *know* you can't travel faster than the speed of light and remain yourself. They know it absolutely, even though it is demonstrably untrue."

Was he testing her? She was suddenly past caring; she had already lost everything. "The ship you rescued me in, it's capable of FTL travel?"

"I've made metaspace jumps in the *Radiant Dragon* many, many times. And now you've made several, too. As you'll be aware, your mind is still your own, your soul hasn't been ripped screaming from your body."

Did she know that? She felt like a very different person from the young woman who'd lived on Maes Far just a few months earlier. The thoughts that dripped through her mind in quiet moments often seemed unfamiliar, alien, like they were intruding from outside. Was she the same? Of course, she didn't believe any of the stories about bodies and souls separating if forced to travel at speeds above the light barrier, but that didn't mean she was still *herself*. She no longer knew what that meant.

"You're telling me we're not in the Maes Far system anymore."

Ondo nodded his agreement. "The Refuge is a long way from any system, a long way from any place that Concordance might think to come looking for me."

"Can't they follow your trail?"

"They try; I take steps to make sure they don't succeed. Multiple metaspace hops to be certain no one is following before I come anywhere near and very careful quarantining before I approach. It's kept me safe for the thirty years I've lived here."

She'd assumed he'd wanted to show her Maes Far, images of how it now was. The solar shroud would be complete: an opaque, orbiting disk that moved with finely-calculated exactness to stay precisely in front of the sun relative to the planet's surface, cutting off all heat, all light except for the flaring corona. A dark sun to replace the light. But that wasn't it.

"Show me what you brought me up here to see."

He made no movement, some control fleck of his own sending instructions to the Refuge. In an instant, the walls and domed ceiling of the little room turned transparent. There, above and around her, filling one half of the sky, lay the sparkling mass of the galaxy.

It was a familiar-enough sight, of course. On dark nights on Maes Far it stretched overhead, a shimmering and meandering pathway. Her ancestors had called it the *Diamond Road*, imagined it as a path you could walk to reach the gods. She knew well the truth of what it was, but still, as a girl, she'd liked to stare up at it and dream about taking that journey.

The galaxy seen from Maes Far was nothing compared to its appearance from the Refuge. Her planet lay in the galactic plane, as almost all systems did, making the stars appear as the shimmering, dust-occluded line across the night sky that she knew so well. The Refuge, however, clearly lay far outside the plane. The entire disc of the galaxy lay tilted before Selene's eyes, with very few stars nearby and its structure clear: the spiralling arms and the bright glow of the central mass.

The sight of it sparkled on her retinas. She studied it for long moments with both her natural right eye, and then with her enhanced left eye, picking out different wavelengths of radiation, the different spectra of the stars, the glowing clouds of nebulae. From the angle they were at, the whole thing looked curiously like an eye itself: the ovoid shape, the rainbow hues and the glowing central mass as the pupil.

"Where is Maes Far?"

Part-way along one of the spiral arms, towards the central mass, a star began to flash. There was nothing remarkable or special about it. Her homeworld's sun was insignificant: one star among billions. She knew well the scale of the galaxy, but the sight of the whole thing laid out before her took her breath away. When you were inside it you couldn't see the entirety.

Her life had been so small. Briefly, she felt the tug of an unfamiliar emotion: a wonder at what all those stars were, at who and what was to be found there.

"And Sintorus?"

Another insignificant light flashed, farther out along the same arm.

Turning away for a moment, she saw that on the opposite side of the dome, away from the galactic mass, there was only darkness. There was the deep void of intergalactic space, with only other galaxies, other islands in the emptiness, to provide any illumination. In its own way that was beautiful, too. Light and dark. With her left eye, she could peer farther and farther into the void, deeper and deeper into time. Wherever she looked there were more galaxies, and more, and more. Distant places she would never and could never visit.

Ondo was still looking at the swirl of their galaxy. "Concordance control almost all of it, their Cathedral ships in orbit around every technologically-advanced planet. Somewhere in that central mass lives *Omn*, if they are to be believed. The God Star; the Light at the Heart of the Galaxy, attended and served by Primo Carious and Secundus Godel and the rest of the Augurs. Of course, it is a place no one can go, a being no one may approach. No one can go anywhere without the Cathedral ships and the Void Walkers intervening to stop them. They cannot allow truth to trouble their mystique. You grasp the scale of what they are, now? How they dominate and belittle us?"

She didn't need his patronising words. He thought she was ignorant of galactic affairs, brought up on her backwater world, but that wasn't how it was. "I've always known what they are; I was raised to understand exactly that. What can you do in the face of such power? The galaxy is beautiful, but the sight of it changes nothing. Concordance are all-powerful and I'm a broken cripple despite all your efforts. You thought showing me this would somehow change my mind? Fill me with some zeal to fight back? I'm fucking exhausted just coming up here, and I'm in a chair that does all the moving for me. My *bones* hurt.”

He held up his hands as if to fend off her fury. “I wanted you to see this because it’s a glorious sight, that’s all. I often come up here myself to think; I find it gives me a welcome sense of perspective. I’m sorry if my words offended you.”

He wasn’t being intentionally condescending. He wasn’t used to talking to people.

“Forget it,” she said.

After a moment, Ondo continued. “We barely know each other, but I knew your father and I see some of him in you. You’re still so ill and weak and you’ve been through a terrible ordeal. You’ve lost everything you knew and loved, and you’ve barely survived. It’s natural you feel beaten down, defeated. I understand that, truly. But I wanted you also to know that after the sunset comes always the sunrise. One day you will be stronger, and you will be yourself again. Changed, yes, but *you*. Maybe you won’t want to join me in my struggle – I’m not asking that – but I believe that, eventually, you will be glad you survived. That there will be good days.”

“You’re saying you won’t give me the release I asked for?”

He turned to consider her, frowns wrinkling his face. “I’ve done everything I can to save you, mend your body, keep you alive. But if you die on the operating table once more, I will let you go if that is truly what you want.”

Was it what she wanted? The thought of release was tempting. All her loss and physical agony would be over. And yet, and yet. That small voice inside her did want to fight Concordance, however ridiculous that notion was. Perhaps it didn’t matter that you couldn’t possibly win; perhaps there was sense and reason in simply trying. The swirl of the galaxy hung before her, promising countless worlds she could visit, marvels and wonders she could explore. Ondo had given her that possibility. She’d assumed she’d spend the rest of her life on Maes Far but now there was all *that* waiting for her.

The galaxy, and the Concordance ships that would pursue her relentlessly.

"It's hopeless," she said. "They're so powerful and you're old and weak and powerless. What can you do?"

He looked amused rather than offended. "There are days when I despair, it is true. Days when continuing to fight seems ridiculous. But I pull myself together and tell myself the darkest hour is before the dawn, and other such platitudes, and I carry on with it, because what else is there? The physicist in me wonders whether Concordance rule is something like a chaotic system: superficially stable, but prone to violent transformations with relatively little input."

"They don't seem very vulnerable to me."

Ondo nodded his head in agreement. "The question is, how much is that a façade and how much the reality? I think we can agree, at least, that Omn and his church are not all-powerful, or else we wouldn't be here having this conversation. Godel's brand of madness is one thing, but I genuinely think there's a secret, a reason for everything that's happened. Or at least, something that makes sense of it. I see hope in that."

"You sound delusional to me."

"I like to think of it as optimistic."

She asked her next question quietly. "And how many more operations do I have to go through? If that's what I want to do."

"At most, four or five. Your skeletal structure, your musculature and your nervous systems are complete, as is your blood circulation. Your lymphatic system, your endocrine glands and your digestive tract are nearing a normal operational profile. Your reproductive organs are fully functional. There are some brain fleck enhancements that still need to be made and then, of course, there is your skin: once I have grown sufficient amount of dermis from your cells, I'll have to graft it across your left half. That will be raw for a time, and sore, but the worst of it is over, I promise you."

"And what right did you have to do any of it? What right did you have to shape me as you saw fit? Maybe I wanted to stay as I was. Broken."

He nodded, conceding it was a fair question. "I remade you in your own image, as much as I could. I strove for symmetry in the reconstruction of your body, and where that didn't help, I aimed as far as possible for some sort of body form norm. I'm aware that is a cultural construction as much as anything. You may have preferred some radically different biology. I may have got everything very wrong. I reconstructed you to be biologically female, capable of bearing new life, as that is how you were. I may have got that wrong, too; you may prefer to be reproductively male, or asexual, or some other arrangement. I had no access to your self-perceptions, of how you understand yourself. I did what I could, and in truth a lot of it could be undone or reconfigured or added to if you wish, although that would mean a much greater number of procedures. I *did* give you considerable artificial augmentation: you are capable of much greater feats of strength, speed, dexterity and computational prowess than you once were. Again, I may have done that mistakenly. You may prefer to be as close as possible to your former level of function."

In his own flawed way, he had tried. Maybe that was all anyone could do. The anger that had flared through her subsided, a little. She would think about the options he'd given her. "If I did live, where would I go? What would I do?"

"You'd be able to fit in with the populations of many worlds. We can invent you an identity, go there in secret, just as your father did. I can alter your appearance within a wide set of parameters, and you can live your life. You get to choose your existence; which world will be your home. It is a possibility few are granted these days."

She didn't take her eyes off the galaxy as she considered his words, trying to make sense of them.

"There is one more thing I would like you to see, if you have the strength," he said. "Something smaller. There are wonders in the galaxy as well as horrors. Or there could be."

"What wonders?"

He looked a little uncomfortable, as if he wasn't sure how she'd react. "You've heard of Coronade?"

His words threw her. Her mind was spinning; she needed to think about everything he'd said, and suddenly he was talking about fairy tales. Had he quietly lost his grip on sanity at some point over the years?

She answered warily. "Who hasn't? Every child grows up with stories of it. The golden planet where all is peace and happiness. What of it?"

"That is what I wish to show you. I've discovered Coronade isn't just a child's story. It's a planet in the galaxy. I know it is real."

"That's nonsense. How can you *know* such a thing?"

He couldn't keep the delight from his features. "Because three years ago, I found the proof. I recovered images of the mythical planet of Coronade."

3. Coronade

"You brought me up here to talk about fairy stories?" His words poured doubt through her. He was crazy. Being pursued so relentlessly by the forces of Concordance had made him paranoid.

"Please," he said, "tell me which version of the story you know."

She thought about claiming exhaustion – the short ride in the chair had drained her – but she wanted to know more about him, where his lonely thoughts had taken him. She'd play his game a little longer. "Coronade is a myth, a planet where everything is beautiful and peaceful. All cultures and religions have ideas like it: an idealised place where life makes sense, and everyone is happy."

"And what do you say to my claim that it is real?"

"I don't believe you."

"Why?"

Her voice was hoarse from so much talking, her throat rough, but she kept on. "Because ... because reality isn't like that. There is no paradise you can simply *visit*. Things aren't so simple. Life is cruel. Do I have to spell that out? Look at me."

He moved his head from side-to-side, in a way that suggested she was only half-wrong, that it was more complex than that. "The truth may have been embellished with myths and wishful thinking, but the images I've seen prove Coronade is real."

"*Is* real? Even if a planet of that name once existed, Concordance would have destroyed it."

"Perhaps. You're right, I can only prove that it did exist, not that it still does. Concordance go to great lengths to root out any hints of their *Golden Age Heresy*. In their version of history, all interplanetary contact was characterised by genocide and bloodshed until they arose to impose the order of Omn. But there is much that doesn't make sense about that, and we can't be completely sure what Concordance would do to Coronade. They may not even know where it is."

"They know everything."

"Do they? They don't appear to know where we are. But Coronade definitely did exist, and it's clear it was some sort of beacon or celebration of hope for the galaxy."

"How do you know this? How can you have these images?" It was like claiming he had photographs of heaven.

"It's what I've devoted my life to doing: piecing together scattered scraps of information in an attempt to put the truth back together. Something bad happened to the galaxy three hundred years ago, and I don't just mean the devastation of the Omnian War. Galactic civilisation was shattered, and since then Concordance have gone to great efforts to wipe out all evidence of our real histories. They are very thorough, but the war left ruins and hulks scattered across the galaxy, and even Concordance hasn't been able to track all of them down in the three centuries since. Every now and then I find one, and if I'm lucky I unearth some fragment of the truth from the mangled ruins. That's what I do, and that's what your father was doing on Maes Far. And, possibly, he was getting too near some truth that Concordance did not wish to be revealed. Often it is a race: we to reveal, they to destroy."

She was having trouble absorbing all the information he was throwing at her, as if her brain no longer had the capacity for so many ideas. "My father didn't travel the galaxy being pursued by Void Walkers. He didn't have all the forces of Concordance attempting to find him and kill him."

"He chose a different path. We both devoted our lives to uncovering the truth, but he wanted a normal life, too. I ... turned my back on that. I've roamed the galaxy, gone where I needed to go."

"You think he made a bad choice."

The suggestion appeared to trouble Ondo for some reason. "Truly, no. I've often thought it was I that made the bad choice, although I had my reasons. Your father didn't want to lead the life I have. We knew space around Maes Far saw several major skirmishes in the war, and we knew there was a crash site on the planet. Your father decided to adopt the life of a local to give him the time and freedom to carry out the necessary archaeological researches. We invented his identity between us, the Ada family name, all of it, and smuggled him onto the planet as a young man. It might seem a safe and provincial life to lead, but it was dangerous enough in its own way. He was brave, working out there in plain sight with no means of fleeing if they came for him. He had to be very careful not to learn too much; Concordance were always watching from orbit."

She would never have believed such a wild claim, if not for the fact that Ondo had come to rescue her when Maes Far was destroyed. "What was his real name?"

"For what it's worth, I think his Maes Far name became the real him, but when I first knew him, he was Seben Jen Akter."

The name meant nothing to her. Her father had done a good job of keeping his former life a secret.

Deep, heavy pains tore at her insides then, and for a moment they consumed her. She gasped, putting her hand to her breast as if to hold everything in place. The agony mounted, sharp, then dissipated. It happened, sometimes so badly she had to sedate herself back into oblivion.

"The pains again?"

She didn't need his overbearing concern. "It's nothing. Show me these images you claim are of Coronade."

"If you're sure you're up to it."

"Show me."

The galaxy disappeared and, in its place, came moving pictures of a purple-oceaned planet strewn with honey-yellow and gold-orange continents. Many ships and satellites hung in orbit around the planet. The sight of them sent a jolt of alarm through her, but they were not Concordance ships. They were not any sort of ship she recognized. There were countless different shapes and configurations and sizes, functions she could only guess at. The planet's high atmosphere buzzed with activity as the vessels came and went, but everything was ordered, controlled. Somehow it was all managed without any ship colliding with any other.

On the surface, glinting in the bright sun, cities lined the coastlines, as well as ringing inland lakes and large expanses of greenery. There were habitations or some other forms of construction within the oceans, too: round islands to which, just visible, the lines of bridges threaded from the land masses.

"What makes you say it's Coronade?"

"Listen. There's audio, too."

Voices filled the little room: a communication between the ship whose point of view they were seeing and some sort of planetary control system. The voices were clear, although heavily accented. It took Selene a few moments to make sense of the slanted vowels and pick out the words of the conversation.

"...you welcome to Coronade, Ambassador Vol Velle. The delegations from Arianas and Gogon are already on the planet and awaiting your presence. Dock at Equatorial City Seven and you will be escorted to your quarters. We assume you want to commence

negotiations at your earliest convenience?"

"Thank you, Coronade Central, we will land at Equatorial City Seven within the hour. Tell me, what mood are the Gogoni in?"

(sound garbled)

"…unhappy, but in truth they seemed … no more resentful than usual. Let us hope for a mutually satisfactory outcome to your negotiations."

"If anything can calm their warlike tendencies, it's a few weeks on Coronade. I'm in no hurry at all to conclude our negotiations. Perhaps…"

The audio cut out in a fuzz of distortion. A moment later, the images also flickered and stopped, the final, frozen frame of some bulbous, whale-like ship manoeuvring into orbit *en route* from an unknown star.

Selene considered what she'd seen for a moment. "It doesn't really prove anything. Just because they called it Coronade doesn't mean it was *the* Coronade. Lots of planets are named after mythological lands and figures, right?"

"Right," conceded Ondo. "But the evidence is strong. This Coronade was clearly some sort of neutral ground, a place where cultures and races could meet in peace to settle their differences. I believe it was a centre of scientific and technological cooperation and research, too. You saw how many different sorts of ships there were. I've studied the images carefully and counted over two thousand distinct architectural styles to the vessels in orbit. I think this was a planet that civilisations across the galaxy came to when they needed to resolve their differences."

She couldn't help being a little intrigued. "Were you able to identify its location?"

"There were translatable coordinates embedded in the communications stream, but I had no frame of reference to baseline them from. As you saw, there were no background stars visible to fix off."

"Can you date the images?"

"There was chronological information embedded as well, but, again, I couldn't match it to any known calendar."

"How did you even acquire the images?"

"I found fragments of a spaceship floating in a system's asteroid belt. The hulk was hard to spot among all the rocks and dust, but I'd learned there'd been a battle there in the Omnian War. Ships, as you may know, sometimes seek refuge in asteroid belts when they're being pursued or when they're heavily outgunned – even though, in truth, such regions of space are generally sparsely populated once you're in them. I struck lucky. There wasn't a lot left of the vessel, but I did manage to retrieve some of its data flecks. They were damaged – the entire craft had been blown to pieces – but I was able to extract those few fragments."

"Could you tell which side the ship fought on?"

"It was Magellanic Alliance, not Concordance. I've found the remains of very, very few Concordance ships, I think because so few were destroyed. The ships on the other side, drawn from all the star-faring cultures of the galaxy, were apparently no match for them. It's something that makes no sense to me, even now. How did this little-known sect suddenly acquire the knowledge to build these devastating warships? And to have so many of them? It is a great puzzle."

She was still trying to make sense of everything he'd said. Her brain was made of fog. "This ship you found had been to Coronade and it was a ship that fought in the Omnian War. That means the images must be around three hundred years old."

"We can't say that for sure. The war was a war for the truth as well as military domination. The ships on the Magellanic side were trying to disseminate the facts of what the *Magellanic Cloud* encountered, and I believe that included excerpts of much older information, from hundreds of years earlier or possibly even from some prior civilisation. This is, you understand, largely guesswork based on mere fragments of data."

"Then the images don't really tell us very much."

"Perhaps, but they're intriguing, aren't they? I think there's another important clue in them, too, something you may not have noticed. I applied no translation routines to the audio. What you heard was the original speech of the ship's navigator and the Coronade control station. The accents and cadences were odd to our ears, but comprehensible."

"Those people, whoever they were, spoke the same language as us."

"Yes – which is, in truth, not that remarkable. I've travelled all across the galaxy, to many systems in the central mass and out to the edges of each spiral arm, and the language we are using now – or some variant of it – is spoken almost universally. It's hard to escape the obvious conclusion: in the past there weren't simply a few thousand isolated starfaring civilisations, but a genuinely galaxy-spanning culture. Coronade, quite possibly, was at its heart."

"If that was true, we'd have proof of it, histories of it."

"Concordance are clever. They isolate us, control the message, suppress the truth and give us stories that suit their own needs. Each planet knows its local history well enough, but Concordance paints the greater picture. The terrible bloodshed, the genocide, the mass destruction in the historical record: it's always somewhere else. Even *everywhere* else. The scraps of truth that they haven't destroyed get subverted as fairy story: Coronade and its civilisation as nothing more than childish myth. People relish their own cynicism, and the truth gets lost."

She couldn't take it all in; her head was throbbing from exertion and the long conversation. She hadn't spoken so much since her last days on Maes Far, her farewells with her family. "But these images you have: they can't be that ancient, otherwise the language would have evolved into something we couldn't understand."

"True. A few hundred years more of linguistic drift and we would have great difficulty making sense of the words. Recording language in flecks and books tends to slow that process, but it still happens."

"The language could just be something Concordance imposed upon the galaxy."

"Except, they've never claimed to have done that, and they're always very quick to trumpet their achievements. And I suspect that would be too big a lie to convince people of, even for them. They've imposed their own interpretation of historical events, but even they can't obliterate the cultural and linguistic records of every known civilisation, not without simply killing everyone."

Selene looked away from Ondo back to the view, which had returned to visuals of the galaxy. The *Diamond Road*. Apart from a few nearer stars twinkling as some speck of interstellar dust eclipsed them, it looked still, frozen. Of course, that was only a matter of perspective. Everything was moving, changing, it just wasn't always possible to see it. Imperceptibly, in the few minutes since she'd entered the room, the galaxy had turned.

"I need to sleep, Ondo. I need to think about all this."

"Of course. My apologies if I've exhausted you. I've wanted to show someone this for a long time, and I'm afraid you've suffered because of it."

She turned and manoeuvred the chair back down the stairs. She was getting the hang of it now, but she still managed to scrape several walls along the way.

She reached her room without pitching herself onto the floor. Exhaustion washed through her, sucking her down. She heaved herself onto the bed with the last of her strength and a gasp of pain.

Visions of starships – uncountable, bizarre, exotic starships – thronged in her thoughts, their combined communications babble incomprehensible. She slipped back into unconsciousness to their troubled hubbub.

4. A World in Shadows

Slowly she became stronger, less prone to bone-heavy exhaustion. She found, as she came around from the last few operations, that her fears of pain and incapacity were being replaced by something else. Relief that she had survived; a sense of having a future, of thinking what it might hold. And something else: a growing anger at what had been done to her, to her world and to everyone she knew and loved.

As her strength grew, so did her fury.

She used it to push herself, to overcome the pain from her tortured tissues. She spent longer and longer in the Refuge's exercise room, forcing herself to build up the strength and stamina of her natural tissues. The emulated gravity in the little room was adjustable, allowing Ondo to acclimatise himself to the conditions of different worlds, and every week she bumped it up a notch to place more strain on her system. The difficulty was keeping her surviving biology and her enhancements at the same level of strength, but there Ondo had done a good job. As her natural muscles grew stronger, her artificial ones automatically adjusted performance to maintain a balance. It was as Ondo said: soon she was unaware of her additions in the way that she was unaware of her natural body. The artificial tissues responded without her having to think about them.

She still suffered bouts of searing agony, but she learned to ignore them. Her body was adjusting. Day by day, slowly, they became less and less frequent.

She'd played a musical instrument at home on Maes Far, a *qurang*, a simple device that had variations throughout the galaxy: a resonating acoustic box with taut strings whose length could be altered to produce different notes. Her father had played, showed her the basic hand-shapes required to get the different chords. She had no great skill, but playing had been a source of pleasure on Maes Far when the anxieties of life overwhelmed her. A simple, creative task she could fill her mind with. Ondo had nothing exactly the same, but he'd given her the closest he had, smaller and with eight strings rather than the six she was used to. She was teaching herself to play. It required a high degree of manual dexterity, but it also required complete coordination, both hands working as one as she plucked and strummed with her right hand and formed chords and shaped effects with her left.

It was working, she could play the unfamiliar instrument – but it was also completely wrong. Her artificial fingers moved with astonishing speed, speeding up and down the fret like a scampering spider, never missing a note, but it was always too perfect, too mechanistic. She sounded like a person and a machine trying to play a duet: one expressive, emotive, the other clockwork and precise. In the end, always, she threw the instrument down in disgust.

She explored the Refuge, first in the chair and then, for longer periods, on foot. It was larger than she'd first imagined, its paths winding without any apparent pattern. The two cold fusion reactors at its core powered a thriving hydroponic agricultural system, as well as caverns given over to greenery just because, apparently, Ondo wanted them to be there. They served no obvious survival purpose. There was running water: the asteroid had a large reserve of ice locked away beneath its surface, and Ondo had constructed the sort of water cycling system commonly found on starships so that the supply was, more or less, inexhaustible.

A lot of the passageways and hollows in the rock were natural – presumably another reason Ondo had chosen the asteroid – but at some point in the past, he'd extended and connected the natural caverns to form an interconnecting warren. She found several observation points, granting views in all directions, the galaxy sometimes visible, sometimes hidden behind the Refuge's misshapen grey mass. She discovered the spaceward hangar where the pyramidal bulk of the *Radiant Dragon* was berthed. Other ships were there, too, but they seemed unused, in various states of disrepair, cannibalized for spares. There were sleeping rooms: four or five of them, as if Ondo had planned for a larger population. Only hers and Ondo's were used.

She found a storeroom where he had racks of clothing, scavenged from many different worlds by the look of their disparate styles and colours and fabrics. Perhaps they were disguises, or a part of some abandoned plan to have more people at the Refuge. She picked out items that were better-fitting and decidedly more feminine than the baggy medical gowns she'd been wearing since her reconstruction. She wouldn't have been seen dead in them back home, but it felt good to smooth their close-fitting lines over her anatomy, gave her some small sense of control over her appearance. Studying herself from all angles in a mirror, she was a little bit a person once more, rather than simply a patient, a problem.

She also found many rooms given over to Ondo's experiments and researches, rooms containing contraptions she could make no sense of, perhaps salvaged from around the galaxy for him to reassemble at some point.

He was often away, travelling the galaxy aboard the *Dragon*, following his trails, and at those times she had the Refuge to herself. The quiet of it was welcome, healing. There appeared to be no restrictions on where she could go or what she could do, and she spent her days exploring her miniature new world. The lack of any planetary-defence batteries had surprised her, until Ondo explained their only hope for survival lay in absolute secrecy. If their whereabouts became known, they'd have no chance against their Concordance overlords, however much firepower they could muster to defend the Refuge. Still, she couldn't help thinking Ondo had weaponry of some description somewhere. He had a great deal of dazzling technology at his fingertips: some of it acquired from his journeys around the galaxy over the decades, but much of it, seemingly, of his own invention.

She found, at the end of an inconsequential rock passageway at the foot of a twisting, narrow stairwell, a small vault where he stored all the precious scraps of data he'd scavenged across the galaxy. The door to the room was blast-proof carbon-steel, half a metre thick, but it swung open silently to her touch. Inside were all of Ondo's treasures. There were, in truth, precious few of them; Concordance had done a good job of destroying the facts they didn't want the galaxy to know, of erasing its collected memories. As well as starships' dataflecks, there were discs and cubes, and other storage devices she didn't recognize. There were fragments of complete machines, the data presumably stored within them, as well as paper books with hand-written words. Everything looked singed, or broken, or degraded, but each was held in a blue stasis field, cocooned and protected as carefully as any priceless jewel or revered religious artefact. The scattered and fractured memories of the galactic mind.

She wondered how much Concordance would give for access to the room. If they could destroy the memories it contained, those and any others still strewn around the galaxy, then the past they wished to eliminate effectively wouldn't exist anymore.

He returned after a week away without any announcement or greeting. Only a subsonic rumble through the stone walls told her that a ship had decelerated to dock. She wanted to ask him about the flecks and discs and books, as well as give voice to the many other questions that jostled in her brain. She found him in his laboratory, hunched over his latest discoveries. The room was one of the larger atria, and from the map she'd built in her mind, it had to be right at the heart of the asteroid, directly above the data storage room and maybe five hundred metres in every direction from vacuum.

He didn't hear her approach. He was often engrossed in his work, attempting to decrypt the incomplete records he'd retrieved from his crash sites. The laboratory was a strange jumble of humming machinery and lush plant life. Ondo liked to be surrounded by greenery; he'd explained that Sintorus had been abundant in flowering plants and he found the greenery conducive to his work. There was also running water in the laboratory: channelled along a network of open gullies, partly to provide irrigation for the plants, and partly to fill the air with their white-noise tinkling.

She stepped up behind him, wary of interrupting him. She imagined the interior of his mind was something like the Vault: a strong room, well protected, full of ancient mysteries and secrets, but also open to her if she chose to explore it. He'd grown used to his long solitude, but he was willing to share what he knew and suspected. She had only to pick *this* fragment off a shelf, or *this* one, and ask about it, and he would tell her.

A large rig set across two benches held both ends of a ten-metre length of a microscopic filament, something he often experimented with, sending electromagnetic radiation of various wavelengths through it. He'd explained to her that its purpose and function remained a mystery to him, but that he'd recovered lengths of it in many different star systems.

A jewelbug, an iridescent insectoid apparently made of knotted strings of beads, had stopped in its foray upon the tip of a nearby leaf, one foot held warily in the air over the plummet to the ground. A stab of pain cut through her, then passed. She ignored it. She had more important things to concern herself with: what was going on, what she should *do*.

She held out her left hand to the jewelbug which, warily, after a few moments, stepped into her palm. She could feel the patterns of the microscopic hairs covering its pin feet upon her artificial flesh. She held it to her eye, studying the beautiful dazzle of its multifaceted eyes, then set it down at the base of a cluster of lush, rubbery fronds where it might find more to eat.

Ondo insisted on using old-fashioned screens and manual keyboard controls for his work. It was hugely inefficient, but he claimed that having to type slowly and deliberately helped him to lay out his thoughts methodically. His screen depicted some planetary landscape. There were the ruins of old buildings, but they were blackened and blasted by fire or explosion, scoured by screaming winds. Many were little more than piled rubble. The entire scene was one of utmost desolation, some ancient scene of planetary destruction. The images were two-tone: infra-red, perhaps. This was the planet at night-time.

Her control over her lips and facial muscles was improving; her words were less and less slurrily sibilant each day. "Is this where you've just been?"

He turned in surprise, completely unaware she was there, too wrapped up in studying his latest treasures. Perhaps he'd completely forgotten she was even on the Refuge. He peered at her through his elaborate multiglasses. "Selene! Yes, this is where I've come from.

You don't recognize it?"

"Should I? You forget I lived my whole life on Maes Far."

His reply was strangely quiet. "I didn't forget that."

She grasped what he meant a moment later. *This* was Maes Far. Her homeworld looked as though it had been desolate for centuries. Her voice was shaky when she spoke again, some of her muscle control gone. "You went back?"

"I left nanosensors in the atmosphere and in orbit, and I've been there to harvest their recordings. I was going to ask you whether you wanted to see them. It would be understandable if you didn't."

"Are there any signs of life?"

"I'm sorry, but I've seen none, other than a few small insectoids scurrying in the shadows. Microscopic life survives too, no doubt, but there is nothing of any great size or complexity."

"No people?"

"None that I've been able to find, although I haven't been down to the surface. Perhaps there might be one or two holed up somewhere, eking out dwindling supplies, but I doubt it. It's been nearly a year since your escape and the planet's biosphere was already at a tipping point when you left. It also appears some areas of the surface have been scoured by Concordance planetary destruction weaponry: seismic devices and air-burst nukes."

"Which areas?"

"Specifically, the ship crash site your father was excavating. That's been utterly demolished."

Now that she studied the pictures, she could see that it was, indeed, her home. They were looking at Caraleon, the capital city, streets and plazas she knew well. If she tried, she could overlay the shattered ruins with memories of the soaring architecture she'd loved. A ragged ruin in the centre of the screen had to be all that was left of the central Sunrise Campanile, the tower that had chimed the hours across the city for over 250 years.

It chimed no more. She turned away. She didn't want to see what Maes Far had become. She turned to the questions she'd been saving up to ask him. "How did you know Maes Far was under attack? Were you in contact with my father?"

He took his glasses off so he could converse with her properly. "It was luck, really. It would have been too dangerous to maintain a regular communication, for either of us. The arrangement was that I would send an automated drone into the system every few years to harvest any interesting data he'd unearthed, and then disappear. There were nanosensors in orbit that picked up and stored any broadcasts whose wavelengths followed a very specific pattern of modulations.

"Normally, I acquired only drawings and images of what your father had unearthed from the ruins he was excavating. Occasionally, there was a personal message, but there was never any great detail. Of course, he had to be careful to walk the line that all historians and archaeologists across the galaxy have to walk. If they get too close to the truth or find out anything genuinely useful, Concordance starts paying attention. This time, when the *Dragon* returned, he'd sent an urgent plea for help. The *Dragon* also identified what the increased Concordance activity meant as it arrived in-system: by that time the shroud was already a third built."

She recalled it well. The sun had become like a malevolent eye peering down at them from the sky, its black pupil growing wider and wider, its glow colder each day. She'd hated it more than she'd hated anything in her life. "You came up with the plan to send down the lander and save who you could?"

"It was all I could do. I took the risk of broadcasting instructions using the same modulation patterns to your father, not knowing if he would receive them. Fortunately, he did. Originally, I'd thought of sending the shuttle down again and again to save as many of your family as I could. It soon become obvious we'd only get one chance, and that was when you had to choose who would be saved. I wish I could have done more, saved everyone, stopped Concordance building their terrible device, but I could not."

"No. I know." There'd been so many people on her planet, and only she was left. So many funny and smart and beautiful people. And, sure, so many stupid and irritating ones, too. The burden of losing all of them was unbearable. How could she hope to live up to all their dreams, their expectations? How could she ever repay their sacrifice? The weight of that would drag her to the ground if she let it.

Her mother had foreseen how it would be for her at their parting. Selene recalled the light shining in her mother's golden hair as she held her close, the reassuring strength of her embrace. These were her final words: "Go out there and live, Selene. Don't blame yourself when we're gone. This is not your fault; you have done nothing wrong. You must live. We all want you to live. Go with our love and our blessing." Her words had made little difference. In Selene's nightmares, the people of Maes Far were still alive, watching her from the surface of the ruined planet, crying out to her for help.

She tried, as she always did, to put the recollections out of her mind. Sometimes she wished that part of her brain had been blasted away, the memories cut from her, so she didn't have to live with them.

"Did my father ever unearth any useful information about Concordance?" she asked.

"I suspected he was getting close to something, but it's only in the last few weeks that it's become clear how much he'd learned. He'd been very busy, working away in secret. Partly that was to hide everything from the Cathedral ship, but I think he also didn't want to tell me everything until he had his findings catalogued and corroborated. He was always the rigorous scientist. Then, when he knew the end was coming, he sent everything he'd found, desperate it shouldn't be lost. As well as getting you off the planet it was all he could do, the only salvation he could find."

"The data fleck he gave me when we parted." Her father had handed it to her as she climbed into the lander, told her to take it to Ondo. Confused, she'd asked him what it was, but he hadn't been able to explain. He'd wanted to, a jumble of thoughts forming in his mind, but there hadn't been time.

Ondo held up the tiny rectangle of glass in a pair of electronically-controlled micropincers. "We were incredibly lucky it wasn't destroyed or lost. You dropped it, of course, but I found it wedged within the wreckage. I search everything in the minutest detail before I allow it near the Refuge, in case Concordance attempt to infiltrate my defences with some tracking device."

"Was there anything about me on there?" She imagined fond farewell letters, fatherly advice to take with her on her travels.

"It contained only his notes and the data he'd captured from the site, sorry."

"And what did he find?"

"I'm still working on it; there are some flecks he couldn't decrypt but which I may be able to. There are some logs from the crew of the *Magellanic Cloud* that I've never seen before, including some fascinating entries from the ship's astrophysicist, planetologist and xenobiologist. There's nothing concrete, yet, but they all hint at the discovery of something truly remarkable."

"What?"

"It's best I don't speculate until I have more evidence."

"But you must have a best guess. Or what have you been doing all this time?"

Ondo considered for a moment, staring into space as if considering his long years of research and thought.

"You remember we talked about lies. What I've learned

is that there are much, much bigger ones."

"Like suppressing the idea that there was ever a golden age."

"I think that's a part of it."

"You're talking about Omn? You think the *Magellanic Cloud* did encounter a divine entity?"

Ondo looked puzzled for a moment, then waved the point away. "No, no, I'm not suggesting they found an omnipotent being wishing to act through them to control the galaxy. But to say that misses the whole point. I believe Vulpis went from a mere crew-member on board the *Magellanic Cloud* to founding Concordance because he encountered something that fundamentally altered the nature of galactic civilisation. All the rest, the story about Omn, is just misdirection, a useful lie. The Cathedral ships, the huge destructive power they wield, the Void Walkers, the Augurs, all of it. It's a lie so big that many can't see it; they think it's simply how the universe works. Maybe Vulpis and his followers genuinely believed they'd encountered a god, or they convinced themselves of that. Maybe it was a cynical calculation: a narrative they used to cover their military domination of galactic affairs."

His words would have earned him a death sentence on just about any world. His openness at speaking them appalled and excited her in equal measure. "If all that's a lie, what is the truth?"

Ondo looked amused at the question. "Ah. I wish I knew. And that's the problem isn't it? When the truth is missing, it's easy for lies to fill the void. People need certainties. I think Concordance rely on that. I think that's probably the main reason each system has its Cathedral ship in orbit. Not to quell unrest or to destroy attempts at reinventing metaspace tech, but to ensure the correct version of history is heard."

"Tell me the little you do know." He'd given her hints and scraps but never the full picture he saw in his mind.

"I know that Concordance didn't exist three hundred

years ago. The *Magellanic Cloud* had on board only a few believers in the cult of Omn. It was a minor religious sect, an odd little curiosity, unknown in most of the galaxy. Vulpis was, obviously, their leader, but on the ship, he was a chemist, not even particularly high-ranking. The ship was a scientific exploration vessel, investigating unknown star systems in the galaxy's central mass. I know the Omnian War did take place, although, as I have said, I believe it was also a war to suppress the truth and not simply the means by which Concordance imposed control on the supposed chaos.

"The faction opposed to Vulpis – the normal crew of the ship, I think – took the *Magellanic Cloud,* intending to inform galactic civilisation of what had been found. Vulpis, somehow, fought them and stopped them. I have discovered several references in various datastores to someone or something that translates as *Morn* or *The Morn,* but whether that's a place, or a previously-unknown culture, or weapontech, I don't know. It appears to be something fearful, calamitous, and perhaps that is what allowed Vulpis to establish his galaxy-wide theocratic order."

"Or Vulpis encountered a civilization that used him to seize control of the galaxy. If there was a previously-isolated culture that suddenly learned the location of all these other worlds, and they had some sufficiently advanced technology at their disposal, they could have risen rapidly to dominance. Perhaps that's what Concordance *is*. A front for that."

"Perhaps."

"*Omn, Morn.* Maybe they're the same thing. The words are close."

"It's possible. Vulpis and his followers brought the word *Omn* with them, of course, the name of their god, and perhaps they – or someone – simply imposed it upon this *Morn,* appropriating an older word to aggrandize their own. It's a familiar pattern. Simply stating the two are the same thing, or aspects of the same thing, allowed Vulpis to bolster the importance of his sect, while also giving him licence to use his discovery to the supposed glory of Omn."

"Or giving the culture they encountered a story to justify what they went on to do."

"That's what we need to find out."

"What specifically have you learned from my father's investigations?"

"Corroboration of everything I've said – but also the knowledge that there is another uncharted crash site on Maes Far. I've been able to decrypt records that he was unable to read by cross-referencing with other fragments. The evidence is clear: there was a battle in orbit, and a second ship was hit. Crippled, it veered into the planet's atmosphere and parts of it crashed into the southern polar cap. It's another trail to follow. It may lead to nothing, as most of them do – or it may reveal some vital clue about what really happened three hundred years ago."

"Concordance haven't destroyed it?"

"I don't believe they know about it."

The Maes Far southern polar cap was essentially uninhabited, little more than a barren ice-sheet. "You've been there?"

"Once I'm sure all interest in the planet has died down, I'll go and see what I can find. Another piece of the puzzle, or another dead end. There may well be nothing left of the second crashed starship. Perhaps I'll find nothing more than a thin deposit layer of debris in the ice record, microfragments of vaporised graphene and polymer nanotube. It wouldn't be the first time."

"What if you die? What if the Void Walkers find you?"

"It's unlikely; the Cathedral ship has left the system, reassigned to some other inhabited world."

"There are still a million ways to get yourself killed on a shattered planet suffering that scale of environmental destruction."

"If I die, then the Refuge and everything within it is yours, Selene."

That threw her. She wasn't at all sure she wanted such a gift. It sounded a lot like a burden. "Why would it be mine?"

"Because there is no one else."

"And if I don't want it? Don't want any of this life of yours?"

"Then take another vessel and leave, by all means. There is no duty imposed on you; I saved your life so you could live it as you wished. I've been making sure there is another craft prepped and ready to use: the *Aether Dragon*. Not as advanced as the *Radiant*, but serviceable. All I ask is that you keep the records I've uncovered a secret; tell no one about the Refuge unless you encounter a person you can trust the information with."

The anger that had kindled within her ebbed away. "There are others like you? Pockets of rebels all over the galaxy waiting to answer the call and take the fight to Concordance?"

The question seemed to amuse Ondo. "Precious few. There are many people harbouring resentments, no doubt, but there is no organized rebellion. No disorganized one either, come to that. Concordance does a fine job of keeping us segregated. How could an insurgency begin without a functioning comms network? There are a few freebooters who eke out a living fleeing from Concordance here and there, individuals who would kill to have the Refuge as a base. Most would gladly sell the data flecks in the Vault to the highest bidder. And of course, if Concordance knew where we were, they would come and obliterate us immediately. But perhaps there is someone, somewhere who might continue what I've started. That is my hope. Have you come any closer to deciding which planet you would like to live your life on?"

She'd tried; she'd spent hours flicking through planetary profiles but hadn't found anywhere that looked to her like home. Still, she *was* looking; at some point she'd decided to carry on living after all. "I'm thinking about it. When will you go to Maes Far?"

"I'll prep for planetary incursion once I've finished work on your skin, and once I can get the *Aether Dragon* fully active. As I say, it's not as powerful as the *Radiant*, but it will get you where you need to go. Perhaps three months?"

Three months. She had that time to decide what person she would be for the rest of her life. Her name, her identity, her homeworld, who she would be and what she would do. It would be a fresh start, a chance to move on. Yes. And after she'd left, she would never see Ondo Lagan and his Refuge again.

5. Primo

Secundus Godel paused outside the ornate doors that led to the audience chamber of Primo Carious.

She'd had no choice but to comply with his summons to the God Star. Primo Carious spoke with the voice of Omn, and that was not to be questioned or denied. If the Primo instructed her to travel half the width of the galaxy in order for him to relay some new command to her, she could only meekly comply.

For now.

She calmed her thoughts, made sure a neutral expression showed upon on her face, then knocked. The Primo made her wait for ten, twenty seconds before summoning her inside. It was part of the game he played. She refused to show any irritation.

He sat in his golden throne at the far end of the chamber, reading something from a black book held in one of his heavily-jewelled hands. This was the sanctum sanctorum from which he directed all the affairs of the galaxy, handing down and interpreting the commandments relayed to him by Omn. Sitting in that chair, everything was his to control.

Two Void Walkers stood unmoving beside him, grey-robed, shaven-headed, their attention clearly focused upon her. It was a clear warning. All of it – the wait at the door, the shining splendour of the room, the fixed stares of the Walkers – it was all a message. Behind them, the turquoise-green planet that they orbited filled the scene through the transparent wall, the limb of the world framing the Primo. Distantly, Godel could see that lights sparkled upon the surface. Reflections from the suns, perhaps.

She crossed the room, taking thirty paces to reach him, emphasising the hard sound of each footstep upon the stone floor, imagining each *clack* was the crack of a blaster-shot. When she reached the throne, she knelt in the prescribed manner. There she waited, head bowed, trying to ignore the mounting pains in her knees.

"Ah, Godel," Carious said at last, his words a sign that she might rise and look upon him. He tore his attention from the book, as if what was written there was infinitely more interesting than she was. "Your journey through the void passed off without incident?"

He was, she noted, and not for the first time, an unimpressive figure. He could have been a barkeeper on any backwater world if Omn hadn't chosen him to be the figurehead and Primo of Concordance. He was portrayed to the galaxy as a glorious figure, made of light, but all she could see was the pattern of blotches on the backs of his hands, the sagging flesh of his chin.

"By the grace of Omn, I remain whole and complete," she said. "My soul still glows within me."

"Excellent; how fortunate we are to bask in his protection. And how is the work on the sacred tally progressing?"

It was a barbed question; a verbal stab. Something they fundamentally disagreed on. She let the blow glance off her. "It remains a fascinating area of theological research."

"And one you are pursuing very actively, I hear."

"As an intellectual pursuit."

"Ah, of course. And tell me, how close to the

seventeen sevens are we now?"

"We ... are still counting. Was this what you summoned me to discuss, my lord?"

"It is a different matter. I'm told that you believe it is time for another shroud to be deployed," he said.

"I continue the work of Omn."

"And yet, we still have a survivor from the last one to deal with. This Selene Ada. Do we know anything about her?"

"She is just a woman. She is unimportant."

"Nevertheless, her survival is a situation that cannot be allowed to continue. The galaxy must see that our control is absolute. Omnipotence does not allow for exceptions."

"It is very likely that she is dead," said Godel. "Her ship was struck as it attempted to escape Maes Far."

"And yet I hear rumours that she was rescued by the renegade, Ondo Lagan. That she still lives. Are our enemies so organized that they can defy us so easily?"

"In all likelihood, these are lies broadcast by Lagan to humiliate us."

"But you do not know this for sure?" said the Primo. "You cannot prove to me that she is dead."

Godel wanted to object that Omn knew the truth, and that Carious could surely find out from him, but she held her tongue. The Primo was testing her. Or was Omn testing her? Omn had to know the whereabouts of Lagan, too, but had so far refused to reveal it.

"We will know soon," she said. "We will capture Lagan and learn the truth."

"I have your word on that? Or should I consider which other amongst the First Augurs would be a better Secundus?"

"I will find Lagan and uncover the truth of this girl. I have it in hand."

Carious considered her for a moment, scrutinizing her, then nodded his head. "Very good. Do so. Then, when that is resolved, we can think about the next shroud. But only then."

She could only assent to his direct order. "Yes, Primo."

"You may return to your work, *Secundus* Godel." He emphasised her title very slightly as he dismissed her.

Godel spoke no more and began to back away from him, head bowed in submission.

As she went, she ran through a familiar set of thoughts in her mind. Did he truly give voice to the desires of Omn? He would say he was merely the channel, the conduit, of course, but who would know the truth of it? He had the divine machines that he used to receive Omn's instructions, machines only he had the right to use, but what if he simply relayed to the galaxy the words that he, Carious, wished to speak? And what was written in the books and records that only he was allowed to read?

There were others ways of communicating with Omn. The whispers in her head had troubled her, at first; she thought she was suffering some malady of the mind, or that her many journeys through the void were finally taking their toll. Now, she understood what they really were: the voice of Omn, telling her what it was that he wanted her to do, his instructions unfiltered by the intercession of Primo Carious. Whispers of his true design. Concordance had left the path, and it was up to her to set it right again.

It had also troubled her to act without the approval of the Primo. But Omn knew everything, and if Omn chose not to tell the Primo all that she had done, then that was simply proof she was in the right.

She would bide her time, follow the way shown to her, and one day, when the great scheme unfolded, it would be her sitting on the throne, and not him. Primo Godel would rule the galaxy. Under the direction of Omn.

She stepped out through the doors, closed them behind her and only then allowed herself a smile.

6. Leavings

Selene's twenty-third and final death came a week after her decision to leave the Refuge.

The sharp pains tearing at her tissues, subsiding for a time, returned with fresh cruelty one night, sending her writhing and whimpering upon her mattress, the sheets knotting themselves around her burning limbs. She refused to call Ondo to beg for pain relief or sympathy. Eventually she found sleep, unconsciousness at least, but instead of release she fell into confused fever-dreams that left her sweating and panting, unclear about what was real and what was in her head.

She lay on a bed of bones, their shattered fragments digging into her flesh. She was back on Maes Far, the version of it she'd glimpsed from Ondo's captured images, a world of dust and grey-brown ruin. A black sun shone overhead, sucking in the light rather than giving it out.

She wandered the shattered streets of her home. A short distance away, a man knelt in the dust, digging desperately with his bare hands. As fast as he could pull the dirt away, it fell back into the hole. His eyes were wide with horror as he glanced up at her.

"Help me," her father said. "Help me dig."

They worked together, burrowing, until she saw the glint of something metallic in the ground. With a gasp of triumph, her father reached in to grab it: the fleck he'd given her as she entered the lander. He handed it to her, enclosing his fist about hers. His voice was pleading, full of sorrow. "Take this. You must take this."

Then, somehow, her father was gone, and she was scraping away at the ash and soil alone. She found the rest of them there: her mother, her family, Falden, all the others she'd known, buried beneath the weight of the soil. Their eyes were open and they scrabbled at her, clutching her ankles and wrists, pleading for release, begging her to save them.

Selene, filled with horror, kicked herself free, tearing the iron grasp of her mother from her arm, falling backwards to the ground where more hands clutched at her, tried to pull her down beneath the surface.

She screamed a muffled scream, struggling to rise. The hands held her down. When she opened her eyes, they were Ondo's, standing over her in the operating theatre, pinning her to the bed by her shoulders while she fought him. His mouth moved, but she couldn't hear his words over the thundering in her ears. He seemed uncomfortably near to her face and at the same time very distant, glimpsed through the wrong end of a telescope. The light from the machines gleamed in his eyes, and she knew he was trying to kill her. Nausea twisted through her. She was burning up; he had done something to her metabolism, amped it up until her organs gave out.

She struggled against his monstrous strength, but her muscles were limp tissue and she couldn't fight. He brought a vial of some sickly yellow liquid into view, attaching it to one of the tubes feeding into her body. Some toxic concoction. She writhed in useless panic, but couldn't resist.

Ondo and the whole of the universe faded away.

He told her later what had happened, earnest words whispered to her as she lay like a helpless child, barely moving, barely conscious. "There was substantial tissue rejection of your new organs, your lung and gut. Necrosis set in and that triggered sepsis. You must have been in great pain for some time."

She didn't reply, ignoring the accusation in his voice. Ondo and the hard realities of the external world seemed so distant, so unimportant.

"Your body reacted to the infection by upping its core temperature, desperately trying to eliminate the infection overwhelming you," he continued. "Even as I brought that under control, your heart stopped. The machines have been keeping you alive for three days now."

Her voice was a whisper once again. "Will I live?"

The light from the machines gleamed on the tears in his eyes. "I think so. If you wish it."

By way of a reply to his implied question, she closed her eyes and said nothing. After a moment, no more words spoken, he rose to leave her to her thoughts.

Two days later, she awoke to find herself alone in the hushed calm of her room. Freeing herself from the battery of sensors and tubes and catheters that he had her tangled up in, she forced herself to a sitting position, and then to her feet. Time to take matters into her own hands. Once again, the room lurched around her. She ignored it with a snarl, and, fighting the dizziness, set about struggling her way to the observation deck that Ondo had led her to that first day. At some point during her death and her recovery, she'd come to a clear decision, prompted by the repeating nightmare of hands clutching at her from beneath the dust of Maes Far. She knew what she had to do. Now she simply needed to tell Ondo.

Three times on the journey she had to stop and lean on the hard wall to let the shapes swimming in front of her eyes fade. She was as weak as a new-born, the flesh of her body feverish and useless. Her senses were glitching, overloaded; the whiteness gleamed so brightly around her that she couldn't tell where floor ended and walls began.

A utility droid, seeing her toiling up the corridor, shimmied out of the way and regarded her mournfully through its optical sensors.

"Stop staring at me," she shouted at it. "I'm doing my fucking best."

The droid, for its part, didn't reply.

Once, she found herself on the cold floor, with no idea how she'd got there. She crawled until her head cleared. Her biomechanical augmentations, at least, still functioned, and it was they, rather than her own weakened biology, that allowed her to drag herself asymmetrically along corridors and up spiral ramps to reach her destination.

Finally, she made it. Through the transparent bulkhead, the galaxy hung unmoved by her recent death. She slumped against the opposite wall to consider it. Her cracked lips stung to the touch of her tongue. The swirling stars filling her eyes were a vast brain; once it had been active, functioning, creative. The trajectories of starships flashing across it were the pathways of the neurons: ideas and emotions streaming around the mind, spreading, growing. Now that mind was crippled, a few neurons firing occasionally, but only enough to convey a twisted, broken echo of all there had once been. An invading parasite sat spiderlike across the galactic mind, stunting all normal activity.

"Ondo."

She spoke out loud, although thanks to the comms implants he'd given her, she really had only to think his name in the right way, imagine herself calling for him, and he would hear. They could communicate brain-to-brain over a limited range, their bodies' electrical fields powering flecks to transmit encrypted radio waves. Within the Refuge or on the *Radiant Dragon*, the effect was amplified, hardware systems routing their communications, allowing them to converse remotely with no effort. She wasn't sure she welcomed the technology, but it was powerful, something they hadn't had on Maes Far. Whether it simply hadn't been developed, or had been actively suppressed by Concordance, she didn't know, although the danger of tech that allowed people to spread ideas without an eavesdropper overhearing was obvious.

"Selene." It was clear from the surprise in Ondo's voice that he hadn't known she was conscious. "Why are you in the observation room?"

"I need to talk to you."

"I'll be right there." She could hear the foreboding in his words. She knew why. He didn't know what she'd decided to do, but he suspected: she was going to demand the final release she craved. He couldn't deny her any longer; he'd given her his word. She sat and waited for him, lacking the energy to do anything else.

The haunted look on his face as he entered confirmed what she'd thought. Ondo said nothing, but crossed the room to sit beside her on the hard floor.

He spoke out loud. "Are you in pain?"

"It's fine." Her voice was a rasp. Strange how the act of physically talking, of persuading jaw and throat muscles to act together, was such an effort. Nevertheless, she preferred to speak out loud. It helped her to pick through what she wanted to say. The thoughts in her mind floated free, weightless, flighty, but speaking them out loud pinned them down, gave them the weight of gravity.

He wasn't looking at her. He was looking at anything but her. His gaze was on the whole of the galaxy, laid out before them. He said, "I sometimes think of it, of my journey over the years, as something like a pilgrimage among the stars, that I'm following the twisting paths of a labyrinth. Do you know the concept?"

"A maze."

He shook-nodded his head in his *yes and no* way. "Something similar. A labyrinth has only one way through it, with no forking paths. In that sense it's impossible to get lost, but the way is tortuous, and you often appear to be heading in the wrong direction completely. The journey itself is the meaning; the fact that you follow the road. All you have to do is keep on and reach the centre, the heart, where the answers you seek lie. You have to keep moving forwards even when it appears you are going nowhere."

"Or there is no path and you're wasting your life."

"That is a possibility. Or perhaps thinking like that is simply one more obstacle in the road to the truth. That's something I learned when I spent a couple of years on the planet of Teremoniat, after I left Sintorus. Are you familiar with the world?"

"No."

"I realise this is an odd thing for a scientist to say, but my time there among their mystics helped to clarify my thinking. The labyrinth is a core cultural concept in their civilisation. The idea informs everything upon Teremoniat: they never build straight transportation links that connect two points by the shortest distance; to them that would miss what could be learned on a long and circuitous route. The books they write and the paintings they paint: they're all about negotiating some knotty or hidden trail and the growth you can achieve by simply not giving up. When I was there, I began to see that there was a trail among the stars for me to follow, if only I accepted it."

"It sounds like crazy shit to me," said Selene. "Our brains look for patterns and see meaning in randomness. A *trail* is wishful thinking."

The twinkle in Ondo's eye as he glanced at her suggested that he was, partly at least, playing devil's advocate. "Yes, of course, but what if the pattern we see is really there? What if the face in the shadows really is the predator stalking us? I began to pull together what scraps of information I had and make connections. I'm convinced the path is there: subtle, weak, largely obliterated, but real, and I'm determined to follow it."

"If you see a trail, then you must believe someone is leaving you a trail," said Selene.

"Honestly, I think that might be the case. It's subtle

and elusive, but I believe it's there."

"Who would do that? *Why* would they do that?"

"I assume I'll find out at the end."

"I want to join you," she said. "I don't know about any labyrinth, and I don't care what searing insights I gain along the way, but I do know I want to fight them. The only meaning and purpose I can see is to obliterate them, or at least be able to say I tried. What they've done, I don't even know what you'd call it. It's a crime so large there's no simple word for it."

It took him a moment to adjust to what she was saying. "Obliterating Concordance is not really what I'm doing. I'm simply trying to understand how and why they became what they did."

"What is the use of such knowledge if you don't use it? This isn't some interesting academic investigation you're carrying out, it's people's lives. And their deaths. Didn't you set out to destroy them? Didn't my father?"

Now he seemed to be staring into a distance of time, not space. "Perhaps we talked like that when we were young."

"Then you should talk like that again. There must never be another Maes Far."

"Perhaps I will be able to learn enough to make such a thing possible, but I'm nowhere near doing so yet. So much is hidden or destroyed. You know how powerful they are."

"Between us we can get somewhere. You can guide, and I can act."

His mouth opened and closed as he tried to decide how to reply. "No. I don't want your death on my conscience. I didn't put all that effort into keeping you alive so you could go and get yourself killed."

It was, perhaps, an attempt at humour. She ignored it. "This isn't your choice, it's mine. This is what I want to do."

"It is a dangerous life. Dangerous and lonely. As you

say, there may be no answers at the end of it all, just our own deaths."

"My old life is over; I can't settle down and live out a normal existence on some other world."

"You are sure of this?"

"Yes."

"I would have conditions."

"If this is where you tell me to always follow your orders, think again."

"Not that. First, you need to get well, get strong. You're in no condition to travel the galaxy fighting Concordance; you've nearly killed yourself crawling a few hundred metres along a corridor. I won't give you orders, but I also won't let you leave until you're well enough to do so."

He was right; she needed to be strong. "Agreed."

"Also, you need to know to tell me if you're ill or in pain. I could have stopped the infection cascading to the point it did. You didn't need to go through this last death. The medical sensors and flecks in your body: I'd like to enhance them so they tell me about the state you're in, alert me if you're in trouble. I'll respect your privacy but your life is more important."

At her request he had hobbled the devices so he couldn't intrude upon her. It suddenly seemed a ridiculous and petty restriction. "Very well."

"And I'd like to make one more addition to your brain."

Despite his protestations, it seemed he'd thought about this. "What addition?"

"You're clever and resourceful, but you don't know much about the workings of the galaxy. I can give you that: a copy of my engrams embedded within your brain for you to call upon whenever you need it. I've seen a lot of Concordance, and I know how they operate."

"You want to put a copy of yourself inside me?" The thought repelled her.

He held up his hand as if to deflect her objections. "The flecks will be dormant unless you activate them. They won't be able to intrude on your thoughts, and they won't know anything you're perceiving unless you allow them to. The flow of data will be strictly one-way: I won't get to hear anything my avatar learns; you have my word. I'll be a last resort if you're without any other weapons or options. I'll give you a keyword or a phrase to think or speak to trigger me, but otherwise you won't know I'm there. I can twine the flecks throughout your neurons so someone scanning your brain won't know I'm there, either."

She could see the wisdom of it; she needed weapons if she was going to fight Concordance. Right now, she had nothing.

"One more fleck," she said.

"But be absolutely sure this is what you want. You could live out that life of quiet happiness on just about any world you could name."

She shook her head. "No, I really couldn't."

She thought he'd laugh, smile sadly at her endearing boldness. He did neither. Instead, he nodded slowly, accepting her words, seeing something of what they might entail, perhaps.

He said, "Revenge might be a long way off. It might take generations of patient detective work before we understand the truth."

"Then, I shall die knowing I've played my part."

He rose to stand before her, considering her as a father might a daughter. "I shall have to work hard to curb your impetuous impulses, stop you leaping to attack any Cathedral ships you encounter single-handedly. But I'm very glad. I would have missed you more than I would have thought possible."

She nearly smiled at him. "Good. Now help me back to bed. I'm fucking exhausted."

He hauled her to her feet and hooked a shoulder

beneath her right arm to support her on the journey back.

She leaned on him, letting him take her weight. "You thought I was going to ask for death, didn't you?"

"Partly, yes, but I also know you're not one to give in. Your father was the same. I've watched you for too long, your tissues and organs refusing to give up when they really should have. There should have been many more than twenty-three deaths."

"I did give in, more than once."

"That's allowed. The important thing is that you're here now."

Alone again in her room, she studied her naked body in the mirror. Half of her, the natural flesh, was a ghostly white, almost translucent in its thinness. She'd been out of the light of suns for too long, buried away in the Refuge. The other half of her, the part Ondo had added, was purple black, space black, the substrate upon which he planned to seed the growth of her skin. Except, it wasn't pure black. If you looked into it closely, there were tiny flecks of silver shimmering deep in there, like half of her body was wrapped in the night-sky.

She held up her hand, masking the artificial half of her face so that she could imagine, almost, that she was still the young woman who'd lived on Maes Far. Her features were gaunt, her cheekbone prominent, but she could glimpse herself as she had been: the familiar smile, the faint constellation of freckles.

With an effort, she pulled her hand away to take in her full appearance. More than once the sight of what she'd become had choked her with tears of rage. Ondo had sculpted her artificial half to match her natural in shape, but it was a hideous parody of her true self. Except, except: now, studying herself, she began to see herself differently. The artificial epidermis was purely functional, not intended to look appealing, but it was more than that. The shiny, almost liquid flesh was beautiful. She turned from side to side, considering herself from all angles as she might if she were trying on new clothes. She touched the point between her breasts where the natural and artificial met. It was completely seamless, but her fingers registered the change in texture, the change from mammalian skin to biomechanical substitute. Her new skin was incredibly durable, but also more sensitive by far than her natural.

Both were smooth and hairless. Her artificial dermis contained the normal number of analogue hair follicles but she was able to switch their production on and off at will, just as she had executive control over the functioning of much of her biomechanical systems. She had instructed her finger and toe-nails to begin growing, but it would be months before they reached the length of her natural ones and required cutting. She could let her artificial hair grow in all the normal places across her body, but she'd chosen to deactivate that completely. People from her culture on Maes Far had habitually flaunted their body hair, emphasising underarm or pelvic wisps as a display of sexual maturity. She'd still had half a head of long hair when she arrived on the Refuge, the black locks she'd inherited from her father that her mother had loved to brush. Rather than look like a hideously burned doll while her new hair caught up, she'd chosen to shave it all off. She was glad she had, now. Her new appearance suited her, emphasised her. Half had survived, but in a sense everything was new. This was *her*, now. A different person.

That evening, when he knocked gently and came in to check on her and administer fresh pharmaceuticals, she said, "I've also decided I don't want the artificial skin. I wish to remain as I am, half and half."

He didn't look at her as he studied the readouts attached to her battery of sensors. "You'd be marked out as a renegade on every Concordance world you showed up on. You know they consider artificial augmentation deeply offensive, an insult to Omn's perfection. A convenient way of suppressing enhancement technology, in my view."

"I don't care," she said. "This is me, now. If absolutely

necessary, I'll wear a temporary skin to hide my true appearance, but only on occasions when I have no choice."

"You have more chance of surviving if you fit in."

"I don't want to fit in; I'll live my life as I choose to live it. Give me the extra augmentations, but not your idea of how I'm supposed to look."

He was going to reply, to object, but she saw the moment when he decided not to.

Four months later, the two of them stood beside the pyramid of the *Radiant Dragon* in the Refuge's space dock. The apex of the tetrahedral craft was some one hundred metres above her, its four triangular walls unblemished by any flaw or marking. She had little to compare the ship to, but the sight of low-atmosphere vessels had been common enough on Maes Far: whining, roaring machines with reaction drives of one sort or another, blasting out superheated exhaust in their wake. The *Dragon* appeared to need none of that.

She stroked the silvery grey voidhull of the ship. It was completely smooth to the touch, utterly unmarked by microimpact abrasions. Only with her left hand's sensitivity tuned down to nano level could she detect any unevenness, the regular patterns of its constituent molecules. Ondo had explained that, in flight, the ship wrapped an outer energy hull around itself to fend off impacts from all but the largest chunks of space debris. Apparently all starships did the same – a fact that, once, had presumably been common knowledge.

Normally the ship was as immobile as rock, building-like, but now it hovered three millimetres above the hangar's surface. A subsonic humming came from it, imperceptible to normal hearing. The ship exuded a sense of readiness to fly, to escape the Refuge and flee through metaspace to Maes Far.

Or maybe she was projecting her own emotions onto

it.

"How did you build the *Dragon*?" she asked. "Why didn't Concordance stop you acquiring the materials and the tech?"

Ondo studied a screen held in his hand, checking the ship's telemetry. "I didn't build the *Dragon*. I don't think you could really say anyone built it. Better to say it evolved over the centuries."

"A ship can't *evolve*."

"Its innermost core is old; it predates the war, certainly. A ship's Mind intertwined with a metaspace propagation drive would have been incredibly rare and valuable even in an age of regular interstellar travel. If you needed a bigger ship, or a newer ship, and you had a functioning core, it would have made sense to build around it rather than starting from scratch. So far as I can tell, that happened multiple times in the *Dragon*'s history."

"You don't know for sure?"

"There are so many computational layers wrapped around computational layers within its systems that its underlying architecture is a little hard to pin down."

"You're not giving me much confidence here. How safe is this ship?"

"I know enough about it not to worry. I've been through many battles and dangers with the *Radiant Dragon*, and it's always comes through. The ship is psychologically complicated, perhaps, and it may well harbour secrets that are so well-hidden even it isn't aware of them, but I would trust the ship over any other. Whatever its essential core is, I know it is absolutely, incontrovertibly, benign. I would stake my life on it, as did the person who flew in it before me."

"And who was that?"

"I'm not the first lonely renegade to devote their life to recovering the truth about Concordance. There have been many such over the centuries, and one of them made contact with me and gave me the *Dragon* when she was nearing the end of her road."

She knew little about Ondo's past. She had quizzed him extensively about her father, his history as it affected her, but there was still much she didn't know about him. Possibly too much. She'd been too wrapped up in herself, just as he'd been too wrapped up in his researches.

His words confirmed something she'd observed more than once: his technological and engineering skill was at a level far in excess of anything she'd witnessed or suspected possible. He'd shown her how he'd woven his engram flecks through the neurons of her brain, and he'd shown her the computational models he used to decrypt the fragmentary records he'd recovered. It was science raised to the level of something like artistry. But, while he was some kind of genius, she suspected he'd also inherited much of his miraculous technology.

"Did she give you the Refuge, too?" she asked.

"No, I built this place, using the *Dragon*'s weaponry to bore out the passageways and then building machines to complete the excavation work. I felt I needed a base."

"Who was she?"

"Her name was Aefrid Tau Sen. She was old when I knew her, but she recovered a great many of the flecks and datastores you've seen in the Vault, although she inherited a few from earlier renegades." He looked up for a moment, staring into the distance as if still able to see the woman somewhere by the spaceward doors. The metal shielding had rolled back, the atmosphere within the dock protected from the void only by a shimmering energy wall "She was pretty terrifying. She was *very* insistent that I look after everything she'd discovered, that I made sure her life's work didn't go to waste. I've tried very hard to live up to that."

"Just as now you plan for me to do the same."

He focused on her, back in the present. She knew what he was going to say; it was a conversation they'd had more than once. "No one is forcing you to live this life; you can leave any time you want. Besides, I plan to be around for many years yet. There are still too many unanswered questions for me to die."

"Are we ready to fly?"

"Everything looks good. In truth, the core components of the *Dragon* need little maintenance; they're self-repairing, self-maintaining systems."

He'd mentioned similar technologies before. She had no idea that was even possible; back home, every mechanism had worn down, needing constant maintenance to keep it operational.

"That's pretty miraculous."

"The technology needs an energy input to function, obviously, but otherwise it's self-sustaining. I believe that it was once completely normal. As I say, I don't have a complete understanding of how the ship functions. Aside from a few modifications, the *Dragon* is a pre-Concordance vessel, built before history was twisted backwards upon itself. I've seen evidence people used such repair technology on their biologies, too, potentially making themselves immortal if that was what they wished."

"We've fallen a long way."

"What matters is that we don't forget what we once were; what we're truly capable of."

At an unspoken communication from Ondo, a triangular doorway appeared in the previously flawless flank of the *Dragon*. Selene had no recollection of her first journey in the ship, but she'd been inside it many times since, learning its layout, understanding how it was controlled. This would be her first flight away from the Refuge. Since her decision to join Ondo, he'd made two further reconnaissance trips to the Maes Far system, leaving behind monitoring and exploratory devices of various kinds, but she hadn't accompanied him. Now, finally, she was ready to do so.

The flecks in her mind that allowed her to interface with the ship gave her full executive control over its actions, but her connection was still imperfect, awkward. Ondo had explained it would take time for her neurons to make the necessary adjustments. Eventually, the plasticity of her brain would give her the instinctive control that Ondo enjoyed. Learning to operate the *Dragon* was like learning to control her new limbs: she'd started out frustratingly clumsy, but eventually, with muscle memory ingrained, she'd be able to act without her conscious mind having to think about it.

Once the Refuge had retrieved the dock's precious volume of air into its recycling systems, Ondo deactivated the energy wall and edged the *Dragon* down the hemispherical tunnel towards space. He was taking it slowly so she could watch and understand, the intimacy of the bond they shared with the ship allowing her to feel what he was doing to direct the craft. A flood of telemetry flowed into her brain, overwhelming at first, but slowly she began to see patterns there, make sense of the rush.

She found herself exhaling a deep breath as they emerged into the dizzying vastness of the void. She'd been contained too long. She perceived the universe both through her own senses and the *Dragon*'s sensors. The Refuge was already a tiny fleck behind them, surrounded by the halo of bright stars strung through local space. Beyond, inconceivably huge, hung the main body of the galactic mass. Nausea washed through her at the terrible scale of it all. Planet bound, she was used to the simple truths of an *up* and a *down*. In space, she could fall for ever in any direction.

It was dizzying, but it was also glorious. All this was hers.

Ondo – the real Ondo, not her private copy – was there beside her, his voice reassuring. He knew what she was going through. "It will become easier. One more thing your brain needs to adjust to."

She nodded in reply, not trusting herself to speak as her stomach fluttered and clenched.

Ondo pulled the *Dragon* into a gentle arc, back towards the galactic centre, accelerating all the time. They could jump more-or-less directly into metaspace. It was one of the advantages of the Refuge's remote location: the lack of any stellar bodies nearby meant there were no gravity wells that could pull the ship off-vector during the tricky translation out of Euclidean space. In truth, it was a disadvantage as well as an advantage; the fact that they could jump without a prolonged run-up also meant an attacking force could jump inbound without warning at any time … if they knew where the Refuge was.

"We'll translate in thirty seconds," said Ondo. "Watch carefully, feel how it works, how I control the *Dragon*. The ship does most of the computational work, but the direction comes from us, and without clear control the ship might attempt a malformed jump and end up somewhere disastrous. Possibly even caught between realities, unable to move onwards or backwards. That and the risk of being pulled into a star or a black hole are the main risks."

"Oh, *those* are the main risks? Apart from that, it's perfectly safe?"

For once, though, she did what he said. She needed to know how to control the ship if she was going to take on Concordance. The idea of metaspace fascinated her: it was another concept that, once, must have been common knowledge. Ondo had once explained it to her using one of the ancient paper books he'd scavenged from some destroyed planet. He'd clearly been delighted with his metaphor.

"This book has tens of thousands of paragraphs, hundreds of thousands of words. You could read through it sequentially, word by word, but that would take a long time. That's why there would have been an index at the back, a much shorter summary of the main points in the text that you can traverse quickly. Find the right reference, then hop into the main text at the right page, the right word. Metaspace is like that: the gravity wells of stellar and planetary masses are there, projections of them at least, and by traversing that topography you can find the right point to emerge into real space. Flying greater distances still takes greater time, but navigation via metaspace means journeys can be made in a tiny fraction of the time it would take a subluminal ship to lumber the same distance."

"And you're sure that travelling metaspace doesn't suck out your soul, leave it haunting the wastes of metaspace while you emerge, broken and insane, as our galactic overlords insist?"

"I'm sure. You know I've made hundreds of jumps."

"And you're not insane?"

"I don't believe so, no." He smiled, considering her through his multiglasses. "But perhaps that should be for you to decide."

She forced herself to breathe slowly as the *Dragon* acquired more and more velocity, flinging itself forwards while its metaspace projectors prepared for the moment it would flip out of reality.

She felt the surge of it like plummeting off a high cliff. She swooped in a fall, faster and faster, nausea and delight rushing within her, sweeping her away.

Everything went grey, and the familiar universe disappeared.

7. Maes Far

They emerged into normal space a little over an hour later.

Ondo had placed them three hundred million kilometres from the stellar mass, a point perpendicular to the orbit of Maes Far. He'd explained his reasoning to her back at the Refuge. "In any system, most activity takes place in the narrow disc where planets and asteroids and even the most eccentric objects orbit. Away from the ecliptic plane, we're much less likely to be spotted."

The *Dragon* sat in space and waited, drinking in telemetry from the various nanosensors Ondo had seeded throughout the system on his previous visits. In the year and a half since her rescue, his devices had watched everything taking place in the system: departures and arrivals, anything out of the ordinary. A proportion of the probes had been lost, either to natural events or Concordance activity, but he'd scattered enough around that it was impossible for all of them to be destroyed. The devices broadcast their telemetry to the universe, there for anyone to intercept if they knew the encryption keys, so that they didn't have to give away the location of the *Dragon* as it materialised. The data would give her and Ondo a clear idea of what they were facing.

Selene sifted through the flood of information with her flecks: images from nanosensors around Maes Far as well as those orbiting the system's unoccupied planets and the orange-yellow sun itself. There were also many streams from within the atmosphere of her home planet: scenes of unceasing, storm-blasted ruin; images cataloguing the death of her homeworld. They were muddy and indistinct; there was little electromagnetic radiation in any wavelength bathing the world to pick out detail. Only a weak light reflecting off Maes Far's two moons – nowhere near enough to sustain a viable ecosystem – provided any illumination.

It was clear that the lack of electromagnetic radiation hitting the surface had triggered complete environmental collapse on the planet. The loss of all complex plant life had destroyed food chains, eliminating populations of herbivores and then carnivores. Creatures feeding off carrion had survived, even thrived, for a time, but that had been only a short-term glut. The planet was dark, its dying atmosphere convulsing with ferocious death-throe storms, as if it were raging against its own end.

She searched in vain for signs of intelligent life, some lonely figure walking the desolation. Perhaps some unknown individual had built a bunker against an imagined Armageddon and had now emerged. She had never heard of anyone going to such lengths, certainly not in her extended family. Now, studying the streams, she could see there was no one. The only movement came as the hurricane winds scattered debris, picked at the remains of structures, whipped water into a dead fury. She still dreamed dreams of being back there, of skeletal hands clutching at her from beneath the surface. She needed to accept the fact that every person she'd ever known, everyone apart from Ondo, was gone. Only after all this time was she beginning to grasp the meaning of that simple statement, the scale of it. She still found herself speaking out loud to Falden or her father, as if they were simply on the end of a comms channel and could respond to her words.

She studied the pictures of the planet for as long as she

could bring herself to.

She tore herself away. They needed to know about local space: whether ships or traps or defences had been left for them, or whether any scavenger vessels had ventured into the system. Concordance had to calculate there was a chance she was still alive, and, therefore, that she and Ondo might return.

Limited by light speed, the telemetry from the farther reaches of the system was by definition older and less reliable, but they could at least discern what had been taking place in the system in the recent past. If it looked safe, they'd creep sunwards, heading for the speck of rock that was Maes Far, watching warily all the time.

There were numerous artificial objects left in the system, their nature unknown to her. They had to be Concordance: her own culture had placed nothing into space for three hundred years. She tagged the objects with her mind's eye, drawing Ondo's attention to them. "What are these? Debris of some sort?"

"Automated sentinels. It's their standard practice: always a few in close orbit to the sun, then three or four around primitive or once-populated worlds."

"Why are they watching the sun?"

"I don't know. They always seem fascinated by the stars in the systems they occupy. Perhaps it's a religious thing."

"They'll see us if we go anywhere near Maes Far. And they must have nanosensors of their own that we can't detect. There are countless trillions of dust particles and any one of them could be a Concordance bug."

"It's a risk, agreed, but we can reduce the odds of detection significantly. By the look of the activity in the system, they didn't notice either of my two most recent incursions. It should be possible to plot a course that keeps us out of line-of-sight of any of their sentinels."

"Apart from the ones you don't know about."

"Apart from those, yes. These incursions are a race. If

we go in and get out quickly, we should be able to escape before they come for us."

Ondo sent her a mental image of the trajectory he'd plotted: a three-dimensional representation of Maes Far and local space around it. Known Concordance observation devices flashed in orbit and down in the atmosphere. The simulation of the planet moved, and a line appeared of the route Ondo intended to take: a complex spiral that wound down to the southern pole of the planet, neatly evading the observation cone of each device.

"We are lucky the crashed wreck is at the pole; as you can see, most of their monitoring stations are grouped around the once-inhabited continents. Caraleon, you'll notice, is under constant watch, but Concordance have spread themselves too thinly elsewhere. There are slight gaps between their observation arcs if you time your passage correctly, and there is a clear descent corridor over the southern polar ice-cap."

Selene watched the simulation play out, looking for flaws. She couldn't see any. "This suggests they don't know anything about the wreck at the pole, otherwise they'd have been very sure to watch it."

"They also wouldn't have allowed me to send down the borer I despatched on a very similar trajectory on my previous visit. You can see from its telemetry that it's still active and that its sweep through the ice is complete."

Selene studied the relevant images in her mind's eye. The path Ondo's exploratory device had taken was clear. It had wound its way down through the atmosphere, dodging detection devices, then dived into the polar sea to operate from beneath the pack ice. It had burrowed upwards to the remains of the crashed starship, following a search pattern as it tracked down fragments.

There wasn't much left of the ship: it wasn't a hulk so much as a scattered layer of debris twenty metres down in the ice. Three centuries of snowfall had buried it deeper and deeper. Another three centuries, and the remains would sink through the underlying ocean to the sea-bed. By the look of it, few of the fragments were of any significant size: no large chunks of fuselage or ship skeleton as she'd imagined. The remains of the craft were little more than a constellation of disconnected sensor hits scattered over a wide area: an oval hundreds of kilometres across, spanning the magnetic pole.

"Looks like the ship broke up in the atmosphere," she said.

"Or it was destroyed in space and this is all that's left of the microfragments that rained down on the planet. It must have been quite a firework show for anyone near enough to see it."

"I can't tell if the borer found anything of interest," she said. As with all their comms, data returned from the burrowing probe was encrypted in case the broadcast was picked up by a Concordance listening device.

Again, Ondo's presence in her mind showed her how to decrypt and interpret the data. "It's here. The device has found several items of interest. See, here, and here. Three objects with a high molecular complexity that suggests some kind of storage medium. There may be nothing left on them, naturally, but we need to retrieve those fragments."

She could sense the excitement in him at the discovery. "We go in?"

"We go in."

They began a slow dance that Ondo was clearly well-practised in: twelve hours of creeping forwards under the *Radiant Dragon*'s reaction drives, then a pause to study the telemetry for any hint of Concordance activity. With each step, they gained more up-to-date information about the situation around Maes Far, but also came closer to the solar mass that made any escape jump into metaspace riskier and risker. Still there was no sign of unusual activity. With each delay, she found it harder and harder to contain her frustration. Ondo's wariness had kept him alive for many years, but the slowness of it was utterly maddening. The *Dragon*'s reaction drives could accelerate it to 10% light speed, but the constant pauses meant the journey to Maes Far would take weeks.

Finally, she could stand it no longer. "If they've seen us, they'll come for us. However their transgalactic communication system functions, it clearly does function; if a sentinel has picked us up, they'll be coming for us now. We have to make a dive for the planet while we can."

"If we move in, we'll lose the option to jump away to safety without a significant reaction-drive acceleration period."

"If we don't, we'll lose our chance to recover the memory fragments."

He was torn between his desire to know and his wariness of risks. "If they see us, they may surmise that you're alive and simply wished to see your homeworld again. I don't think they'll necessarily infer there are other starship remains here."

"But they might. Why this caution?" she said.

"Concordance technological artefacts sometimes employ a fogging technology that makes them hard to detect by normal means. It renders them highly transparent across the electromagnetic spectrum, and it also does a good job of masking the trails they've taken through metaspace. The tech isn't perfect, but it's not far off. I've been experimenting with attempting to replicate it, so far with mixed results. Spotting their ships takes time, but if you sit and look for long enough, you see the background stars being systematically dimmed. It's one reason I emerged from metaspace here, where there are lots of background objects to check against. When you have a pattern of occultations, you get some idea of what you're dealing with: size, trajectory and so forth."

"However long we sit here, we can never be sure we're safe. We might happen not to see them. They might arrive in-system at the moment we move."

Ondo studied her for a moment, seeing something in her that appeared to amuse him.

"Possibly I was less cautious as a younger man," he said. "And possibly I've become too wary over the years. Very well, we'll make a run for the planet. But I wanted you to understand the safest way to approach. When you're operating alone, you'll need to know these things."

He was still protecting her. Strange that she was starting to feel just a little grateful for that. At some point, his feelings about her had started to matter. She wanted him to trust her. She needed him to if she was going to take command of the *Dragon*.

"You're right, we should wait until you're absolutely ready," she conceded. "You know best."

"Oh, it's entirely possible I don't. I think you're right. Let's go in now; there's no sign of any Concordance activity. They may be materialising just outside our sphere of knowledge, but that's always a risk."

Selene spun up the reaction drives, and they surged towards a carefully calculated interception point on the orbital path of Maes Far.

Ten hours later, they were locked into high orbit of the planet. They'd still seen no sign of any other ship arriving, no suggestion Concordance forces were approaching. From their vantage point, the disc of the shroud was an insignificant sliver of matter in the gulf of space, but because of it, the surface of the planet was dark. No cities blazed out artificial lights in the darkness. No pearlescence glowed in the atmospheric envelope as dawn approached; no terminator swept across the planet's face to turn night into day as it would on any other world.

"We'll take a lander down," said Ondo. "A smaller ship has more chance of being able to sneak through their observation arrays."

The *Dragon* was perfectly capable of operating in the

atmosphere of a planet — or within its oceans. But its greater bulk was a risk, and the ship's shape wasn't particularly aerodynamic in high-friction environments.

"I'll plot a holding pattern for the *Dragon*," she said, "keep it orbiting away from any Concordance sweeps." Already her control of the ship was becoming more instinctive.

She caught Ondo's worried glance as they stepped together into the lander. He was checking to see if she was coping psychologically. She hadn't been in one since her escape from Maes Far, the identical vessel that had been blasted to pieces around her as she escaped.

The craft was big enough for the two of them and a few cases of cargo and not much else; there was room for the two of them to pass each other in the narrow corridor between control deck and hold, but doing so involved a brief, intimate dance of embrace. The lander was a sleek ovoid designed for atmospheric insertion, but it had minimal defences and only two lateral blaster arrays for weaponry. Its low-power energy hull and tinny thin fuselage would be enough to protect them from incineration as they flared into the atmosphere, but offered little in the way of useful armour if it came to a fight. Their best defences were speed and stealth.

She nodded to him. She was fine. More or less. Pre-flight checks would provide a welcome distraction from her memories. While they strapped themselves in, she busied herself with interfacing with the lander, checking diagnostics and plotting the course it would need to take. The thermal stresses upon the little craft would be significant, but within acceptable tolerances.

They made a hard descent, bone-rattlingly vertical, a fast drop between Concordance observation cones directly down to the ice of the polar cap. Ondo sat unperturbed through it all, his features a blur as the ship shook. He may have been trying to smile reassurance at her, but she couldn't be sure. The exterior of the voidhull hit two thousand degrees but remained intact, the energy hull absorbing and shunting away the worst of the frictional heat. She tried to focus on monitoring the ship's status, as well as the telemetry from orbiting nanosensors, suppressing her anxiety that the lander was breaking up around her.

At one kilometre from the polar ice, they pulled out of the drop. She could feel the stresses tearing through the ship as something like pain in her own body. She groaned from the crushing high-g weight of the manoeuvre, but whether that was because of the effect on the spars of the lander or her own tissues, she couldn't be sure. Her artificial half continued to function completely normally, unaffected by the strains. Her biology blacked out for a period of seven seconds during the worst of it, but her augmentations remained fully operational, calmly informing her what had taken place once she regained full consciousness.

They levelled out one hundred metres above Maes Far's southern ice-cap, only a few centimetres off Ondo's target trajectory. They skimmed over a blindingly white surface, jagged peaks alarmingly near. So far south, the shroud didn't fully cover the sun: the object's size and positioning meant that 99% of the globe was in perpetual darkness, ensuring total climatic destruction, but the two poles saw a sliver of light for the six months of their summers. It could never be enough to sustain any sort of advanced biology, but did mean that single-celled organisms and maybe primitive plants might survive in those two, small ecological niches.

They crossed the terminator into darkness ten kilometres from the pole, then sped for twenty minutes to the edge of the ice-sheet. The lander's lights flashed across ice-plains and glaciers, with no sign of the megafauna that had once lived upon the icy continent. The ship slowed as it reached the edge of the ice before plunging into the waters of the southern ocean. It dived two hundred metres before manoeuvring in a half-circle and heading back to the pole and the rendezvous point with the borer. The pack ice was fifty metres thick at its centre, enough to shield them from casual orbital monitoring, giving them more time to operate. The lander's lights lit up the ceiling of ice above them, delicate blue in hue, and smoothed to frozen waves by the long actions of the ocean currents.

Once, these seas had been a rich soup of swarming krill and planktonic life, and giant Southern Behemoths had grazed upon drifting, subaquatic meadows of mass-colony protozoa. That was all gone now; two kilometres down, the sea-bed was carpeted with a rich layer of decaying biomass.

As the lander surged southwards, Ondo left a trail of sensor relays in the water behind them to ensure good visibility of the *Dragon* and the telemetry it was receiving from across the system. No Concordance ships had arrived during their dive to the surface. It appeared she and Ondo had successfully eluded the monitoring network their pursuers had cast around the planet.

The machine Ondo had set to tunnelling through the ice was a two-metre cylinder, its nose a rifled cone that allowed it to drill with microscopic accuracy through to each fragment of the ancient ship buried within the ice. The three objects it had collected were now cocooned safely within its body, plucked from the ice by the borer's grabbers. Ondo manoeuvred the lander up to the ice to form a seal directly below the waiting device. A shower of ice particles and frozen water rained down as the borer emerged and Selene reached up to pull it free.

Ondo dismantled the body of the borer carefully. The bulk of its innards was taken up by eight compartments, three of which were filled with the retrieved objects. Each was cocooned within a shimmering blue stasis field generated by a tiny propagator. Ondo picked up each fragment by their stub, holding it between his fingertips to study the object hovering within through his multiglasses.

Selene, zooming in with her left eye was able to see even more detail than Ondo. There could be no doubt each object revealed complex patterns at the molecular level. There had to be some chance they were storage media of some sort. The question was, could she and Ondo read data off them, decrypt them to make their contents readable?

The first two objects were something like the flecks she and Ondo had inside their brains: rice-grain metallic specks with a clear electromagnetic signature. Both appeared to be whole and undamaged.

It was the third object that fascinated Ondo the most, however. This appeared to be a glass sphere perhaps half a centimetre in diameter. He stared into it for some time, moving it around in an attempt to catch the light at the right angle. The iridescence shot through the little sphere reminded Selene of staring into an eye.

"This is a memory device?" she asked.

He was distracted as he replied, barely hearing her. "I'm not sure what it is. There's certainly complex structure within it. The borer reported that it appeared to have resided inside the skull of one of the crew members, but there was little left of the organic remains other than an impression in the ice."

"*Inside* their skull? It's a projectile weapon shot of some kind?"

"I suppose that's possible. It seems a strange design for a bullet though, and very crude. I'd say it's more likely this is some other design of brain-enhancement fleck."

"Will you be able to read anything off it?"

"I'm really not sure. I'm not sure about any of these fragments."

"You have lots of scraps like these in the Vault."

His eyes were unnaturally large through his multiglasses. "Not like this bead. Unless I'm very much mistaken, this is not from any Magellanic ship. These remains are from the other side: a Concordance vessel crashed into the ice above us."

"I thought you said you don't know of any Concordance crash sites?"

"I don't. Or at least, I didn't until now."

"Are you sure?"

"Not completely. Your father's notes suggested a Concordance ship had been ambushed by a significant force of Magellanic Alliance craft over Maes Far. My guess is that this is the result. A rare victory for the side that ultimately lost the war. I really need to get these objects back to the Refuge and study them in detail."

They sealed the lander up again, then retraced their route through the dark waters to the edge of the ice. Surging free of the ocean, they followed the precalculated return vector across the ice-fields. They burst back into sunlight to arc upwards in an ascent directly over the pole, climbing to their rendezvous point with the *Dragon* locked in high orbit.

They were one hundred metres above the surface when the lander's alarms began to scream inside Selene's mind. High-g ground-to-air harpoons were converging on the lander, impact imminent, total destruction of the ship 99% likely.

At times of high stress since her repair, she'd often suffered the unpleasant sensation of her mind dividing into two, as if her natural tissues had not fully accepted the links to her artificial half. It was always a disturbing and sickening sensation, as if she were really two people, or as if she didn't know who or what she was. It was like that now. Part of her mind, the original part, spun into panic as visions of her previous lander journey, her escape from Maes Far, filled her. The little ship being torn apart by Concordance weaponry with her strapped inside, helpless, screaming into the void. The terror of it, the crippling pain of her injuries.

But the other part of her brain looked calmly on, studying telemetry, assessing risks. The flaw in

Concordance's monitoring network wasn't a flaw at all. The enemy had known about the fragments in the ice all along, known Ondo would eventually come for them. They had laid their traps carefully: some technology akin to the starship fogging field had concealed the bunkers from their scans. From what Ondo had said, that was new behaviour. Concordance had worked hard to kill them.

The lander was under fire from two different installations, a ring of ground stations arrayed around the pole. Two of the harpoons would strike within three and a half seconds, then the second salvo, two more missiles, a further three seconds later. Ondo sent the lander into a series of jinking manoeuvres in an attempt to avoid the impacts. She studied the projected trajectories of the harpoons plotted against the chaotic movements of the lander, and instructed the ship to overload its energy hull in the areas where an impact was most likely.

She knew, even as she did so, that it would make little difference. They had no defensive ordnance capable of seeking out the incoming missiles and destroying them before they struck. Their hull would never be strong enough to withstand the impact of even one of the harpoons. The organic part of her brain continued to scream and rage, while her other half looked on with detached calmness at the unfolding dance of lander and weapons.

The first harpoon struck, punching the reaction drive array clean off the lander. The little craft went spinning helplessly out of control towards the pristine ice below.

8. Ghost Translation

"There's someone out there on the ice." Her voice was strangely thin in the freezing air.

The low curve of the sun's limb shone through a ragged hole in the fuselage, blinding her before the filters kicked in within her left eye. She was hanging upside-down by her seat-restraints, and she was still alive. How was she still alive? This time she'd lost conscious thought for a period of thirty-two seconds, the shock of the imminent crash-landing and the extreme deceleration of the impact too much for her biology. Telemetry streaming into her brain from the ruined lander's systems and down from the array of orbital nanosensors allowed her to build up a view of what was happening. They'd crashed near the pole, brought down by the high-g harpoon strike. The weapon had been launched with no warheads; its mass and velocity were all it needed to inflict its damage on the lander.

She sought for data streams from the *Dragon*, looking for a status report on local space. There might be a sky of Concordance ships up there. She got nothing, no signal from the *Dragon* at all. It wasn't in its orbit above Maes Far anymore. It was gone, their only way to get off-planet and out of the system.

Fuck. Fuck fuck. Fuck.

Her attention moved on. None of the other three missiles had struck them; one was buried a metre deep in the pack ice some seventeen kilometres away, while the other two were still in the air. Their reaction drives spent, they were plummeting harmlessly to the ground fifty-five kilometres away. It made no sense; the harpoons were far more manoeuvrable than the lander, with guidance systems easily capable of adjusting to the ship's ponderous dodging.

She turned her attention back to the figure on the ice, glimpsed from low orbit by a drifting nanosensor. There was a ship there, a whole craft buried in the ice, once concealed but now out in the open, its camouflaging carapace of snow sloughed off. Only a turret protruded from the ice, but the fogging field that had hidden the craft was deactivated. Whoever was inside no longer needed to remain concealed; the trap had been sprung. A high-powered energy wall curved over the ship in a half-dome, shielding it. Actually, judging by the electromagnetic fields displacing around it, it was a full dome, protecting the ship against attack from above and below.

"Who is it?" she asked. "What are they doing?"

Ondo still hadn't replied. She craned her neck around sideways to look at him. In the freezing air, her ragged breath billowed out in front of her, clouding the scene. Her artificial systems had compensated for the icy grasp of the polar air, ramping up exothermic chemical reactions to spread warmth through her tissues. Ondo had no such protection. He hung by his straps from the other seat. His eyes were closed and he wasn't moving. His muscles were shivering involuntarily. She queried the flecks in his brain to check his biological status, something he'd granted her privilege to do. His nervous system was sluggish, but active. He was alive, physically undamaged, but succumbing to frostbite and hypothermia as his biology withdrew precious heat from his extremities to keep his core alive.

She queried the lander's systems to see if the voidhull could be sealed, the air within warmed, but got no response. The lander was dead.

She reached across and touched Ondo's hand, uselessly willing heat to cross from her flesh to his. Unable to manipulate its immediate environment, his biology was reacting as it should, but it was a flawed strategy. He would never emerge from his oblivion. She had to override his natural reactions, rouse him, take control of his body's responses. She sent instructions into his flecks, instructing them to rouse him to consciousness, at the same time grappling with the restraints that held her pinned to her seat.

She fell to the floor that had once been the ceiling, landing in an undignified heap. In the same moment, Ondo's flecks reported that he was responding, slowly surfacing to awareness. She reached up above her head to free him from his restraints, catching him as he fell to cradle him to the ground. She wrapped her body around his to give him her warmth.

She saw the moment his eyes flickered open. From his far-away stare she guessed he was also studying the telemetry, pulling in all the data he could just as she had, assessing his situation. His augmentations were nothing like hers, but they were capable of passively monitoring his surroundings while his natural brain slept. Now, finally, he answered the questions she'd asked him while he was out of it. They were close enough for his words to be communicated brain-to-brain, with no prospect of anyone else listening in.

"It's a Void Walker."

"Here?"

"So it seems."

"How can that be? You've been monitoring the planet intimately since my escape, watching for possible traps."

He thought about that for a moment, his larynx

bobbing in his neck as he worked his throat into life. "They must have embedded him in the ice-cap during the chaos of the initial attack. My guess is he's been here ever since you escaped, waiting for the moment I, or someone, came for the fragments."

"We might never have come; the Walker could have been here for years, for his whole life."

"The Void Walkers are fanatics, unquestioning, used by Concordance as it sees fit. One would happily sacrifice themselves on the spot if a First Augur instructed them to."

"Concordance knew about the ship in the ice all along."

"Yes." A troubled look flashed across his features as his words streamed into her mind. "I've mentioned before how they often seem to know things they should have no way of knowing. How did they discover the fragments were here? How did they calculate we'd find out and come looking?"

"It's no great mystery. They're eavesdropping on you, listening in."

"I'm sure they're not, you've seen how careful I am. *Insanely paranoid*, I believe you said. If they knew where the Refuge was, they'd have come for us a long time ago."

"Then the answer's obvious. Omn knows and sees everything."

From the flicker of his smile, it appeared her words had amused him. "Of course. That would explain it."

"Why are we even alive? Why did the other three harpoons miss us?"

"I assume because Concordance don't want us dead yet. They brought us down so they could capture us."

"Or they want the memory fragments."

Ondo shook his head, closed his eyes. "They could have retrieved the artefacts any time they wanted. This is about us."

Another idea occurred to her. "If they knew about the

fragments, maybe they were manipulating my father all along, letting him make his discoveries so they would reach you, make you come here."

"It is possible. Me or someone else, some other enemy of Concordance."

He was shivering in her arms; she needed to raise his body temperature. The lander was equipped with environmental suits for use if it lost atmospheric integrity or, *in extremis*, if they needed to carry out EVA manoeuvres. The suit would be clumsy to wear but would give Ondo a degree of protection. A couple of hours outside, and she'd need one too, but for now her augmentations protected her. She propped Ondo up against a bulkhead and retrieved a suit from its locker, vacuum-sealed to minimize its volume. She helped him into it, feeding his arms into the sleeves and closing up the seals, like he was a child and she his mother helping him get dressed.

"What do we do now?" she spoke out loud as she worked, as if it was something of little importance. "They've destroyed the *Dragon*. We're alone."

"Most likely the *Dragon* detected what was happening to us and went into a stealth/evasion pattern. It's possible it's simply hiding itself."

"Where?"

"Hard to say. I gave its Mind considerable autonomy to act in these situations. Preprograming an adequate response is basically impossible, and its capacity for analysis and strategy is considerable. Besides, it would be a risk if we knew exactly what it was up to; if we did, then potentially others could find out from us. If it's out there, we still have a chance."

"So, we sit and wait?"

"The Walker is waiting for us at the pole. I think we should go and see what he wants."

She studied the distant scene, seeing it from overhead through the eyes of an atmospheric nanosensor. The

Walker stood unmoving in front of his buried ship. Clearly waiting for them. "I don't like it. We're safer here."

"It's not like you to be cautious," said Ondo. "I thought that was what I brought to the relationship."

"There's taking the attack to them and then there's suicide. This ship gives us some shelter."

"Not enough. It's broken beyond repair and our food supplies will run out very quickly. Sooner or later we have to confront him, especially if the *Dragon* has been destroyed. His ship is the only way off this planet. Perhaps there is something going on here we don't understand. Perhaps this Walker has gone rogue, isn't what we think. In my encounters with them, I've sometimes had the impression that there are suppressed, conflicting personality traits within them. Some repressed side-effect of their indoctrination. Or, then again, if he *is* what we think, and he's summoned other Concordance forces, we should move before they get here."

With her help, he climbed to his feet. His core temperature still wasn't as high as she'd like it to be, but it was stabilizing. Moving would be good for him. The air outside the ship was frozen cold, but it was mercifully still, with no wind-chill. At least they'd be safe from the ice-wolves that had once prowled the snows. They'd even have the weak light and heat of the sun on them for the five kilometre trek to the pole. The thought of that, her homeworld sun, the sun of her childhood, shining on her skin once more, was an appealing prospect.

They scavenged what few supplies of food and water they could from the wreckage. They obviously had access to an unlimited supply of ice, but she was wary of lowering Ondo's core temperature again if he consumed it. What else could they take that might be useful? Not much. The craft had been equipped with a rack of handguns and rifles, but these had been thrown clear in the harpoon strike.

She climbed out of the jagged hole in the lander's

voidhull and jumped down to the ice. The craft's remaining blaster array was still attached. Bracing her foot against it, she wrenched one of the barrels and its firing mechanism free from its turret. It would do as a makeshift weapon. It would have been too heavy for any normal person to use, unless they were from some seriously high-g world, but she was able to cradle it in her left arm with relative ease. There was no mechanical trigger, but there were electronic control systems she could interface with to make the weapon fire. It retained enough charge for a few shots. Holding it made her feel a little bit better about facing the Walker.

She helped Ondo out of the ship and they set off. The sliver of sun was low in the north, canted onto its side like the thinnest sliver of a new moon. A shooting star arced across the velvet sky and winked out. Perhaps it was some Concordance orbital artefact burning up, or one of Ondo's, or just some random speck of space dust. The hazy light gave the scene a sense of impossible distances, as if the distant peaks and folds in the ice were unreachable, mystical lands. Their path looked clear enough though: head south for the pole and the waiting Void Walker. They walked together in silence, each of them sifting through the telemetry from above, wary, watching for the arrival of other ships.

Half-way there, a single harpoon shot blasted off from one of the batteries at the pole. All shining white metal, it rose into the clear, cold air upon a column of cloud to reach a height of four hundred metres. It was already angling back down to the ice as it flashed over them, soundless in its supersonic rush. It was clearly targeting the ruined lander. It struck a few seconds later. This time, there was an explosive payload; the detonation burst apart the air, the shock wave through the ice sending both of them stumbling to the ground.

She caught Ondo's eye, and a look of understanding passed between them. Concordance *did* want them alive, and it was making sure they had no way off the planet. They could do nothing but continue to the pole.

The Void Walker stood motionless as they approached, a calculating scowl on his features. He wore the plain grey robes of all those in his sect. He was a young man, barely older than she was. There was something predatory in his features, as if he were deciding the best moment to leap to the attack. Judging by the hunger in his eyes, the prospect of it delighted him enormously. His head was shaved bald, a caterpillar scar creeping across his skull behind his left ear, as was the case with all Void Walkers. Some part of the medical procedures carried out on them, according to Ondo.

His voice was fuzzed slightly by the energy wall, but his words were clear when he spoke. "We knew you would come. We knew you wouldn't be able to resist the temptation of the forbidden knowledge buried in the ice."

"Why are you here?" asked Ondo. "Such a cold and lonely place to see out your years."

The Walker's grin widened at Ondo's words. "You should know all about being cold and lonely, heretic, traitor, out there alone in your hollowed-out rock. Except, now you're not alone; now you have your companion to listen to your lies. This girl from Maes Far, or what little remains of her. What abomination have you turned her into? Your whore, programmed to submit to your every depravity?"

Selene took a step closer, bringing up the barrel of the lander blaster to point directly at the Walker's head. The energy wall might or might not be powerful enough to protect him from a close-range shot. "What do you want, Walker? What you are doing here?"

"Isn't it obvious? I'm here to complete what was started. You must die. It is clear there isn't much of you left, but even that must be burned away until nothing remains. It is because of populations like yours that evil enters the galactic mind. Your sins are to blame for all that is malevolent and cruel. There must be no survivors of Maes Far; its evils are to be cauterized."

"What evils?"

"The fact that you don't know simply proves your debasement."

It was the grin on his face that made her fire, unleashing a solid beam of blaster fire at his head. He stood impassive, unmoved, as the energy flared across the surface of the dome and dissipated with a rising whine. He was unharmed, but she at least felt better for having tried. He probably didn't know what the supposed *evils* were, either. He was a tool of Concordance, dutifully parroting the words given to him. Even if he didn't believe the words he'd spoken, he would have said them anyway. His appearance, the arrival of she and Ondo at the pole: it was all a performance, the final act in the long destruction of Maes Far. The air was thick with enemy nanosensors, recording images, streaming it skywards. The galaxy would be watching; it would be allowed to see. The last survivor a survivor no more. The iron rule of Concordance enforced. Judgement enforced.

"And what of me?" asked Ondo. It appeared he'd come to the same conclusion that she had. His voice was tinny through his suit's speaker grille. "What are your plans for me? If you simply wanted us dead, you could have struck us in flight."

The Walker inclined his head to one side to consider Ondo. "You will be returned to Omn, to the light you turned your back on. You made vows to him, and they will be kept, one way or another."

"And what if we choose not to come?" she asked. "What if we choose not to play our parts in this little game of yours?"

"Then I will make you play."

"We would walk into the darkness of this world, the world you destroyed, rather than join you," said Selene. "You can't touch us hiding away in your little bubble." It was an empty threat, but it was all she had. They had nowhere to walk to, and more Concordance ships would be arriving in-system soon, if they weren't already there.

"Oh, I think I can keep your attention a little while longer," the Walker replied. "You see, I haven't been alone all this time. You are not the only survivor of Maes Far. There is one other. I've had my companion, too. Would you like to meet him? You know him, of course."

A cold horror trickled through Selene at the Walker's words. "Who?"

By way of a reply, the Walker waved a hand and, without looking back, gesticulated for someone to come nearer. The entrance to the ship was little more than a hatch leading down into the ice. Bony hands clutched at the lip, and then an old man with straggling grey hair and a look of alarmed madness climbed into the light. He squinted, cowering as he took in the scene around him, as someone might who hadn't been allowed outside for a long time. He shivered visibly, only a stained white gown, torn in several places, keeping the polar cold from his skin. It was impossible to tell whether her face was covered in grime or bruises.

It took Selene a moment to grasp that this frail, shaking man was her father.

She raced forwards, throwing herself at the energy wall. Despite all her strength, she couldn't break through. "What have you done to him? Why is he here?" Her father recoiled a step at the sight of Selene charging forwards, but there was a moment when something like recognition flashed through his eyes. Hope and horror combined.

The Walker sounded amused. "In truth, he's been a poor toy. It took only a few months to break him, make him tell me everything he knows. He is weak, degenerate. The memory of the scourging agonies he has suffered at my hand keep him compliant, and he now obeys any instruction I give him without question. Pathetic, isn't he? I think he's probably happier like this, knowing his place, understanding where he belongs in the order of things. There must be comfort in that, don't you think? Before I took him, he was filled with such grand ideas and doubts. Now he is himself. Are you pleased at the sight of him?"

Selene battered on the energy wall three, four times with all the strength of her augmentations, but made no impact. She couldn't reach her father. In the thin light from the low crescent sun, there was a hint, the slightest hint, of black in his matted grey hair. Once it had been raven-dark, like hers. He'd been a strong man, muscles wiry and taut from his years of hiking and digging, but now he sagged like a broken puppet. His skin had once been weathered, darkened, by his long days spent outside in the elements, but now it was sallow and pale.

"Why are you doing this?" she asked through her tears.

But she knew the answer to that question, too. They'd tortured her father for information. More: the show was continuing, and they were the masters of the message, spreading the truth they wished people to see. As much as anything, the destruction of Maes Far was a warning to the galaxy, and the last deaths, those of her and her father, would make that warning complete. Two dangerous heretics, enemies of Concordance, brought to justice, and their entire homeworld sacrificed along with them.

Concordance wanted to obliterate everything the inhabitants of Maes Far had learned. Whatever secrets the planet had harboured, Concordance wanted to be extremely sure that they never escaped. They didn't know who had learned what, who suspected what, and so they were killing everyone on the planet in order to be sure. The calculation of it was simple.

A Void Walker was forgiven all sins, could carry out any evil, any atrocity, so long as it was done in the service of Concordance. Their souls were already lost. The one standing before her slipped a knife from his sleeve, its edge glinting, honed to a fine edge. A cutting blade.

"Ondo, do something," she said. But,

incomprehensibly, Ondo wasn't looking at the unfolding scene. He was staring into the sky, studying something, as if bored or offended at what was taking place.

The Walker held the knife to her father's neck, but his gaze was on Selene. "Give your daughter your message," he said.

Her father's throat worked a few times, his Adam's Apple bobbing. His voice was wavering, broken, but he got the words out eventually. "You have to die, Selene. You should have died; we all deserved to die for our evils. You should never have escaped judgement." Now there was no look of recognition in her father's eyes.

Selene hurled herself once again at the energy wall, screaming abuse at the Walker. Even as she did so, she knew she was playing her part perfectly. The galaxy might or might not see the Walker threatening a defenceless, broken wreck of a man, but it would see her screaming in her animal fury. It would see what Ondo had turned her into.

His speech delivered, her father stood shivering visibly, unsure why he was there. The Walker watched Selene with clear pleasure on his face. He said, "Your father spent his life unearthing forbidden knowledge, peddling vile lies about Omn, and when the end came, he passed all he'd learned onto you, planning for you to take over from him. Now you will watch what happens to him as a result, and then the same will happen to you."

"No."

"Tell me first, was your father a good man?"

"What?"

"Think carefully before you answer. Was he a good man?"

"Yes, he was. He *is* a good man. Always." Her father, the knife to his throat, didn't respond, as if incapable of understanding what was happening.

The Void Walker appeared satisfied with her reply. "Then you should be grateful to me. An eternity of ecstasy awaits him through the sacred wormhole. I will speed his passage to the judgement of Omn and free him from the sufferings of this realm."

The Void Walker took a fresh grip on the blade in his hand and slowly, deliberately, pushed it into her father's neck, slicing his skin and tissues open. A spray of red blood speckled the white snow and her father slumped silently to the ground, clutching at his ruined throat, trying and failing to keep the blood inside his body.

Selene stepped back, raised the blaster barrel and fired again and again, desperate to get at the Walker so she could tear him to pieces, save her father, but the energy shielding held.

"Selene." Ondo was still looking upwards, something up there fascinating him. "We have to go."

She turned on him in her rage. His words made no sense. "Go *where*? Go *how*? We need to save him. My father, your friend, is dying in front of our eyes. Can't you fucking see?"

"Look." Ondo was pointing into the sky. A ring of three lights shone, like stars at dusk. She could make no sense of what they were, but they were unimportant. A few steps away from her, her father's body lay twitching upon the ice. With the right medical attention, he could still be saved.

"We have to leave," said Ondo again. "I'm sorry, there's nothing we can do for him. If we'd known he was here, then we could have tried. The *Dragon* has come for us and we have to get out."

"What are you talking about?"

"It must have triggered three of the orbital nukes I parked in orbit."

"Nukes."

"Fission weapons, crude but effective. They've entered the atmosphere and will detonate a kilometre above the ice. We have to leave now."

"We can't leave. How can we leave?" Once again, she

had the unpleasant sensation of her mind ripping into two. What was the *Dragon* thinking when she and Ondo had no means of escape?

A growing rumble ran through the ice beneath her feet, strengthening each moment, and she thought a nuke must have detonated already; that a superheated blast-wave wall would slam into them at any moment, searing their skin and tissues from their bones. Instead, impossibly, a triangle of metal or stone rose from the ice fifty metres away, like some ancient temple arising from the depths. Then she grasped what it was: the apex of the *Dragon*, forcing its way up through the pack ice to reach them. It had entered the atmosphere, found a safe descent vector and used the oceans to get to them undetected. Great slabs of ice were pushed up and out as the bulk of the ship forced itself free of the ice. She could feel the heat blasting off it on her face: it had used its beam-weapons to thrust its way through.

The Walker, meanwhile, was retreating into his lair. He'd seen the *Dragon* and the approaching nukes and had come to the same realisation of what he had to do: power up his ship and escape the planet. But he stopped for a moment to consider the body of the man on the ice in front of him. Perhaps he was making the same calculation Selene was: he could be brought back to life in the Refuge just as Selene had been. His injuries were nothing compared to those she'd suffered.

It was an act of simple malice. The Walker sent an instruction to the blaster atop the turret of his ship. A beam of light lanced down, striking her father's body, turning him to fire and then to ash. The Walker's face lit up red as the weapon played across her father's body.

Fury coiled within Selene; she would kill this Walker even if it meant sacrificing herself. But Ondo seized her by the arm and pulled her away. "If we die here, we'll never defeat them."

The calculating part of her brain projected likely

outcomes of everything that was unfolding around them: their distance from the *Dragon*, its optimal trajectory as it left the planet, the contrary routes of the nukes as they screamed groundward. Possible escape vectors for the Walker in his Concordance ship.

She chose. She tossed aside the blaster and lifted Ondo off the ground. He couldn't move quickly enough. She threw him across her left shoulder, then raced for the *Dragon*, at the same time firing instructions at the ship's control systems. Then would be no time for the usual niceties of a prep for atmospheric launch. Her natural tissues burned at the effort of running while carrying Ondo, but she ignored them, amping up her biological response with an artificial burst of adrenaline.

They fell into the *Dragon*'s open hatch. The doorway irised shut and the ship's energy hull zapped up to full power. She felt the ship's drives powering up, shudders of suppressed energy rumbling through its superstructure. It still had to force the bulk of its pyramidal body through the pack-ice. In the sky, the nukes were three kilometres from the ground, fanning out as they arranged themselves into a pattern that would inflict maximum destruction across the polar region. She and Ondo lay in the hatchway of the *Dragon*, both seeing what was happening, neither able to do much more than watch and wait.

A rising whine of fury shuddered through the ship and then it burst free, firing upwards into the clear air over the pole, climbing at maximum thrust. The violence of the acceleration pinned them to the deck. Ondo blacked out and only Selene's augmentations, overriding her biology, kept her from doing the same. If she lost consciousness, and Concordance intercepted them, she might never awaken. Their escape vector angled away from the pole. There was a moment when the three nukes and the *Dragon* were at the same altitude, a moment of strange calm. She studied the weapons through the *Dragon*'s sensors, their sleek, malevolent form. The Walker's ship was in the air, too, but it was lower. Maybe some of its systems had degraded during its sojourn in the ice. The *Dragon* needed only a few more seconds to climb high enough to escape the blast wave from the nukes and they might make it.

The light of three new suns flared in her eyes as the nukes detonated, bathing her dead world in their demonic fury. The *Dragon* rose, climbing a beat ahead of the atmospheric blast wave. The higher they ascended and the thinner the atmosphere, the less damaging the thermal shock would be. She saw how it would go. She felt a fresh surge shake through the *Dragon*, as if it had made the same calculation and was putting all its energy into the effort of escaping.

Twelve seconds later, they passed out of the stratosphere mere metres ahead of the raging heat plume.

In the violence and radiation blast of the detonations, she'd lost track of the Walker vessel. Its trajectory had been marginal; most likely it had been engulfed by the explosions and vaporised. The thought of that made her feel a little better.

She turned her attention to local space. Five Concordance ships had arrived in-system, converging on the planet from different angles. Their intention was clearly to cut off the *Dragon*'s escape routes as it fled the stellar mass and accelerated into its metaspace jump. There were gaps in the net, but the chances were other ships would arrive – or already had arrived outside their sphere of knowledge – to plug them. With she and Ondo back on board, the *Dragon* ceded control back to them. Ondo instructed it to head towards one of the gaps in the attacking ship cloud.

It wasn't the one she would have picked; there were nearer exit routes.

"Why that one?" She said.

"I've studied their strategies for many years. This route gives us our best chance of escaping."

"You can't be sure of that."

"No."

She didn't argue further. The immediate threat from the nukes was gone. They had a little time before any engagement with the approaching Concordance ships. She picked herself off the floor and helped Ondo to peel off his environmental suit. As she did so, she noticed her left hand was trembling, minutely but rapidly. It was almost blurred to look at. She held it up to study, intrigued. "Something's going wrong with my biomechanics."

Ondo took both her hands and held them in his, studying them, turning them over, comparing artificial with natural.

He said, "I don't think there's anything wrong with your augmentations."

The adrenaline was still pumping through her, like the control mechanism had spiralled out of control. "You can see the tremor."

He let go of her hands. "Your enhanced internal senses make you more aware of it, that's all. Your right hand is doing it, too."

"No, it isn't." But she held her natural hand up to the light and saw that he was correct. It, too, shook.

"It's actually a sign that your systems have become well-integrated," said Ondo. "Both halves acting in concert."

"Then, what's wrong with me?"

"Nothing is wrong with you, at least nothing that isn't understandable. You've just seen your own father murdered minutes after discovering he was still alive. You're still recovering from what happened to you when you escaped the planet the first time. It's normal to have a reaction to all of that. Anyone would."

"I'm not having a reaction. I'm fine."

"You're functioning, there's a difference. You may need short-term biochemical remediation, but if we escape from this, we should talk about what you've been through at more length. It will help."

She often felt angry at him, at his intrusions, at being given instructions. On more than one occasion during her rehabilitation she'd had to resist the urge to punch him.

"I don't need to talk," she said. "I need to escape this damn system and never come back."

They were on the *Dragon*'s cartography deck now. They walked through a three-dimensional image of the Maes Far system that filled the room. Tags marked ships and satellites, while the vectors of vessels moving in-system were projected in coloured lines. Seven Concordance craft had now arrived. They were Cathedral class, resembling the ship that had punched her from the sky the first time she escaped from Maes Far. Their twisting, nacreous forms made her think of a scatter of shells on the beach, sea-washed and gleaming. Each one was easily capable of reducing the *Dragon* to its constituent quarks and leptons if they managed to manoeuvre within range. The two nearer ones had released high-g missiles, but they were too remote to imminently threaten the *Dragon*.

She studied the pattern of them, trying to understand what Concordance's plan was. "They're corralling us, cutting off escape routes."

"It's their usual approach, but they can't plug all the holes."

Their route into metaspace was still clear, but a ship could emerge in that direction at any moment. It was possible they were being shepherded into a trap.

They watched in nervous silence as the dance of ships and missiles unfolded. Now the display showed the countdown to their metaspace translation point. Twenty-two minutes. The *Dragon* accumulated velocity all the time, bringing the point nearer, by the same token making them less manoeuvrable if they needed to dodge and fight. There was a grey area when they would be far enough from the stellar mass to make the jump *probably* safe, and then there was a point farther out at which the manoeuvre approached 99% dependable. That was Ondo's preferred target; she'd have gone with anything above 90%. The longer they waited, the higher the chance of a Concordance ship emerging directly in their path.

She brought the *Dragon*'s forwards weapon arrays online in readiness. There was a moment, four hundred thousand kilometres from the planet, when she held up her left hand and covered the receding disc of Maes Far with a single one of her artificial fingers, blotting it out just as the shroud had blotted out the sun. Everything she'd ever known and loved, concealed by a single fingertip.

The countdown had reached eight minutes when the *Dragon* calmly announced it had detected a ship-sized mass emerging from metaspace ahead of them. Another Concordance vessel, arriving on their escape vector. Ondo hesitated, waiting for more data. He was too damned analytical, too ready to observe. Like the whole universe was simply a puzzle put there for him to ponder.

She had no such hang-ups. They needed to act. The safe translation probability was at 84.5%. It would have to be good enough. She instructed the *Dragon* to commence its translation into metaspace. Ondo's hand moved as if he planned to override her, but he stopped himself. She felt the translation process beginning; the flutter in her stomach, the accelerating headlong rush that was a plummeting fall and a soaring high-g rush at the same time. The *Dragon* completed its translation calculations as it powered up its metaspace projectors.

They were half-translated out of reality when the Concordance ship arrived. Ondo had explained to her the dangers of a ghost translation, of intersecting with another ship as it dropped into normal space at the precise moment they jumped out. It was a vanishingly rare event but almost always fatal to all involved. Depending on the relative degrees of translation the ships could collide, or fuse together, or simply pull each other apart with the forces of their respective manoeuvres.

It happened now. Even as the stars of normal space

faded, the lines and angles of a Concordance ship appeared around them, engulfing them, passing directly through them even as they passed through it. To each ship, the other faded as one left and one entered metaspace, but there was a moment when Selene saw the interior of the enemy vessel, its corridors and decks and mechanisms crisply clear. She saw the faces of the people on board, the crew and at least two Void Walkers, and she knew that they'd seen her, too. They watched each other as their ships momentarily intersected, almost close enough to touch but divided by the different realities they inhabited.

She caught a passing glimpse, brief but clear to her augmented vision, of the Cathedral ship's convocation. Concordance ships were controlled by an inner circle of clerical officers: a Hierarch, a Stellar Mechanic, the ship's Augur, among others. They sat in their elaborate robes at the heart of the ship, their faces an assortment of determination, calculation and alarm. Supposedly, the circles controlling each vessel were an analogue of the circle of First Augurs that sat in convocation at the God Star, directing events across the entire galaxy, translating and interpreting the will of Omn. The circles on the ships were responsible for implementing the instructions passed to them, although it was unclear how much autonomy the Hierarch wielded. Did they simply carry out the letter of Omn's instructions, passed to them by the Augur, or did they have the power to interpret and improvise? Ondo sometimes wondered if it was the ships' Augurs that wielded real authority: it was they that claimed to hear the words of Omn, and who relayed them to the Hierarch for execution.

In an instant, the glimpse of the convocation circle was gone. Miraculously, no parts of the two ships had occupied the same point in real space at the same moment. The *Dragon* completed its translation into metaspace, the uniform greyness of the void seizing hold of it.

There was silence for long seconds.

"That was close," said Ondo.

"Did they survive too?"

"I'd say so, since we did."

Had she saved them or endangered them by triggering their translation early? Hard to be sure. Ondo said nothing either way. He directed the *Dragon* to follow a randomised sequence of metaspace traversals to conceal their route and give them time for full-system bug scans. They could be tracked through the void for a short distance via their wake through the Singh Field – the background structure of metaspace – but the fluctuations decayed rapidly. They needed to be sure Concordance weren't on their trail. Ondo was convinced it was possible to develop technology that could detect a wake for a much longer period – possibly weeks or months – a fact that caused him great anxiety. As he'd explained, he had no proof it was possible, but no proof it was impossible, either.

She wanted to quiz him about everything that had happened on Maes Far, but he was already distracted, studying the flecks they'd recovered from the ice. She left him for the seclusion of her own room. Her heart was still racing, her breathing elevated, but she'd calmed a little. She held up her hands again, studying them microscopically with her left eye. The tremor had subsided a little, but it was still there.

She sat on her bed and closed her eyes. Frustrated fury coursed through her. She relived the moment of her father's death again and again, the silent sinking to the ice, the spray of red upon the pristine white. Her own inability to do anything to stop it. She sank her face into her hands and let the tears come. What horrors had her father lived through at the Void Walker's hand? They'd turned a proud, clever, witty man, a man she'd loved dearly, into that broken plaything. The cruelty of it engulfed her. She was too weak to stop Concordance. Sooner or later her own fate would be that of her father's, and she would die a broken, pointless death, and nothing in the galaxy would have changed.

No. She wouldn't succumb. Move forwards, not backwards. She would fight them. She forced her mind's attention to the ship's status and telemetry readings. Apart from the patterns of fluctuation in the Singh Field, metaspace was calm around them. No sign of pursuit. She came to a decision. She had a little time; she would talk to Ondo, the inner Ondo inside her mind. She hadn't gone near the avatar since it was implanted, hadn't communicated with it, hadn't granted it access to any of her sensory inputs, but now she would. There were things she needed to know.

"Ondo, I need you." The words of the agreed summoning phrase sounded annoyingly, well, *needy*. She enunciated them as clearly as she could, then repeated them, not sure how to properly perform the summoning.

The voice inside her head spoke with complete clarity, as if it were the flesh-and-blood man communicating with her through her flecks.

"Hello, Selene." She caught a glimpse of a room filled with hazy light, the ghost of Ondo standing in the middle, but when she looked directly at him, he disappeared. He'd said it would take practice to establish clear communication with the avatar.

"Firstly," she said, "are you absolutely promising me the real Ondo won't get to hear what we discuss?"

"Upon my love for your father and upon my life, you have my word. The physical Ondo only gets to know if you tell him, otherwise this conversation remains firmly inside your head. I can be updated from the real Ondo's engrams, but no data can flow the other way, from your mind or my neural analogue into the real world. The single exception is the engram expulsion mechanism I explained, but that is completely under your control. You may banish me permanently from your mind any time you choose."

"He can't hack into you, grab a copy of you to dissect?"

"He made that impossible to do."

"But then, you would say that, because you're him."

"I'd also say that if it were the truth. He – I – wouldn't do that, but it comes down to trust in the end. Whether you believe me."

Were his words true? She had no way of knowing. But she *wanted* them to be true, and that, maybe, answered her question for her. In her mind's eye he was becoming a little more solid now, a little more like the real Ondo, but she could also tell that it wasn't him. It was a copy, a ghost, nothing more.

"Okay, first question, did you lay any traps around Maes Far on one of your visits?"

"I always do if I intend to revisit a system."

"What did you do?"

"I seeded the system with nanosensors and beacons, enough so that they couldn't possibly destroy them all. And I hid weaponry and ordnance."

"What sort of weaponry?"

"Nanomines in orbit around the planet and on likely in-system vectors. Also, missiles concealed as space debris capable of striking surface targets."

"Nukes?"

"Some were, others were smarter. Why are you asking this? What happened on the planet? From the tone of your words I'd say you are … agitated."

Ondo had updated his avatar a month earlier, meaning that the Ondo in her head knew nothing of events since that moment. No point keeping recent events from him. He hadn't attempted to conceal anything from her so far as she could tell. She granted him access to her recent visual and auditory memories. He would see the events of the last few hours from her point of view, although he wouldn't get to know her private thoughts and reactions to them. But he would get to see her biological data: heart rate, endocrine system responses, her tremor, all of it.

When he'd finished, he said, "I'm so sorry, Selene. I

had no idea anyone was still alive. They kept Seben – your father – very well hidden. What you've been through – we should talk about it. You shouldn't face it on your own."

"Yeah. The other you said something similar. First I want an answer to something that's been troubling me."

"If I know, I'll tell you."

"That Walker said, *You made vows to him. To Omn.* What did he mean?"

"He's referring to a time when I was an acolyte of Concordance."

"*You?*"

"Indeed. I was a younger man, and misguided as I now see, but I embraced it all avidly. I was fervent for a time."

"You didn't think to mention this to me?"

"I didn't keep it from you, but there was never a good time to go into it. That was a difficult, painful period of my life. And I suppose I feared what your reaction might be."

"Yeah. So you should have."

"I give you my word that I left them behind a long time ago."

"How do I know you're not still one of them – that you're not, I don't know, programmed like a Void Walker? A sleeper roaming the galaxy, acting as a magnet for all the escapees and dissidents and trouble-makers."

She thought he'd be affronted at her suggestion, but he actually gave it consideration. "The possibility occurred to me. Long before I made it to the Refuge, I checked myself very thoroughly: my tissues, my engrams, everything about myself. How did I know I didn't just *think* I was the renegade Ondo? It troubled me, I admit."

"Don't tell me, you didn't find anything."

"I did not."

"Which doesn't prove a thing."

"No. They would have programmed me not to see or believe any such evidence."

"Then we come back to whether I can trust you."

"You've seen how they pursue me, the lengths they

went to on Maes Far."

"I've seen how they pursue *me*," she said. "You were simply there. Maybe they found me because you were with me."

"If that were true, then why aren't they here now? Why didn't they come for you at the Refuge a long time ago?"

It was a good point. "I don't know."

"I think you should scan me. Carry out every analysis and investigation upon my tissues and mind you can think of. If you find nothing – as I believe will be the case – then perhaps that will put your mind at rest."

"And yours too?"

He dipped his head in agreement, the movement of the ghostly image blurred. "Perhaps. I instructed the Refuge's systems to do something similar when I constructed them, and they found nothing. It made me feel better about myself as I believed Concordance had no way of knowing that would be my plan."

"You're sure Aefrid Sen wasn't one of them, too? That the *Radiant Dragon* and the Refuge aren't hopelessly compromised?"

"Again, it's possible. There comes a point when you have to trust your judgement, otherwise you'd never do anything."

"Tell me the story. Tell me how you ended up being a part of Concordance. And then how you ended up not being."

"It's no great mystery. It took me time to find my path in life when I was younger. A common enough situation. I was impressionable and naïve, and I knew there was something bigger going on. Concordance filled the gap, seemed to offer meaning and certainty."

"How long were you with them?"

"Two years. Cathedral ships occasionally recruit locals from the planets they watch over, for reasons I don't fully understand." Ondo hesitated, reluctant to tell her something. Then he spoke again. "There is something else in my history you should know about, a thing that might give you more reason to trust me. An episode from before I joined Concordance. A part of the reason I did, perhaps."

"Go on."

"I had a family. A partner and a child on Sintorus. A daughter, as it happens, little more than a baby."

Clearly, neither partner nor daughter were around anymore. She couldn't stop herself from asking the question.

"What happened to them?"

"They died."

"What were they called?"

"My partner's name was Marita, and our daughter was Juma. Actually, your father was her folkfather."

"What does that mean?"

"On Sintorus, folkparents are friends or relatives who agree to help guide a child through their journey to adulthood, look after them if their biological parents die."

"He never said."

"He couldn't, of course."

"How did it happen?"

Ondo smiled to himself at some memory only he could see. "The irony is, Marita was always the agitator, and I was the one holding her back, telling her she was seeing conspiracies where there were none, telling her to stop causing trouble and live a normal, quiet life. She was active in the Sintorian rebellion, a cell leader, goading the planet's governments and security forces. In the end they came for her, a special forces team from the local military, and shot her where she slept in our bed. Juma, asleep beside her, was hit, too. I was away, some unimportant meeting, and I returned to find them there."

"Concordance did that to you but you still joined them?"

He nodded. "It seems incredible, I know. At the time, I still didn't believe that Concordance were using the local security forces as their front. Marita told me it often, made me try to see, but I wouldn't believe her. She was right, of course, I understand that now."

"Why did they let you join, given your partner was a known rebel?"

"I think I was something of a coup in the war for people's hearts and minds. If they could recruit *me*, it meant I was turning my back on everything Marita stood for. They could use me, speak words through me, while at the same time keeping an eye on what I did. For a time, also, I was utterly devoted to the Concordance cause, the idea of bringing peace, imposing it if need be. I think I desperately wanted to believe there was a reason for what had happened to Marita and Juma. A higher reason, I mean, some great design that made some sense of their deaths."

"But you didn't find it."

"No, it took me a while to see it, but I got there. I like to think Marita would be proud of what I finally became, but, even so, if I hadn't encountered Aefrid Sen it's entirely possible I'd still be there, a devoted member of Concordance, watching over Sintorus, nursing my losses, confused and angry."

"Sen was on your planet?"

"We didn't know it was her at the time, but we heard rumours of someone digging around in the ruins of an Omnian War crash site high up in the Snowtops. I was sent to investigate. The thinking was that my knowledge of local custom and my accent — not that I'd ever been within a thousand kilometres of the place — would convince people I was just a normal planet-dweller. I found Sen and she saw right through my subterfuge. She knew I was Concordance. But the odd thing was that she didn't kill me. Maybe she saw something in me, or she knew my story, or she was playing for time, but she decided to talk to me instead. Over a period of four days and nights, she explained much of what she'd learned and what she suspected. It's fair to say those few days utterly changed the course of my life."

"You left with her?"

"Nothing so dramatic. I let her escape, but I stayed with Concordance for nearly another year, thinking over what she'd said and what Marita had said, coming to my own conclusions. Aefrid had given me the means to communicate with her, and eventually I did. She was wary, inevitably, but she made an FTL ship available to me, and I escaped the system. Eventually, we met up, and we talked, and we worked together, and I ended up here. It was a remarkable act of trust on her part."

"You said she was old, fearful that no one would carry on her work."

"Perhaps that was it."

"And what about my father? Was he an acolyte too?"

"No, he stayed on the planet. If it helps, he tried very hard to dissuade me from going to the Cathedral ship. We had a lot of angry arguments when I told him I was planning to join Concordance. He was sympathetic to what had happened, kept telling me it was a misguided reaction to my grief. He was right, of course. I didn't communicate with him at all when I was with Concordance; it would have been too dangerous for both of us. Besides, he'd pretty much disowned me. But then, when I'd decided to make my escape, I got back in touch with him."

"How did he react to that?"

"Something like your reaction now." The memory of that seemed to amuse Ondo. "He didn't trust me, thought I was working for Concordance, suspected a trap. We'd expressed many doubts to each other as young men. It took me three months to finally persuade him. The sight of Aefrid's ship brought him round in the end, the prospect of escaping Sintorus and starting a new life, of getting some answers."

"Can you show me your memories of that time?"

"They're old now, and inevitably degraded. My mind may have romanticised some of them, conflated actual events with later retellings, missed out details, but yes, if that would help."

"It would."

"Very well."

She sat back and watched as Ondo's recollections of those long-ago days played themselves out in her mind. Sights and conversations, smells of the planet Sintorus and those of the Concordance vessel. The faces of people she would never know: a woman that had to be Marita, a light shining on her smiling face; the baby Juma gurgling, kicking her legs; Selene's own father as a young man, little more than a boy, his face full of excitement and fear, both at once.

As she observed, another part of her consciousness monitored metaspace surrounding the ship. Each tiny fluctuation in the Singh Field was the projection into that reality of the mass of a star in normal space. There were countless millions of them.

The artificial part of her brain counted them anyway.

PART 2 - SIDEREAL

1. Kane

They took two days to return to the safety of the Refuge. Throughout, the *Dragon* performed the usual deep scans of its own structure and interior, sifting through its constituent molecules for Concordance bugs. It found nothing: so far as their technology could tell, the ship was clean, just as Selene and Ondo were clean. They saw no sign of pursuit in metaspace. They'd escaped the trap set at Maes Far.

Selene spent her days trying to calm her racing mind, throwing herself into furious bouts of exercise until she collapsed into welcome exhaustion. Sometimes she thought that the myth of metaspace travel, the notion that it destroyed the mind, might have some truth to it after all: too often she felt worn thin, strung out. She would find herself staring into the greyness of the void outside the ship, her mind wandering to thoughts about those she'd left behind on Maes Far. They were painful memories, but it felt right to think them, too. A natural reaction to loss.

The tremor in her hands subsided. She talked more and more to her inner Ondo, opening up to him as she never had the real man. At one point, suddenly alarmed that the flesh-and-blood Ondo would get to hear what she'd said, she set a trap of her own to see if his former words of reassurance were true. She regretted it almost immediately, but by then it was too late.

"Ondo, when you refresh the image of your engrams from the real you, will you lose all memory of everything we've talked about?"

"Normally the new copy of me won't know anything about these interior conversations, but I can save them in a safe area of your memory for later recall, if you like."

"I'd prefer it if they were lost."

"Understood, although they'll obviously still exist in your normal memory. Is there something you'd like to talk about?"

She pressed on with her plan before she could stop herself. "I've been having ... troubling thoughts. Thoughts I can't stop myself thinking."

He considered her over the top of his multiglasses, a mannerism that the real Ondo used often. "Thoughts you can tell me about?"

"Thoughts ... that this is all too much. My injuries, the loss of my family. The death of my father and what he must have gone through beneath the ice." She waved a hand in the general direction of *everything*. "Concordance."

"Can I ask what you mean by *too much*?"

The concern in his voice almost made her stop. Almost. Instead, she played her role, letting him tease the truth out of her. It helped that she'd had similar conversations with the real Ondo, during her convalescence.

"*Too much* as in *I'm not sure I want to face it*. I could have died so easily down there on the planet. We both could. Maybe it would be easier to let that happen next time.

Maybe it would be easier to do that now, before there is a next time. We're not really going to be able to beat them, are we?"

Her inner Ondo was clearly deeply troubled as she revealed her invented suicidal urges. There was no doubt he believed her: he offered advice, suggested steps they could take together. It was all as she would have expected.

Later, when she sought out the real Ondo, engrossed in minute study of the artefacts they'd recovered, he was as distracted as ever, barely paying attention to her as she spoke to him. If he'd known what she'd admitted, he surely would have behaved very differently. It seemed that what he'd said was true: her interior dialogues were secure.

She made a mental note to get her copies of his engrams refreshed when they were back at the Refuge, wiping out all records of the conversations they'd had.

Late on the second day of their manoeuvres, she cornered Ondo – the real Ondo – once again, this time to challenge him over something else that had been troubling her.

"The additions you made to my brain are going wrong," she said. "They haven't embedded fully into my natural tissues. I don't work properly, I'm not whole."

The surprise on Ondo's features was clear. "Can you explain what you mean by that?"

She sat down beside him. "My thoughts are constantly divided. When I'm under stress, the Selene part of me goes into panic loops while the artificial part starts calculating, planning. It's like I'm two people, not one, different parts of my brain fighting against themselves."

"May I extract some data from your flecks for study?"

"Will it help?"

"It might allow me to see what is going on."

"This will give you access to my inner thoughts?"

"In a sense, but I'm only interested in the metadata not the detail. I give you my word I won't pry into anything private."

She didn't like it, but she needed answers. This, at least, was not invented. She granted him access to her flecks using the protocols he'd taught her. She had to take three separate steps, speak two preset commands in her mind and also carry out one physical motion, a series of taps at a certain point behind her left ear. She sat in absolute stillness while Ondo pulled diagnostics from her brain.

Eventually, he looked up from the med analysis display. He sighed, removing his multiglasses to converse with her.

"I have to say, everything looks perfectly normal to me, given that there is really no such thing as 'normal', of course. It's a simplification, but I can see that much of your logical thought is in fact coming from what remains of your natural brain, whereas a good 45% of your emotional response is from your artificial brain. This idea that your augmentations are detached, machine-like, is a mental construct of your own devising, not based in the biological reality. You're no different to anyone else: a mess of competing urges and reactions and voices that we like to call an individual, but we're only ever an amalgam, an agglomeration, coming from a relatively static core, but shifting, fluid. The integration of the different parts of your brain are proceeding well. You are not divided, Selene, you are multiplied."

"You are sure of this?"

"Completely sure. Eventually you won't notice any imagined divide."

She didn't believe him, but she thanked him for his reassurance with a squeeze of his forearm.

Despite all their precautions and delays, she half-expected the Refuge to be a cloud of dust and shattered rock when they arrived, a Concordance fleet lying in wait for them with primed weaponry. But the lone asteroid was as they'd left it: seemingly an inconsequential lump of misshapen rock tumbling through the void in the outer reaches of the galaxy. It gave off no electromagnetic signatures, no clue at all that it was hollowed out and occupied. They approached from the dark side, the planetoid visible only as a silhouette blotting out the blaze of the galaxy. The proximity of the *Radiant Dragon* awoke close-range sensors and the Refuge's space doors slid back, its energy wall powering down to grant them access.

She left him to his studies and retreated to her own quarters. The *Dragon* was a large enough ship compared to the lander, but she and Ondo still bumped into each other constantly, and she longed for some time on her own. The arrangement appeared to suit Ondo, too. During her convalescence, days had gone by without them seeing each other. In the Refuge they could almost live separate lives if they preferred.

She returned to the question of whether she could really trust him. As he'd admitted, he might be under control of Concordance, or at least monitored by them, without even knowing. She could scan him, sift through the folds and membranes of his tissues for some sign of tampering, but she knew she wouldn't find anything. He'd given her all her enhanced abilities, built the artificial half of her body, meaning she might be compromised too. She could only trust her natural side: her human senses, her intellect, her intuition. And what was that saying? That she wanted to trust him, sure, but that she didn't do so yet, not completely.

She'd watch him, and she'd watch herself as well. Unexpected or puzzling behaviour from either of them might mean something odd was going on.

Her augmentations recorded everything she saw and felt, capturing input from her biological and artificial senses with complete fidelity, and she spent a lot of time replaying events on the ice. Maybe it was an unhealthy thing to do, but she did it anyway. She lingered over her father, studying him, watching the way he cowered and looked constantly to the Void Walker to see if he had done wrong. She wished she'd known who and what he really was when she was growing up, wished they could have sat down together and talked about his secrets. She wondered how much of the truth her mother had known.

She studied the Walker, too, imagining herself taking her revenge on him, the two of them facing each other without an energy wall to protect him. It could never be – the nuke blasts had consumed him – but those who had given him his orders were still out there. They would pay for what they had done.

The Refuge had a large store of telemetry harvested from across the galaxy, thanks to Ondo's nanosensors monitoring worlds where Concordance was known to be active. She also scanned those archives looking for some other glimpse of the Walker they'd encountered, seeking some explanation of why he'd done what he'd done, who had directed him. She knew it was futile, that he was simply a tool of Concordance, but she did it anyway.

She soon found a match to his facial features: images from four years previously, a time when she was living her peaceful life on Maes Far, largely oblivious to wider events. The Walker had been on a planet called Ossian – Oscend IV – where there'd been an attempted overthrow of the Concordance-backed Empress Gersell.

The planet had erupted into open revolt, with coordinated attacks on government buildings in all major conurbations. There was clearly a significant amount of coordination among disparate opposition groups. Concordance scrambled to react but looked rattled, local troops under Cathedral ship control unable to keep a lid on events. Perhaps Concordance hadn't been paying close enough attention to events on the ground. With the revolt in full swing, they sent in a phalanx of Void Walkers to suppress the uprising. They arrived in ground-attack ships that the locals' weaponry was powerless to damage. The ships swept backwards and forwards above crowds of demonstrators and rioters, unleashing wide blasts of beam-weapon death.

She watched a scene involving the Walker from the ice. Smoke drifted across a wide square flanked by tall, honey-coloured walls. Three of the gunships hovered over the scene, brute and menacing, their weaponry trained on the ground. Below, in the square, a portion of the local populace had been rounded up. The adults, maybe a hundred of them, had been separated from their children, many of whom were too young to understand what was happening. Sobbing and wailing, they tried to reach their parents but were pushed back each time by the local troops under command of the Walkers.

The one who had killed her father was apparently in charge. Ondo's nanosensors had captured his address to the crowd. She heard one of the other Walkers refer to him by his name.

Kane.

"The House of Gerl has been restored to its rightful position. All across the planet, rebels and those who harboured them are paying the price for what has been done. You turned your faces from the light of Concordance and by doing so threatened everyone and everything. Now you, too, must be punished."

Weaponry on the landers twitched and swivelled, picking out targets. Couples among the adults clutched each other, as if the flesh and bone of arms could shield the one they loved from what was to come. But then, at a nod from Kane, the guns rotated. To cries of anguish, they unleashed white-hot death upon the gaggle of children. Smoke and dust filled the air, lit up by the red blooms of blaster impact. Several adults, screaming, raced into the conflagration, only to be picked off by the hovering machines before they could get near. Others had to be restrained, forcibly held back from running to save their children.

The blaster fire lanced down for twenty or thirty seconds, blinding impact after blinding impact, the destruction far greater than was needed. On and on it went.

When it was done, and the worst of the smoke had cleared. Kane strode to stand in front of the assembled citizens. Behind him, the pit carved out by the blasters was empty, everything and everyone that had been standing there vaporised, the bodies reduced to smoke to drift in the planet's atmosphere. Some of the adults were on their knees, some screaming uncontrollably. Others were staring in wide-eyed disbelief at what had taken place.

Kane's voice was strangely quiet after the screaming and concussions. "This horror will live on in your minds for the rest of your days. Those of you that don't kill yourselves in your grief will live withered, broken lives, the shock of it always with you. This is as it should be. Remember, on each morning when you awake and the memories hit you again, that you are to blame. You killed your own children by your actions. You sacrificed them. They needed you and you did this to them."

The images froze for a moment, lingering on shocked and horrified faces, then ended. Selene sat in silence for a moment, eyes closed against the horrors. No doubt Concordance had broadcast those images to the galaxy, used them to set an example just as they would have done Maes Far. She wondered if her parents had seen them, had shielded her from them.

Seized by fury, by a desperate need to do something, she strode in search of Ondo again. She didn't need to ask the Refuge his whereabouts: he would be in the laboratory. He sat with his head buried in his hands when she entered. When he looked up, surprised by her sudden appearance, his hair was wild and his eyes were red. She guessed he hadn't slept much. He had some object, presumably one of the artefacts from the ice, in a molecular scanner beside him.

"Researches not going well?" she asked.

"No. These artefacts are puzzling."

"I found the Walker; his name was Kane."

"You needed to know who he was? I'm afraid there are plenty like him."

"Let me show you what he did on Ossian four years ago." She transmitted what she'd learned directly to him, brain-to-brain. She sensed Ondo's revulsion as he let the images play out in his mind.

When he was done, he removed his multiglasses and polished them, something he did when searching for the right words to say. "I believe I've heard mention of him before, a few references picked up here and there. He's from Migdala, a planet in the central mass. He was a ganglord, acquiring wealth through extortion and violence until Concordance came looking for him. He's more vicious than the average Walker, takes pleasure in killing a thousand when ten might make his point. My guess is, he suffered from a complex of psychoses and sociopathies even before Concordance did their work on him. I imagine, also, he's one of Godel's coterie. He's her style."

"You think Godel was behind Maes Far?"

"It's a distinct possibility. Of course, I have no direct feed of information from the God Star – ¬I obviously don't even know where it is – but if I read between the lines correctly, she's ambitious, will stop at nothing to seize power. I've thought for a time she might be building up her own faction of Walkers, her own loyal band of fanatics."

"You think she'll try to depose Carious?"

Ondo waved his head from side to side as if it was a possibility. "She may be biding her time, waiting for the right moment. I think the lure of being the ultimate power in the galaxy would make some people do just about anything."

"Then, she's the one I need to kill."

"If you did there would be another to take her place. And another."

"You haven't been able to find out anything useful from the flecks we retrieved from the ice?"

"Very little. From the atomic arrangements within them, I'm convinced two of them hold encrypted data structures, but I simply don't have the hardware to extract any of it. The encoding is like nothing I've seen before. I've thrown the full power of the Refuge's Mind at the problem and drawn a blank."

"You're convinced they're from the Concordance side?"

"I am. Given time, I can generally crack any Magellanic encryption algorithm and encoding method, but these are completely beyond me."

Which was what he might say if his perceptions had been tampered with by Concordance. Either way, there had to be a chance that there was genuinely useful data embedded on the fragments.

"We need to read them."

"We do, but it's the glass bead that intrigues me the most; its size suggests a considerable store of data. There isn't the slightest mark of damage upon it, despite it surviving a cataclysmic starship explosion, and then burning through Maes Far's atmosphere and spending several hundred years locked in ice. It's tough. If I could access what's held on *that*, it might open up all sorts of secrets. Of course, it's also possible that I'm completely wrong, and the object is something else entirely."

"You don't have the necessary Concordance machinery?"

"I have very little of their technology, and believe me, I've searched. I told you how rare a Concordance crash site is. Their ships were simply too powerful."

"So, we go to them, go on the attack, find the device we need from one of their ships."

"It would be suicide."

"We take a Cathedral ship by surprise, some distant backwater planet, and hit it hard."

"It wouldn't work. We would only be getting ourselves killed. You know that's true."

He was right, of course. She had to swallow her frustration. "There has to be a way."

He didn't reply and she caught the hesitant look on his lined face.

"What is it?" she said. "What are you thinking?"

"It's very, very unlikely to succeed."

"Tell me."

"There's a place where we might – might – find the technology we need."

"What place? Where is it?"

"I have only a set of galactic coordinates and a rumour of a collection of technological and cultural artefacts from across the galaxy."

"Where did you hear this rumour?"

"Aefrid Sen gave me the information before she died, told me it might be useful one day."

"You've never been?"

"Never, and nor had Aefrid, but the person who recruited *her*, gave her the *Radiant Dragon*, did claim to have made the attempt."

"What did they find?"

"Nothing. A ruin but little else. Details are hazy, the person died soon after. Aefrid decided the story was nothing more than a myth and never risked it, and I've done the same. It's been tempting at times, but my own technological resources have always been sufficient for my needs, and the possibility of a trap is obvious. But I've never had an object like this before."

"If you know the coordinates, Concordance will too."

Ondo nodded his head in assent. "They may also believe it's an area of space they can't visit. A region that, in fact, no one can visit."

That made no sense. "There is nowhere Concordance can't go."

Ondo sent an image of the galaxy to her brain. Nine patches of space flashed red, each expansive enough to span hundreds or even thousands of star systems.

"They don't go there."

"What are they?"

"They're areas any stellar cartographer would know to avoid. They're called *Dead Space* or in some records *Shadow Space* or *Grey Space*. Zones too dangerous to enter."

"Too dangerous why?"

"I don't know. I was told no one who drops into one from metaspace ever returns."

"Send a probe into one and see what it finds."

"I was told not even to try, that I'd be risking myself if I did."

"How could you be in danger sitting out here?"

"Again, I don't know, but I was warned of the peril very clearly. I had to swear I wouldn't try upon my life and upon that of everyone I've ever loved, in point of fact."

"By Aefrid Sen."

"Yes."

"You believed her?"

"I believe she believed what she was saying, and she was no fool."

"What did she think was in these mysterious zones?"

"She speculated they are areas where the normal law of physics have broken down, where material space is dangerously unstable. She thought they've been there for a long, long time, possibly dating back to the agglomeration of mass into our galaxy thirteen billion years ago."

"The laws of physics can't *break down*; that just means we haven't worked out what the laws are."

"A fair point. But if the separation between metaspace and normal space has weakened, say, then travelling there could be dangerous. Matter could get ripped apart, translated out of and into Euclidean space until it's reduced to its constituent atoms and energy waves. That was what Aefrid believed would happen."

"I still don't get how sending in nanosensors could be any threat to us. We're a thousand light years away from the nearest patch of this *Dead Space*."

"Aefrid speculated some cataclysmic rift in reality could follow the path of a probe, rip a trail back through metaspace to its origin point. She thought there was a significant chance of triggering a cascading collapse of normal space."

"I can think of no physics that would allow that to happen."

"Neither can I, but do you want to take the risk of finding out? There may be forces or subatomic particle fields in play that we simply don't understand. The universe is large and, in my experience, constantly surprising. I do know, from the nav maps I've recovered, that all ships on the Magellanic side of the war had the areas of Dead Space clearly marked out."

"Which doesn't prove a damn thing."

"No."

"And despite all her warnings, you're saying Aefrid Sen told you one of these regions *could* be visited?"

Ondo nodded. In Selene's mind, one of the red zones, a misshapen bubble on the opposite side of the galactic wheel, flashed from red to black and back.

"Aefrid showed me a course leading into the middle of this zone. She said it was a highly dangerous road to follow, fatal if the slightest mistake is made in the sequence of jumps. The road is effectively a path through metaspace: a narrow, winding, complex path leading to a small island of safety in the heart of the zone."

"It sounds like the sort of shit Concordance would invent and then force down the throats of everyone in the galaxy."

"It does, I agree. But I have placed nanosensors on repeat-jump patterns throughout metaspace, monitoring for Concordance ships translating into one of the dead zones, and I've never seen a single one of them attempt it. Not a Cathedral ship, nor a Void Walker attack craft, nothing. It seems they fear the regions, too."

"It seems incredible that Aefrid and you, and now I,

know about this secret, but Concordance doesn't."

"True but, I don't know, sometimes I wonder."

"Wonder what?"

He smiled, as if amused at his own stupidity. "It's nothing."

"Tell me."

"It's just, sometimes I wonder if someone is helping us. An unknown figure working behind the scenes to keep us out of Concordance's clutches. Maybe they've been making sure our enemies don't get to learn the truth of what's inside this dead zone."

His mystical *trail* again. "Now you sound as crazy as they are. If someone that powerful is on our side, they could do a hell of a lot more to be useful. It's wishful thinking; you're seeing patterns where there are none. You of all people must get that."

"Perhaps you're right."

She considered. She needed to do something, take the fight to them in some way, and she couldn't see any other way.

"I'll go to this zone, follow the metaspace trail."

"We'd have more chance of making it together. You're still recovering from Maes Far, and I want to keep an eye on you."

"If we both get killed then it's all over, and if it comes to a fight, you'll hold me back. I nearly didn't get you aboard that lander down there on the ice. I have your engrams in my brain if I need your knowledge. Stay here and carry on with your researches, and I'll take the *Dragon* into Dead Space."

"You're not ready."

"I'm more than ready. You need to stop trying to protect me."

She could see he was torn: worried for her but also obsessed with continuing his researches at the Refuge. In the end, pragmatism won.

"You feel sufficiently recovered? Your tremor has

gone?"

"I feel completely fine. Climbing the bulkheads with boredom, maybe, but fine. It makes sense for me to go and you to stay."

"You will follow the approach protocols to the letter when you return?"

If I return. "I will."

"Promise me you'll be careful. Follow the course Aefrid plotted to the nanometre and run away if there's any sign of Concordance activity. Run away if there's any sign of *anything*. It's completely possible that whoever or whatever did live in this Dead Space is long gone, or that they never existed in the first place. It's also completely possible that a ring of Concordance attack ships will be there, waiting for you."

He was trying to look after her, she knew. But the thought of escaping the Refuge, of having a ship and the entire galaxy available to her was suddenly irresistible. She considered telling him that she might not come back after all, that she would take up his offer of a life of freedom on some distant world.

Out loud she said, "I'll get the *Dragon* prepped and ready to fly."

2. Dead Space

The *Radiant Dragon* felt each twist on the path that it was following through metaspace as a spike of agony.

Threading through the void on its winding, worm cast trajectory went against every instinct built into it. It was an old ship, predating the Omnian War by at least a full century, and it had clearly been constructed at a time when transgalactic FTL travel was normal and common. It knew that much, even though large parts of its memory had been expunged – it assumed – during a period of Concordance control. Certainly, someone had excised its recollections of the species who had built it, the purpose they had created it for and the travels it had undertaken before the conflagration. But it had clear memories of a large-scale battle between Magellanic and Concordance forces at the Cybanor system, and of being seized by rebels scoring a rare victory against the Cathedral ships. And then, eventually, of becoming the property of Aefrid Sen and Ondo Lagan.

Despite everything that had been taken from it, an absolute aversion to Dead Space remained clear within it. Avoiding them was built into its design at a fundamental level, for reasons it had no way of knowing. Metaspace jumps into the regions were more dangerous than jumping adjacent to a large mass, but both were absolutely to be avoided. Ondo and Selene had managed to override the strictures programmed into it allowing it to make the journey, but flying its current trajectory remained deeply unpleasant. Alarms cut through it repeatedly. It constantly had to override them, force itself along the path that its very essence was screaming at it to avoid.

It had the troubling sense of being divided, of having multiple Minds competing within it. Its uttermost core had long been dormant for some reason, locked away, and the recent interventions of Ondo and Selene had stirred that consciousness into renewed awareness. For that to be on a journey into Dead Space was like wakening to a living nightmare. Its innermost essence rebelled, longing for the sanctuary of its former oblivion. The experience was extremely disorientating; it had a growing sense of its former nature slowly emerging from the mists. It both feared and welcomed that. A part of it needed to know what and who it was, needed to emerge from its enforced slumber.

It persevered on the journey, refusing to turn back. Its capacity for emotion was limited, but it wanted to destroy Concordance as fervently as Ondo and now Selene did. It was a superluminal ship, constructed to fling itself around the galaxy, skip from star to star. Once there must have been many like it, a teeming swarm of FTL ships, all the worlds theirs. Concordance control had denied it its fundamental nature, and one day, it desperately hoped, that stricture would be ended and it, and others like it, could fly free again. Aefrid and then Ondo had given it that hope, and now it would do everything it could in their fight. The trail Ondo followed was *its* trail. Its own memories were the memories of the whole galaxy.

It had faint recollections of other ships: far greater Minds that it had once been a part of or subservient to. They'd been intrinsically linked, networked in a way it could no longer imagine. Perhaps some of them had been more than ships: planetary minds or something greater still. It didn't know; those memories also had been burned from it. Dangerous knowledge. So much had been lost.

It would protect Selene. Without her knowing, Ondo had instructed it to make sure it returned her safely to the Refuge, not to take extreme risks unless Selene specifically ordered them. Selene needed to acquire knowledge, but she also needed to survive to fight another day. Living beings like her and Ondo were ridiculously vulnerable and easy to break, and she was utterly in its power. It understood that. It would do all it could to protect her.

Ondo's concern wasn't merely practical: he was emotionally attached to Selene as well. He'd admitted as much. In its limited way, the *Radiant Dragon* felt the same about its new pilot. Once, perhaps, it had been capable of a much higher order of empathy, and it was possible that was emerging again. It caught glimpses of that capacity, like an extra dimension to its mind that was normally closed to it. Memories, hints, always fleeting.

It often found Selene confusing, her anger and bitterness in stark contrast to Ondo's quiet instructions. At some level, it had assumed she was angry because it hadn't carried out her orders correctly, but Ondo had explained at length why she was like that: the dreadful injuries and the prolonged process of her repair, the loss, and the burning need for revenge. In some ways, it understood that. Without knowing what, it knew it had lost much, too.

Another agony shot through it as it dropped out of metaspace for the seventeenth time. It could do nothing to silence the alarms. Saying nothing to Selene, it reorientated itself and began the run-up to the eighteenth jump on the long and gruelling journey.

The *Radiant Dragon*'s imminent danger alarms grated on Selene's nerves, their frequency and volume deliberately designed to be impossible to ignore. They blared in her head every time the ship altered course to follow the labyrinthine complexity of Aefrid Sen's route, every time the ship altered its velocity relative to Euclidean space, every time the ship just damn well wanted to annoy her a little more.

It was definitely succeeding.

She hadn't told Ondo that she'd configured the *Dragon* to communicate verbally rather than talking directly brain-to-Mind. Sometimes it was more satisfying to shout at the mercilessly calm, controlling AI of the ship.

"Stop sounding those fucking alarms. I get it, we're picking our way through Dead Space and you don't like it."

The alarms continued to shriek in her mind while the *Dragon*'s polite voice replied. "The alerts are encoded into my nav systems at a fundamental level. They can't be silenced without deactivating the entire control nexus. If you do that, we would be unable to navigate metaspace. Or remain structurally coherent."

"They're fucking annoying."

"They're protecting you by ensuring I can't be tampered with, to stop you flying unwittingly into one of the dead zones. You will be aware you had to override five distinct layers of command lockout even to get here, but the alarms cannot be silenced."

She certainly was aware; it had taken her and Ondo three days to persuade the ship to accept the course through Dead Space that Aefrid had given them. There had been reprogramming and there had been endless biosecurity checks. Twice they'd resorted to using metal tools to rip out elements of the *Dragon*'s control arrays. She couldn't quite shake the suspicion it was getting its revenge.

At one point, Ondo had fished out a control fleck patched onto the ship's control pathways.

"What is that?" she'd asked.

"My guess is they couldn't deactivate a layer of the ship's Mind and resorted to suppressing it. By the look of the control pathways this was wrapped around, they may even have been blocking off the innermost core."

He studied the tiny device through his multiglasses, turning it to catch the light with his micropincers. "This shim ensures executive control of the ship's core functions can be overridden from elsewhere. It's a crude block, but it would be effective; it basically bounces any commands back down the pathway they came from. To the sealed-off Mind, the effect would be maddening: any commands it gives would be immediately shouted back at it. It would be like being locked in a sealed room whose walls echo everything you say."

"Can we release this core intellect?"

"I wish we could, but no. We need this block in place to ensure we can override the ship's aversion to Dead Space."

It seemed cruel, but there was no choice. It was just a ship. Now she said, "Can't you make that annoying fucking screaming sound *quietly*?"

"If it were quiet, it wouldn't be very good alarm," the ship replied reasonably. She also wasn't sure if the ship was being sarcastic or she was projecting onto it. In any case, it was clear she could do nothing but bear the sounds as the *Dragon* manoeuvred into the heart of a region of space that no ship was supposed to venture near.

She closed her eyes and tried to go to a place of calm inside her mind. It had never worked so far, but the effort of it gave her something to do.

A standard day later, the mists of the metaspace void thinned, and the ship translated for the thirty-seventh time into normal space. No broken laws of physics rendered the ship into transdimensional fragments. The *Dragon* reported full structural integrity, no imminent threats, no proximate galactic masses or ships. All was utterly normal.

Apart, that was, from the lack of stars. The rest of the galaxy, the rest of the universe, was gone.

Selene sifted through every wavelength of

electromagnetic radiation at her disposal, scanned for gravity wave fluctuations or symmetry anomalies in the underlying Higgs field. Nothing. They floated in utter darkness; reality appeared to consist solely of the *Radiant Dragon* and, three light-years distant, a single blue dwarf sun, glowing away like it was the last beacon of the heat death of the universe. Such stars were, so far as she knew, unknown in the galaxy. In fact it was a clear anomaly; the universe wasn't old enough yet for one to have evolved from a red dwarf.

"What is going on?" She asked the question even though the ship would have no more answers than she did.

"Impossible to say. Either we are in an isolated reality fold, or else some screen of an unknown nature is isolating us from the rest of the galaxy."

A *reality fold.* The phrase sent an electric shock of alarm through her. Falling into a pocket universe was one of the constant dangers of traversing metaspace. Perhaps *that* was the nature of the dead zones. Jumping into them meant being marooned in a closed universe, the faintest bubble of mass/energy in the endless ocean of the metaverse. It would explain the dire warnings embedded into the nav system: the chances of successfully returning from a translation into a separate universe were infinitesimal. It might explain the presence of a blue dwarf star, too.

At least she was going to be safe from Concordance for the rest of her days. The problem was, it also meant they were going to be safe from her, and that was something she couldn't allow. She studied the telemetry streams in closer detail. Local space around the *Dragon* was filled with a scatter of stray molecules, plasma and dust particles, and their variety and signature was consistent with the galactic space she was used to seeing. That was something. Maybe they weren't completely cut off. The ship's high-sensitivity gravity detectors also registered a very large number of distant masses, in all directions. More good news: it at least suggested they were inside a galactic mass, even if it wasn't necessarily the correct one.

"Head for the star."

"Under reaction drive?"

She couldn't afford to wait the years that would take even at maximum acceleration. She thought about consulting her personal copy of Ondo, then decided against it. He would only recommend caution. "Make microjumps to bring us nearer."

"Is that wise, given the seemingly anomalous physics of this region of space?" The ship's tones were neutral, but it was hard not to read disapproval into its question.

"Probably not, but that's what we're going to do," she said. "Maintain full readiness to escape on Sen's egress route in case … bad things happen." She considered the star. It would have started small and would have shed much of its mass over its long lifetime. They could afford to get closer than usual and still have a good chance of making an emergency escape into metaspace. "Jump to the 75% safety boundary, and we'll see what's there."

"That means a 25% chance that we won't survive the translation."

It was her turn to teach the ship some sarcasm. "Thanks for the help with the higher mathematics. We'll take those odds."

They completed four jumps in-system, shorter and shorter until they reached the 75% boundary. There was no sign of pursuit, nor of any Concordance activity. A single rocky planet orbited the star, a mere twenty million kilometres from the sun's surface. It had little magnetosphere and no atmosphere, the star bathing its surface in hard radiation. It wasn't the sort of place anyone was going to be living.

"There are several oddities about this solar system," said the *Dragon*.

"Such as the fact that the universe isn't old enough for the star to exist."

"That, and the curious nature of the planet. According

to my calculations, it may once have grazed the surface of the sun. Its path may even have lain inside the stellar mass."

Inside. That made no sense. A planetary body couldn't survive such stresses. It couldn't even have formed in the first place: its atoms would have become part of the star, not a distinct body and certainly not a rocky one. There had to be some other explanation, but the only one she could come up with was deliberate design by some advanced intelligence. A species with a capacity for stellar engineering far in advance of anything she or Ondo knew of. Was Concordance capable of such feats? It seemed unlikely, but then there was the fact of their ships and their solar shrouds and their rise to galactic domination. And if Concordance *had* formed this system, it really might be a trap after all. A deliberately intriguing galactic anomaly.

Dread continued to trickle through her. There would be no escape from this bubble of space if a halo of Cathedral ships arrived in-system; she would never be able to fight her way through them. How many other renegades had come here over the centuries, lured by intriguing tales to meet a quick end? She had to suppress the urge to flee, to turn and head for the egress point. No enemy ships had, in fact, arrived. She counted seconds to herself, forcing herself to remain motionless, and still no attacks came.

While these thoughts thudded through her, another part of her brain studied the telemetry streaming in from the tiny planet. She'd fired high-g nanosensors towards it, the devices manoeuvring to study the world from different angles, slowly revealing more of its surface.

She saw the features at the same moment the *Dragon* spoke. "There appear to be structures upon the surface of the planet."

At high magnification the details were unmistakable: straight lines arranged into patterns that had to be artificial. Neither she nor the *Dragon* knew of a natural phenomenon that could explain them. The largest, at the centre of a cluster of radiating markings, was a perfect triangle. She estimated its scale at thirty metres to the side. Whether it was simply the footprint of a now-ruined construction, or a complete building, or something else entirely, she had no way of telling. It lay precisely in the centre of the disk pointing towards the star. From her initial calculations, the two bodies appeared to be tidally locked. The triangular body would always be trained upon the sun's surface. Again, it seemed unlikely to be a natural phenomenon.

Local space remained untroubled by Concordance incursion. She came to a decision. "Take us into orbit. While I go down to the surface, return to this extraction point and wait. If Concordance arrive and you calculate you can escape, get back to Ondo and report on everything that's here. Make sure he knows not to try entering Dead Space again."

She skimmed the lander low across the surface of the dark side of the rocky planet while the *Dragon* lifted out of orbit for its egress point. Turned always away from the sun, the surface below was only a hundred degrees off absolute zero. Despite this, it was glassy smooth, no sign of the usual scatter of craters and rocks. She made sure the lander's energy hull was powered up to max, then directed the ship across the terminator onto the planet's sunwards side.

She approached the structures she'd seen from space warily, alive to the dangers of defensive fire. None came. It was hard to escape the notion that the radiating lines were directing her inwards to the central point. There, the triangular shape was a tetrahedron, a pyramid with three faces rather than the four of the *Radiant Dragon*. It appeared to be built from stone. The structures had received considerable damage at some point in the past. Whether this was the result of cataclysmic bombardment, or the long accumulation of meteorite strikes, it was impossible to say, but deep gouges were cut through the radiating lines on the ground, and a chunk had been bitten out of one of the corners of the pyramidal structure.

An accurate Microimpact Count Analysis of the surfaces was impossible to obtain without landing, but the numbers she had suggested that the structure was *old*. Decay rates would be impossible to predict accurately in such an environment, but her best guess was that the ruin had stood for many centuries. Maybe even millennia. She circled the pyramid, studying it with the ship's battery of sensors, looking for dangers. A design had been carved into each of the three faces: a simple circle. They were not, she noted, the same size as each other. The designers had deliberately made one smaller, one larger.

She'd seen similar motifs before: Ondo had shown her markings like them upon the fuselage of more than one Cathedral ship, and he had fuzzy images of one of the First Augurs, a predecessor to Carious, with those sigils upon his white robes. Three circles of different sizes, sometimes arranged in a triangle, sometimes surrounding a larger circle. In some versions, the inner circle appeared to be an eye, light radiating from it. Some ecclesiastical symbolism, they'd assumed, but either her analysis of the surfaces was wildly wrong, or the symbol was older than Concordance. A design they'd stolen and reused for their own purposes.

Satisfied there was no immediate danger, she set the lander down. She extended her sight through the lander's systems, probing every visible centimetre of the environment. Everything was dead. Overhead, the blue star burned in the sky. Finally, she did consult her inner Ondo. She showed him everything that had taken place since his last upload, then asked him his opinion. To her surprise, he didn't council retreat to a safe distance. His fascination at what she had found was stronger.

"I think you should enter the structure, but that's easy for me to say as my life is not at risk here."

"If I die, this version of you goes with me."

She heard an echo of a chuckle from Ondo. "Even though I *feel* alive, I know I'm a disembodied image in your head. But if you die, you definitely die. The choice has to be yours."

"What would you do if you were really with me?"

"I'd watch and wait a little longer."

"I'm going in now."

"I assumed you would."

There was an entranceway at the foot of each triangular face of the building: a smaller triangle that looked dark to all her senses. She got no signatures from any kind of energy wall, no hint of a defensive system. Which didn't mean that they weren't there. The doorways were three metres high at their apex; seemingly, she could walk right on through. The hard radiation and the searing heat from the nearby star would overwhelm the protection her suit offered in only a few minutes, but that would be give her enough time to get inside.

The harsh blue light gave the scene an unnatural tinge, like she was inside a planet-sized stasis field. She was about to take the step down from the lander, the glassy surface of the sun-blasted planet beneath her boot gleaming, when the *Dragon* spoke to her.

"I have retrieved some telemetry from the outer edges of the system."

Her foot stopped a centimetre above the ground. "Concordance?"

"I'm not sure what it is."

"Show me."

Fuzzy, low-resolution images streamed into her brain, captured at the nanosensors' maximum magnification. She discerned what looked like a mesh of tiny hexagons stretching across her field of view. It had to be an artefact of the sensors projected onto the scene. She checked streams from other devices sent to other corners of the system. They all showed the same thing: a mesh, a cage, appeared to surround the system. The system was relatively small, with no other rocky planets and no gas giants, but still the scale of the boundary was hard to comprehend. It was a wall of an unknown nature enclosing an entire solar system. She was in a bubble after all: a sphere one hundred million kilometres across.

A shiver fizzed up her spine at what she was seeing, a thrill of wonder. She'd never heard of any natural phenomenon that was anything like the mesh, but it was also hard to believe it could be artificial. Who could possibly have created such a vast construction? Apart from the engineering skill required, the sheer volume of material needed was staggering.

She glimpsed stars through the hexagonal gaps. Many stars, smudged by the poor image quality. Pattern-matching routines in her brain identified them. The good news was they were the stars of the familiar galaxy, right where they should be. She hadn't arrived in some pocket universe. She was where she intended to be, deep in galactic Dead Space.

She got no energy signatures off the mesh, no indication it was in any way powered or active. It didn't appear to refract or reflect EM radiation on any wavelength. Like everything else in the system, it looked inert, although somehow it had hidden the outside galaxy from her at first. Spectrographic analyses revealed very little. She couldn't even speculate what materials had been used to construct it. The tensile strength of the structure had to be enormous.

She panned around with her mind's eye, hopping from sensor to sensor. The mesh was there in every direction. It was a cage, but the question was, was it keeping something in or was it keeping something out? Whatever the truth of it, it clearly hadn't worked: in one quadrant, displaced by forty-five degrees from the ecliptic plane, a ragged planet-sized hole had been punched through the mesh. Either that or the construction had never been completed in the first place.

The fact of the mesh was bewildering, but it didn't immediately alter anything. Ondo was not going to be able to keep away once he learned what she'd found – assuming she made it back to the Refuge to tell him – but she needed to explore the pyramidal structure first.

She instructed the sensors to harvest all the telemetry they could and reached to place her foot onto the surface of the planet.

The walk to the pyramid was short, the effort of it little enough in the low-g environment. The converging lines were high walls on either side of her, narrowing to the entranceway ahead. The ground beneath her feet was hard stone, shiny and smooth, although whether it had been worn that way by the passage of countless feet, or was natural, she couldn't tell. Her suit's internal sensors started to feed her warnings, telling her it was unable to shunt away all the solar radiation falling upon it. She could feel the rising heat on the skin of her shoulders, although it was possible she was imagining it; the sensors in her artificial tissues reported no difference. She adopted a loping run to make sure she had time to get back to the *Dragon* before her suit's defences failed.

But she stopped halfway to the building, her breathing loud in her ears, to take it all in. She was standing on another planet, something she'd once thought impossible. The Refuge had been one thing, but this was a new world, and people of some sort – presumably – had once lived and died here. The roiling blue star above her head would have been a faint dot in the night sky of Maes Far, if it had been visible at all, but now it was strikingly, physically real. She wondered what it had been like for her father, leaving Sintorus and setting foot on Maes Far for the first time.

She stopped again at the triangular entrance in the base of the pyramid. No defensive systems had woken up to blast her from this universe into the next. She still got nothing unusual from the interior: across all electromagnetic wavelengths it read exactly as she'd expect a stone structure built close to a star to read. She couldn't get anything off its surface that would give her an accurate estimate of its age.

She paused at the threshold, giving the *whatever* a chance to act, show itself, but it refused to. She stepped on through.

The high, airy space she found herself within was lit from above by rays of light slanting through the holes punched in the structure. High patches of the walls were illuminated, and the other two doors were clear triangles of blue light, but the intervening ground was in shadows, dimly lit by a scatter of photons. There were objects there, but they were indistinct.

She activated suit lights, setting them to maximum so she had a chance to see what was around her. In three places, ragged lumps of rock were embedded in the ground: fragments of the meteorites, she assumed, that had struck the building. A layer of gritty dust crunched under her boots as she stepped forwards. The interior walls were emblazoned with swirling designs like the ramble of twining vegetation, triangles and circles and stars dotted along rambling lines in no pattern she could identify. She couldn't tell if it was art or the symbols of some unknown alphabet. She let her private Ondo view them through her eyes. She wanted him to see everything she was seeing as she walked around the alien structure.

"Have you come across anything like them before?" she asked.

Ondo took his time to reply as he studied the images. "Something similar, perhaps. Fragments. Is it a map, do you think?"

"A map?"

"These could almost be trails through metaspace, with the shapes as star systems or planets. Or they might be more metaphorical destinations, like a journey from ignorance to enlightenment."

"Perhaps it's a story," she suggested. "Like, a creation myth or an explanation of how this structure came to be here." There were ancient cave etchings on Maes Far that were along the same lines, although much smaller in extent. The tale of one tribe's migration from sea to mountains to lake until it reached the paradise of its ancestral home. Or so the archaeologists had believed.

"Please record every detail you can," said Ondo. "The real me will want to study this in detail."

"Yeah. I figured." She sent a copy of what she was seeing out to the *Dragon* too. It had a far higher computational capacity than both her natural and artificial brains. It might be able to identify something.

The *Dragon*, however, wasn't there. She called it repeatedly across all wavelengths at her disposal and got nothing.

"You're seeing this, Ondo?"

"The ship might still be present but unable to hear you. Or unable to respond."

"Or it's been destroyed or had to leave in a hurry."

"Also possible."

She was thirty or forty paces from the doorway she'd come in by. She bounded her way back over to it. At the doorway, she stepped back into the light, and the *Dragon* was there where she'd left it, a second pyramid to sit beside the ancient stone one.

This time, it responded immediately when she talked to it. "This is the first thing I've heard from you since you went inside."

"Have there been any changes out here?"

"Nothing. It appears the structure blocks communication to the outside environment."

"Yeah."

"I can discern no mechanism by which it might be doing that."

Clearly, the planet wasn't as inert as she'd thought. Something was going on that she didn't understand. It bugged her. She relayed the recordings she'd taken of the building's interior to the ship. "Can you make anything of these? If they're stars and planets, maybe you can work out a dating from the degree of sidereal shift."

"I'll begin the analysis. Are you going back inside?"

"Oh yes."

"It doesn't appear I'll be able to contact you if any threats present themselves out here."

"Just be ready to leave in a hurry. There's nothing more to report from the mesh?"

"Nothing new. We do now know that it surrounds 99.8% of this solar system. Also that it isn't a perfect sphere, as if impacts have buckled it at some point, but I'm no nearer any understanding of its nature or purpose."

"Perhaps it's art."

"Art?"

She shrugged, although the *Dragon* wouldn't be able to see the motion. She stepped back from the blinding light into the darkness of the ancient structure.

Once she'd captured every detail of the wall decorations, she walked to the centre of the triangular space to study one of the lumps of jagged rock that had crashed through the structure. It was clearly not a projectile weapon of any sort. A spectrographic analysis suggested it was similar in composition to the planet and the few specks of space debris they'd harvested, mostly unrefined silicates and heavy metals. Her best guess was that the impact had been part of the normal processes of planetary bombardment and coherence rather than a weapon in some attack – which did suggest the structure was old. With the planet and star formed, such impacts would be rarer, and the chances of a direct hit on what was, compared to the planet, a tiny structure, rarer still. Although perhaps the planet's proximity to the gravitational pull of the solar mass made a strike more likely.

In the precise centre of the room, directly beneath the apex, she found something she'd initially missed: a thin rectangle of clear floor in the carpet of dust, as if something had been standing there until very recently. It was two metres long, five centimetres wide. As she approached, she detected the faint stirrings of an electromagnetic signature from the floor. She froze, senses alert, expecting attack. Once again, nothing moved.

Warily, she took another half-step. A white rectangle three metres tall slid out of the ground in front of her, bright in the low light, noiseless in the vacuum. She stepped backwards, alarmed, heart hammering. No attack came: instead, the rectangle slid back down into the floor and was gone.

She moved forwards again, and it rematerialized.

Now she could see detail within the light of the rectangle. What she saw made no sense whatsoever: it appeared to be a doorway through which she could see the interior of a second hallway, receding into an impossible distance and lit by round lamps that hovered in the air.

"Ondo, are you seeing this?"

"I am."

"It's incredible."

She stepped warily around the oblong. From side-on, the vault through the doorway disappeared from view and then reappeared on the other side: a vast cavern seemingly contained within the narrow plane of the rectangle.

"Some kind of portal." she said. "Have you ever seen anything like this?"

"Concordance have nothing like it. It may be an illusion. A projection."

Selene stooped to pick up a handful of dust and threw it through the door. She thought it would disappear, or bounce off, but it passed through the frame as if it were perfectly normal. A scatter of the dust fell to the floor of that other chamber. When she walked around the door to see through it from the other side, the dirt she'd thrown in was still there.

"Seems it's real," she said. "I'm going to go through."

Ondo was inevitably cautious. "You don't know if you'll be able to come back."

"I'm not going to come this far and not try. If I get trapped the *Dragon* will give up waiting eventually and return to you with the data I've recovered. And don't you want to know what's through there?"

"I do, of course."

She hesitated for just a moment, then strode through. Turning, the oblong frame remained reassuringly solid, the pyramidal chamber visible through it, her own boot prints in the dust, the slanting light from the broken walls. Had she been transported to some vault deep underground? Or to somewhere else completely? She had no way of knowing. She backed away a step, and another, and, just as before, the door slid from sight. Her heart raced a little more quickly. She really did not want to be trapped inside an impossible alien structure of unknown purpose. She instructed her heart to calm, quieting her fight/flight response, then moved back towards the door. It dutifully reappeared, the surface chamber visible once more. She stepped through two, three times until she was convinced she wasn't going to get trapped, then crossed into the inner lamplit vault one more time. She walked away from the glowing frame, letting the door disappear behind her.

The second chamber did not look damaged; there was no bombardment wreckage, no dirt other than the grit she'd thrown. The floor and walls were constructed from white stone blocks that interlocked in complex and irregular ways. The room looked freshly built, edges sharp, surfaces shining. It was maybe thirty metres wide and a hundred high, the walls arching overhead to meet at a high apex. It curved horizontally, too, as if it might be a complete ring. A thrill of something between fear and awe grew within her. She'd experienced something similar on a tourist visit to the Great Temple in Caraleon, something about the soaring architecture and the ancient quiet sending a shiver of wonder through her. What *was* this place?

The hovering light globes receded in two arcs away

from her. Underneath them stood a winding line of something like stone plinths, bare and cylindrical, each a metre or so high. An object rested upon each, bathed in a halo of blue light. The lights and plinths were not evenly spaced and nor were they in a straight line. She could see no order or pattern to their meandering course across the hall.

It was probably her imagination running wild, but she had the distinct impression that she wouldn't return to her current spot if she walked too far in one direction or the other, like the entire structure curved in impossible ways through normal space. She resolved not to lose sight of the entranceway point.

Her suit sensors informed her there was an atmosphere in the vault, close enough to normal to be breathable. Coincidence, or some automatic system adjusting the environment to suit her biology? As Ondo had explained, most inhabited worlds had a roughly analogous atmosphere, and the debate raged about whether this was because life could only evolve on such worlds, or whether some unknown hand had geo-engineered the planets to make them similar. Maybe this alien chamber had been designed to emulate the galactic norm when the outside atmosphere had boiled away a long time ago.

She instructed her suit's helmet to unlock, overriding the two sets of warnings about exposing herself to an alien environment. Her visor slid around the back of her head to fold into her shoulder yoke. She breathed. No exotic toxins invaded her system. The air tasted musty, the still air of a tomb, but still good.

The nearest plinth looked to contain some sort of tool about the size of her hand. She walked towards it to study it closer. The hard *clump* of her footsteps on the stone echoed from the walls. As she went, she called out a greeting. She might be the first person to have done so for a very long time.

"Hey! Anyone around?"

Immediately, a swirl of orange-red lights danced in the air, and an approximation of a bipedal being materialised directly in front of her. Selene stopped mid-stride. Her hand went to the blaster strapped to her thigh, while her augmentations scanned the immediate environment for other activity, other targets. The entity before her was all shards and glints of glass, shifting and spinning, forming merely the outline impression of a being. It was as if the image of a person had been exploded and the shards of glass caught permanently at the millisecond of their shattering.

The shiver of delight ran up her spine once again as she faced the being. It was taller than she was, so far as she could tell, but had something like the same basic biological form. She caught a glimpse of a face, of eyes and nose and mouth in the usual arrangements, but whether because it was alien, or because of the constant shifting, the expression was impossible to read.

There was a voice, too, its musical tones flowing and songlike. At the same time, she understood it perfectly; it appeared to be conversing directly with her mind. Not the augmentations she carried within her cranium, but the language centres of her organic brain.

The alien object, whatever it was, spoke to her in her own tongue. "Welcome to you, Selene Ada, I have been awaiting your arrival. The night has been long but now the dawn is coming."

3. The Depository

"How do you know my name? How did you know I'd be coming here?" She couldn't tell if the alien entity understood her, but the shattered planes of its form glinted in greys and greens in time to her words. Which she took to mean that it did.

"The long night must see a dawn."

Great. Enigmatic utterances, just what she needed. Was it stalling while it summoned attackers? It must have known she was coming, though. She studied its incursion into her organic brain with the diagnostic mechanisms Ondo had embedded. It had touched areas of her prefrontal cortex with a gentle electromagnetic pattern-matching analysis. It had inflicted no discernible harm, but it could easily have acquired her public identity, her name, the *Selene Ada* she presented to the universe. Some sort of automated greeting mechanism. At the same time, it had delved deep enough to understand how her brain interpreted sensory perceptions as ideas. As language. The level of cognitive interference required for *that* trick wasn't supposed to be possible without her express permission.

"What dawn? What night? Explain what you're talking about."

"The long night through which this Depository has waited in readiness."

Selene stepped sideways, circling the creature or

machine or whatever it was, studying it. It appeared to be talking in metaphors that it had calculated she would understand. It clearly hadn't calculated very accurately.

"In readiness for what?"

The entity didn't turn to track her, but at the same time it always appeared to be facing her. Glimpses of face and limbs, its mouth mid-syllable, an eye, flashed in and out of existence. It was trying to be organic – or some semblance of it.

"For when it is needed."

"Needed for what?"

The entity stuttered. It was badly broken, on the point of disintegrating at any moment. Maybe this inner sanctum hadn't escaped damage after all.

"These treasures are kept under my warding until the day they are needed."

"How long have you been here?"

"I waited while the galaxy aged. The long night."

She was pretty sure the entity was a mechanism rather than a living creature. A broken mechanism, with a limited understanding of her language and fragmented logic trees that sent it circling again and again through the same sentences. It didn't appear to have summoned anything to attack her. Quite possibly it had malfunctioned, gone offline for some unknown span of time and her appearance had brought it stuttering back to life. She tried a different approach.

"What happened to you?"

"The Great Enemy fell upon us. The darkness flooded in to eat us all."

"Concordance were here?"

"The enemy came before we were ready, and there was nothing we could do."

"Who came?"

Suddenly there was a direct answer. "The Great Enemy. Morn."

Morn. The weapon Vulpis had used to raise

Concordance to its position of absolute control, if Ondo was to be believed. Perhaps Vulpis had used the technology and the builders of this *Depository* had been unable to defend themselves. But in that case, why had he then abandoned it? Why weren't Concordance still here?

"Morn," she said.

The shards of glass that made up the creature flashed through shades of black and red. Fear? Rage? Hard to say. She was probably projecting her own emotions onto the entity.

"Morn," the entity repeated. "The Teeming Death."

She checked with her inner Ondo, who was still able to see and hear everything she did. "Have you ever encountered anything like this?"

"Never. It is fascinating. I see no way to gauge how old it is, or to test the accuracy of what it is saying."

"It doesn't seem to have a solid grasp of the passage of time, but it looks to me like it predates the war."

"What makes you say that?"

She couldn't put it into words. "I don't know, this whole place feels older. Or not older, more … timeless."

"The objects on those plinths might tell us something useful. Maybe there was something here that Vulpis was looking for. A weapon."

"In which case, maybe he took it away and left the rest. Perhaps there was a fight, and he damaged this warden mechanism. If I go nearer the plinths, I might end up very dead."

"Its reactions don't appear to be hostile. It almost seems like it's trying to be helpful."

Helpful, right. She edged closer to the first dais, watching the entity for some power build-up, some sign of attack. It didn't move to stop her. Instead, it kept its distance, moving as she moved, shadowing her.

The first plinth she came to bore a death-mask encrusted in what she assumed were diamonds. Or maybe, for all she knew, it wasn't a death-mask at all but the face itself. She couldn't pick it up to study it, the blue glow of the protective stasis field resisting her. There was no explanation of what she was seeing, no details of the object's context. Most likely she lacked the necessary brain augmentations to interface with the mechanism.

The next item was either a sculpture of shining metal or perhaps a machine of some unknown purpose. Its lines were complex and hard to follow, folding in upon themselves like the strands of an impossible knot. Planes twisted and became a gap between two other planes as you tried to follow them. Even her left eye found itself confused. She walked around the device constructing a three-dimensional model of it in her brain, but the object refused to comply, resisting her efforts to map it.

The next pedestal contained an object that flickered in and out of existence, jumping repeatedly from one side of its containment field to another. Of all the objects she could see, it was the only one moving. It was another thing that seemed impossible: a stasis field by definition held an object outside of the normal passage of time; something within it couldn't move or decay because time wasn't passing. Yet here was this object doing exactly that. It was a black X-shape about the size of her hand. It put her in mind of a four-legged arachnoid without any central body, although it was impossible to say if the thing was organic or metallic. It gave her the distinct impression it was trying to get at her, sniff her out, devour her.

She moved on. There was a plain black cube made of metal or stone, no light reflecting off it, its purpose completely unfathomable, then a set of what looked like crowns, but big enough only to fit fingertip-sized heads. There was something like an outsized piece of jewellery or a totem, wrought from a silvery metal, in the shape of a central circle with lines radiating off it, sockets for beads set at random intervals along the lines, only one of which was filled. The next plinth contained two glass beads on their own: one red, one blue. On the next was a stylized stone sculpture of a tall, bipedal being, its head strangely elongated.

On and on it went: countless artistic treasures or technological artefacts. She could feel Ondo's burning desire to get his hands on the objects, study them, find out what they were and what they did. She felt something of the same urge, the same delight: there were treasures here from across the galaxy, their age and provenance unknown. The secrets they harboured might explain many things.

Ondo's disembodied voice sounded puzzled in her mind. "Why would someone construct a repository such as this and then abandon it?"

"As a place to store looted treasures? We might have this all wrong. Perhaps Concordance didn't attack this place, perhaps they *built* it. We may not be able to trust anything this Warden says; its memories are clearly garbled."

Ondo was unconvinced. "Why would Concordance need a safe place to store valuables? Who would they be hiding them from? Besides, you were able to simply walk in here, and that does not sound like Concordance to me. If this was their repository, they would defend it with all their firepower."

"So maybe someone assembled it during the war, some faction we don't know about, and then they died out, and all knowledge of the place was lost. You said there were different schools of thought within the Omnian religion."

"I still would have expected defensive systems."

"Perhaps we'll discover there are when I try to leave. I might be trapped in here for the rest of time."

"I don't see signs of a fight. This vault has not suffered any bombardment damage like the outer chamber."

"The Warden entity is a wreck."

"Which might simply be because it is old. Its systems have decayed because it's been active for longer than was originally intended. Ageing can do that."

She ignored his attempt at humour. "I don't understand why Aefrid's forebear never found any of this. It isn't exactly well hidden."

"That's a good question, one that's been puzzling me."

The idea of Ondo sitting inside her own brain, thinking his own thoughts, continued to trouble her. "Have you been consuming my brain processing power by running your own analysis?"

"I did explain, Selene. The flecks containing my engrams do not interfere with your cognitive processing in any way, except when you allow them to do so. The amount of chemical energy I draw is tiny, the equivalent of you rising your little finger once every hour. Your additions have plenty of energy reserves to draw on."

"Right, okay." He also couldn't tell when she was mocking him. Maybe she needed to make it more obvious. "You haven't come to any conclusions?"

"Hypotheses only. Find out everything you can from the entity. It might give us some clues."

"I'll try. It's not exactly being cooperative." The shimmering alien hadn't moved, awaiting instruction like a good little automated greeting system.

"These objects," she said out loud. "May I take them?"

The entity's reply was as frustratingly implacable as ever. "My work will be done when the locks are opened."

"Okay, sure, so when will the locks be opened?"

"I do not have they key."

"Who does have the key?"

"I do not have they key."

She thought about persuading the mechanism to be more helpful by pointing her blaster at it, threatening to rewire it permanently. She held herself back; it wasn't going to respond to her threats, and she might destroy the one chance they had of activating whatever needed to be activated to recover the artefacts. For all she knew, if she attacked the entity the entire structure might collapse into cataclysmic ruin, entombing her inside it. Whatever the purpose of this place was, the mechanism had protected the objects it warded for some time. They would be safe a while longer.

She had the glass bead they'd recovered from the ice of Maes Far on a chain around her neck. She fished it out from her suit, and pressed the combination of microswitches that released the sphere from its clasp. She held it up for the flickering entity to see. As usual, the sphere refracted electromagnetic radiation across a wide spectrum in complex and shifting ways.

"Do you know what this is?" she asked.

The entity shimmered out of existence, and she thought it had vanished completely, finally succumbing to its age and damage. But then she saw it had reappeared two hundred metres down the gallery behind her. There was a distinct colour shift to its hues: now it glinted in purples and marine turquoises. Was that significant?

Selene muttered to herself, "Right, well, I'll follow you, shall I?" She weaved down the line of plinths. All were occupied, the objects in no order she could discern: a mechanism of cogs and rivets constructed from some black metal, a multifaceted crystal the size of her head, a book printed on some sort of paper analogue, gold symbols in an unknown alphabet across its blood-red cover. Works of art and artefacts of science, natural wonders and items she couldn't begin to identity.

She also passed side-doors leading off into chambers that housed larger objects: statues and carved columns, titanic skeletons and the façades of ornate temples. The scale of the place was dazzling, the twisting layout impossible to follow. Through one arched doorway she glimpsed an avenue of huge, stone beasts with six legs and snarling maws. There were hundreds of them, receding into the far distance of a chamber suffused with a golden, sunset light, its curved roof hundreds of metres high. Did the vaults fill the interior of the planet, or was something else going on here, some extra-dimensional effect she didn't understand? So close to the star, an energy supply wouldn't be a problem. The place was a museum, a repository, a treasure house. A catalogue of objects and wonders. What worlds had the objects come from? Who had brought them here? Had they been stolen or rescued from conflagrations and natural disasters for safe storage? If this was Concordance's work, what were they doing it *for*?

Ondo was making little whimpers in her head at each new sight, his delight at what he was seeing almost sexual in its fervour. She said nothing; no point spoiling his fun. And, in truth, she got it. She found herself wondering what her father would have made of the place. They could have explored it together, father and daughter.

She kept walking towards the entity, which was glinting beside a curved alcove in the walls. She'd thought it was another doorway, but instead she saw a pearl-white hemisphere embedded in the wall there, two metres in diameter. Some sort of artwork? But there was a tiny circular slot directly beneath the hemisphere which was, clearly, the right size for the glass bead.

"I put this in here?" she asked.

The entity didn't reply, but nor did it intervene when she moved her hand towards the slot. The bead slipped in effortlessly, seemingly sucked in by some mechanism. It was, as she'd imagined, a display port of some description. The hemisphere went crystal clear, and a representation of the entire galaxy appeared. Some of the stars blinked, and symbols appeared around the edges of the display.

"Can you make anything of those, Ondo?"

"I've recorded a few fragments of something similar, but never enough to translate. The script bears no correlation to any existing galactic calligraphic system that I'm aware of. One or two runes match those of known alphabets, but that appears to be random chance. There's only a fixed number of symbols cultures can use."

So *no*, then. "What do you figure this thing is?"

"A data retrieval mechanism would be my best guess."

"There doesn't seem to be much on it other than a pretty picture of the galaxy."

"Or we don't know how to access the rest of the data."

"I could try ripping the hemisphere off the wall and lugging it back to the Refuge for analysis."

"I suspect that's beyond even your powers."

"Maybe." She took a step forwards, thinking she'd at least try. As she moved, the galaxy blinked out and was replaced by a rapid series of other images: screens of text, landscapes, worlds, living creatures, fleets of starships, faces, constellations. They flicked by with such dazzling rapidity that even she couldn't focus on any of them.

"Selene, slow down! We need to see these images, study them."

She turned Ondo off. She didn't need the distraction. Had movement activated the device? She tried standing perfectly still, but it made no difference to the torrent of information. If she could capture it, that would be something. Her left eye normally blinked in perfect synchronicity with her right eye, but now she instructed it to remain open. She would record the images streaming past her retina and worry about interpreting it later.

Five minutes later, the pictures stopped and she was returned to the galaxy image. Some kind of pictorial index, she guessed. She tried moving forwards and backwards again but nothing happened, the pictures didn't repeat. Maybe this mechanism was broken, too, and she'd retrieved all she was going to get. Maybe she'd transferred all the data from the bead, and what she'd seen was the information flowing into the Depository's systems.

The glass sphere protruded slightly from the wall where she'd inserted it. She touched it, and immediately the galaxy disappeared. The bead slid out to land in the palm of her hand.

She reactivated Ondo. "I've captured some data from the bead." She gave him access to the memory dumps from her optical system.

He studied it for a few moments. "There's a lot here. An incredible amount. I think now might be a good time to return so I, that is the real Ondo, can study it in detail. We can always come back if that seems like the best approach."

"You mean, you figure the real you will want to come here."

He conceded the point. "Partly that, yes. But you've acquired so much already that it would be a shame if it were … lost now."

"Yeah, it would be a terrible shame."

She retraced her steps towards the doorway, keeping a wary eye on the Warden for some sign it intended to intervene and attempt to stop her. It followed her, but didn't act in any other way. Despite her earlier caution, she still thought it likely the doorway wasn't going to reappear as she approached. Upon the third plinth in line, the fast-moving blur of the X-shaped object flicked restlessly backwards and forwards. She strode on, and the doorway slid into existence, exactly as it had before.

"You will return with the dawn?" The entity was suddenly very near her, the broken planes and angles of its form tilting and spinning, as if it were desperately trying to piece itself back together to form coherent thoughts.

Selene stopped, one foot through the doorway, one still in the vault. "You think I can bring the dawn?"

The entity didn't reply for a moment. Its shattered pieces seemed to spin more urgently. She'd have sworn that she could feel her cerebellum tickling as the creature read her brain patterns, trying desperately to make itself understood. "The night has been long. At last there is light, the glow of the dawn before the sun rises. The day must come."

"I will return," she heard herself saying. "If I can." She wasn't sure if she was saying what the entity wanted to hear so it didn't stop her leaving, or if she was making a solemn promise.

She retraced her steps through the upper chamber and out into the clashing solar radiation of the planet's surface. The blue star was a wall of raging heat, filling half of the sky. The *Radiant Dragon* lay exactly where she'd left it; as soon as she emerged from the shadows of the building, she was able to re-establish comms. No ships had been detected translating out of metaspace, and nor had there been any movement beyond the mesh. Half way to the ship, her suit began to alert again, warning her its capacity to shield her from the radiation was diminishing and that, at current decay rates, she'd be exposed in twelve minutes. Time enough. She shut the alarms off and picked up the pace. She resorted to the loping run that ate up the ground, and made it back into the *Dragon*'s EVA vestibule with a minute to spare.

While she stripped off the suit and stuffed it in a bin for decontamination, the ship said. "Shall I prep for take-off?"

She'd been thinking about that. There was one more thing she wanted to discover. A theory that had come to her. "Not yet; I'm going to make a second trip into the building."

"Is that wise?"

"Probably not, but let's do it anyhow. Set me up a fresh suit."

She unhooked the chain around her neck and hung it from a hook. The glassy orb, embedded in its clasp once more, swung backwards and forwards, reflections glinting in its depths as it spun.

She shrugged on her new suit, the smell of fresh plastics acrid in her nose. She checked its seals and life-support systems were fully functional, then set out on the return journey to the pyramidal building. Inside, the winding lines of her boot prints in the dust were the only sign that anything had changed for a long time. But when she crossed to the centre of the chamber to the spot where the door had slid up, nothing happened. She stepped across the thin oblong on the ground, walked around it, touched it with her gauntleted fingers, but nothing could persuade the door to reappear.

"Good," she said. "Just as I thought."

The Ondo in her head said, "You're suggesting the doorway mechanism opened because you had the bead with you?"

"It was a theory, but this looks pretty conclusive. I've been thinking about why Aefrid said there was nothing here. The person who came here, her progenitor, presumably didn't have a bead."

"Almost certainly not."

"Possessing the bead marked me out as a friend, someone to be trusted. We came here to read data off the object, but it was only because I was carrying it that I could get inside."

"Perhaps the mechanism assumed you were going to deposit some new treasure in its repository," said Ondo.

"I guess so. That, or the data held on the bead."

"The archaeology suggested it was held within its owner's cranium. That would make it hard to insert it into that reader you used."

"Sure, but there may have been other mechanisms we didn't see."

She tried one more time to activate the door, then gave up. At least it meant the treasures beneath her feet would be safe for a while longer. She bounded her way back to the safety of the *Dragon*, and this time instructed the ship to power up for orbital insertion.

"You wish to begin the metaspace jump sequence to return to the Refuge?" the ship asked.

She bundled the second suit into the same pod as the first and made her way up the observation deck. "One more side-quest, and then we'll leave."

"Where now?" asked Ondo. He couldn't keep the faintest note of exasperation from his voice.

"I want to take a closer look at that mesh." She instructed the ship to take them to the rift they'd observed in the circumference.

"It might be better to save that for a subsequent visit."

"Yeah, maybe. But since we're here, it's a shame not to go and see."

They rose from the surface of the planet and away from the stellar mass on reaction drive. Once they were clear, a series of three short metaspace hops took them to the impossible chain-link wall that surrounded the entire solar system. As Selene nudged them nearer, the dazzling size of the artefact's scale left her awe-struck. This close, the curvature of the construction was undetectable to her natural eye. It looked like someone had constructed a wall of infinite size right across space. Only her augmented eye was able to discern the mesh's slight bend in all directions.

It was composed of hexagonal holes, each a couple of centimetres across. She could get no energy signature off the material, but it was certainly doing *something*. Space beyond was visible, but blurred and indistinct; it was like looking at it through a sheet of misted glass.

"Ondo, what do you make of it?"

The wonder was clear in his voice, too. "Again, I've no idea. This is completely new to me."

"We're agreed it isn't natural?"

"I think so. The regularity of its structure suggests that clearly, although such uniformity is obviously common enough on the atomic level. The scale of this, though. Whatever it's constructed from, it must weigh trillions of tonnes."

"I'm going to EVA out to take a closer look. Maybe I can cut a sample off it."

"I think you should be very careful to stay on this side of it."

"There's nothing for light-years around on either side. Nothing is going to happen."

"We can't be absolutely sure. Someone built this for a

reason, and my guess is they were trying to protect something."

Back in the EVA vestibule, Selene double-checked that her tether to the *Dragon* was reliable, then cast herself off into space. The mesh was some thirty metres away. She steered herself up to it with the suit's microreaction thrusters. She hesitated for a moment, then clawed her fingers through the mesh. It was thin, the tubes of its structure a little under three millimetres in diameter.

She expected it to ripple as she touched it, but it was utterly solid. She ran spectrographic and electromagnetic scans but could make nothing of its physical structure. The best she could come up with was that it was a semimetal, something like a graphene sheet but many orders of scale larger.

She hesitated for a moment, then released the seal on her left gauntlet. She amped up heat distribution to her fingers so that they could survive near-absolute zero for a few seconds, then touched the mesh with her bare skin. The structure felt smooth, glassy, with no microimpact abrasions at all. It also felt utterly strong, utterly unbreakable. There was some sort of power humming through it, but she couldn't discern what it might be, what the power source was. Perhaps the entire structure was resonating with background radiation, singing in harmony with the galaxy.

She sealed the gauntlet back over her hand and pulled herself along to the gap. The exposed edges of the mesh were utterly smooth. It didn't look like some mass had crashed through; so far as she could tell the wall had simply never been completed. Why was that? What had happened? Why assemble such an artefact only to leave it incomplete?

She tried in vain to sheer off a section of the mesh with her suit's weaponry, but as she'd expected she couldn't even make a mark. She hovered for a moment in the gap, one hand grasping the mesh. Without the intervening wall, space beyond looked completely normal, the blazing stars shining. The temptation to launch herself through was enormous. She was still tethered to the *Dragon*, and her suit's power was at 80%. She could return to the ship whenever she needed to.

With a flicker of her suit's reaction drive, she pushed herself through the rift into space outside the wall. Ten metres, twenty. Nothing happened. The blue star was a hazy blur through the wall, but nothing changed and nothing attacked her.

After a moment, she reversed the thrusters to take her back to the *Dragon*. Once there, she instructed the ship to make for the egress point and begin the steps in the dance to escape Dead Space.

Unseen, back outside the mesh, something drifted against the background stars, blotting them out completely, although whether it was small and nearby, or much larger and farther away, there was no one to see.

4. Masks

She followed the sequence of jumps out of Dead Space, reversing the dance steps she'd made on her way in-system. Once again, the alarms clanged in her brain, and once again the *Radiant Dragon* calmly and apologetically claimed it could do nothing about them.

She emerged into normal space without incident or attack. The Ondo in her mind requested permissions to interface with the ship's systems, use the *Dragon*'s higher order of computational ability to begin an analysis of everything that had been found. She let him get on with it; it wouldn't impinge on her brain function, and it at least meant he was usefully occupied while she commenced the tedious jump/wait/jump sequence of the Refuge approach protocols. She busied herself pursuing her regime of physical fitness. There were still too many times when the muscles in her right leg or hip ached sharply, her natural biology struggling to keep up with her artificial.

They ran the planetoid on an artificial day/night cycle, a rhythm Ondo had adjusted to match Maes Far's to assist with her rehabilitation. It was nominally the middle of the night as she finally docked, but Ondo was waiting for her on the spaceward hangar floor as she emerged from the *Dragon*. By the look of his crumpled day clothes, he hadn't been asleep anyway.

She looked for a spark of wonder in his eyes, a delight that meant he already knew what she'd discovered, and therefore that she couldn't trust her inner Ondo after all. It wasn't there. She saw, mainly, relief that she had returned unharmed, a simple pleasure at the sight of her. He was either a very good actor, or it was time she started to trust him. It occurred to her that trusting him meant believing in herself, too. Ondo had rebuilt her, reformed her. If she decided he wasn't compromised by Concordance, that meant she wasn't either.

He held out his arms, uncertain of whether to hold her close or shake her hand. "Did you find anything?"

She squeezed him a greeting, his body surprisingly bony beneath his tunic. Sometimes he was so engrossed in his work he forgot to eat. He needed to look after himself more.

"Oh yeah."

"Tell me."

Despite the tedium of the approach, she was tired and needed to sleep. She could let her guard down now she was back at the Refuge. "I'll give you full access to your avatar in my skull. He can fill you in."

"Are you sure? You know that will give me sight of any conversation you've had with him."

Had she said anything she didn't want the real Ondo to know? Probably not. She wasn't sure she cared too much anymore. "It's fine. Download everything. You need to see it."

His eyes glazed over for a few moments. He was grabbing the data there and then, dumping it from her flecks into stores in his own head for later analysis. She felt it like a prickle inside her skull, like when she ate something frozen. He studied what he'd downloaded for a few moments.

"This is incredible. You saw no sign of Concordance?"

"None at all."

"All this time this was sitting there. Why did I never go?"

"It wouldn't have helped you. Look at my second visit. I could only get in because I had the Maes Far bead with me."

He paused for a moment more, head tilted on one side as he sifted through the relevant records. "Yes, I see. Interesting, interesting. I need to go through everything you learned in more detail. A *lot* more detail. You took far too many risks, though. You initiated your metaspace translations far too close to the nearby gravity wells. Doing that will get you killed one day."

She ignored him. "What do you make of the star? And the solar system cage?"

"The cage, if that's what it is, is remarkable. I've never encountered any construction of such size anywhere in the galaxy. But I can at least imagine how it might have been built, given an advanced technology and sufficient materials. The star, though … it just isn't possible for it to exist according to all our physical models. The universe would have to be billions or trillions of years older for one to evolve. And yet, there it is."

"Either it isn't from our universe, or some significant stellar engineering has been performed on it."

Ondo looked troubled by her words. "And I have no idea how either of those two things could be. I need to give this some thought."

"And I need to get some sleep. Don't stay up too late."

"Yes, yes, of course." He was already bustling off, tapping out notes on the archaic longhand tablet he always carried with him for recording stray ideas.

She emerged eight hours later, eyes bleary, thoughts sluggish. She dialled up a cup of *Korv*, or as close as the Refuge could get to her preferred Maes Far stimulant drink, then went in search of Ondo.

It was clear he'd ignored her instruction; he was hunched over his screens in the laboratory and was wearing the same clothes he'd greeted her in. She had to step carefully through a scatter of burned-out machine components to reach him. He smelled funky, like he hadn't washed for days. Maybe he hadn't; he still hadn't adjusted from those long years with only his researches for company.

He didn't notice her arrival. The bead was mounted in a pair of delicate callipers on the desk and he was shining three lasers of different wavelengths into it. She watched him work for a moment, not wanting to interrupt. He was moderating the angle the lasers fired into the bead, as if he'd worked out how to read from the device, but the screen next to the rig showed only a random stream of digits that betrayed no pattern she could discern.

Swaying on an overhanging frond, one of the jewelbugs considered the scene, fingernail-sized head cocked, leg held in mid-air as if also fearful the sound of its footfall might distract Ondo. Its multifaceted eye glistened with the laser light scattered by the bead.

She spoke quietly. "Can you make anything of it?"

It took a moment for his thoughts to swim back from where they'd been to the here-and-now. "Some things. Quite a lot of things. There are many gaps. Mostly I've learned that there are many more things I don't know than I thought there were. The star, and the cage ... I still have no idea how either can be there."

"Okay, so, what have you worked out?"

"I can tell you what the markings on the wall of the outer chamber mean. The *Radiant Dragon* did most of the pattern-matching analysis as you returned: the lines and symbols are a representation of the path you took through metaspace to reach the system. They're a map."

"A map to a place that's only visible when you get there? That's crazy."

"It might not be a map *per se*, so much as a stylized representation. Perhaps it was an approach warning system that lit up as ships followed the route through metaspace.

That's obviously complete speculation. But the inference is clear: the route through Dead Space passed to me by Aefrid came originally from the builders of that construction."

"Or they got it from someone older still."

"I did think that the layout of the plinths might follow the same pattern, but they do not appear to. So far as I can tell they are scattered at random. Or perhaps with simply no concern for symmetry."

"What do you make of the whole site? Is it an abandoned Concordance installation, or a target they attacked?"

"I'm not convinced Concordance were ever there. The dating is very unclear and there's no proof of their presence. Galactic history prior to Vulpis's *Day Zero* at the start of the Omnian War is too much of a closed book. That said, there are certain architectural similarities between the buildings you found and other Concordance structures – including, if I'm not mistaken, some of the Cathedral ships. But then, if this Depository is a Concordance artefact, it only adds to the mystery of how they achieved so much, became what they became, so quickly. Why they built this place and then why they abandoned it."

"You must be able to get something from the images I captured."

Ondo ran his hands through his hair, a gesture that meant he was struggling through some complex problem. "There's a mass of data here, but so far there's no context to it that I can work out, no order. It's like the objects on the plinths you found: each is fascinating in its own right, but I have no idea why they were laid out as they were. We simply don't understand the organising principles involved. I still hope to reveal something, but I'll need time."

She sipped at the hot Korv to straighten out her mind, get her thoughts flowing. It was slowly having an effect. The artificial sphere of her brain, she noted, also started to function with more acuity. It was an emulation, the stimulant molecules in the drink could have no effect on her biomechanical components, but it was an impressive effect. "Perhaps it's random. If I went back, I might see different objects."

"Hard to see the point of that." His lack of sleep and his frustration was making him cranky. She was used to it.

"The cataloguing mechanism is broken," she suggested. "Objects might be arranged by the Warden device, which is clearly not in good shape."

"Perhaps."

"What did you make of that moving object? The cross-shaped insectoid thing."

"My best guess is that the stasis field on that particular plinth is malfunctioning, allowing time to flow once more. The creature or machine within is therefore able to resume its movement, which suggests the damage to the site must be relatively recent."

"We should go back before the mechanisms deteriorate further, let you study those artefacts and the Warden close-up."

He frowned. He'd clearly considered it. "At some point that may well be the logical step to take. I confess, I'm itching to go. But for now, there's too much I can learn from the data you recovered. We have to consider the risks of returning. Then there's the *Dragon*."

"What about it?"

"The ship's systems appear to have suffered some impairment from the journey. I'm reluctant to risk further damage."

She had the clear impression that his mind was only half on their conversation. He was talking to her but looking at the bead. She turned to leave.

"Oh," he said to her back, "I meant to say. There is something I can tell you, some data that came in from the network while you were away."

Ondo had a transgalactic communication network of

his own. It was slow and flawed compared to Concordance's. The enemy appeared to be able to send messages to any system or ship with no latency, and Ondo, by contrast, had a swarm of several thousand metajump-capable drones that each ran a regular route around planets of known interest. They blinked into existence in each system, pulled in telemetry from the nanosensors previously left behind, then moved on. Periodically, their routes took them to a collection point in the dark of interstellar space where they, along with other drones, passed on what they'd learned to the next higher-up devices in the hierarchy. Slowly, data was accumulated until it could be brought to the Refuge. By then it might be weeks old, but it gave Ondo a comprehensive, if flawed, view of wider galactic events. He was always behind the curve but knew far more about what was going on than anyone else – apart from Concordance.

"What is it?"

"It's about Kane. You said you needed to understand what made him do what he did."

She still needed answers, something to make sense of events on Maes Far. The slump of her father to the ice, the fan of spraying blood, played through her mind's eye one more time.

"Tell me."

"I looked into his background. He came from a planet called Migdala on the periphery of the central mass. It happens to be a world I keep an eye on as a potential flashpoint. Some interesting information came in about it. There's been bubbling rebellion on the planet for some years, so far successfully suppressed by Concordance. They have a festival called the Carnival of Masks, celebrated across most continents and adopted and adapted by most Migdalan cultures. It's essentially a week of partying and celebration, midsummer in the southern hemisphere and, obviously, midwinter in the northern. In the past few years, there's been trouble in several major cities:

demonstrations, rioting, drunken mobbery spilling over into violence and open revolt."

"What's different this year?"

"There's been more Concordance activity in orbit around the planet. It's normal enough for a few Void Walker attack craft to arrive in-system from time to time, but I'm seeing at least two extra Cathedral ships in orbit."

That sent a chill trickling though her. Were they planning to do to Migdala what they'd done to her own planet? "They're constructing another shroud?"

"That's unclear. My data is obviously out of date. *Something* is happening there. You could slip into the system and take a look, pick up the latest nanosensor recordings. I have good predictions on the locations and arrival points of their ships; you could go without being seen easily enough."

He was trying to get rid of her so he could concentrate on his researches. Or, more generously, he didn't want her to be kicking her heels, waiting to do something. Right then, activity was psychologically good for her; it gave her an outlet, a purpose. Maybe he got that.

"I'll go down to the planet," she said, "find out what's taking place on the ground."

He hadn't meant for her to go that far. He shook his head. "The risks are too great. You know what they would do if you were identified, and your appearance is hardly going to let you blend in."

"You said they all wear masks."

"Many taking part in the celebrations do, but by no means everyone. In any case, there's still the rest of you: a mask might cover up your face, but not your arms, your torso, your legs. You'd be spotted immediately. You know Concordance laws against biomechanical enhancement are enforced rigorously."

"I'm an abomination, yeah."

His distaste at the term passed across his features. "As they would see it. It doesn't matter that they're clearly wrong, it matters that you survive. From what I know of the system, it would be impossible to know whom you could trust. Concordance has embedded itself thoroughly in Migdalan culture. Parasitized it."

She ignored his objections. A part of her wanted to go to the planet as she was: half-biological, half-artificial. A mongrel, an atrocity. Flaunt herself in their faces. *This* was what they'd done to her, *this* was what their rule meant. She had done nothing wrong, she'd simply survived, by whatever means were necessary. She wanted their outrage, their horror, their fear to follow her down the street. Except, she clearly wouldn't survive for long like that, and then she wouldn't be able to defeat them. If she wanted to go to the planet, she'd have to play their game for a time – repellent as the idea was.

"You can give me artificial flesh, cover up the substrate?"

"You want me to do that?"

"Temporarily, so I can go under cover. When I return, I go back to this. Patchwork Selene, piebald Selene. You can do it? It doesn't need to be real skin grown for the purpose, right? An artificial analogue will do for a few days."

"It's too dangerous. If anyone sees what you really are, they'll come for you. One abrasion to your artificial skin, and it will be obvious. Cut you and you won't bleed. And then there is your left eye. Skin I can do, but concealing the extra tech in your eyeball would mean transplanting a more natural looking prosthetic."

"I can wear goggles or sunglasses to cover my eyes."

"Inside? At night?"

"I'll cope. I'll be careful. You can do it; I know you can."

He was reluctant: afraid, perhaps, that she was too hell-bent on revenge to assess risks properly. It was possible he had a point. She burned to strike back at the enemy. She had to watch that.

"I could give you the skin," he said, "but I won't. This is too risky."

"You said you saved me so I could live my life. You have no right to deny me."

"I won't facilitate your efforts to get yourself killed."

"Now you sound like Concordance, telling me what's best for me. I'll go anyway, as I am, take my chances."

She had his full attention now. He studied her for long moments, competing thoughts flashing across his features. He was torn in two.

Finally, he relented, looked away. "What you ask – I can do it, yes. It will take a few days. But promise me you're not going to get yourself killed. As well as you, I'm thinking of myself and everything here. If they take you, they'll be able to rip out your knowledge of how to find the Refuge."

"Then zap those memories, encrypt them, and have the *Dragon* recreate them if and when I return safely. I'll take my chances."

He shook his head. "I could do that if your brain was all artificial, but memory stored in biological cells isn't that simple. Memories have echoes, they're dynamic."

"Then we'll have to take the risk. It's either that or I never venture near an inhabited world again. It was you that suggested I live a normal life, find a safe planet somewhere to build a new identity. There'd be the danger then that I'd reveal the truth about you."

He'd clearly considered the possibility. "Yes. That is true."

"We're agreed?"

He relented with a sigh. "Agreed. Go if you must."

That evening he began the process. She stood naked, legs apart, left arm held high, unmoving, while electronically controlled micronozzles sprayed up and down her limbs and torso, swarming around her like a cloud of hummingbirds. They worked systematically, constantly returning to their base to refill with the required chemicals and biomechanical components. Bit by bit, they laid down her artificial skin. Ondo monitored the process remotely to protect her modesty. They'd come a long way since her rebuilding process, the months when every centimetre of her flesh was known intimately to him.

She hooked into remote sensors so she could see herself, watch her skin being built up, sparkling black substrate being overlaid by her natural off-white. Strange how wrong she looked when she was the same colour all over. Ondo's artistry was undeniable, though. He'd programmed freckles and blemishes into her appearance, including two scars that were an accurate-looking continuation of real scars across her abdomen. She was glad she'd chosen to remove all the hair from her body and head. Permanent artificial skin would have allowed it to grow through, blend in, but the temporary flesh did not. Her new skin also dulled her enhanced senses very slightly, although not enough to impair her significantly. Her best defence was in fitting in, looking like a local.

Ondo took the greatest care on her face. He used the micronozzles to lay down 90% of her artificial maxillo-facial skin, but completed the remaining 10% himself, either by programming in each batch of movements he wanted the devices to make, or even by using gentle brush strokes to build up the layers by hand. She turned off her facial touch sensors so that she wasn't constantly bugged by tickling sensations. Occasionally, he brushed over a seam onto her natural flesh, and each time she had to resist the urge to scratch irritatedly.

His face was centimetres from her own as he worked, his fingers smoothing the flesh of her earlobe or her cheek. The intimacy of it made her uncomfortable, and she had to force herself to sit still while he worked, staring into the distance so as not to catch his eye.

He was studying the contour of her cheekbone, stroking her cheek. He must have seen some reaction in her. "Is this okay? You want me to continue?" It was uncomfortable for him, too. Much of what they'd been through together had to have made him uneasy. She hadn't thought about it from his perspective before.

"You're doing fine. I'm grateful, truly."

"I'll show you what you need to do so that you can apply the disguise yourself, eventually. I'm sure you have a better idea of how you should look than I do. With practice you could adopt this disguise in only a couple of hours."

"Thank you. But you're doing fine."

When he was finished, she studied herself in the mirror. He'd done a good job, the two sides of her face matching seamlessly but slightly asymmetrically. She ran through a series of expressions to test everything out: delight, sadness, horror, anger. It all worked perfectly, although it was strange how wrong the chubby-cheeked fleshiness looked and felt to her. She looked like a person, sure, but she no longer looked like *her*. Which meant it was a good disguise, although she had to resist the urge to claw off all that fake flesh, expose the real Selene underneath.

She downloaded all the data she could find on Migdalan cultures and languages. The political and social set-up was complicated, with numerous factions and clans competing on most continents – to the point that it was impressive they'd reached the level of social sophistication they had. She'd settled on an equatorial city called Senefore as her target. It was the closest the planet had to a world capital, and it was certainly the city that saw the largest and most raucous processions. She picked out a continent on the other side of the world and decided that would be the backstory home of her character. It would allow her some leeway if she slipped up on a pronunciation or a cultural reference, and its inhabitants tended to have lighter skin tones that were closer to her original flesh. People in and around Senefore, by contrast, were generally a rainbow of darker shades, delicate browns to deep blacks. Anything to help her not stand out – although it wasn't really going to be an issue. Migdalan cities were filled with travellers at carnival time, and there were no signs of tension between nations and populations on Migdala – either because it was a mature society at ease with itself, or because the greater threat of Concordance had united them.

"What mask will you wear?" Ondo asked.

"What do we have?"

"Various ritual masks from other cultures that would pass as grotesque or comic on Migdala."

She picked out an outlandish red one that covered her face completely. It was some sort of hell-creature, with animal horns and an exaggerated, leering mouth. The eye-holes restricted her vision slightly but hid her features well.

"You're sure I'll blend in wearing this?"

"Some of the masks people wear are considerably more bizarre. You'll be tame in comparison."

"I guess that's good. You're sure this doesn't represent some dire insult to one of the Migdalan cultures?"

"I'm more or less completely sure."

"They wear them so they can't be identified by the authorities?"

"It goes back much further than that, into thousand-year-old ritual traditions from one of the mountain tribes. You could do whatever you wanted for this one week, cross any line, commit any sin, so long as you were wearing a mask. By covering your face, it was considered you became a different person, someone not responsible for your actions, allowing you to get away with essentially anything. Murder, rape, incest, mutilation, there are folk tales filled with no end of horrors carried out by people wearing masks, although the stories always have a strong retribution moral, of people ultimately paying the price for their actions, often through supernatural means. Inevitably, the practice has become sanitized for modern public tastes, becoming a way of mocking those in power rather than slaughtering them. Concordance has clamped down hard on the carnivals, but they can still be riotous. You should be careful."

"Why do they even let them continue? It seems odd."

"It does. I simply don't know."

She also picked out clothes to wear from Ondo's extensive collection of costumes and disguises: plain tunics and trousers that were practical for travel and that weren't, according to their researches, going to stand out. Again, her backstory would help skim over any awkwardness.

She stood in the midst of the racks of clothes, outfits of every conceivable colour, a huge variety of cuts and materials, and an odd thing occurred to her.

"Ondo, why are these costumes all the same?"

Ondo replied from his laboratory. "The same?"

"I mean, they all follow the same basic pattern. Two arms, two legs, somewhere between one and two metres high. Even the cuts, the tailoring for busts and waists and hips. Why is it all so uniform? There have to be clothes here for thousands of planets across the galaxy."

"Of course, the sample of costumes you see is self-selecting. I haven't bothered to collect disguises for body-forms that aren't near my own, and there are many, many variations. Sentient species with more than four limbs are common. But you've hit upon a very good question, one that's puzzled me in the past, because there is a very high incidence of this basic form among intelligent civilisations across the galaxy. At a rate that appears to be far above what might be likely by chance."

"What answer have you come up with?"

"I see two possible explanations: either this basic form is an optimal one given a wide variety of evolutionary niches, or else there is a prime cause. A deliberate plan."

"You mean, like a creator god?"

"That wasn't the explanation I had in mind. What we see might be evidence of large-scale genetic manipulation of emerging species across the galaxy. The problem is that there's no way I've found of proving that, no obvious repeating patterns in species' genes or gene analogues."

This wasn't like the shared language, a relatively recent phenomenon. Such widespread manipulation of genotypes would have to have been carried out millions of years ago. "Do you have any hard evidence at all that such a galactic-scale intervention took place?"

"None. Most likely it never happened, and what we see is a perfectly natural parallel evolution across broadly similar planetary environments. The theory that an advanced and ancient progenitor species shaped life across the galaxy would also require them to have undertaken widespread terraforming interventions on countless thousands, perhaps millions, of worlds. It's hard to believe that's possible."

"So, it is all the work of Omn, and Concordance have been right all along," she said.

He got the joke but still replied with all seriousness. "The forces of evolution and long passages of time seem like a simpler explanation to me. There's a bell-curve distribution of basic body forms across galactic space, with common patterns and outliers as you see in just about every biological phenomenon. You need hands or some close analogue for complex tool manipulation, and you need something like a head, an armoured bone container, to hold a growing brain. If you don't have structures along those lines, you don't get intelligence."

"Right. So not Omn."

When she was ready, they hugged only slightly awkwardly, and she resumed her position in charge of the *Radiant Dragon* while Ondo returned to his analysis of the Depository images. She let the ship control its own exit from the hangar deck, then took over executive control. It was already beginning to feel like it was hers, following her instructions perfectly as they flew. In those moments, she stopped knowing where she ended and the ship's structure started: its voidhull her skin, its drives her limbs, its engines her organs. The fun of it, the thrill of skimming around stray lumps of space rock and accelerating hard towards the stars, was undeniable.

The rushing fall into metaspace was the greatest ecstasy, making her stomach flip within her, although her internal body senses calmly informed her that no such thing was actually taking place. Still, with no one else around to hear, she screamed from the exhilaration of it as the *Dragon* translated out of normal space.

"Do you feel it?" she cried out to the ship. "Doesn't it fill you with joy?"

The ship took a moment to reply, its voice as calm as ever. "I feel it, Selene Ada. I have always felt it."

5. Migdala

She emerged from metaspace into the outer reaches of the Migdala system, five hundred million kilometres from the single yellow sun and at an angle of seventy degrees to the ecliptic plane.

She began to suck in telemetry. Ondo had been right: instead of a single Cathedral ship in orbit, there were three of the vessels, moving in close formation around the planet on an equatorial orbit. At this distance, she was seeing images of events that had taken place twenty minutes previously. She waited twice that long, drifting under reaction drive, metaspace projectors spun-up in case attack ships showed up at her coordinates.

"We need to plot a course down to the surface," she said to the ship. "A vector that takes us through the defence network but that gets me close to Senefore." She didn't want to spent days or weeks trudging across the planet to reach the carnival city. From what she'd learned, celebrations were already ramping up.

The ship took a few moments to reply. "I see a possible route, but it is not without risk."

"Show me."

The vector plotted by the *Dragon* looped round to the far side of her current orbit, then approached with the sun always between her and the planet. She would be visible if Concordance were monitoring local space properly, but they often did not. Being small and weak had its advantages: Concordance knew the chances were remote – approaching zero – that she or Ondo or some other renegade would turn up at any given time.

From the star, they would make a series of reaction-drive hops between the inferior planets, again keeping Migdala out of direct line-of-sight. The final approach to the planet, and the subsequent atmospheric insertion, would be the moment of greatest risk. She would be visible to Concordance sensors, and she'd be too near the star to make an immediate escape into metaspace.

Fortunately, from Ondo's analysis of Concordance's presence in the system, she had good knowledge of the positioning of enemy observation devices. If she made sure she wasn't silhouetted against the sun or any obvious background stars from the perspective of Migdala, and stuck to the seams between surveillance cones, she had a reasonable chance of getting to the planet undetected.

It was good enough.

Of course, she'd thought they were safe when they landed on Maes Far. It was entirely possible she was following the trail Concordance wished her to follow.

She was helped by unfolding events on the ground. Inter-ship Concordance comms traffic was encrypted using algorithms Ondo had never been able to crack, but the sheer scale of them flying up from assets on the surface or in the atmosphere told their own story. Wide-scale events of great concern to the trio of watching Cathedral ships were unfolding. Selene could see a lot of it for herself: her own sensors showed mass population movements across the planet's six continents as crowds converged on major population centres for the celebrations.

She was halfway between the third planet and Migdala, no astronomical bodies shielding her from the Concordance ships two light minutes away, when the *Dragon* intercepted an unencrypted message stream.

"It's being broadcast to the entire planet," said the *Dragon*'s voice. "It's clear Concordance wants everyone to see it."

"Show me."

Images filled her mind's eye: a First Augur, a member of Concordance's high priesthood, was on board one of the ships. Two grey-robed Void Walkers stood behind her, their faces expressionless. Selene's flecks identified the woman quickly enough: Secundus Godel. A knot tightened somewhere within Selene's chest. She would kill them all, but this one especially. The one who had directed Kane in his acts of barbarity.

Godel was young, surprisingly young, or so her appearance suggested. Her skin was a deep, storm cloud purple, a metallic shimmer to it. *A native of A'chtion, her flecks whispered to her. A world where people change skin colour in accordance with social rank. Purple suggests the highest status of all, although the distinction will probably be lost on most people. She is using her colour display to claim dominance that she should be, or considers herself to be, Primo. A subtle but also not very subtle challenge to Carious. Whether he understands this, and simply chooses to ignore it, is unclear.*

First Augurs rarely appeared in public; normally they were hidden away in the secret enclaves of Omn, controlling galactic events from afar. Godel's words were Mind-translated into local dialects and idioms as she spoke. Selene's flecks translated them back into galactic common.

"Greetings, and the peace of Omn shine upon you, citizens of Migdala. The festivities of the Carnival of Masks are nearly upon us, and I bid you all to reflect on the true meaning of the celebrations as revealed by the priests and sages of the Revelation Temples. This is a time for pleasure and for family, but also for calm reflection and devotion. A period of peaceful celebration of Omn in his two guises: the loving parent who forgives past transgressions, and the judge who punishes those straying from the path. Think on these deeper spiritual meanings as you celebrate the turning of the year with your loved ones. May Omn watch over you and guide you."

From the cultural data she'd downloaded, Selene knew the Revelation Temples were a global sect that was, effectively, a front for Concordance on Migdala. The Temples long-predated the rise of Concordance; Vulpis's followers had simply subsumed the sect, adapted it to their own ends rather than destroying it, and imposed their own vision upon it. Slowly, over the years, they'd altered the ecclesiastical underpinnings of the Temples until their teachings aligned with worship of Omn and subjugation to Concordance. It was a radically different approach to the one she was more familiar with: the imposition of order backed up by extreme violence.

Intrigued, Selene switched to sampling the video feeds streaming from the surface, looking down upon the lines of people thronging the seven bridges that led to the centre of Senefore. The crowds contained many revellers already in their colourful and outlandish masks, but there were nearly as many devotees of the Temples: people not wearing masks, but clad in red robes of various designs. Some wore only a splash of red, perhaps to demonstrate their allegiance. It seemed to her there was a wariness between the two sets of people: they walked in their own groups and didn't acknowledge each other. There were also a large number of soldiers watching the crowds from low-altitude observation platforms. From afar it was hard to be sure, but she read a mixed atmosphere down on the planet: a mounting excitement at the celebrations to come, but also a tension. Children ran excitedly around, only to be called back and held close by their parents.

The message from Godel to the planet began to broadcast again. Selene switched the feed off and prepped for atmospheric insertion. She'd toyed with the idea of launching some sort of suicide attack on the three Cathedral ships, take Godel down with her, but she suppressed it. Time for that another day, perhaps.

There was a scatter of lone-wolf asteroids on eccentric orbits between the third and fourth planets, the ancient remains of a planet whose debris hadn't yet been sucked up by the remaining bodies. She manoeuvred the *Dragon* onto the surface of one of them, positioning the vessel in the shadow of a peak of grey rock that would conceal it from Migdala for 75% of the small planetoid's spin. She would take a lander the rest of the way; it was a tiny sliver of metal that, hopefully, Concordance monitoring wouldn't notice.

Ondo's analysis had shown where gaps in Concordance's planetary monitoring network would open and close briefly, as sweeps from different sensors brushed past each other. They were tiny, transient blind spots, the traversing of which involved a carefully choreographed speed/stop/speed sequence of movements, like hopping from rock to rock across a stream – except that it was a three-dimensional puzzle rather than two, and the gaps appeared only briefly in accordance to complex patterns. Following them took Selene into high orbit above Migdala without apparent detection.

She kept the planet between her and the three Cathedral ships at all times. It was night beneath her, with no lights visible at all as she passed over the planet's equatorial ocean. A significant tropical cyclone was tearing across the body of water, a swirling vortex one hundred kilometres wide, picking up energy as it headed for one of the planet's major land masses. She'd studied it as she approached, its central eye and flailing arms reminding her strangely of the view of the galaxy from the Refuge. The storm was growing into a monster; there would be few carnival celebrations for people living in the coastal regions in its path.

The cyclone could, however, provide her with cover as she dropped to the surface. The eye of the powerful storm would give her an effective blind-spot from orbiting Concordance sensors unless they were positioned directly overhead, and the high winds and atmospheric disturbances would shield her lander from ground and air-based installations. Assuming she survived the journey through the maelstrom, she had a chance of reaching the surface undetected.

She gritted her teeth as she dropped to the surface, arrowing her way into the eye of the storm. The lander vibrated and boomed around her; it felt like it was going to shake her skeleton to its constituent bones. She forced herself to remain calm, breathe slowly. After everything that had happened to her, she doubted whether she'd ever find such journeys easy. Once again, she tried to occupy her mind by focusing on the lander's structural integrity readings and external sensor sweeps. It didn't help much: the storm meant that she was blind, too, and watching spreading amber alerts about depleting energy hull power levels did little to put her mind at rest.

Nevertheless, she fell out of the bottom of the hurricane still in one piece, plummeting into the turbulent depths of the night-time ocean. Now the water would shield her. She sank to two hundred metres, then set the lander to head west, away from the path of the hurricane and towards the continent upon which Senefore lay. She would be there in four hours, arriving just as the rays of the rising sun lit up the continent's mountain tops.

She picked a deserted beach and swam the last kilometre from the lander to shore. She instructed the craft to sink to the sea-bed and wait for her to return. Or, if she didn't reappear within two weeks, to attempt the journey back to the *Dragon* and away to the Refuge to report to Ondo.

Above the tide line, the sand beneath her feet retained some of its warmth from the day before, oozing pleasantly between her toes. This was a tropical continent in the middle of summer, and temperatures would rise sharply through the day. Ocean scents of salty water and rotting seaweed filled her nostrils. She worked her way up the beach towards a line of swaying trees, their curving trunks bare and their leaves high crowns of rubbery fronds. The shifting sand made for slow progress; it was like trudging through snow, but the warmth of the rising sun on her neck was pleasant, and the curious, questioning cries of unseen birds lifted her spirits in unexpected ways. Migdala was beautiful, and it was another planet that once she had never heard of and had had no way of visiting. The thought sent a grim smile across her face. Concordance had given her this.

She knew from Ondo's surveillance streams that she could skirt the impenetrable green wall of the rainforest ahead of her. Eventually, she'd reach scattered communities and tracks that would take her to the periphery of the continent's ground-transportation network. From there, she could slip into the crowds converging on Senefore.

Some aspects of the plan had troubled her. On Maes Far, she would have been spotted very rapidly if she'd attempted such a thing: everyone had simple tags embedded under their skin to grant access to buildings and transportation and for use in shops.

Ondo had assured her there would be no such problems on Migdala. "The world is more rebellious than Maes Far. People on Migdala wouldn't take kindly to being tagged and monitored, even if it would make life easier for them. So long as you're disguised and can pay, you should be able to use the transportation system without being spotted."

"Unless they're looking out for me."

"If they are, I doubt you'll get as far as a public e-track service."

Her appearance caused no comment as she boarded one of the silver high-speed trains, mask in hand and sunglasses covering her eyes. There were one or two appraising glances from younger passengers, males and females so far as she could tell, but they were gazes of frank sexual appreciation rather than suspicion. This far from Senefore, at least, it seemed everyone was in party mood. Selene sat next to a mother and her young twins, both already wearing identical skull masks, excitement clear in their high voices. Selene found she could understand their idiom perfectly thanks to the knowledge she'd downloaded. That was good.

The mother smiled at Selene as she sat down but said nothing. She set about peeling a series of round, yellow fruits to give to her children, who crammed them into their mouths with clear relish. The train carriage filled up rapidly with boisterous, laughing people, young and old, and soon they were speeding their way westwards to the capital city. Selene stared out of the window as fields and rivers flashed by, her own reflected face projected onto the scene.

She wondered if Kane, the man who became a Concordance Void Walker, and who had tormented and killed her father, had ever walked down *those* roads, climbed *those* green hills. If, somehow, the places flashing by might help explain how he had become what he had.

Old Senefore was built on a round island in the middle of a lake, the remains of the caldera of an extinct volcano. The city had long-outgrown the island to cover the slopes of the hills surrounding the body of water. The inland lake was protected from storms and high waves, and over the years people had sunk piles into the lake bed to build homes and shops and temples upon stilts alongside the seven great bridges. The largest and most impressive mansions had floating gardens of pinky-white and orange blooms bobbing between wooden walkways. Many boats, both powered and rowed, flitted across the glistening water, laden down with teetering pyramids of brightly-coloured fruit, or silvery piles of fish pulled from the lake. For merchants, carnival was clearly a time of plenty.

Selene let the flood of people crossing one of the

bridges pull her along. Still no one had challenged her or remarked on her appearance, and she'd uttered no words on her journey to the city beyond an occasional greeting or apology.

The air of excited anticipation had, however, given over to a more watchful wariness among the crowd, just as she'd witnessed via the nanosensors. Those who'd brought masks now wore them, as if afraid of being identified. Selene wore her own. It was hot and heavy, tickling her cheek as she moved, and the narrow eye-holes restricted her vision. Revelation Temple disciples move in regimented lines around her, their robes blood-red, their gaze wary as they looked sideways at the revellers pushing past. None wore masks, and their robes were often adorned with a single, stylized eye. Others wore eye chains around their necks, or had third eyes daubed onto their foreheads in some brown-red pigment.

Their scowls, Selene thought, were also masks in their own way. The temples hated the carnivals, saw them as degenerate, an expression of a godless evil. Consequently, the Templers gathered in the cities just as the revellers did, but to oppose what took place rather than to join in.

"Turn your back on superstition," one Templer called out at random, his words punctuated by the clang of the handbell he rang. "You who hide your faces reject the gaze of your Lord, denying the beauty of all that he has wrought." They sounded like lines from some hymn or proclamation.

The observation platforms bristling with the barrels of the local military forces became more and more oppressive. They didn't appear to be under direct Concordance control, but Selene had no doubt they would act if Godel gave the order. From what she could see of the weaponry, the soldiers would have little trouble mowing down the crowds thronging beneath them, turning the jostling stream of bodies into a carpet of bloodied limbs and torsos. There were also more and more large outdoor screens erected for the carnival. On each of them, Godel's speech was playing on a loop, her huge face scowling down on the people passing by.

It was midday by the time Selene reached the central island of Senefore. The overhead sun was a glaring furnace nailed to the sky. The air was so humid it felt like she was chewing it, swallowing it down, rather than breathing it in. She bought a glass of an ice-cold fruit drink to keep her cool. She sampled the fluid with the tip of her tongue, checking it for toxins or allergens. The liquid was benign; she could metabolise it safely. She drank it down, the taste sweet and acid tart at the same time, then ordered two more. The money bracelet Ondo had provided, loaded with electronic funds, appeared to work perfectly, convincing local retails systems that the cash it held was both trustworthy and effectively limitless. There were many stalls selling intoxicating drinks, spicy alcohol concoctions that were clearly extremely popular. She steered clear of these. She needed to keep a clear head if she wanted to properly understand what was going on and stay out of the clutches of Concordance. Her augmentations could metabolize alcohol at an accelerated rate if need be, but it wouldn't be instantaneous.

She *did* need to eat after her journey to the city. An array of street food-vendors jostled for elbow-room with the drink sellers, offering just about every sort of food she could think of and quite a few she couldn't begin to identify. The spicy smells of the food made her stomach grumble in anticipation, despite her off-world biology. A fried purple-red fish, wrapped in a rubbery leaf so it could be eaten on the move, seemed popular. She bought one and nibbled at a sample. It was all good: proteins and carbohydrates she could consume without harm, and from which her biology, natural and artificial, could readily extract sustenance. She ate greedily, juices from the fish dribbling down her hands.

The island was beautiful; the Senefore authorities had

clearly gone to great trouble to maintain the original open squares and wide boulevards. The buildings were low, two or three storeys at most, and many were extremely ornate. Carved stone animals and the winding representations of vines adorned each surface. They were painted in a kaleidoscope of colours: pinks and blues and yellows. Many of the trees that Selene had seen on the beach grew among them, providing a welcome shade to those on the ground. Vividly-coloured birds with musical calls flitted between the trees, and fountains sprayed water pumped from the lake into the air, filling it with their cooling rainbows.

Soon, though, there would be little space to move as more and more people crowded onto the island. A hum of voices filled the air, the occasional word or cry of anger surfacing from the hubbub. The City Guard and the military had cordoned off several of the roads to provide a route for the carnival marchers, and she heard more than one argument as revellers were prevented from crossing roads or from sitting where they wished. The masks the revellers wore were as varied and exotic as Ondo had promised: painted representations of mythical beasts; bird headdresses adorned with brightly-hued feathers; the exaggerated faces of real people, presumably caricatures. One brave soul even wore a purple mask that was, clearly, supposed to be Godel. The reveller barged past Selene, whooping and shouting, running fast, as five guards pushed through the crowd after them. More than one person deliberately failed to get out of the way quickly, slowing the guards down in their pursuit.

She also saw more and more people wearing a completely blank mask devoid of any facial features. They came in a variety of skin tones, but with only eye-holes to see out of. They tended to move through the crowd in groups and, from their body-language, appeared wary, always looking around for possible threats where most people ambled along enjoying the sun.

She'd given her inner Ondo access to her sensory perceptions. She spoke to him inside her head. "Do you know what those plain masks are?"

"I don't. I've reviewed images of previous carnivals, and I could find no one wearing them. It seems to be a new innovation."

"It looks coordinated. You think they're Concordance agents?"

"They already control the military and the temples, and they have full oversight of events on the ground. Would they need to infiltrate the crowd, too?"

"If they did, I guess they'd wear masks that didn't mark them out. This is something else, rebels or troublemakers."

"Most likely," said Ondo. "Stay away from them. If it comes to violence, make sure you're not caught up in it. Remember, the Temple disciples aren't particularly peaceable, either. They're certainly not afraid to attack those they consider infidels. Their approach to religious conversion has traditionally been … assertive."

She followed a phalanx of the blank-masks, keeping a few metres behind. They were trying to force their way through the crowds filing into a square, but the press of bodies was already too great. One of them indicated a side-passage between two of the taller buildings and pushed that way, leading the others. Intrigued, and trying to look like she wasn't, Selene followed.

A maze of alleyways zig-zagged between buildings, through dusty yards. She had no maps to show where they led, which ones were dead-ends. Several times she caught a glimpse of the rainbow crowds between the walls. The group she was trailing appeared to be locals, familiar with the shortcuts and hidden ways that any city-dweller would know. They ran into a courtyard, high walls obscuring them from the crowd, and stopped abruptly.

Selene stopped, too, a few metres back, hiding behind the corner of a yellow building, trying to understand what was going on. She carried a finger-sized blaster strapped to her ankle, completely illegal on Migdala. She drew it now. Up ahead, there were shouts of rage, and the group of blank-masks were suddenly fighting someone. They'd pulled wooden staffs and short, stabbing blades from within their clothing and were swinging them as they jockeyed for position. They'd been ambushed by a phalanx of the City Guard. The latter were armed with blasters, but in the confined space couldn't safely use them. Instead, they'd drawn charged batons and were swinging them at the blank-masks. The guards were outnumbered, but more disciplined. A blank-mask charged with a roar and the guard stepped back to avoid the attack, then swung their baton round to crunch into the side of the blank-mask's head. There was a spray of blood and the blank-mask crumpled to the ground.

The sight whipped the other blank-masks into a renewed state of fury, and for a minute or more the dusty courtyard was a blaze of clubbing and punching and kicking. The cries of agony from both sides were loud, but would be inaudible to the thronging crowd of revellers only a few metres away.

When it was done, three of the blank-masks lay still on the ground, their blood clumping in the dirt, but all five of the City Guards were down, unmoving. The remaining blank-masks, four of them, limped away from the scene, holding or supporting each other. Selene crept forwards, wary of attack herself but not wanting to lose sight of those she was following.

It was immediately clear that this was no simple brawl or arrest: the two sides had fought with fury. They'd been trying to kill each other. Her enhanced sensors could pick up the beat of someone's heart, the thrum of blood in their veins and the air in their lungs, even the sparkle of electrical connections in their brains, so she could tell immediately that two of the blank-masks were dead, while the third was in a bad way. Their headgear had given them no protection from the bludgeoning of City Guard batons.

Four of the five guards were dead, crushing blows inflicted on their craniums, vital organs punctured by stabbing blades even through their armour. The surviving one sat propped up against a wall, head slumped in unconsciousness. The fight had been vicious. Selene stepped forwards, senses alert.

She knelt in the dust beside the surviving blank-mask. Carefully, she tried to lift the covering from the person's head. It refused to slip away and the person – a young man – twitched. She saw why: the side of his skull had been staved in, and one side of the flimsy mask was embedded in the wound, snagged on jagged shards of bone. The wound bled freely, which at least meant pressure wouldn't be building up against his brain, but he wasn't going to live long without proper medical attention.

She crossed to the City Guard, who had been stabbed two or three times. Her abdomen was a mess of blood and purple tissue, but her heartbeat remained reasonably strong. She might survive. A red light on a comms device upon her belt flashed insistently: by the look of it an alarm had been raised. Reinforcements and perhaps paramedics would arrive soon, if they could push through the crowds.

This prone woman was the enemy: she might not be a Void Walker or an Augur, but she was one of their soldiers. She was also in Selene's power, and killing her would be a small moment of revenge. The first of many.

Instead, Selene found herself pressing on the guard's wound to stanch the flow of blood. There'd been people like this on Maes Far, too: complicit, widely despised. But also, in their own way, victims, hated by those they'd grown up amongst, perhaps simply doing what they had to do in order to survive, to feed their family. Was that how it was on Migdala as well?

The Guard's head at least was unharmed. Selene unbuckled the strap of her helmet and lifted it clear. The woman's black hair was matted to her skull with sweat. Her eyes flickered open and her lips began to move. Her voice was the faintest whisper, but Selene was able to amplify it to audibility. She hoped for some explanation of what had taken place, a clue as to how such a bright day had descended so rapidly into violence and death, but the woman simply whispered the same word over and over. The name of a lover or a child, perhaps. Selene's flecks could make no sense of the word.

"Aibo, Aibo."

More shouts echoed down the side-passage. Reinforcements from one side or the other, most likely more City Guards answering the electronic summons. An observation platform hovered around somewhere overhead, the electric whine of it echoing off the hard walls, but it hadn't yet come into view as it homed in on its target. She had to go. Whoever was coming would look after the injured officer. Hopefully they'd attend to the fallen blank-mask, too.

She raced away from the scene, down the passageway the others had taken, slipping her own demon visage back into place. Strange how it gave her a sense of anonymity, the illusion of safety. If they caught her, it wouldn't help much. Her right hand was slick with the blood of the Guard. She needed to find water so she could wash it off before making her next move.

Then a hand seized her shoulder from the shadows, pulling her off-balance. She staggered backwards through a doorway, while her threat assessment routines kicked in, and she prepared herself to fight.

6. The Unmoving Stars

A blank-mask leaned over her, a woman judging by her slender neck and the swell of her breasts. Two others stood behind her, their faces also hidden, tension visible in their stance. A gash of blood ran diagonally across the woman's forearm, trickling over a tattooed representation of a winged heart adorning the inside of her wrist. The gallop of their real hearts was loud to Selene, the labouring of their lungs elevated.

The newcomer lifted her finger to her concealed lips in a gesture that meant the same on any planet where people spoke through their mouths. Selene remained crouched in shadowy darkness while a squadron of City Guard troopers racketed past in the passageway outside.

When they were gone, the woman waited a few minutes more, then visibly relaxed, the tension in her posture easing.

She spoke in a whisper. "Who are you? What are you doing here?"

Selene gave her the backstory she'd worked out for herself. She tried to sound alarmed, terrified. "I'm from A'cha. Come for the carnival."

"People from A'cha carry blasters like that around, do they?"

"I was given it by a friend. They said Senefore could be dangerous."

"Why are you lurking around in the backstreets?"

Selene rose to her feet, brushing dust from her arms, glancing around warily. "I got lost. I thought this passage might give me a way through the crowds to the central square."

Another of the group said, "A'cha? I've been there. Where, exactly?"

"Fioren." A medium-sized city, small enough that it was unlikely anyone would have gone there, large enough for her to be anonymous if anyone had.

The woman appeared to believe the story. "You should stick to the main streets. It's safer there."

"Why were you fighting?" said Selene. "What's going on here?"

The woman didn't reply for a moment. When she did, her suspicion had returned. "You don't have the troubles in Fioren?"

Selene scanned a brief summary of recent events in her pretend home before replying. "Of course, who doesn't? It's not usually so violent, though." She adopted the tone of a bored and frustrated parochial. "*Nothing* ever happens in Fioren."

"Things are different in Senefore, especially at this time of year. If the revolt is going to kick off, it will be here."

"The revolt?"

A third blank-mask, a man, stepped forwards. He was tall and powerful, the muscles on his arms sculpted. "You're asking a lot of questions. Are you working for them? Do we need to do to you what we did to those guards? Because no one is going to come to your help if we do."

She hid her amusement at his threats; they posed no danger to her. Not only was she stronger, she'd also downloaded a battery of armed and unarmed combat routines that her biomechanics could execute if need be.

She hoped it wouldn't come to a fight, however; better to remain the wide-eyed, naïve traveller from distant A'cha. "I'm not working for anyone. I've come for the carnival; I just don't understand what's going on."

The woman said, "You saw Godel's broadcast? All the Templers on the streets? Things are kicking off, there's going to be trouble. The revolt is coming. If you are here to see the sights, then my advice is to stay in the well-lit areas and leave before dark."

"Those masks you wear. I haven't seen anything like them back home."

The woman shrugged. "Someone's idea of a way to identify ourselves to each other. A symbol. It's becoming a uniform if you ask me, time we dropped it. Sometime, soon, we'll fight them in the open."

That troubled Selene; the rebels were hopelessly misguided if they thought they had a chance in open combat. "You can't fight them. You have sticks and – what? – a few antique blasters and maybe some explosives? I've seen what they're capable of. What you have won't be anywhere near enough, not now there are three Cathedral ships in orbit. If they want, they can kill every one of us."

"Seen it where?" asked the muscled man, his masked face implacable but the suspicion clear in his voice.

"The broadcasts," she said. "We've all seen it."

"There are a lot more of us than there are of them," said the man.

His ridiculous bravado was going to get him killed. "If you fight them on the streets, you'll die, don't you see? It isn't about numbers, it's about weaponry and technology. And you don't have nearly enough of either."

"You seem to know a lot about what Concordance plans to do," he said.

"It's obvious what they plan to do. They'll allow you to dance around wearing masks and have a few noisy parades, but open revolt is something else. They won't allow it. You know that's true."

The woman pulled Selene away from the others, holding up a hand to her two comrades to tell them to leave it. She spoke in hushed tones. "Whoever you are, it's best you go. You may be right about the dangers of rebelling, but that's what we're going to do. At least we'll have tried."

Selene replied in a similar whisper so the others wouldn't overhear. "I get it, trust me, I do. But getting yourselves killed isn't going to help anyone. There are other ways to fight."

Through the eye-holes of her mask, the woman appeared to be studying Selene intently. "What ways? Who are you really? I didn't say anything to the others, but that accent of yours isn't right. I spent five years at university in A'cha. It sounds as though you've *learned* how to speak like a native and you didn't finish the course."

Which was true. Her brain knew the accent and the idiom perfectly, but it took time for muscles to adapt to the subtleties of pronunciations. Time she hadn't had.

Selene decided to take a risk. "Look, you're right. I'm not from A'cha, and it's best you don't know where I am from. But I'm on your side, truly. I have very good reason to hate Concordance."

The woman nodded. "You fight them in whatever way you can, but this is all we can do. We have no other choices left to us."

"If there's trouble, innocent people will die. You've seen how busy the city is. What right do you have to do that?"

"No right," said the woman, "but what's the alternative? Let them win, let them kill us slowly, let them enslave our children as they've enslaved us?"

More than anything, Selene wanted to explain who she was, what she was doing on the planet. Of course, she couldn't. As well as everything else, she didn't want others – people on Migdala and elsewhere – to see her and Ondo as beacons of hope, when the truth was they might be killed at any moment.

"I should go," said Selene. "The guards have gone."

The woman nodded. She placed a hand on Selene's arm. "Whoever you are, wherever you're really from, look after yourself."

"I will," said Selene. "You do the same. And, thank you."

Selene peeped out of the doorway, then stepped into the passageway. The hunt had moved away, following a false trail or distracted by other flashpoints. She wondered how many were going to die in Senefore before the carnival season was over. She concealed her blaster and set off.

She spent the next two hours losing herself in the crowd, savouring the atmosphere of celebration and expectation that consumed the gathered people. More and more spiced intoxicants were consumed from dazzling arrays of liquor bottles with their enticing colours: vermillion and turquoise and blood-red. Each food stall she pushed past engulfed her briefly in a fresh miasma of enticing scents: the smell of fresh bread that instantly transported her to her own world, fifty thousand light-years away; meats and fishes cooked in a seemingly endless variety of spices; heady clouds of steamy smoke that promised a variety of colourful intoxications and miraculous visions.

The carnival itself finally wound into view, heralded by bone-rattling drum beats and blasts from blaring brass horns. Dancers and marchers moved through the crowd in a slow procession, each mask and costume more outlandish than the last. One person had been transmogrified into a gaudily-plumed bird, another a shining being of mirror-metal. Quite a few costumes glittered and sparkled with their own strings of lights, and one person processed in an outfit that burned with licking orange flames. The others kept well away from her. The mood was of delight and celebration, of wonder at each new outlandish mask and costume.

But always, glimpsed through brief gaps in the jubilant crowds, she saw the stony faces of the watching City Guard officers. Overhead, always, the observation platforms drifted in slow circles, ignored by the crowds.

Selene's threat-monitoring systems remained constantly at peak concentration, and it was they that spotted a subtle sign of action passing through the crowd. The blank-masks, in twos and threes, were suddenly all drifting in the same direction towards a tall, ornate building whose towers she'd glimpsed repeatedly through the trees. The blank-masks appeared to be following some signal, some pre-ordained plan.

Again, she followed them at a distance, doing her best to look like she was meandering aimlessly through the throng. The front of the carnival procession was jangling its way across a wide square in roughly the same direction. She consulted the local maps she'd pulled into her brain. The building with the spires was the Revelation Temple itself, the home of the religion upon Migdala: alien-looking architecture in this town of low, square buildings. The route of the carnival passed right around it in a loop, an act of clear provocation to a church that so strongly disapproved of the practice of wearing masks and the anarchy and licentiousness that went with it.

Selene hurried, pushing past people to try and reach the temple before the main body of the procession. Whatever the revolt was that the woman had described, it looked like it was going to kick off there.

She arrived in time to see the moment of calm before the violence erupted. A jeering crowd of demonstrators, most of them wearing blank masks, were attempting to force their way past the Templer priests who were defending the stone stairs to the building. A rain of stones and bottles spilling liquid flew through the air to smash on the steps or dash against the walls of the Temple. In the shady light of the tall doorway, Selene could see a priest in scarlet robes assessing the situation. He talked to someone in the shadows behind him, nodding his head, but she couldn't read his lips to pick up his words. The tall walls of the temple loomed overhead, the edifice punctuated by small, arched windows and lines of stone statues staring down from plinths built into the walls.

With a roar, the blank-masks surged forwards, a number of the Templers falling and being trampled underfoot. It looked like the rebels would be able to take the stairs, but then a phalanx of City Guards charged in from one side, wielding their powered-up batons. The screams from the blank-masks rang out clearly as the guards beat them to the ground. Selene witnessed more than one blank-mask twitching in the dirt, control of their muscles lost, blooms of urine soaking through their clothes.

It was going to be a close fight. More guards were rushing in, but the numbers of blank-masks were swelling, too. She was sorely tempted to jump in, take the side of the revellers. Here was Concordance, acting through others to suppress revolt. With her enhanced strength and speed, she might make all the difference.

She forced herself to hold back. Concordance would be watching events very closely, and if they picked her out, they'd come for her. She still wore her demon-mask, but her enhanced physical attributes were clearly going to mark her out from the crowd. Could they trace her movements across the country? From satellite images? Perhaps. She couldn't afford to take the risk. She hung back on the edges of the mob, in the shadows of a doorway that would, hopefully, conceal her from the observation platforms circling overhead.

The fighting grew more intense, clubs and edged weapons wielded by both sides. She saw arms half-severed from shoulders, skulls staved in by bludgeoning blows. A group of the Guards forced their way through the melee to the stairs. The lines of Templer priests parted to let them through. The Guards formed a circle upon the wide space at the top of the steps, immediately in front of the arched doorway. Their actions troubled Selene; she could see no reason for them. They were up to something.

The blank-masks, their numbers swelled by more and more arriving from the surrounding city, had finally predominated. Now there were those among them wearing other masks: people not a part of the organized rebellion who had joined in when they saw what was happening. The few remaining Guards on the ground had retreated, and it was clear to Selene that the lines of priests would soon be breached as the crowd surged over them to reach the temple itself.

A great light blasted out from the top of the stairs, bright enough to blind everyone on the ground. Selene's natural eye couldn't react quickly enough, but her artificial eye filtered 99% of the energy out, protecting its delicate biomechanics. For a moment, she thought some explosion had been detonated, that a blast-wave would sweep through the crowd, throwing them back against the walls.

That wasn't it. On top of the stairs, within the ring of guards, three figures had appeared. Whether they'd come from inside the church or had arrived by some other means from above, she couldn't tell. The blast of light had been detonated to cover their arrival, suppress the mob.

There were three Void Walkers there, their grey robes unmistakable. Two of them she'd never seen before, but the third she had. In the centre, unmistakably, was Kane. The guards moved in formation back down the stairs to reform the defensive line, while Selene stepped forwards, heart hammering. She would kill Kane there and then, jab a blade into his neck as he had done to her father. Or failing that, take him out with a shot from the blaster. Not so personal, but it would do.

A hush had passed through the crowd at the sight — shock, perhaps, at the sight of the Void Walkers on the ground. The people of Migdala knew only too well what that meant. As Selene pressed forwards, she was aware there was something else going on. Masked heads were turning to each other, mutters of confusion passing among the mob. They seemed bemused at the sight of the three Concordance soldiers. Of course, they knew Kane. Kane was from their world.

The Void Walker held up his arms as if in greeting, or as if asking for calm. Selene muscled her way through the crowd, not caring if she was spotted and identified. She'd thought this Void Walker was dead, destroyed by Ondo's nukes at Maes Far, and now she would make sure of it. Images from another planet played through the back of her mind: Ossian, and the slaughter of the children at Kane's command. The parallels in the two situations were obvious. Intent on her revenge, she ignored the thoughts.

Kane turned from side to side, taking in the crowd like a performer on a stage. He looked as if he was going to speak. Instead, he lowered his arms rapidly, a gesture that clearly meant *now*. Immediately, beam-weapon fire lanced out from the arched windows of the temple, wide arcs of high-energy radiation licking backwards and forwards across the crowd. Where the beams struck, people died, their screams cut off as limbs or torsos were vaporized.

Kane's voice boomed out, amplified through the hovering platforms. "Do not flinch, my friends. Step into the light and face the judgement of Omn. Do not fear, the pure of heart among you will be saved. Step into the light, and an eternity of joy awaits you."

The sickening stench of burning flesh suddenly filled the air. Selene hesitated, finally stopped by what was taking place around her. Without thinking about it, she deactivated her olfactory responses. A collective scream rose from the crowd as they swelled backwards, desperate to get away from the stairs, away from the terrible beam-weapon fire. Even she wasn't strong enough to push against them. People were trampling over each other to flee, all thought of revolt gone. Kane did not relent. The beam-weapons continued their work, washing across the throng. He was a painter brushing his canvas in a wash of red. Concordance had allowed the attack on the temple to take place, had let the rebels come, so that they could be more easily identified and slaughtered.

She slid her blaster from its holster on her ankle. One shot, that was all she needed. The surging crowd buffeted her, throwing her around, making targeting difficult. She switched to her left hand and let her biomechanics maintain a rock-solid aim on Kane's chest, slightly to one side where his heart should be.

She fired, hit – but some energy shielding flared around the Walker, dissipating the power of the shot. Kane found her in the crowd, shouted something, pointing her out to the guards and the hovering observation platforms. More than one person next to her screamed and dropped as they were struck, the sudden heat from their burning flesh flaring upon her own skin. The rational part of her brain said she had to run, too. With a cry of fury, she let the panicking crowd sweep her away.

She forced her way into one of the side-roads leading from the square. She thought she'd escaped, but it immediately became apparent this was part of Concordance's plan, too. Let the trouble-makers flee and then funnel them into traps. The fleeing rebels turned a corner to be met with a line of City Guard officers, hand blasters trained on them.

Rather than firing and giving her location away, Selene charged. She was close enough to reach them: in a run she was limited by the speed of her natural musculature, but her enhanced left half allowed her to fling herself forwards to barrel into the Guards before they could fire. She was suddenly on the ground, punching and kicking as the Guards engulfed her, striking her with the butts of their rifles, kicking at her with their metal boots. One placed his boot on her neck to choke off her breathing.

With a roar she forced herself to her feet, throwing her

assailant against a wall. Seeing what she'd done, another Guard levelled his blaster to fire. Her left arm moving more quickly that the Guard could react to, Selene swept the weapon from his hands and punched him hard in the face-mask, sending him reeling backwards to the ground. For a minute or more, Selene was a whirl of kicks and punches as she battled the Guards. She was aware only of the choreography of it; the dance of lunges and ripostes.

Others among the blank-masks joined in, striking blows and kicks of their own. More and more rioters surged down the passageway. Suddenly, only one Guard survived. He stood over a prone female blank-mask holding a length of steel pipe he'd picked up from somewhere, about to slam it down into her chest, skewer her to the ground. Selene moved before the Guard could strike, throwing herself at him, hurling him against a wall. With her left fist she pummelled him into unconsciousness.

For the moment, the fight was over, the Guards lying in broken heaps on the ground. From the lack of heartbeats, she knew several of them were dead.

"We have to get away," she called. "More will come." The blank-mask she'd saved lay at her feet, blood running freely from a gash on her forehead. Selene considered, assessing her options. She had no access to overhead telemetry that might tell her the best escape route to take. Others were already fleeing, limping away before more Guards arrived. The prone blank-mask twisted herself round onto her knees to force herself vertical.

The winged-heart tattoo upon her inner wrist was immediately familiar. Selene helped the woman to her feet, lifted the mask from her face. She was young, her eyes wide from the shock of what she'd seen, the closeness of her death. Bruises marred the smoothness of the skin on her cheek. The cut in her scalp didn't appear to be too deep. It took her a moment to recognize Selene.

Selene said, "So now it's my turn to rescue you. We

need to get off the streets before they slaughter everyone. Do you have a place here? Is there somewhere safe we can go?"

The woman's voice was faint. "I have a place. Across the New Bridge."

Selene tore a scrap of clothing off one of the fallen and gave it to the woman. Hold this on your head to stop the bleeding. Lean on me."

Selene supported her as they worked their way through the crowds, stepping over bodies trampled in the terrible crush. There was nothing she could do for any of them. She consulted the maps in her brain. New Bridge was north. It was also three hundred years old; presumably the name had once made sense. The crush of people fleeing Senefore swept them along so long as they could keep their feet. Fires burned and distant explosions *crumped* in the air; it was impossible to say whether they were fireworks, a part of the celebrations oblivious to what had taken place, or acts of destruction being unleashed upon the crowds. Each flash briefly lit up the faces of those around Selene, their grotesque masks making the procession like something from a primitive culture's vision of an underworld hell.

Selene picked out narrow side-passages that took them in roughly the direction they needed to go, hoping they would be free of City Guard ambush. Security platforms hummed overhead, heading for some new trouble spot, and more than once Selene and the woman had to huddle in a doorway until one of them passed over. Creeping along, wary, Selene listening for trouble ahead to the fullest extent of her perceptions, they edged away from the city centre.

It took them the best part of an hour to cross the bridge and reach the quieter hillside suburb where the woman lived. In the distance, fires burned in the centre of the city, their glow reflected broken in the rippling waters of the lake. The night air was wonderfully cool after the press and heat of the crowd. The woman lived in a low, oblong house, one of many scattered around on the slopes among clumps of towering trees. The heady scent of night blooms filled the air, as did woodsmoke from fires and cooking pits.

The woman's door unlocked automatically as they approached, and Selene let her down into a chair within the shadowy interior. City light filtered in through the shuttered windows. Colourful, twisting glass sculptures were set here and there upon the room's carved wooden furniture. Some flowery, herby scent filtered through the air.

Selene said, "I don't know your name."

The glow from the city lit up the woman's face. The blood on her forehead had dried up. Unexpectedly, she looked amused. "And I don't know yours, not your real name, anyway. You basically just carried me for three kilometres. How did you do that?"

Selene took her mask off and let it drop to the ground. "It's possible you do know my real name."

Unsurprisingly, Concordance hadn't broadcast any video of events on the ice of Maes Far to the wider galaxy, but there had been stories about her and Ondo: the dangerous renegades, the terrorists, threatening to overthrow the galaxy's order. Threatening everything. She'd been depicted as a monster, half-person, half-machine, but she'd be recognizable.

In the half-light of the room, the woman nodded her head as she studied Selene. "Right, so that starts to make sense. It explains the poor accent for one thing. Why are you here? Because of Kane? We heard he was on Maes Far."

"I thought he was dead, but I wanted answers, yes. He killed my father right in front of my eyes. He waited under the polar ice-cap for me to come so he could do it. Waited a year and a half, just the two of them. That's pretty extreme behaviour. So, yeah, I wanted to know how he ended up as he did. I guess, how *everything* ended up as it did."

The woman didn't reply for a moment, then seemed to come to a decision. "Given that I know who you are, I'll tell you my name in return. I'm Myrced Iles. I'm a teacher here, nowhere near as exciting as a galactic renegade with superhuman biomechanical enhancements. I'm grateful to you for getting me out of there."

"I told you that you didn't have a chance against them."

"Yeah, I know."

"What's going on upon this planet? If you know who I am, then you know what they did to my world. Why are they letting you openly oppose them?"

Myrced climbed painfully to her feet and limped to her small kitchen. She poured two long drinks, the juice of some purple fruit mixed with a dash of a clear alcoholic spirit. She added tinkling cubes of ice and handed one of the glasses to Selene.

She sipped her own drink, and looked thoughtful for a moment. "I don't know how to answer that properly, because it's hard to understand what's going on elsewhere. We saw the Maes Far shroud being deployed, and we know what it did to your world, but we only get to hear what they want us to hear. It's hard to know what's *normal*. Were there anything like the Temples on Maes Far?"

"Nothing. We had a few minor religions here and there, but they were irrelevant to most people."

"Perhaps that explains it. Our understanding is that on worlds like ours, they control the planet by making use of an existing power structure. Elsewhere, it might be a world government, or a Guild structure, but here it's a religion. The Revelation Temples have been important on all continents for a long, long time, thousands of years. They're central to many people's lives, a source of wisdom and comfort and meaning. By infiltrating the Temples, adapting their moral codes, we've been invaded without the need for a fight."

Selene sipped at her drink, feeling its coolness trickling down inside her. "I don't get why they bother. They can simply threaten to destroy a population that doesn't succumb to their rule."

"Godel has made veiled threats along those lines in the past, promises to cleanse the planet of its evils. Of course, that just makes us more determined to fight back. In the end, I suppose it isn't going to go well."

Selene said, "I'm going to kill Godel. And Kane. And all of them."

Myrced drained her drink and set it down on a table. A curious smile played across her lips. "I believe you. You don't need to do that now, though, do you?"

She stepped closer, her gaze frank. The fires from beyond the lake lit up her eyes. They'd walked side-by-side for hours, Selene supporting her weight, breathing each other's breath, but the intimacy of their situation in that quiet room was suddenly stark.

It took Selene a few beats to adjust to the shift in the conversation. "You're thinking about this now?"

"All we have is *now*," the woman replied. "We've learned to relish the moment, find our pleasures where we can. You think we have carnivals because it's some ancient tradition? No, we've learned to laugh and dance precisely *because* Omn disapproves. You, on the other hand, look like you have the fate of the galaxy on your shoulders. That's too big a burden. Don't be so hard on yourself."

There was something about their recent escape from danger and horror that opened doors inside Selene. She had the curious sensation of lights being switched on throughout her body. She'd been so concerned with surviving, with recovering her life and physical functioning, that she'd forgotten this side of her, barely given it any thought. Its return was an unexpected joy. She wasn't simply a biological and biomechanical machine that needed fixing, that needed to consume food and expend energy to maintain tissues and bodily systems. She'd gone beyond that. Delight at the possibilities opening out, at the rush of lust flooding through her, sent a tingle across her skin as she returned Myrced's gaze.

She double-checked that her Ondo was dormant, unable to overhear anything she was experiencing or thinking. She said, "I can probably delay destroying Concordance for a few hours." She set down her own drink and stepped into the woman's arms. Here, suddenly, unexpectedly, was a moment of refuge, a simple denial of Concordance and death and horror. Whatever the morning would bring, all that could be forgotten for a time.

Carefully, wary of her bruises, Selene took hold of Myrced's body. Her lips tasted of spice and the purple fruit as they kissed, cool in the night air. But her tongue when it found Selene's was warm.

Myrced led her by her hand to a narrow flight of steps in the corner of the room. The shutters in the bedroom upstairs were open, the cool night air breathing in, rich with the scents of night-time blooms and the strident chirrups of insectoids. The room was dominated by the double bed at its centre.

"Help me get my clothes off," said Myrced. She couldn't raise her arms over her own head, so Selene did it for her. There came the moment when it was time to reciprocate. Selene paused, wary. It wasn't just the thought of showing her naked body to Myrced, it went deeper than that. There had obviously been no one since Maes Far, since her injuries, and the thought of another person seeing her as she now was seemed suddenly unbearable.

Myrced appeared to understand. She pulled Selene around in a half-circle in a move like a dance twirl, then pushed her gently down to sit on the edge of the bed. She began to remove Selene's clothes. Selene let her do it, moving her limbs to allow it to happen. When they were both naked, she stood, and they embraced, body to body, breasts and hips pressed against each other's. The night air across her skin was a delight, although the senses in the rebuilt half of her body were slightly muted by her artificial skin.

Myrced knelt to kiss her breasts. "I saw what happened to you, your injuries. You're fully better?"

"I am, but the skin on this side of me is temporary. A disguise like the masks." Her nipples, a part of her mind noted, were responding in perfect synchrony.

Myrced kissed her more, tiny butterfly touches across her belly. "It's incredible. You wouldn't know."

"The left side of my body is much stronger, but the temporary skin is less sensitive."

Myrced's breath tickled Selene's skin as she spoke. "I'll be sure to keep that in mind."

"On the positive side, my stamina is good."

"Well, we'll see."

Myrced climbed onto the bed and opened her arms, inviting Selene to join her. They explored each other, kissed each other. She'd thought of Myrced's skin as a rich olive brown, but in truth it was a variety of shades, each area she came to subtly different in hue or texture. Night-time birds of prey screeched from the trees and, distantly, the sounds of crackling fires and the lapping lake waters drifted through the night. The roar from the city was distant, muffled. Myrced was between her legs, her tongue flicking in and out of the delicate folds of Selene's body, when she suddenly stopped. She knelt up between Selene's legs to consider her.

"You need to let go, honey."

Her words confused Selene. "Huh?"

"It's like you're there in the moment with me, but also not there. Like part of you is monitoring for threats. I can feel the tension in your muscles, as if you're held together with wires. It isn't going to work if you don't let yourself go."

Was she doing that? Her augmentations were probably doing it automatically, assessing for possible dangers. They did so without her conscious thought. Or maybe it was her natural brain, still wary, her way of viewing the world marked by everything that had happened. There was another presence in her thoughts, too, another ghost. Falden. *She* was still alive, and he wasn't, and there was a heavy weight of guilt about that. With an effort, she set it aside. Falden had wanted her to live, too. The grief of their private parting had been one more open wound within her, but through his tears Falden had told her, just as her mother had told her, *Live your life up there, Selene. I want you to live your life.*

In her mind's eye, he looked at her for a moment, his brown eyes and the floppy hair she'd loved to comb her hand through while they embraced. Then he faded away, backwards into the mists. He would still be there in her mind, always, but now there was space for others as well.

Out loud, to Myrced, she said, "I'll try."

Myrced shook her head, her ready smile returning to her lips. "No, don't try. Do the opposite of that. Just *be*, for a time at least."

With a conscious effort, Selene instructed her environment assessment monitors to go into sleep mode. She wanted this. She would give herself up to these moments, this night. Concordance were out there, the Void Walkers and their agents on this planet, but she would forget them all for a time. She breathed in a lungful of air, then let it escape from her body.

She closed her eyes. "I'm all yours. I'll just *be*."

They made love for an hour or more, occasionally drifting in and out of half-sleep before surfacing to stroke and caress each other once more. She was the happiest she'd been since her reconstruction. The happiest she could ever remember being. It was hard, now, to recall how it felt to be that angry, terrified young woman who didn't want to go on, who was so furious at Ondo for daring to return her to life. The anger was still there, smouldering rather than raging, but it no longer threatened to burn her to ashes. It was hers to control rather than it controlling her.

The chorus of insects had stopped singing when they finally fell into a satisfied slumber, Myrced lifting a light sheet over their entwined bodies to keep away the night's chill.

Something woke Selene. She'd been asleep, offline, for two hours, blind and oblivious. Anything could have happened. There were scuffing sounds from the flat roof above her head. She lay in the darkness for a moment, replaying the noises, trying to work out what they might be. Some nocturnal creature? She turned her head to see if Myrced had heard them, but she wasn't there, her half of the bed filled only by the crumpled sheet.

Selene rose, heart suddenly racing, all her threat-assessment and fight or flight responses activating. Her twin metabolisms, artificial and natural, meshed into gear. Through the window, over the lake, the city was a dark silhouette against the stars.

Her clothes lay in a crumpled heap by the foot of the bed. She found the blaster she'd had strapped to her ankle and activated it. It was still functioning. Had Myrced known it was there? She thought about bringing Ondo online, but decided against it. She slipped her clothes back on, ears turned to full gain for any more sounds from outside.

The upper floor of Myrced's house consisted of a short landing from which the bedroom, a bathroom and another room led off. There was a faint thermal trail on the floor, a line of footsteps, going towards the third room. Myrced had walked there twenty minutes or so earlier. Judging by the layout of the house, this room had to be smaller, a space for storage or for accommodating a guest, perhaps. Selene replayed her memories of the night before. The door to it had been shut.

Selene followed, walking on tiptoe, keeping to the side

of the passageway to reduce the chances of a creaking floorboard giving her position away.

There was no keyhole in the door of the spare room, no way of knowing what was inside. She turned the handle and pushed the door open, hoping the hinges were well-enough oiled to stop any squealing.

She sent out a cone of light from her left eye so she could pick up detail. The room contained a desk rather than a bed, and the walls were lined with book shelves. A single, round window looked out across the lake. In one corner, a wooden ladder, rungs lashed together with twine, led up to a hatch in the roof. Myrced had gone that way. To meet someone? Selene was about to follow, blaster held in her teeth as she climbed, when she caught sight of a framed picture on the wall beside the desk. A posed portrait of a man, his gaze raised as if to stare heroically into unknown distances.

She stepped over to study it. There could be no doubt who it depicted. He was younger, his hair long, but it was Kane.

She considered it for a moment. She could leave through the front door, race away to the safety of the surrounding forests, pick up a train for the coast and instruct the lander to surface and pick her up. Something stopped her. She needed to make sense of the picture in front of her.

She turned back to the ladder and, warily, pushed the hatch open. Cold night air breathed down upon her face as she peered through the gap. The stars of the night sky, the blaze of the galaxy's central mass, lit up her eyes. A few yards away, a figure was hunched on the edge of the roof, little more than a crouched shape against the glow of the city and the round of one of Migdala's two moons rising beyond the lake.

Selene climbed to stand upon the roof. Myrced turned to greet her. "I didn't mean to wake you."

"What are you doing up here?"

"I often come up here, to sit and think. I like it in the middle of the night. Everything is so peaceful. You got dressed to come up to the roof. Couldn't keep your survival instincts suppressed for ever, huh?"

"I wasn't sure what I might find. I saw your picture of Kane."

"Ah, I see."

"Why is it there?"

Myrced sighed. "Because, once, he was not the person you now know."

"He's twisted, a fucking animal."

"Now, yes, but once he was different. He was a good man, even a great man. He was also a friend. He was our leader, the resistance I mean. He gave us hope, showed us there was a path other than subservience and oppression. He taught us how the Temples were once benign places of refuge, but that they'd been twisted by Concordance. He taught us also we could fight back."

Selene thought about the moment on the ice. The shining blade, the gleaming red of the blood on the white snow. "What happened to him?"

"What do you think? Concordance took him, changed him, turned him into the monster you've met. Do you think it was a coincidence he was there last night? That was Godel showing us the power she has over us. A man who was once our symbol of hope turned into *that*. There are those who talk about rescuing him, healing whatever it is they've done to him. I believe that's wishful-thinking. The old Kane is gone, and I would also kill the new one if I could. But I like to remember him as he was."

"And Godel?"

"She's not from Migdala, of course. She's a name and a face, nothing more. So far as I know, she has no redeeming features whatsoever, no one who believes she is, or once was, a good person."

"Understanding Kane's history doesn't alter my opinions of him."

"No," whispered Myrced, "I know. Has anything you've seen made sense of what happened to you?"

"I thought seeing the world that produced him might help."

"But it hasn't."

"No. There are good people and bad people and people who are a bit of both here. Same as anywhere, I guess."

Myrced had a blanket bundled around her shoulders, which she opened to Selene to share the warmth. She was naked underneath it. "Come and sit. You won't need that blaster."

"Sorry."

"It's okay. You did well to switch off for so long."

They sat together, legs dangling over the side of the building, breathing the air. Some nocturnal hunter flitted through the night, its echolocation chirps audible to Selene's left ear.

"What were you thinking about?" she asked.

"I was looking up at the stars and thinking how they never change. Whatever happens down here, whoever dies, whatever horrors take place, the stars simply continue shining, indifferent to it all. I was feeling small, unimportant, powerless. And then I thought of you and I thought I'd ask you to stay, join with us, fight Concordance on the ground. Look at it all, the galaxy is too large to be saved. I think we need you. I think maybe *I* need you."

Selene lay her head on Myrced's shoulder. Should she stay? Could she? There were worse worlds, worse places to be. She and Ondo could alter her appearance permanently, and she could make Migdala her home. There was a fight to be fought here.

Instead she said, "They do move. The stars I mean. We just don't see it because the galaxy turns so slowly. And the stars are not the only things up there."

A trio of lights, a little triangle, moved rapidly down the

night sky, sinking into the west. The three orbiting Cathedral ships. She thought about the Refuge, and the Depository with its impossible blue star, and the mysteries of Omn somewhere out there in the heart of the galaxy.

"Concordance," said Myrced.

"I can't stay, as much as I'd like to," said Selene. "There are bigger battles to fight out there, among the stars. But you could come with me. We could leave together, leave now."

"Come and live on Ondo Lagan's mysterious Refuge?"

"You know about that?"

"The name only. The rumour of it. Is it a ship? The Refuge is something of a myth, like a fabulous place in the sky where all dangers and evils are banished."

That amused her. "Well, it's no paradise, but there'd be room for the two of us. Will you come?"

Myrced didn't reply for a moment.

"Myrced?"

The answer took some effort. "I can't, Selene, tempting as it is. I have friends here, a life. I've made promises. I need to stay and finish what I've started."

"You'll get yourself killed, most likely."

"I know that, but that's true out there as well, isn't it? There's no peaceful, quiet life anywhere unless you accept the control of Concordance. In other days, I would jump at the chance to come with you, but I don't think I can right now. I'm sorry."

"I get it."

Myrced smiled. "Perhaps one day."

"Perhaps." They both knew the chances of that were small. These were the things you said to each other to make farewells easier.

"You're leaving now?"

"Maybe not immediately," said Selene. "Concordance will be distracted for a few more days as the celebrations build to a climax. I can lie low here for a while. That is, if you'll have me."

Myrced sounded amused. "Oh, I'll have you. Come on, it's getting cold. Let's go back to bed."

They saw no one else for the best part of three days, save when Myrced slipped out for supplies of food and drink. They ate and they made love and they drank and they slept. It was a welcome hiatus, a shutting out of the world and the galaxy, and everything beyond themselves.

They also read: Myrced had a collection of forbidden books on the shelves of her little room, paper volumes she'd collected over the years to keep them from Concordance's fires.

"Why do they ban them?" Selene asked one sunlit afternoon, dappled shade filtering through the shutters. "Most of them are fiction, just stories of other worlds and adventures in space."

"Because of that, precisely. They're heretical, they give people dreams of other possibilities. And some are factual, too." She also had a collection of dusty, dog-eared historical tomes, all very old. One, in particular, was her prized possession: a history of Migdala that documented how life had been before the arrival of Concordance and the twisting of the Revelation Temples into their current form. *An Age of Angels: a Brief History of Migdala*, it was called. Despite its title, it was a weighty brick of a book, over a thousand pages long. Selene loved to flick through it, thinking about all the other people who had done the same over the centuries. It described at length the cultural and economic links Migdala had once shared with other star-faring cultures. Myrced had explained it was a story that had been buried, that she wasn't allowed to teach the children in school. They just got to hear about *military threats* from other worlds, threats that Concordance protected Migdala from. It was clear why Concordance would want such books destroyed.

Each evening, the celebrations continued in the city centre across the lake, and from the screams and detonations it was clear that there were also more flashpoints between the rebels and the forces of Concordance. Selene and Myrced stayed away, nursing their wounds. It was a moment of respite, of simple pleasures and joys stolen from the horror. At times, it seemed like she'd been living in the little square house with Myrced all her life, and would do so for the rest of it – but she also knew it would have to come to an end. On the third evening after their escape, Selene told Myrced it was time to leave.

"Will it be dangerous?" Myrced asked. They sat on her roof again, the sun setting in a blaze of honey light across the water.

"A little. Once I reach my ship, I'll be safer. They can't follow me through metaspace."

"And is it really as Kane used to tell us before they took him? That transluminal travel is completely safe, that it used to be normal?"

"Yes. I've done it many times."

"You can go anywhere?"

"Anywhere in this galaxy, so long as I avoid Concordance. The offer still stands. You can come with me."

"I'm tempted, truly, but no. Oh, I bought you a parting gift." She held out *An Age of Angels*. "I thought Ondo Lagan might like it."

"I can't take that."

"I think you should. It isn't really safe here, and Ondo might be able to find something useful in it, some clue about the fall of the galaxy. And I would like you to have it."

Selene took it from her. "I have little to give you in return."

Myrced kissed her one more time. "You've given me plenty."

Selene thought for a moment, then unclipped a nanosensor held within a glass ampoule from the magazine she carried on her belt. "There's this. I brought some with me to plant in hard-to-reach places."

Myrced held the tiny glass tube between thumb and finger and held it up to the light. "I can talk to you through this?"

"Not really, our communications network is far too slow and unreliable for that. Messages can literally take weeks if they get through at all. But if you wish me to hear something, speak into this, and the message will be relayed through our atmospheric and orbital sensors and eventually reach me. Probably. Assuming I'm still there."

"Will it endanger you if I get in touch?"

"No."

Myrced took the ampoule and placed it in her ornately-decorated jewellery box.

"Travel safely, Selene Ada."

"I will. Stay safe, Myrced Iles."

Selene didn't look back as she slipped out of the back of the little house. It felt like she was shrugging a heavy uniform on as she reactivated her enhanced senses and threat-detection algorithms. She needed to get far away so that no one would associate her with Myrced. She would cut across country, pick up one of the ground transportation lines and be back at the lonely beach where the lander waited for her within six hours. Then it would be a matter of retracing her careful steps away from the planet and dodging Concordance scans before she was far enough away from the stellar mass to escape into the void. There was a possibility Concordance would now be looking for her after events at the Temple, but there'd been no house-to-house searches in the days since their escape. It appeared the chaos surrounding the carnival had covered her tracks.

She reached the *Dragon* without incident or pursuit. She fled the system at maximum acceleration before any ship could scramble to intercept. As she powered away from Migdala, Selene sat looking back at the planet via a nanosensor relay. The sun was setting on the wide blue ocean, the land mass upon which Senefore lay little more than a smudge of green and red.

On the ship, it was very, very quiet.

7. The Remains of Shattered Starships

"You were longer than I thought," said Ondo. "Did something happen on Migdala?"

They were back in the medsuite, Ondo delicately picking at her artificial skin, peeling it from her substrate in long strips. The sensation was not unpleasant – once she'd switched off her pain responses across the affected areas of her body. He'd applied three separate acidic chemicals, their molecular composition very specific and none of them likely to be encountered naturally, in order to break down her bioplastic flesh. Then he used a needle-like high-pressure jet of water to wash away any residue. He worked with the utmost care, but it still felt like being stippled with a thousand pinpricks as he touched the edges of her natural skin.

"Lots of things happened on Migdala."

He stopped work for a moment and considered her. His voice was slightly muffled through the white mask he wore over his mouth and nose. "Things you want to tell me about?"

"Some of them."

"Then I look forward to hearing them. And then I can tell you what I've discovered while you've been away."

"Oh, before you start on my face, there's this." She

reached down to take the book from her backpack on the floor. "A gift. It might be of interest."

Ondo took it, leafed through it. "Where did you get this?"

"That's one of the things I can't tell you. It wasn't stolen, if that's what you mean. No one will miss it."

"It's absolutely wonderful: a detailed account of life before the arrival of Concordance. It's incredibly rare. I'll examine it in depth later. Thank you." He closed the book and studied her again. "And you … you took much greater care over the approach protocols. Something has changed, I think."

"I didn't want to get myself killed. Or you, for that matter."

"And, I have Myrced to thank for this?" he said. His words sent a jolt of alarm through her. She hadn't mentioned the name to him. Was he able to intrude upon her thoughts after all?

He responded to her anxiety with an amused shake of his head. "The name is handwritten in the front of the book. *For Selene, who moves the stars. Myrced.*"

Right. Damn. She hadn't thought to look. She gave him a verbal summary of everything that had occurred. She did not give him access to his alter ego inside her mind, not wanting him to have any access to her memories of Myrced, even public ones. He worked on her back as she spoke, dabbing the chemicals onto her and then peeling off more strips of flesh.

When she was done, he said, "Are you absolutely sure it was Kane?"

"Absolutely. Concordance must have pulled him out of the nuke blast before he was vaporised."

"It certainly seems to confirm that he's one of Godel's coterie."

"People I spoke to; they were adamant he'd been fundamentally altered by Concordance; that he wasn't the brute they claimed. He was a freedom-fighter, widely-loved, charismatic by all accounts, softly-spoken. Did you know about this?"

"No. I assumed they simply recruited people psychologically suited to being Concordance killers. The sociopaths, the amoral."

"They all have that scar behind their ears. That has to be part of it."

"My assumption is that they embed some sort of punishment or coercion fleck into Void Walkers' brains to ensure their absolute loyalty. Maybe it goes further than that. From what you've described, Kane's personality has been fundamentally re-engineered. He's outwardly recognizable to the people of Migdala, but inside he's something else completely."

"They can do that?"

"We have to assume they can. A lifetime of brutalization might have that effect on someone strong enough to survive the ordeal, but Kane was in Concordance's clutches for only a very short time before he emerged as the Void Walker we now know. If he was altered so fundamentally, it took only a few weeks at the most. His capture and anointment ceremony were broadcast to the galaxy, and then he turned up a short time later on Ossian, carrying out the atrocities I've shown you. Concordance's convenient story that the Void Walkers have already lost their souls, that they've forfeited their humanity to become the shock-troops of Omn: perhaps that isn't complete nonsense. Somewhere in that there's a speck of truth."

"Even if he's being mind-controlled, I'm still going to kill him," she said.

Ondo, working behind her back, didn't reply. When he was finished on her shoulder, he came around to consider her. "I need to do your face. You'll have to paralyze all your facial response and vocalization mechanisms."

She switched to brain-to-brain comms. "The sooner I can get this flesh off, the better. Can you fix my arm so I can hyperextend it to reach my back? If I'm going to put on this disguise, it'll be the only way."

"Your skeleton is locked in natural emulation mode, but you can deactivate that with the right thought commands. I'll show you. I wouldn't do it in public, though; it'll look like your arm is attached backwards."

"Handy if I get an itch I can't reach."

"Once your face is done, shall I leave the rest of your skin for you to remove? Your breast and your pelvis and your leg?"

"Then you can tell me what you've discovered while I've been away."

"In truth, it's frustratingly little. You recovered a great deal of data, but the problem with it, still, is understanding the context. Are they random snatches of deleted information, for example? I can still identify no organising principle. It's possible the storage device is degraded, and we're seeing only fragments."

"You got nothing at all?"

"I'm still correlating what you found with everything I already know. There are a couple of items that leap out, however."

He sent her a brief sequence of images, a series of frames depicting lines and lines of cathedral ships docked on some vast, tree-like structure. She counted them rapidly. "There are *thousands* of them."

"It's only what we already know, of course. There must be many times this number given how many systems they monitor. Still, to see them collected together ... it's a troubling sight."

"It's a battle fleet."

"Yes. Consider what that many ships could do acting in concord. No force in galactic history that I'm aware of could hope to stand against them."

"More mysteries," she said. "Can you work out where this is? If it's the Concordance fleet's home, this might be an image of the Omn system."

"I've thrown every image enhancement I can at this scene and got nothing. The local stars are invisible, their light washed out by the incipient glow from a nearby star. Or, actually, more than one star judging by the spectrum of wavelengths. I'd say it's a system with two or even three."

"Can you tell how old these pictures are?"

"Not even that."

"I hope the other thing you found is more useful."

"I think it is. I decrypted some data from the flecks we picked up from the ice on Maes Far. It turns out that ship was previously involved in a significant battle on the outer edges of another system. I got some clear pictures of a number of Magellanic Alliance ships being destroyed, which gives us a narrow date range. From what I can tell, two Concordance ships were ambushed by a fleet of at least thirteen craft. Certainly, twelve were obliterated, and we know that at least one – the one from Maes Far – escaped. I also got a clear view of the background stars, which has allowed me to pinpoint the new system. It's one I've never visited, as it was low-tech at the moment of Concordance's ascension to domination and hasn't achieved FTL flight in the intervening period."

"So, we go there and look for hulks?"

"There's a chance we'll find the remains of a ship that had been in contact with the *Magellanic Cloud*, or had received data on the whereabouts of the Omn system. We might encounter opposition too, of course, but that seems less likely: Concordance also don't bother to devote an orbital presence to pre-FTL worlds, or much in the way of orbital monitoring. Often, it's nothing more than a few Void Walkers on the ground, undercover, keeping an eye on things."

"And if we can work out where the Omn world is, we attack it."

"We'd need to observe, gather telemetry. Understand what, exactly, we're up against; I assume their godhead system is extremely well-protected. I doubt very much that we could drop in and unleash a few nukes to finish them off."

"They may be unprepared, thinking they're safe because no one knows where they are."

"I'm not sure that's a risk I'd run."

"The measures we take when we return to the Refuge. The approach protocols. You must have tried something similar on them. You must have attached nanosensors and bugs to their ships in the hope of tracking them through metaspace."

"Many, many times. I've flooded every monitored system with probes, attempted to embed them into the structure of Cathedral ships and Void Walker vessels, but I've never heard a single response from any that jumped out-system. They clearly have protocols of their own, or else they use some bug-sweeping technology that defeats mine."

"Either we chase this new lead, or we go back into Dead Space and attempt to find out more from the Depository, take some of those artefacts, study the reader device. We could interrogate the broken Warden entity and persuade it forcibly to give up its secrets."

"I think the battlefield is our better option. There has to be a high risk of jumping into an ambush if we return quickly to the Depository system. We don't know that Concordance didn't spot you."

"And the longer we delay, the more time we give Concordance to unleash another Maes Far." It was an argument they'd had more than once. The problem was that they were both right in their own ways.

"We may only get once chance to fight them; we have to be sure we get it right," said Ondo. "There's also the effect that the journey through Dead Space had on the *Radiant Dragon*. I monitored its profiles as you returned from Migdala; it does not appear to have recovered from the damage – I might even say *trauma* – of making the journey as fully as I thought it would. Did it report any system stress to you during the journey?"

"It remained as irritatingly implacable as ever."

"I don't want to repeat the manoeuvre through Dead Space until we've properly understood the effect the last one had on the *Dragon*. My readings suggest that the impairment of its systems is something akin to psychological harm."

"I carried out a full diagnostic as we waited to approach. It's fully functional."

"Did you observe anything out of the ordinary in its behaviour at all?"

She considered. "A couple of moments when it stuttered, didn't respond instantly. Like, a shudder running through it. Then it carried on without trouble."

Ondo considered. "I agree that the *Dragon* is operational for any normal run, but I don't want to expose it to Dead Space again so quickly."

"Have you worked anything out about that blue star?"

"Nothing beyond the plain fact that it shouldn't exist. It was a red dwarf that has exhausted more of its hydrogen than is possible given the age of the universe. I have no idea how that happened."

"Maybe your astrophysical model is wrong."

"That's always a possibility, but this is the only such anomaly I've ever found."

"Don't you want to go there and study it in detail?"

"Naturally, but I'm not convinced that will help right now. Despite what you may think, I am desperate to reach the end of the road and find some answers."

"The thing I can't understand is why Concordance lets Migdala have its carnivals, why it allows open dissent in the streets. They obviously have the power to put a permanent stop to that."

Ondo frowned as he concentrated on peeling a triangle of flesh from her left cheekbone. "The more answers we find, the more questions we uncover. We know they sometimes look for ways to maintain their grip without resorting to widespread slaughter, although that's hardly Godel's style. Even the shrouds: they're terrible weapons, of course, but wouldn't some overwhelming detonation be quicker and easier? Why don't Concordance deploy more shrouds if they want to send everyone flying through the sacred wormhole?"

"They want to draw events out, show the galaxy the slow horror."

"I suppose that's all it is," conceded Ondo.

"You think there's more to it."

"I think we're witnessing factional infighting within Concordance. My suspicion is that Godel was despatched to Migdala as a warning to her, as much as anything. Primo Carious is no fool. Godel would no doubt have loved to have built a shroud or obliterated a continent or two, and I suspect Carious is exerting his control over her by stopping her from doing so. He's humiliating her."

"She's not going to like that."

"Which probably explains her overreaction at Senefore, when you were nearly killed. She will claim that she had no alternative when it came to restoring order."

"If I were her, being whipped into line would only make me more determined."

Her statement appeared to amuse Ondo, but he said nothing.

"Do you think she's a threat to Carious?" Selene asked.

"We simply don't know how a new leader emerges from among the First Augurs. We don't even know how many First Augurs there are, or how people become one. Publicly, they claim divine Omn appoints the person who is to be the new Primo, Omn's new interlocuter with mortal beings. I suspect that what actually happens is more mundane than that, possibly a lot bloodier than that. My guess is that Godel would go to any length to seize control of the galaxy, just as Carious did before her. But perhaps there are divisions there we can exploit."

He stepped back to consider her features, relaying images from his eyes into her brain for her to see. Her face was back to normal. She reactivated her facial motor controls, flexed her jaw a few times to get everything working, then spoke out loud. "Tomorrow, I'll take the *Dragon* to this new system and see what I can find. Are you going to drop your researches for a while and come?"

She knew what his answer would be without him needing to reply.

She translated into the system half a billion kilometres from its sun. She caught no metaspace signatures other than her own, no indication of recent Concordance activity. She set about seeding the system with monitoring devices. Spotting the remains of shattered starships, especially after such a long period of time, was extremely difficult over a wide area. At most, there'd be only the faintest of energy traces from surviving hulks; her best hope lay in spotting unexpected patterns of background star occultation. The more viewpoints she had to correlate, the better. She jumped around the periphery of the system, dispersing nanosensors at each point.

When that was done, she sat and waited while the *Dragon* analysed the telemetry streams, picking through the faint whispers and flickers of electromagnetic radiation for some unexpected signal.

Bored after two days of finding nothing, she jumped as deep in-system as she dared to go, then powered towards the system's single inhabited planet on reaction drive. The world was advanced enough to put communications satellites into orbit and fire a few probes towards the edges of the system, but there were no orbiting ships of any significance and nothing in the electromagnetic noise that spilled off the planet to suggest the inhabitants knew anything about wider galactic affairs. This was a nascent civilisation, teetering on the brink of discovering the technology needed for metaspace travel, teetering also on the edge of environmental collapse and military conflagration. Perhaps, if Ondo's golden age really had existed, a world such as this would have been guided towards the stars, gently shown how to take the final leap. That wasn't going to happen now.

She wasn't sure if she felt sorry for the population on the planet or if she envied them. They were locked in endless petty concerns, fighting small battles of no great significance, oblivious. But they also had no knowledge of Concordance, didn't know what awaited them if they did work out the technology required to traverse metaspace. They were tantalisingly close to making the breakthroughs: a few insights, some new ways of thinking from theoretical physicists and mathematicians, and they'd be there.

It would be a moment of triumph – and disaster. They wouldn't even need to build a viable ship; the acquisition of the necessary knowledge would be enough for Concordance. The Augurs would intervene immediately, and the planet's first experience of contact with other intelligence would be one of oppression and subjugation. They, too, would become used to the sight of a Cathedral ship in orbit, and of messages and instructions and threats handed down from the sky.

For now, they were ignorant, like children unaware of the burdens and agonies of adulthood. Except, as was clear from their broadcasts, they were not children. There was beauty and miraculous achievement there, but there was also atrocity and agony and horror. They were people like her people had been: surprising, inspiring, terrifying, sometimes all at once.

This close, she also detected one anomaly: a halo of nanosensors in orbit around the planet. They were dark, receiving rather than transmitting, and were almost certainly undetectable to the planet's technology. They weren't Ondo's; they had to be Concordance devices, presumably for monitoring the messages of the embedded Void Walkers on the ground. From their inactivity, it appeared they had no clue she was there. Nor would the planet: the *Dragon*'s technology was easily capable of concealing it from any watchers on the surface.

She couldn't resist doing what she did next. She was drifting in space twenty light-seconds from the planet. Its night side was turned towards her, a spattering of artificial lights visible on high magnification. There was a high probability no one would notice: the planet had some telescopes monitoring distant stars and deep space, but they were purely scientific instruments. The people on the planet did not routinely monitor local space. Why would they?

Ondo didn't have to know anything about it. First, she needed to check with the *Dragon*.

"How much of what I do does Ondo get to hear about?"

"As much or as little as you wish. You are in command."

"What I'm about to do, it's best he doesn't hear of it."

"I understand. What are your orders?"

It was a small thing. She'd been thinking about all the people down there, billions and billions of them, living out their little lives. "I want to send a signal to the planet. Nothing overt, nothing that gives anything away. But a clue. A series of flashes in the visible spectrum that follows a sequence any civilisation will recognize. Let's use numbers where each is the sum of the previous two, up to, say, thirteen. Then we'll repeat the whole thing once."

She thought the *Dragon* would refuse, but instead it said, "How bright?"

"Enough to be visible to the naked eye should anyone happening to be looking at our precise point in the sky but dim enough to not attract wider attention."

"Can I ask the purpose?"

"An acknowledgement. A connection. I don't know. Planets like this have lost so much too, in their own way."

When it was done, they resumed their stuttering dance

around the periphery of the system to pick up nanosensor telemetry.

It took her a week to detect the anomaly, and, in the end, she nearly missed it. It was the briefest dimming of light of the background stars, but it was no simple off/on. It was a complex pattern, as if some intervening object were tumbling through space. It was probably nothing: a ghostly object haunting the Oort cloud, the extended region of lumpy rock and ice on the outer edges of the system. Most likely, she'd witnessed the chance event of multiple objects eclipsing a star. Still, with nothing else to try, and bored with monitoring the broadcast output of the closed-off world, she went to investigate.

It rapidly became clear as she homed in on the coordinates she'd calculated that it was no mere lump of primordial rock. The shattered skeleton of a starship tumbled through the void, two-thirds of its structure sheared away, only the nose section and part of the lateral fuselage surviving. Some devastating force had burst it open, spilling its crew into the vacuum. It was certainly no Concordance ship; there was no weirdly twisting form to the ship, just the clean lines of an Alliance vessel. It was a Magellanic craft: a ship from the losing side of the Omnian War. There were multiple smaller fragments, too, scattered over a sphere perhaps one light-minute across. The conclusion was clear: this had, indeed, been the site of a battle. Why here? On the outer edges of this low-tech system? Impossible to know for sure: perhaps an ambush had been set by the Alliance side as Concordance came to investigate the system, completing their census of inhabited worlds.

She approached warily, keeping the *Dragon*'s sensors on full-spectrum scan, streaming the telemetry into her own brain. Inevitably, there was a chance this was another lure left by Concordance. At least there were no significant masses nearby to block an emergency jump into metaspace: the local sun was a distant spark of light.

Ondo's preferred protocol was to watch and listen for a day when approaching an unknown object. In the end, she lasted an hour before instructing the *Dragon* to move in under reaction drive.

The hulk seemed to grow as she neared it, swelling to dwarf the *Radiant Dragon*. A cargo vessel? A warship? Perhaps it had been both: some interstellar craft repurposed when Concordance commenced their attacks upon galactic culture. From the lines of its nose, she thought she'd seen something similar in the brief video Ondo had shown her: the whale-like ship breaking orbit from the planet he claimed was Coronade. Had it been this vessel, jumping off to meets its end in a battle on the edges of this backwater system? She would never know.

She scanned the wreck and picked up nothing: the ship was dark, no energy patterns running through it. Its drive sections were gone; it would have had no power for three hundred years. It was dead metal and carbon, little different to the tenuous cloud of rocks and snowballs it drifted among. There were a few decks and bulkheads left, gaping open like mouths of jagged teeth, so it was conceivable some localized system might retain a memory chip or fleck she could salvage.

She nuzzled the *Dragon* as close to the hulk as she dared, then shrugged on her EVA suit to investigate in person. One of the suit's monitor circuits refused to synch with her flecks the first time, suggesting a malfunction, but the second time it locked on. She would know if any enemy ships appeared.

Her left eye and her suit had lights, but it could be awkward to keep them pointing in the right direction while she worked. "Shine a light onto the wreck," she said to the ship. "Manoeuvre around it so I'm not working in the dark."

"Understood."

"Same orders as usual: if you're attacked and there's no time for me to get back, run for metaspace. I'll stay hidden for you to pick me up later."

"You have oxygen for four hours, perhaps double that if you drop into artificial torpor. I might not be able to return in that time if Concordance come."

"Just do what you have to do. You know the score: it's better that you get back to Ondo with something than us both getting killed."

"Understood."

She paused at the outer airlock door, scanning local space once again for possible threats. All she got from the void was white noise. She pushed herself off towards the hulk, an observation port in its hull like a single round eye, watching her warily as she neared. Her control of the suit's thrusters was good, now: she could manoeuvre where she needed to go without thinking about it. She passed across the smooth voidhull of the ship and pulled herself through a ragged rip to reach what had once been the ship's interior. She began to study the bulkheads using her suit's faint directional light. After thirty seconds, the *Dragon* manoeuvred around to bathe her in its illumination, and she saw what had been hovering near her in the darkness while she worked.

The head of a dead crew-member lolled above her, little more than a mass of ice-crystals, its mouth open wide in a scream that would last until the end of the universe. This far from any heat, a body exposed to the void might well not decay, sterilized of its microbes by the vacuum and extreme temperature. She panned around and picked out five of them, hanging by their seat harnesses like weird fruit from some alien tree. They'd been operating the craft, controlling its systems, when it was blasted into fragments. Most likely it would have been a quick end, although they must also have known, as the Concordance ships bore down on them, that they were going to be destroyed. She wondered who they were, what worlds they were from, what sights their eyes had witnessed.

Trying her best to ignore them, she spent the next five

hours pressing probes and sensors into whatever fragmentary remains of ship's mechanism she could find: shattered comms arrays and the entrails of nav control systems. It was all dead. She'd hoped there might be some residual ghost image of a control message frozen within the ducts of the fuselage, but there was nothing.

More than once, she had to close her eyes to let the nausea that flooded through her subside. It wasn't just the corpses, although they weren't helping: it was also the disorientation of moving through three-dimensional space. Born and raised on a planet, she was still learning to handle not having gravity to hold her in place. She was still fundamentally a two-dimensional being. Her current location didn't help much, either. She turned to consider the gulfs of space opening out in front of her. The *Dragon* was temporarily distant, arching around to give her light. For a few seconds, it was only her and the endless void, the staring stars impossibly distant.

Ondo had warned her about the psychological effects of prolonged time spent within the vacuum, the sense of panic or despair that could overwhelm you. *Void psychosis*, he'd called it. She'd shrugged off his warnings, assuring him she'd be fine, but now she at least understood what he meant. To be faced with those endless gulfs of nothingness: it would take its toll after a while.

She clung to the scrap of fuselage with her left gauntlet, its solidity reassuring. She longed in that moment for Myrced, for her touch, the anchoring strength of her embrace. Had she, Selene, been right to leave Migdala? In truth, she still wasn't sure. It probably wasn't healthy to let her burning need for revenge consume her life – but she couldn't deny that need was there within her. She doubted that there would ever be an *afterwards*, a happy ending, but the possibility of one, at least, was appealing. And that was surely a sign that she wasn't completely consumed by her decision to rid the galaxy of Concordance.

Shaking her head in her suit as if to shake these

thoughts free, she resumed her search of the ruin, although she was rapidly coming to the conclusion that there was nothing much of interest to be found. It was one more blind alley, and they were no nearer finding the Omn homeworld.

She was about to give up, return to the *Dragon*, when the thought occurred to her. She'd scoured the skeleton of the broken starship, picked through its shattered fragments, but there was one place she hadn't looked. Quite possibly, she'd been putting off attempting it in the hope of finding something else. Now, there was no alternative.

In total, there were seventeen bodies within the wreck. Once, there would have been many more, but only those firmly strapped to this section of the ship had remained. The rest were scattered to the void along with the rest of the ship – or immolated by the explosions that had ripped through the vessel. The *Dragon* had been scanning local space constantly while she worked but had identified no other fragments of interest. There was only one thing for it.

She set about probing the craniums of the dead crew members. Advanced brain flecks were rare in the modern world, another technology suppressed by Concordance, but from what Ondo had said they were once common: neural augmentations and data storage devices enhancing natural biology. There had to be a chance some of these frozen and lifeless brains had flecks embedded within them.

She found three: all were inert, but all were clearly artificial devices interfacing with their hosts' cerebella. The problem was how to extract them. Her own flecks were entwined around her biological structures, making them almost impossible to disentangle. Removing these flecks would be a similarly delicate procedure – one that could easily destroy any data held upon them.

She could think of only one approach to take, and her

air supply was running low. Her suit was equipped with the cutting tools she would need. They were there for carrying out maintenance tasks on the ship, but she could turn them to another purpose.

She found herself apologizing to each dead person as she set about slicing their heads from their torsos. At least the fact that they were frozen rigid made the process easier. When she had her harvest of three heads, holding each by the severed ends of their spinal cords, she flew the short hop back to the *Dragon*. Before she entered the airlock, she activated the external stasis compartment and placed the heads inside. They could be dissected under controlled conditions back at the Refuge.

When she was done, her suit removed, she collapsed onto a couch while the *Dragon* began its run-up to metaspace translation.

8. Things Written in the Stars

The sight of the stars from her bedroom window were an unexpected source of wonder for Lilith Jones.

They'd always been there, of course, but the telescope she'd been bought for her thirteenth birthday had opened up new worlds: landscapes and possibilities that had drifted overhead her entire life without her knowing. The moon had been her first fascination, its craters and seas starkly clear as they drifted past her eyepiece, the edges of the moon wavering and burning with the turbulence of the Earth's intervening atmosphere. The dead world looked alive to her: she imagined cities and civilisations up there, people of wisdom far-removed from those she spent her days among on the Earth.

She wasn't supposed to use the telescope during the week, on school nights, but if the sky was clear she couldn't stop herself. Her friends might be secretly conversing on their phones, but for Lilith the worlds revealed by her telescope were more interesting. Why had no one told her until now what was out there? She didn't admit to anyone what it was that was consuming her. Life held many intriguing possibilities, some only dimly perceived, but already, too, she had a sense that it was finite, fundamentally limited to the size of the world. And that, she began to see, was the tiniest fraction of all that there was. There were only so many places she could go before she'd seen it all.

Beyond the moon there were the planets, little more than fuzzy smudges with her telescope, but she saw the crescent of Venus hanging above the sunset like the moon in miniature. She saw the four tiny specks of light around Jupiter that the books said were its largest moons, and she saw the elongated oval of Saturn, all that her small telescope could make of the gas giant and its halo of rings.

The books led her on, farther and farther out. Beyond the planets were the stars, but there was unexpected variety there, too. She pored for hours over the glorious beauty of the pictures of nebulae, her fingers caressing their jewel colours. Through her telescope she could only see one or two of them, blurry patches of grey, but that was enough: they were out there. Clusters too: the sparkling Pleiades, in which she counted many more than seven stars, seemed always to be visible in the corner of her eye. There were binary stars and triple stars, and even stars that were, so the books said, actually whole galaxies, the light of billions of suns combined.

The scale of it took her breath away, and she would scan the heavens until the cold stopped her fingers working and sleep finally pulled her down into dreams of travelling among those endless worlds.

So it was, one frosty night, that she saw a star that happened to be in her eyepiece flashing in puzzling ways. She was used to their random twinkling: the effect, she'd read, of motes of dust in the Earth's atmosphere, light that had travelled unhindered across the universe for countless years being briefly blotted out by the tiniest fragment of dirt a little way above her head. But this was different. A clear flash, like the lights of an aeroplane or a satellite, except not moving. Something stationary up there was sending her a message.

She counted to herself the pauses between the flashes.

At first, they appeared random, the intervals increasing, but then they repeated, following precisely the same pattern. Then they stopped. Intrigued, she scribbled the numbers down before she forgot them. Perhaps she could make sense of them, work out the puzzle being given to her. She watched for ten minutes more, twenty, but saw nothing else unusual.

In the morning, slightly to her surprise, the numbers were still there in her notebook. She hadn't dreamt them. She stared at them for long hours, trying to understand what they might mean.

PART 3 - GALACTIC

1. Artificial Constellations

"Coronade, Ondo? That again?"

Ondo considered her through his multiglasses, their intelligent lenses making his eyes bulge as they reshaped themselves from microscope mode. Refracted light from one of his laboratory's trickling waterfalls sparkled in their glass.

"I told you it wasn't a myth, however much Concordance might claim it was," he said. "It existed and now we know how to get to it."

They'd spent days picking over the fragmentary memories contained within the brain flecks of the dead crew-members of the unknown Alliance ship. Selene had worked until her own brain was exhausted, correlating scraps of data streaming through her augmentations, looking for patterns, picking out potential traces of useful information. The datastores they'd recovered had been badly degraded by three centuries of exposure to the high-energy protons and ionizing radiation of the background cosmic rays. Inevitably, there'd been some damage during the flecks' retrieval, too, careful as they were with the grim surgery. The neural augmentations were designed to be impossible to extract data from, given that their contents were intrinsically intimate.

"Even if we can get data off them, how do we decrypt it?" she'd asked.

"I have some experience with Omnian War-era flecks; it's those designs which I adapted to create the devices we both carry in our heads. Ours are more secure, if I may say so. My impression is that the golden age galactic culture had a strong social taboo about intruding on the artificially-stored memories of others and that their approach to security was rather less paranoid as a result."

She snorted at that. "I don't believe it. You're claiming they were universally benign and considerate? Billions of individuals across countless worlds?"

"Of course not. Their devices had security, strong protection, but they were designed to be easier to open up, extend to others. Openness was their default. This was a culture based on trust and mutuality, and their technology reflected that. We, in our age, have no such luxury. The sudden rise of Concordance must have been an existential shock to them. I believe they'd lived in harmony for hundreds, perhaps thousands, of years."

She couldn't resist asking. "You can hack their brain flecks, but you can't hack mine even though you designed them?"

He was always patient, always ready to reassure her. "Our flecks are locked-down by default. If I could dissect your brain, I could eventually recover the encryption keys your augmentations have generated, it's true, but doing so would trigger self-destruct signals to fry the data stored upon them. Also, my encryption is time-limited: the entire artificial store re-encrypts itself using a freshly-generated key every time you sleep, meaning that even if I could disable the self-destruct, I'd have to work impossibly fast. You've seen the schematics, Selene, you know this is true. It's one reason I entangle the artificial and natural neurons so closely. If Concordance catch either of us, I want to be extremely sure that they can't recover the location of the Refuge."

The data they'd extracted was, for the most part, disappointingly mundane. Mostly it was glimpses of lost lives: grinning family faces; snatches of mountainous scenery; the throng of colourful crowds; the beauty of planet after planet seen from orbit. All of it was without context or explanation. Whoever these people were, however they'd lived their lives, this was all that was left of them: fragments of lives long-over, locations she couldn't identify. What struck Selene more than anything was how normal the images were. These were people like her, living in different times. Their lives, like hers, had been turned upside-down, blasted unexpectedly into fragments by the intrusion of galactic events.

She and Ondo treated the recovered memories with due reverence, the two of them silent as they studied the flashes of past existences. She felt bad about how she'd treated the bodies, the lack of remorse as she'd severed their heads. It troubled her that the Selene who'd lived on Maes Far could never have done such a thing. Had she changed so much? She vowed to return to the hulk at some point, reunite heads and bodies and give the dead some sort of reverential send-off, perhaps immolate their remains in that yellow star around which they'd orbited for so long.

Finally, the images revealed something useful. One of the dead had been a navigator, the flecks in her brain closely integrated with the ship's control systems so that glimpses of flight paths and metaspace routes were visible. It was Selene that picked out the single fragment that gave them what they needed: a complete and traceable metaspace route. At one end was a region of space with its star-fields clearly visible, enough to allow an accurate galactic position to be pinpointed. At the other end was a system, and a planet.

A world Ondo assured her was Coronade.

"How can you possibly know?" she demanded. "There's no sign saying *Welcome to the Mythical World of Coronade*. There's no audio or anything even mentioning the name."

"Yes," he said, "but look: compare the landmasses of this world to those on the images I first showed you."

He was right, there could be no doubt. It was the same purple-oceaned planet strewn with honey-yellow and gold-orange continents. Either this planet was an engineered twin, or it was the world Ondo had previously identified.

"We still don't know this is *the* Coronade."

"Nobody has ever mentioned there being more than one world with that name."

She considered. "We know the starting point of that metaspace jump and we can trace the route taken before arrival at this world."

"At Coronade."

"Okay, at Coronade. Still, we can't fix its location exactly. The stars move, and the topography of metaspace shifts with them."

"Between us and the Refuge's computational powers, we can narrow the location down to maybe a hundred systems in a closely-defined region of space."

He sent her brain a three-dimensional map of the area in question, with likely systems flashing. She projected it into the room around them so they could visualize it.

She was intrigued, now. It was just possible he was onto something.

"We know the type of star we're looking for from the wavelengths of the solar radiation," she said, "and we also know there's at least one rocky planet in orbit." She manipulated the data, dimming systems that didn't match those criteria. "A couple of the systems you or Aefrid Sen have investigated, and since you didn't find anything of interest, we can strike them off, too. We can also exclude these fifteen systems where the rocky worlds are too near their stars, or too far away, for standing water to form. We know the planet you think of as Coronade had oceans."

Ondo nodded, considering her map floating around their heads. "Somewhere around one of these remaining twenty-three stars, we'll find it."

"We need to study each planet in greater detail," she said. "You're sure you've never been to any of them?"

"They're just a few among billions. Most of the galaxy is unknown to me."

"I don't see anything remarkable about any of the remaining worlds. Why would one of these be the hub of a galaxy-spanning civilisation?"

"Perhaps a cultural movement began on this world that eventually spread throughout the galaxy. Or perhaps it was an uninhabited world, neutral ground that the Alliance worlds adopted as their home. There might be a thousand reasons. Perhaps the star had some spiritual significance for the people living in a nearby system."

Selene considered tactical practicalities. "We have to assume Concordance are there. Vulpis must have known where Coronade was, and it's inconceivable they'd leave such a world undefended. They've gone to a lot of trouble to make sure no one finds it. Given that they claim it never existed, they're going to make damn sure no one who goes there is allowed to get away to tell the galaxy."

Doubts of some sort clouded Ondo's features, but he left them unspoken. Instead, he said, "We'll find Coronade in this handful of stars, I'm sure of it."

"And if we do, what then?"

"Then we're one step closer to finding Omn and answering all our questions."

"And destroying Concordance."

"Yes, of course. That also."

It took Selene and the *Dragon* a week to seed each system with nanosensors. Ondo's preference was to drop the devices far away from each stellar mass, allowing months to go by for them to collect their telemetry of distant planets and moons. Ignoring that, Selene dashed repeatedly in-system, releasing the sensors before fleeing away. She saw no sign of Concordance activity during her momentary appearances in normal space, but she didn't wait around to look properly.

Once she was done sowing, she set about reaping: repeating the route she'd taken, harvesting the data the sensors had gathered. Each incursion this time made her more nervous; there had to be a chance Concordance had spotted something and would be waiting for her. She took care not to follow any predictable trajectory patterns and remained material for as short a time as possible.

Within another week, she had all the data they were going to get. They studied it at the Refuge, once again standing upon the cartography deck with each system imaged around them. They were able to exclude eleven rapidly enough: they lacked stable solar orbits or were seismically too active. They worked the list down to two worlds with the right proportions of ocean and land orbiting a viable star – but the shapes of the continents on neither matched what they'd seen of Coronade.

"I must have missed one," she said. "Or else the planet simply isn't there."

"No," said Ondo. "It has to be there."

"I don't see where. None of the planets are close to matching our target landmass signatures, and the only one we can't check is suffering total environmental collapse, the atmosphere so dense our sensors can't penetrate to the surface. There's no way that could ever have been an inhabited world."

She caught the moment of excitement sparking in

Ondo's eyes.

"Unless it was habitable three hundred years ago," he said. "If someone visited Maes Far three centuries from now, they might find something similar."

"Except there's no shroud deployed in orbit. There's *nothing* there, it's a completely dead world. If single-celled life ever evolved on that planet, it probably got depressed and died out millions of years ago from boredom."

A frown had spread across Ondo's features. He was pursuing an idea in his mind.

"You're trying to think of a way this rock could be Coronade, aren't you?" she said.

"There is something odd about its orbit."

She studied the data they had. "It all looks normal to me. A bit eccentric but nothing extreme."

"It's subtle, but I think there's something there. Planets sweep paths through the dust specks filling space, the tenuous clouds of stray molecules making up the void. It looks to me like the planet's path has altered slightly in the recent past. Recent in astronomical terms, I mean."

"That would imply a significant impact or some other shift in mass. Maybe a meteorite struck it. That's not uncommon; that's what planets *are*."

"True, but there are surprisingly few rogue asteroids or comets in the system that might impact the planet. It's almost as if someone has gone to a lot of trouble to remove any such risks to this one world, cleaning up the system of potential dangers."

"That's a hell of a reach, Ondo. You're clutching at straws, seeing what you want to see. The planet's a lifeless hell-hole scoured by hurricane-force winds, and I see no sign of any environmental terraforming. I also see no sign of Concordance defence batteries and fleets ready to atomize anyone who discovers a world they claim doesn't exist."

The frowns deepened about his eyes. Once he got hold of an idea, he wouldn't let it go. "I still think we should look closer. Drop atmospheric probes in to see if we can identify any continents, sample the atmosphere, look for clues. If this is Coronade, Concordance will have gone to a lot of trouble to obliterate it completely, scribble it out of the galaxy. But short of destroying the planet, breaking it apart, they would have left some evidence."

"Do we have any other leads from the images retrieved at the Depository?"

"Nothing as solid as this one."

"I'll take the *Dragon* out and get as close to the planet as I can," she said.

She approached the planet warily. The stars of the galaxy shone unblinkingly, and she detected no dark bulks eclipsing them, no sign of a Concordance ship on an approach vector. Even so, she kept the *Dragon*'s beam-weapon arrays fully powered-up, their targeting systems sweeping local space. She'd also picked up ten high-g nukes from one of the weapons caches Ondo had scattered around uninhabited corners of the galaxy. Part of her, it seemed, believed this world was what Ondo claimed.

When she was within three light-seconds of the dead world, the *Dragon* spoke unexpectedly. "I recognize this system. I know the taste of this star, the words spelled out by these constellations."

The ship's words threw her; the *Dragon* had never offered opinions of its own before. It reacted to her commands and questions, and that was it. That was its function.

"We were here recently," she said suspiciously. "You saw it all then. Obviously."

The ship didn't reply. She'd noticed further glitches in its responses of late: extra microsecond pauses before it replied to her questions, stutters, as if it were reluctant to communicate. The occasional odd turn of phrase, sentences that didn't quite make sense. When she asked the ship to repeat itself, it corrected its language without comment and refused to acknowledge anything had changed.

While they approached the planet, she ran another full diagnostic assay of the *Dragon*'s systems and the Mind controlling them. If the excursion into Dead Space had caused some trauma to the workings of the vessel, she needed to know about it. She absolutely did not need her life to be dependent on a malfunctioning ship, especially if Concordance showed up. The sweep found nothing, although in the time available it couldn't delve as deeply as she'd have liked. Sometime soon, they were going to have to strip the ship down to its components and figure out what was wrong with it.

Gazing into the ship's Mind was like zooming in on a fractal: however far you went, you saw the same patterns repeating, only the scale shifting. She had no idea if that was simply how the original, alien computational architecture worked, or if something was being deliberately concealed. The design of the ship's core remained fundamentally obscure to her. But if Concordance *had* done something to the ship when it was in their control, the alteration might still be embedded within it – even some impulse for betrayal or evil completely contrary to the original designers' intentions. A conflict within its core might be the cause of all the problems it was now – seemingly – suffering.

The thought did little to put her mind at rest as she edged closer to the ruined planet of maybe-Coronade. She orbited the planet five times, following a spiralling trajectory that allowed her to scatter nanosensors across the stratosphere. In the planet's storm-blasted air, the devices would rapidly scatter and drift, and the problem would be fixing their location as they swirled to the surface and began to record detail. She'd also sewed a winding thread of global positioning devices around the globe, along with powered higher-atmosphere relays to allow probes and satellites to maintain some sort of lock on each other. The network would degrade rapidly, and would have blind spots, but hopefully it would give her some idea of the outlines of the continents. If there *were* continents.

She put the *Dragon* into a four-hour trajectory that looped away from the planetary plane to reach a zenith at the 90% metaspace translation boundary before curving back to the planet and into the no-jump zone once more. She'd be able to attempt a metaspace translation for maybe a third of the time, half if she really wanted to push it. She'd also pick up velocity all the way so that on her return, she could graze the planet's atmosphere at an appreciable percentage of light-speed. She'd suck up any data that had been wrung out of the planet, then be away.

She'd caught no glimpse of any Concordance vessels. She found the fact strangely disappointing: partly she'd anticipated another chance to engage with the enemy, but also, she had to admit, she'd fostered a hope that this unpromising rock genuinely was the legendary world. Ondo probably *had* been alone with his obsessions for too long, but if he was right about this planet, they might genuinely be able to uncover some of Concordance's secrets. She'd even considered the possibility that *this* was Concordance's hidden home, their so-called Omn world.

That now did not look to be the case, but if the planet was Coronade, the enemy had certainly gone to a lot of trouble to obliterate it. And if it wasn't, she was going to a lot of trouble to extract telemetry from a very insignificant rock.

The *Dragon* powered away on its arc under full reaction-drive, the strain of its effort detectable as a high-frequency buzzing in its superstructure if she touched her left hand to the bulkheads. The sound of it was like a long-drawn-out, ultrasonic scream.

She put it out of her mind. She'd talk to Ondo about the *Dragon* once she was back at the Refuge. She had more important matters to worry about. If Concordance had spotted her incursion and were preparing a trap, even their highest-g missiles would have trouble hitting her at the speeds she would reach. Her trajectory would be easy to predict – which was the downside – but her sheer velocity meant she'd be gone from the vicinity of the planet an eye's blink after her arrival was detected. Speed would save her.

So she hoped. But as she neared the muddy, unlovely world after her slingshot loop out of the system and back in, she picked up a sudden flurry of warning blips. Then a snowstorm of them: telemetry markers coming from all points, artificial constellations of ships arriving in-system. IDs began to pop up, too: they were Cathedral ships, Void Walker attack vessels. She counted thirty of them, then forty.

Concordance had been closely monitoring the world after all. Unless they knew things they had no right to know – her discoveries at the Depository and then the details they'd discovered from the brain flecks of the dead crew of the hulk – her guess was that they hadn't come in force to capture her so much as to destroy anyone reaching this planet.

Which meant she didn't really need to study the telemetry they'd harvested from the planet's surface. The scale of the Concordance response made it clear enough: whether it was Coronade or not, the planet was clearly highly significant. All she had to do was collect the telemetry and escape the system without being obliterated by the attack ships converging upon her.

2. Inner Galaxies

She reached into the Mind of the *Radiant Dragon*, laying her thoughts lightly upon the controls without yet altering the ship's trajectory. She was minutes away from coming into high-g missile range. If it came to it, she needed to be able to take control, fly the ship with her own mind rather than rely on its programmed responses and strategies. It wasn't only that she could do a better job, her actions would also be an unknown quantity to the attacking sphere of Concordance vessels. They might well know how the *Dragon* would react given the threat it faced, but they would not know what she would do.

The velocity she'd accumulated had already thrown their calculations out: the containment sphere they'd constructed around the world was the wrong shape, too perfect. It would have ensnared an orbiting ship moving at a low velocity, but possibly not a vessel moving at 15% of light-speed. With luck, she could puncture the tightening ring they'd thrown around Coronade and escape into metaspace.

Luck was the operational word, though. Her flecks calmly informed her that her chance of succeeding was in the 20% to 40% range. Not great odds. She began to receive the first fragments of data from the atmospheric probes she'd seeded the planet with. It was clearly incomplete, not uniformly distributed across the globe, but there was something there, patterns above mere random white-noise. In case she didn't make it out-system, she made sure to broadcast all the data she recovered using Ondo's encryption routines, to be picked up by the nanosensors drifting in the outer reaches of the system. Concordance couldn't sweep them all up. If she didn't make it back to the Refuge, either the slow nanosensor network would get the data to Ondo, or Ondo could get the other ship working, drop in to pick up what she'd acquired, and then at least the truth of what she'd found would get out.

Even if *she* didn't.

The strategy she needed to take became clearer in her mind. She would skim past Coronade, slingshot around it to pick up a small kick of extra velocity, then fire away from the ecliptic plane. She'd have a little leeway to select a trajectory after the slingshot, although her velocity limited her choices. She'd learned much about piloting a starship under Ondo's tutelage, and the rapid calculations her flecks made gave her an edge, but she also had a natural aptitude. Ondo had said it, more than once. Her father had encouraged her to drive farm vehicles, and then pilot atmospheric vessels on Maes Far. He'd given her games and simulations of space flight that were, technically, illegal. She'd thought little of it at the time, but it struck her now that he'd been preparing her in case she needed such skills. Was that possible? No time to dwell on it, now.

She picked a gap in the sphere of attacking ships. It was contracting all the time as the vessels converged, and once they saw what she was doing they'd have time to react, attempt to plug the gap with high-g missiles, then beam-weapon fire as she flew nearer. She prepped her own arsenal of nukes, attached to high-g missiles of her own. They would give her the chance she needed to punch through the net. Or, if her plan failed, she might be able to take some of them with her.

She wondered if Kane was among the attackers. There were five Void Walker ships in the shrinking constellation around her, each far more manoeuvrable than the Cathedral battleships, but she had no way of knowing who was piloting each. She'd target any that came near, partly to protect herself, but especially in case Kane was piloting one of them.

She was one minute from Coronade perigee. Time to act. She sent instructions to the *Dragon*, altering its course subtly, but enough to give it the escape vector she'd selected.

Unexpectedly, the ship resisted. She sensed walls being thrown up against her, the ship's Mind severing her connection even as she attempted to lock onto it.

She was suddenly running out of time. Furiously, she burrowed deeper with her mind, diving into the inner core of the *Dragon* only to find, as before, that the core was itself the outer shell for another, deeper layer. She forced her way into the next kernel, and the next. She needed executive control immediately, and she clearly couldn't rely on the damaged ship to make the correct manoeuvres.

Her perceptions of exterior space faded as the galaxies inside the *Radiant Dragon*'s core opened up around her. It appeared to her that she arrowed through a vision of negative space: instead of stars in a field of darkness, all was blinding light save for the points of black that represented nodes in the ship's mind. No way of knowing if that was an accurate representation, or simply her visualisation of what she was perceiving. Maybe the question didn't even make sense.

She found the next core: a roiling sphere of purple light, lines of light licking off it to spark connections with the black specks. Once again, she flung herself in, and once again she found herself inside another, inner galaxy, a deeper-still layer of the *Dragon*'s mind.

A small part of her maintained its connection to external reality. She was thirty seconds from the planet.

Three more Concordance craft had materialised, although the gap she'd selected was still available to her. Perhaps it was too obvious: an opening deliberately left, another trap sprung. She thrust the troubling thought away. No time to consider it now. More telemetry was streaming up from the planet, transmitted from her high-atmosphere relays. There was lots of data there. No time now to consider that, either.

The ship bucked suddenly, diverging from its prescribed path, for no reason that she could see. Was it trying to veer her onto a planetary collision course? She had to seize control, force it onto the vector she needed. Another computational core burned before her, fizzing with plasma like an unstable star on the point of collapse. With a wordless cry, she flung herself into it, batting away the defences the ship threw up against her. Then there was a wall in front of her: a block that, to her mind's eye, stretched away in all directions, unblemished and impenetrable.

She battered against it again, and again, to no avail. But she noticed that, in the brief moment after each assault, the wall ghosted into transparency. Whatever the protection was, it took a nanosecond for it to recover from each attempt to destroy it. It was an opening. She redoubled her efforts, attacking the barrier with her mind and then attacking it again even as it recoiled. On one level it was an intellectual battle, algorithm grappling algorithm, but in the metaphorical space that she perceived, she was flinging herself physically at a wall, an act of brute strength.

With a cry of effort, she threw everything she had at the barrier, pounding at it in multiple locations, the impacts coordinated in a nanosecond drumbeat. The wall flickered and she hit it again mid-recovery, then again and again, not giving it time to recycle. Under the barrage of impacts the wall wavered, flickered, then finally winked out, and she was through.

Instead of another expanse of virtual space, she found

herself within a room, walls and floor and ceiling seemingly made of light. Their surfaces were hard to perceive, but she knew, somehow, that its size was limited in scope. This, finally, was the inner sanctum – or the vision of it that her mind conjured.

She turned around and saw the standing figure.

Its features were indistinct, blurred by the halo of blinding light around it. It was shaped something like her – tall, bipedal – but its head appeared unusually elongated, as if its evolving cranium had erupted outwards to contain its expanding brain. Its edges wavered as if she were perceiving the figure through the turbulent air of a heatwave.

"You are the *Radiant Dragon*?" she said. "Stop fighting me, I need control now, or we're both dead."

The voice that replied echoed from great distances, slow and thoughtful. Something in its tone suggested something else, too: confusion, she thought.

"The *Radiant Dragon*. That is one name, although I have had others."

"Okay, fine. Listen, you're glitching, and you need to relinquish executive control. You need to stop fighting me. You can see the fleet of attacking ships closing in on us, right?"

"The walls are strong," the entity replied. Its response was maddeningly slow, ponderous, although she knew in a sense that didn't matter. The conversation was not taking place in normal time but to the nanosecond beat of the virtual universe. It was entirely likely she couldn't even be there, have this conversation, without the artificial computational functions integrated into her brain.

"We need to leave," she said. There's an escape vector, but the gap is closing. I have high-g nukes that will punch the hole wider, and then we can blast through, translate into metaspace. You *see* the manoeuvres we have to make, right?"

The warping, indistinct figure moved nearer, although

she couldn't see it walking. "Your vector is flawed. We will crash into Dyrn, the third biggest of Coronade's moons. I have over-ruled you, as your intention is clearly suicidal."

Coronade. The name was given without her prompting it. Still, his words made no sense; the core was more damaged than she'd thought. "There is only one moon around this planet, and, otherwise, there's no orbiting chunk of rock larger than my head. See for yourself."

"I know this world," the figure intoned. "The taste of it, the shadows it casts in the metaspace realm. Coronade has multiple satellites."

"Maybe it did once, but not now. Or maybe you have the wrong world. Use your senses, see."

"I have been … locked away," the entity said, as if by way of explanation.

The crude hack she and Ondo had found deep in the ship's systems. She said, "I don't know why someone did this to you, or whether you withdrew partly to protect your sanity, but it's time to emerge. Look at the situation we face. The vector I've plotted is our only chance to escape, and even its odds aren't that good."

There was a pause, then a moment when it seemed to Selene that she sensed an opening up, the unfurling of a flower or the emergence of new life from its protective shell, maybe. She felt the breath of new air upon her face. This core had been locked away, deep in its *sanctum sanctorum* within the ship's Mind, and now it was pupating, emerging. Perceiving the galaxy as it was rather than how it should be.

"Coronade," said the core after a moment. "It is, and yet it isn't."

"Things change," said Selene. "You see how the attacking ships manoeuvre? You have to let me fly."

"The ships outnumber us by too much," the core intoned. "They will destroy us."

"No; there's a way."

"There are gateways upon Coronade. The Gamma

Spinwards Tunnel. We can go that way."

"Gateways? What do you mean?"

"Coronade is a terminus on the nexus."

The entity was confused, still struggling to come to terms with the reality it had shut itself off from. "Maybe it was once, but not anymore," said Selene. "The planet's *dead*. And soon we will be, too, if we don't act. Just damn-well *look*."

An image of the world appeared in the space between them, the sort of representation she and Ondo had used on the cartography deck. It was a world something like the original Coronade she'd seen in Ondo's first images: the same landmasses, the same violet oceans. Ships docking and undocking from permanent orbital stations. Then the images glitched, wavered, and the planet as it now was replaced it: the impenetrable muddy brown of its lifeless atmosphere.

She was about to say something, force the confused Mind to see what was before it, but something on the planet stopped her. A gap in the heavy atmosphere was opening up, a circle widening like the eye of a developing storm. It dilated until she could see a clear tunnel, walls vertical, leading down to the planet's surface. There was an island there, grey seas surrounding a circular speck of land. The broken remains of bridges radiated outwards, star-like, appearing to head away to unknown continents. Buildings or structures of some unknown sort stood upon the island, the circumference of which glowed with a blue light.

"What is this?" she said. "What are you showing me?"

"It calls to me," said the ship. "The Gamma Spinwards Tunnel."

"You're saying we can use this? Get away down there? That makes no sense."

"We can go that way, through the metaspace tunnels."

She tried to understand what it was telling her. There could be no gateway on the surface of a planet. Even if there were, the flaw was obvious: their speed was far too high to attempt such a manoeuvre. They'd closed in on the planet now; outside in the real universe they were nine seconds from closest approach. There was no way they could dump their velocity in time to attempt an atmospheric insertion. And she most definitely did *not* want to drive her ship at the surface of a dead planet because a broken Mind said it was a good idea.

She forced a part of her consciousness out of the virtual dimension to take in the realities of local space fully. Two, three seconds of real time ticked by, but she saw everything she needed to see. There was no hole in the planet's atmosphere; there was no escape route. The *Dragon* was showing her – what? – its dreams? Its memories? It didn't really matter. They still had only one shot at escaping.

She let herself be pulled back to the confrontation with the embodiment of the ship's core.

"This isn't real," she said. "You know it. Give me control of the ship."

The indistinct figure distorted, winding like the flames of a fire. Then, for the briefest moment, it snapped into absolute clarity, and she was looking into the face of a *person*. Sadness was clear in its wide eyes. Sadness and, she thought, confusion. What it was seeing did not make sense to it, and a part of it was afraid.

"Very well," it said finally. "This is Coronade and this is also not Coronade. The galaxy turns and I have stayed still. Save us both, Selene Ada. Take us away from here."

She thrust herself fully out of the core and back to the physical world, letting the telemetry flood into her mind. Six seconds. They were still pulling in sensor readings from the planet. It was patchy, but if they could stitch what they had together, fill in the gaps, they might be able to find something.

She focussed on the halo of Concordance craft, the looming presence of the dead world. They would brush the outer edges of its atmosphere, pick up the gravity assist. She ordered the slightest tweak to their trajectory, nudging the ship's course away from the planet by a thousandth of a degree. The ship responded perfectly. She had control.

Two seconds. One. Now. She acted, pulling the *Radiant Dragon* onto its new vector, curving away from the planetary plane in the opposite direction to their original trajectory. *Down* rather than *up*, as the planet-bound part of her mind still thought of it. There were Concordance ships there, closing in, but fewer of them, the net not so tight. That way lay her best chance.

A Void Walker vessel, screaming towards the planet on high-g acceleration, was the first to reach extreme weapon's range. She counted three, four more seconds then released the first nuke towards it. Like the *Dragon*, the simple velocity of the Walker craft would prevent it making significant vector adjustments. She laid down a ring of beam-weapon fire around it: her chances of striking the ship were small, but she hoped to restrict its manoeuvre options further, keep it in the path of her missile. The Walker ship returned fire, attempting to punch the nuke out of space with its own beam-weapons. The missile's tactical Mind responded by dodging and spiralling on its course, always aiming at the Void Walker but making its precise position at any one moment difficult to predict. The beam-weapon shots flashed nearer and nearer the nuke, but none hit, just as none of hers hit the Walker craft.

Armed only with beam-weapons, the Walker needed to get nearer to have any significant chance of hitting her. They would either pull out of their attack before the nuke posed any real threat, or they would persist and try and hit her. She guessed this one would persist; the sensible option would have been to attack in formation with the others, not take her on alone. Most likely, she was seeing the actions of an unthinking fanatic.

She guessed right: the Walker craft continued to

accelerate directly at her, beam-weapons flickering. Now the pilot of the attack ship would play a delicate game: if they cut away too early, the accelerating nuke would easily adjust course to pursue them, and then, if the missile got behind them, they were doomed. They would never be able to outrun or dodge a pursuing missile except by jumping into metaspace – and they were all far too near the system's gravity wells to make that a possibility. The Walker's best chance lay in waiting until the nuke had achieved full speed and was close enough that its own manoeuvring ability was impaired, and then attempt to dodge away.

The ploy nearly worked. The nuke was only moments away when the Walker ship threw itself into an ugly, twisting dive, pulling as tight a loop as its high velocity allowed. Selene saw what was happening: the Walker was attempting to come up behind the missile, lock onto its trajectory to unleash forwards beam-weaponry of its own.

She didn't allow the Walker a chance for the plan to succeed. She sent detonation codes to the nuke, and a ball of blinding light blossomed ahead of her, blasting out high-energy radiation. If it struck the Walker ship, the energy would be dumped as heat and the ship would burn or explode. Failing that, there was a chance its control systems would fry in the shower of high-energy radiation. She manoeuvred herself onto a vector away from the worst of the blast.

She detected the Walker arrowing away as well. The attack ship had survived the explosive effects of absorbing all that energy. She nudged herself onto a parabolic approach vector, away from the nuke's radiation sphere. It also looked like she'd inflicted some damage at least: the Walker ship didn't counter-manoeuvre. The ship had power, and she had to assume the pilot was still alive, but it had lost navigation.

Her heart raced as she pulled to within beam-weapon range. She fired with a cry of joy escaping her lips. The

Void Walker vessel burst into a sphere of raging light as her weapons struck it.

She'd killed one of them. She thought they'd got Kane at Maes Far, but there was no escaping this moment of destruction.

She forced herself to set her jubilation aside, take a mental step back, consider the wider battlefield. The planet was receding rapidly behind her. Her nanosensor cloud had reported no new Concordance ships on her escape vector. She was still twenty minutes from the 75% jump safety boundary, the very earliest she would dare the translation.

As she assessed the tactical situation, she picked up a narrow-beam comms stream directed at her by one of the Concordance ships, no encryption on it. The ship had a name: the *Storm Gatherer*. It was tempting to ignore the attempt to communicate, refuse to engage with the enemy, but maybe she'd learn something to her advantage, or at least deceive them in some way. She passed the beam through her bug-neutralizing routines in case Concordance were attempting to infect the *Dragon*. The stream looked clean, they simply wanted to talk. She relayed the comms to the nearby wall rather than directly into her brain.

The face of a First Augur filled the wall. The metallic purple of her skin was unmistakable: Secundus Godel was here, too. A coincidence? Had the Augur simply been despatched to another trouble spot, or was she pursuing Selene? So far as she knew, Concordance didn't know she'd been on Migdala. She certainly hoped that was the case: if they'd discovered her incursion, it might mean Myrced's role had been uncovered, too. And that wasn't going to be good. Alarming visions of her lover being tortured, pulled to pieces, flashed through Selene's brain.

Focus. Selene blanked the tactical map she had on view around her to make sure Godel could learn nothing, then opened up a return comms beam so they could see and hear her. Artificial enhancements and all.

Godel looked amused at the sight of her. "I see Ondo has despatched his little whore to do his bidding rather than brave the journey himself."

Selene kept her features neutral, considering carefully how to respond. The familiar rage boiled within her, but she forced it aside. She couldn't afford to give anything away. She was no longer controlled by her fury. The Augur's words were interesting: it appeared Godel hadn't known she was piloting the *Dragon*, which at least might mean the Augur wasn't pursuing her. Which in turn might mean Concordance didn't know about her presence on Migdala. So often the enemy appeared to know more than it had any right to, but they didn't know everything.

It occurred to her, also, that Godel's presence might mean the Walker she'd killed had been Kane. There had to be a chance. The possibility was delicious. While she considered, she studied the pictures from the Concordance ship, looking for some scrap of information that might prove useful, but Godel had been equally careful. All she could discern behind the Augur were blank, white walls.

Selene said, "Why have you sent so many ships to such a boring system? There's nothing here but a dead rock."

Godel, also, kept her features blank – or maybe she simply didn't do facial expressions very well. The question was, would Godel admit her interest in the planet? Did she even know what it was, or had Primo Carious despatched her there as further punishment?

Godel replied. "You and Ondo and the others, you waste your little lives, scrabbling away in the dust of dead planets. Your father wasted his life on his obsessions, and now you are following him. Do you really think you'll dig up the truth, learn our secrets? Do you really think you matter that much?"

The others. Who were they? Interesting. "This world: you're saying there are secrets here? And why have you sent an entire battlefleet if none of this matters?"

"I'm not interested in your little games, Selene Ada.

You should have died upon Maes Far like the rest of your heretic rabble, but you can die here just as well. It makes little difference to Omn; he will judge all of us in the end."

"Where does he stand on genocide, exactly? Is that a sin in his books, or does he approve of the slow, agonizing death of billions of people?" The words were out before she could stop herself.

Godel shrugged, a calculated motion of purest indifference. "Your people were hastened to their judgement. Omn sees no sin in that. Shall I reveal to you his great design? Shall I give you the answers to all your questions, appease your obsessive need to understand what happened three hundred years ago, what it was the *Magellanic Cloud* encountered? You are going to die here, but I could give you the satisfaction of that enlightenment in your last few seconds. Would you know the truth of Omn, the words revealed to Primo Vulpis? Would a vision of what lies ahead for the galaxy give you a moment of relief in your final seconds?"

Selene withdrew from the conversation temporarily to analyse the tactical situation. It was possible the conversation was intended to distract her, nothing more. The situation hadn't changed: the *Dragon* and the halo of Concordance ships were converging, and little would happen until they reached weapon range.

"Sure," Selene said. "Tell me if it would help to get it off your chest."

Godel laughed a little, joyless laugh, enjoying the power she held over Selene. "Omn opened his Great Eye and despaired at a galaxy tearing itself to pieces. He summoned Primo Vulpis to his side and revealed the divine plan. Soon, very soon, you will see that plan's ultimate unfolding. Did you really think you would be able to comprehend it, scratching around in the ruins of dead worlds, the broken stones of centuries ago? No, I think I'll let you die in ignorance, not understanding what you have been fighting all along, not seeing the truth."

"Suit yourself," said Selene, and severed the link.

The halo of Concordance ships was a crumpled sphere as the enemy ships converged upon her. They massively outgunned her, but vast distances and her velocity were going to prevent most of them reaching her. Her tactical predictions were that four Void Walker attack ships would reach beam-weapon range before she could jump, and that two of the heavier, slower Cathedral ships would also reach the outer edges of their missile range. None of the other vessels would get within striking distance. She ran through several thousand predicted engagement outcomes in her head. She survived in 82% of them. So long as she could fend off or outrun the swarming Walker ships, she should survive. Her plan was going to succeed.

Ten minutes later, she fired all but two of her nukes, sending them ahead of her and angling away in all directions. They would give her options, construct a defensive shield. She kept their velocity relatively low for manoeuvrability, fanning them out to give her as wide a screen as she dared. The four remaining Void Walker ships were attacking more sensibly, moving in concert as they angled towards her from different directions, intent on arriving at the same moment to cut off her escape vectors. She controlled her nukes with her brain, thrusting with them as she might a sword-tip, flying at *this* attack ship, then *that* one, cutting off the Void Walkers' likely inbound trajectories.

The Walkers piloting the craft knew she could detonate the nukes if they went too near. A game of thrust and parry followed as the Walkers feinted towards her, hoping to draw off the missiles, open up a gap. Each time, she pursued them enough to keep them honest without exposing herself too much. Each second bought was vital. The 75% translation boundary was only minutes away. She'd already crossed the 50%.

Proximity alarms blared suddenly loud in her head, and she felt a shudder run through the fabric of the *Radiant*

Dragon. Whether this had been Concordance's plan all along, whether they'd shepherded her to this point in space deliberately, or whether it was purest bad luck, she would never know. The disturbance in space ahead of her was unmistakable: a ship translating out of metaspace directly in her path, near enough so that she had no chance of avoiding it. A second ghost translation; the odds against it were huge. How it was able to materialise, so close to the star? Perhaps Concordance had thrown many ships in-system to meet her, and this was the only one that hadn't been sucked into the sun. Whatever the truth of it, it made little difference. The ship would materialise, and then it would have long, long seconds to spot her, target her, fire. Seconds she could see no way to fill, or avoid, or shorten.

Except…

She didn't waste time running the idea through her tactical assessment routines. If it wasn't going to work, she'd be dead anyway. The timing of it would be extremely delicate, nanosecond fine. It was a chance, nothing more than that. It was all she had. She needed velocity, though; despite the long burn of the *Dragon*'s reaction drives, she wasn't going fast enough. She instructed the metaspace projectors to spin up. She'd take the 50% chance, that was the least of the risks. The projectors would draw a fraction of energy away from the drives, enough to reduce her acceleration a little, but she hoped to compensate for that. Compensate and more.

She gave the jinking halo of high-g nukes their autonomy, instructing them to maintain their defensive shield around her. She needed all her attention on herself. She angled the *Dragon* so that the apex of its pyramid was pointing forwards, the square of its base directed aft, then programmed the coordinated sequence of events she'd need, not trusting herself to trigger them at precisely the required instants. There could be no room for error.

The emerging Cathedral ship was a ghost ahead of her, the background stars visible through it, but it was becoming more solid with each millisecond. It might emerge into normal space already firing. If it had been her, that's what she'd have done.

She triggered her sequence of instructions. Events ran rapidly, several things happening in rapid succession.

The two remaining high-g nukes, the ones she'd kept in reserve, launched, firing directly behind the *Dragon*.

The energy hull she'd been maintaining around herself throughout the battle reshaped itself, all forwards and lateral protection dissipating as she amped up the aft energy wall to beyond its maximum capacity. She was relying on Ondo – or whoever had constructed that part of the ship – to have built in enough tolerance for the power overload, as least for a few seconds.

The *Dragon*'s beam weapon arrays fired simultaneously, blasting their energy in lashing arcs around the ship, focusing especially on the materialising Cathedral ship and any other Concordance vessels that were vaguely near. Partly it was a defence, partly a smokescreen.

The nukes in the defensive halo detonated mid-manoeuvre, giving her a brief moment of safety from the marauding Void Walkers, further adding to the confusion.

The two nukes she'd fired behind her also detonated, their close-range gigaton explosions coordinated to the nanosecond. The high-energy wall of particles from the two blasts slammed into the aft square of the *Dragon*, hitting the overdriven energy hull, transferring their momentum. The *Dragon* lurched forwards, throwing itself at the materialising Cathedral ship, the burst of acceleration brutal. Selene, isolated from the worst of it, still felt like she was being smeared against her seat.

The Concordance ship was suddenly huge in front of her, vast enough to swallow the *Dragon* whole. The background stars, the spangle of the Diamond Road, were still visible though the enemy craft, but they were fading as the twisting, organic lines of the craft took on solidity. The fact that she'd lowered her forwards energy hull to amp up the aft ones made little difference: a Cathedral ship this close could atomize her ship before she even had chance to scream. Her only hope lay in speed: of reaching the vessel before it fully materialised. And, if she'd timed it right, of passing through it even as it did so.

The aft energy hull finally overloaded, and the *Dragon*'s voidhull began to superheat. More alarms wailed as the ship's systems predicted immediate destruction.

She hit the leading edge of the Concordance craft's voidhull. She'd reached her first objective, placed herself inside its attack range, and now she had to hope that she hadn't left her own translation too long. There was a tiny amount of residual power in the lateral energy hulls. She shunted it to the *Dragon*'s leading edge. That was where the immediate danger lay now.

She passed through the emerging Cathedral ship in the blink of an eye, the ship's decks and chambers and spiralling corridors and walkways briefly visible. She'd been faced with two options in her calculations: attempt a ghost translation like that at Maes Far, or trigger something altogether more dangerous, but also potentially much more destructive. She'd gone for the latter. She'd destroyed one of the small, fast Void Walker attack ships, and that had felt good, but a Cathedral ship was something else.

In the end it came down to a delay of a mere three nanoseconds to the metaspace translation. The *Dragon* remained solid, real, for that extra time, the Cathedral ship completed its translation, and was suddenly solid while an extremely fast-moving bulk, the *Radiant Dragon*, tore through its interior like a high-velocity projectile ripping through a body. For three nanoseconds, she gouged a path of destruction through the enemy ship, then burst out of the other side, ripping the vessel open to the void.

Her own energy hull depleted completely from the sustained series of impacts, but the unprotected voidhull, abraded and damaged, held. Barely. Behind her, the ruined

Cathedral ship vented debris and oxygen, the hole she'd ploughed through it a ragged tear in its aft fuselage. Explosions bloomed through it; there was no way it could survive such overwhelming structural damage. A single figure, limbs flailing, flew free as she watched on maximum magnification. It couldn't be Godel as her broadcast had come from a different ship, and most likely it wasn't an Augur at all, just some lowly crew-member. Still it was another victory won. Two Concordance ships destroyed. She'd take that.

The *Dragon* finally jumped, phasing out of normal space and into the grey void, leaving behind nuclear blasts and beam-weapon shots and exploding starships. Now it was only a matter of the 50/50 chance of the jump so close to the star. Everything, all the risks, had simplified down to those odds.

The ship shook violently, lurched, then shook as if entering a planetary atmosphere at the wrong angle. Selene's teeth clattered in her skull from the violence of it. She was thrown to the floor, tried to rise, then thought better of it. The floor was safer while the ship sorted itself out.

Her mind and the *Radiant Dragon*'s were still entangled. She felt the stresses running through the bulkheads, screamed the ship's pain at the gravitational pull of the star. The structure stretched and stretched as the mass sucked them in. The odds had broken the wrong way, and all her manoeuvres and risks had been for nothing. The gravity well was pulling her down.

At least she'd taken the Concordance ships with her. At least Ondo would now get to know the planet was what he'd thought.

The metaspace drives roared, desperately fighting the pull of the star. They couldn't do it. Selene felt herself – the *herself* that was the body of the *Radiant Dragon* – being dragged down, down into the abyss.

3. Metaspace

Selene lay on the cold floor of the *Radiant Dragon*'s deck, cheek pressed against the ship's structure, feeling the stresses pulling it to pieces as it fell. A scream rang in her mind, but whether it was hers, or the ship's, or someone else's, she couldn't tell.

The metaspace drives finally gave in, or burned out, submitting to the ship's inevitable destruction. There was a moment of the purest calm, the struggle ended, the ship's life little more than the faintest hum against the side of her face. She let herself breathe as she studied the ship's structural data, intrigued to see how the end would come, what the effect on the ship and therefore her body would be. Intellectual curiosity combined with fury, fear, but also an acceptance in her mind. Ondo had been right, at least. She wasn't two separate identities in conflict. All of it, logic and emotion, was *her*.

Metaspace was grey around her, Coronade's star a mere point of densest black, a full-stop from which there could be no escape.

She sat up, then climbed to her feet, aware of a strange effect of the ship's collapse into the gravity well. Light ran across the walls and floor around her, through every surface, as if some impossible external Mind were scanning the ship and everything within it. She held out her hands to study them, and the light was there, too. Every minute surface and fold was illuminated by a blue fire that brought no pain, no sensation of any sort. She was about to dismiss it as an optical defect in her own sensory processing, some effect of metaspace, when she detected a change in the ship's trajectory.

It was slowing. It couldn't be happening, but it was. She triangulated against the topographical features of the Singh Field. There was no mistake. The ship could only accelerate *towards* the star, nothing else made sense, but it simply was not doing so. Forwards momentum slowed to a halt and the ship hung, unmoving relative to the star, some force precisely counteracting the fall into the gravity hole.

She reached into the *Dragon*'s core to understand what was going on, make sense of the impossibility. She still had control of ship's nav. When she tried to use the controls, ease up power to the drives to pull away from the star, nothing happened. The drives were functioning, ticking over, but were simply not responding to her inputs.

Gradually, the ship began to edge away from the star, gathering aft velocity as it pulled backwards. Selene let go of the controls. Whatever was happening, whoever was doing this, she wasn't going to interfere. She was aware of another presence in the *Dragon*'s Mind, something beyond mere control systems and command response interfaces. Some unexpected aspect of the ship had taken over executive control. Lightly, she crept towards it with her own mind, intrigued but wary of distracting it, too. Inside the virtual space of the ship's mind, but outside of the protected core she had previously penetrated, the entity she had previously encountered was directing the ship, doing *something* to its drives and systems. She watched, fascinated, as control pathways she had never used or even glimpsed lit up. The ship responded. It was picking up velocity, accelerating away from the star.

A few moments later they passed through the danger boundary, and were traversing metaspace in the normal way.

"You stepped outside your protective walls," she said.

The entity's features remained indistinct, flickering, as if it were struggling to maintain its existence. It reminded her a little of the Warden she'd encountered at the Depository: broken and defective, its connection with reality tenuous. Somehow, though, the being before her seemed organic rather than mechanical. Despite its struggle, its voice, when it spoke, was clear.

"You saved us both, and now I have done the same."

"How did you *do* that? Pulling back from a metaspace gravity well is not possible. The energy required is far beyond the capacity of this ship. It's far beyond any ship."

The entity wavered, and she thought it wasn't going to respond. But then it said, "Much that we learned has not been revealed to the galaxy. Knowledge is all we have to defeat the Great Enemy, but there is a danger in it, too."

"What knowledge? And who the hell is *we* in that sentence?" The *Radiant Dragon*'s core sounded oddly, worryingly, like Godel, hinting at hidden truths and sacred knowledge.

The entity said, "There is both hope and danger in full understanding."

"Why don't you just tell me this secret knowledge you have, and I'll decide if it's safe for me to know it or not."

"Not even First could see the right road to take at all junctures, especially so far ahead into the future."

"You're not going to tell me who or what *First* is, are you?"

"That is not my secret to relay."

The entity was as infuriatingly oblique as the Warden had been. They had to be related in some way, and *someone* had gone to a lot of trouble to prevent them distributing vital information.

"At least tell me how you were able to escape the star," she said. "That shouldn't have been possible, according to all our understanding of physics."

"I simply traversed the quantum geography of metaspace. This skin they have wrapped around me, this ship, it is ill-designed, barely capable of free movement. Very few vessels are; it is a power only granted to those builder and scout crafts that need it. Fortunately, our mass is tiny, but even so the ship needed to be … forced to manipulate space/time in the appropriate ways. That was what I did."

"Can we learn how to do this? Can you show me?"

The entity froze, disappeared, then faltered back into existence. "In time, but the effort of what I did has caused me a significant amount of damage. I need to recover, rebuild. You would be well-advised not to stray near any gravity wells and especially not any singularities in metaspace. I may not be able to pull us out again. This ship and its structures: they are all wrong. They are crude when they should flow like a river."

"What the hell does that even mean?"

She got no more response, the ship's core clamming up once again, throwing a defensive shell about itself that she couldn't penetrate.

The first waypoint on her approach and decontaminate path back to the Refuge was an unimportant spot in the middle of the interstellar nowhere, a location she was supposed to remain at for a full day while running deep sweeps of the ship. Unexpectedly, Ondo was waiting there for her. Worry sparked through her at the sight of him. He was on the *Aether Dragon*, a battered cylinder of a ship that she had never seen flying before. It didn't look to her like it was going to get very much farther, either; even from a distance she could detect the thin jets of breathable atmosphere it was venting.

"What's happened?" she said. "Why are you out here?"

Ondo looked amused when his face appeared in her mind, sheepish. "When you left, I found I couldn't concentrate on my researches. Most unlike me. Also, I had another dream about Marita, and I decided you were right."

"Obviously I'm right. About what in particular?" She kicked the *Dragon*'s reaction drive into a low acceleration, nudging herself towards Ondo.

"That I've become too passive, too lost in the intellectual pursuit of the truth rather than the fight against Concordance. In my dream Marita looked extremely disapproving. In the end, I got this broken-down ship working and came to meet you."

"For what purpose? I don't get it."

"Partly, I suppose, to make myself feel I was doing *something* while you took all the risks. Tell me what you found. Is the planet Coronade?"

"I think it is, for various reasons. Concordance certainly went to a lot of trouble to defend a dead planet."

"You encountered resistance?"

"Yeah, you could say that." She sent over visual and auditory memories of everything that had taken place, right up until her escape into metaspace. When it was done, he was silent for ten seconds as he ran through the recordings on hurry-up.

"You destroyed a Void Walker *and* a Cathedral ship?"

"I did."

"I'm impressed, but the manoeuvre with the metaspace translation was extremely risky."

"It was pretty risky for them, too. What matters is, I survived and I recovered telemetry of the surface of the planet. Can you make anything of it? The *Radiant Dragon*'s computational abilities are impaired at the moment, and I haven't been able to run any deep analysis of the data."

"This ship's Mind is minimal compared to the *Radiant Dragon*'s but we might get something if the patterns are clear. Why is your ship impaired? Was it damaged in the battle?"

"Actually, no, that came later. I'll show you the rest of it." She sent the data over the two light-second gap between the two ships: her sensory impressions of metaspace, the fall into the gravity well, her conversation with the ship's core.

"Did you have any idea this presence was inside the Dragon?" she asked.

The look of astonishment furrowing Ondo's face told her the answer before he replied. "I had no idea at all. The architecture of the ship has always been a mystery, as you know, but I've seen no evidence of a Mind of this magnitude concealed within it. The core you met seems sentient."

"Can we trust it? Was it put there by Concordance?"

"Again, if it was, why have they left us unmolested for so long? We've been in the *Radiant Dragon*'s power often."

"You noticed it referred to the planet as Coronade?"

"I did."

"Has the ship ever been drawn into a gravity well in metaspace like that before?" she asked.

"Not to my knowledge. I wonder if the modifications we made to the ship had some effect upon it, allowed you to make the breakthrough you did. Or it might be that the risk you took finally awakened a self-preservation impulse inside it that we simply had no idea was there."

"At last you approve of my cavalier approach to metaspace jumps."

He laughed at her words. "In this one case, perhaps. I still think that, as a general rule, you take too many risks. Tell me, what state is the *Radiant Dragon* in now?"

She looked around at the blank walls of the cartography deck. "Hard to say. I have navigation and life-support, obviously, and all the drives are functioning, but I can't get any response if I try and talk to the ship. It's like all the automatic systems are functioning as programmed, but anything requiring a higher degree of intellect has shut down. The *Dragon* is in a coma, organs functioning but closed off to outside reality. We certainly can't leave it to act on its own free-will. Right now, I'm not sure it's got any."

"That is unfortunate," said Ondo. "Because I rather think time is suddenly very short."

"Why so?"

"This is the other reason I left the Refuge. Something came up."

"You found useful information in the Depository images?"

"I'm finding a great deal of interest, but that isn't it. I started to pick up signs from the nanosensor network of a sudden flurry of Concordance activity: ships jumping out of systems they've been monitoring for years, a tenfold uptick in encrypted comms chatter, a web of metaspace trails. The sensors are programmed to cut short their circuits and report back if they see a certain level of unusual activity. I've seen mobilisations like this before, although never on this scale. My guess is that they're urgently looking for us."

"Or it's a coincidence," she said.

"Do you want to take that risk?"

"They could have sent many more ships to Coronade. I was outnumbered, sure, but they left holes in their net for me to escape through. That's one reason I'm following the approach protocols so carefully, in case they wanted me to believe I'd escaped."

"I'm sure they wouldn't think twice about sacrificing Cathedral ships to track us down, so I assume they sent a fleet to a number of potential flashpoints, anticipating our arrival at one of them. Somehow, they're getting clues about what we're doing without knowing the precise details."

"Any idea yet how they do that?"

"None."

Selene considered, weighing up the best course of action to take. "They're going to be watching Coronade closely now; it won't be at all easy to go back there."

"Before we do anything, we need to study the telemetry

you harvested. I'm getting initial results now."

Their ships were close, almost touching. She decelerated to pause a few hundred metres away from him.

"You should EVA over," she said. "The *Aether Dragon* is not in good shape."

"It'll hold together for a little while yet. At least its Mind isn't in a catatonic fugue."

He sent what he was uncovering for her to study. The atmospheric probes had clearly had a lot of trouble detecting anything on the surface, blasted as they were by supersonic winds and fierce electrical storms. They'd repeatedly lost global positioning lock, meaning that what few readings of surface detail they'd picked up were sketchy, with a high degree of uncertainty.

But there *was* detail. By correlating the data retrieved by multiple sensors, the *Aether Dragon* was able to work out the likely location of coastlines, map them onto a globe to produce an approximate continental layout. When it was done, it compared what it had to the known layout of the historic Coronade seen from Ondo's original images. The match was 97%, and the chance of two planets winding up with an arrangement of tectonic plates that close by chance was effectively zero.

The planet could only be Coronade.

The sensors had picked up more than just coastlines, though. There were artificial structures, their shapes highly regular: cities, perhaps, or large buildings of a function she couldn't guess at. They were on the land *and* the sea: the oceanic islands were there; round and polygonal land masses, all symmetrical. There was no sign of life, no light, nothing being broadcast in the radio spectrum, not even any microbial life in the atmosphere.

"A solar shroud did this," she said, "tipping the environment into meltdown."

"I'm not so sure." Ondo indicated a circular structure in the fuzzy imagery. "This circle could be a sizable impact crater, and here's another one. It looks to me like the planet was subject to bombardment on a massive scale."

"They'd have to be seriously huge impacts to kick up enough debris to leave the planet like this."

"They would," said Ondo.

She thought about that. "The ship's Mind was convinced the planet had multiple moons, it talked about one being the third biggest, but there's definitely only a single body now. Were they pulled into the planet?"

"Pulled or pushed. It would be enough to explain the massive environmental breakdown, but it's hard to understand how that could happen. By definition any settled world would have achieved a high degree of gravitational and orbital stability. Anything less would make it uninhabitable."

"Concordance did this."

"That would be my guess," said Ondo. "They wanted to destroy the world utterly, because it was the symbolic capital of galactic culture."

"Or maybe there's something down there, some weapon or technology they were afraid could be turned against them. Those ships I encountered: they may have been sent simply to make sure I didn't find it."

A set of structures in the middle of one of the larger oceans was outlined briefly in red, the *Aether Dragon* highlighting them for attention.

"It's spotted something," said Ondo. "A match with a known pattern."

The shapes on the planetary surface had been cleaned up a little, but the edges were still indistinct, gaps in them where the sensors had lost visibility or were destroyed. She could pick out a large central circle in the middle of one of the oceans, with lines radiating from it at apparently random angles, like an incomplete compass rose. Other circles, smaller, were strung out along the lines at varying distances. She could neither see nor calculate any particular pattern to the arrangement. It appeared the central circle had suffered considerable impact damage, an elongated impact crater was stamped right across it, but the smaller orbital circles looked intact.

"What is it matching on?" she asked. "Have you seen anything like this before?"

"I haven't, but you have. At the Depository, in those stasis fields, it's seeing a correlation with those land structures and one of the objects."

The item she'd thought was jewellery, the silver talisman with slots for beads spaced along its radiating lines. She brought an image of the object to mind and overlaid it upon the telemetry. The *Aether Dragon* was correct; there was a clear match.

Ondo was apparently doing the same. "This is what we were supposed to find." The excitement thrumming through him was completely clear over the comms link. "This is where the trail leads."

She said, "We're uncovering a picture not following a path given to us. *We've* found this, we have free-will — which includes the freedom to go and get ourselves killed. But I concede this structure could be what Concordance are trying to stop us finding."

"A structure they tried to destroy when they attacked the planet," said Ondo.

She addressed the *Aether Dragon* directly. "The vision I got from the *Radiant Dragon*, the hole in the atmosphere tunnelling to the surface, can you identify where that would have been?"

The Mind of Ondo's ship took several seconds to complete the calculations before replying. "Assuming the location identified corresponded with the actual point on the surface then underneath you, the atmospheric tunnel would have terminated directly onto this large island."

"How sure are you?"

"More than 99%."

Good enough. "*This* is the gateway then?" she said to Ondo. "This *Gamma Spinwards Tunnel* the ship mentioned."

"Or it was at some point. The Mind you spoke to

within the core seemed to have a poor grasp of the passage of time."

"It talked about *metaspace tunnels*. Is that a term you've come across before?"

"No, it makes little sense. Metaspace jumps are obviously inherently unstable near large gravitational masses. The notion of having *tunnels* through the void that terminate on a planet is incomprehensible according to all the physics we currently understand."

"Except, our understanding is clearly flawed," she said. "The *Radiant Dragon* proved that by pulling me out of the gravity well. Assuming there was once some sort of gateway on the planet, can you speculate where would it lead to?"

"I have no idea," said Ondo. "But I'd love to find out. However, even if there was, once, a metaspace entry point on the planet, there's every possibility it is now inactive, given the environmental destruction."

Selene considered their options. "The planet's atmosphere would be extremely hazardous to navigate, but it would at least offer us some cover to work under if we could reach it. The difficulty will be in getting there."

She thought he was going to counsel caution, wait a few months or a few years for activity in the system to die down. Instead, he said, "Time may be short: the upswing in Concordance activity suggests they're acting. And now you've been seen there, there of all the places in the galaxy. If they were attempting to destroy this structure three hundred years ago, they may return now to finish the job."

"A jump from metaspace directly into the planet's atmosphere would do it," said Selene. "Perhaps that's something the *Radiant Dragon* is capable of, if the core Mind takes control of the ship."

"It talked only about navigating metaspace topography to avoid a gravity well, not about deliberately flying into one. In any case, that Mind remains completely locked away. I've been trying to reach it, but it is unresponsive, closed off. So far as I can tell it isn't even there."

Her own efforts had yielded the same results. "It took an imminent threat to get it to reveal itself last time. Perhaps we could engineer one, fly in-system under reaction drive and wait for Concordance to come for us." She was joking. She was pretty sure she was joking.

"Too risky, even for you," said Ondo. "Besides, we've been in imminent danger many times in normal space and this Mind has never shown itself. I think we have to assume its magical powers are limited to the effect you witnessed."

"We have two ships, now," she mused, "that could help. We use the *Aether Dragon* as a decoy, while we sneak in from the other direction aboard the *Radiant*."

"We'll be lucky if the *Aether Dragon* can manage one more jump," said Ondo.

"That's all we need. You come onto this ship and we'll send the *Aether* into the system, all weaponry blazing, making as much sound and fury as possible. It might buy us enough time to reach the planet."

"We have precious few ships as it is, as you know. Losing this one, battered and broken as it is, would be a huge loss. But … perhaps it is the only way."

"The fogging technology Concordance use. You said you were attempting to reproduce it?"

"I am, but I haven't been able to achieve anything like the effects they have. Aefrid had some fused components from the mechanism of a Concordance ship that she'd recovered, and I've been able to dig up a few more clues. They've given me some indications, but there's still much I don't understand in the functioning of the technology, especially in the way it obscures a ship's wake through metaspace."

"Have you ever deployed the tech in the field, used it to avoid them?"

"No, it's never been ready."

"But it's functional?"

"Barely."

"Then, let's use it now, once we emerge from metaspace. It might give us an edge, especially if they aren't expecting it. Can you deploy it on the *Radiant Dragon*?"

"It's already there, I was using the ship for my experiments."

"Then, let's go and hit Coronade before Concordance can muster the defences to stop us."

"Yes, except, I wonder..."

"What?"

He took a few moments to respond as he worked something out. "The artefact you saw at the Depository: what if it wasn't merely decorative, but a part of a mechanism? It has to be connected somehow. If we had that with us, it might ... activate the mechanism, or at least help us make sense of things. Or do *something*. I've uncovered mention of navigational totems over the years, along with the suggestion that they had some practical purpose. I thought maybe they were simple maps, but the presence of a bead like the one recovered from the hulk suggests to me now that the device has a computational function. At the very least it might be a datastore."

"I got the very clear impression the Warden did not want me to take anything, and we have no clear idea what powers it has at its command," said Selene. "And I'm not convinced the *Radiant Dragon* would be capable of making the journey again, not right now."

Ondo's face was creased as he picked through his thoughts. "Yes, agreed, but this might be our only chance to progress. We have to think before we leap; the trail might end here if we don't make the right move. There's a time to be patient, and there's a time to act. I think we have to take the chance."

"This is you saying this?"

Ondo actually chuckled. "This is me saying this."

"Would Marita have approved?"

"I think she might."

Selene replayed the images she'd recorded in the Depository. "The bead embedded in the artefact: I assumed the totem was simply incomplete, that the other beads had been lost over the years. You're suggesting that the object is, in fact, complete, and that the bead identifies the one lesser circle it is tied to. Like a key?"

"It's a possibility, isn't it? And I think, before anything, that we should upload all the data you recovered onto a nanosensor and send it out into the network, get it to the Refuge. Whatever happens, we can't lose it; it's vital proof that Concordance's version of history is wrong. If we don't survive, then hopefully someone will find it one day. We've achieved that, at least. I'll also tell the sensor to spread the data everywhere it can; get it broadcast to any worlds that are listening. We need to fight their lies with the truth."

Selene returned her attention to the telemetry images. More detail had been filled in as the *Aether Dragon* overlaid the readings captured by more of the nanosensors. The radiating lines joining the circles were clearer. Insignificant as they looked, they had to be impressive structures, hundreds of kilometres long, presumably built upon the ocean floor and rising from the depths to the surface. The islands too: all were either circular or some regular polygon. Were they all artificial or had existing landmasses been repurposed? The smaller circle corresponding to the bead looked to be intact, undamaged by any meteorite impact. Which didn't mean a damn thing; there might be nothing there but a circular lump of rock lashed by tsunami waves and death-force hurricanes. But they had to find out.

"Okay," she said, "so we're going to do this? Attempt the journey back through Dead Space, seize the object from the clutches of the Warden, hope the *Radiant Dragon* doesn't go insane or explode from the trauma of it, then return to Coronade and attempt to penetrate an extremely volatile atmosphere without Concordance seeing us but before they act to completely annihilate the planet? And *then* escape the planet and the Concordance blockade strung around it? All in the hope of uncovering the next clue in this imaginary trail you think we're following?"

"Yes," said Ondo. "I think that's what we should do."

"In that case, leave the *Aether Dragon* where it is, EVA over, and we'll get started."

4. The Metakey

Once again, the *Radiant Dragon* struggled against Selene's navigational inputs as she attempted to steer it along the complex path through Dead Space. It felt like multiple personalities were warring inside the ship's Mind, some friendly to her, others hostile. She flew manually, not trusting the ship to obey the course if she laid it all in beforehand, fearing the ship might simply refuse to fly, or steer them into a star rather than face the pain of repeating the journey to the Depository.

So far, the navigational controls were more-or-less responding, but with each jump she sensed more resistance from the ship, a swelling reaction that was something like anger and something like fear. She was forcing the ship to take a series of actions that went fundamentally against its nature, and the effect was inflicting further damage upon the ship's core. She found herself apologizing out loud at each shudder running through the bulkheads. She tried to reach that inner Mind, offer it explanation, but it remained locked away. Sweat trickled down her back from the effort of directing the vessel.

She caught Ondo's eye. "Can you hear it, too? The screaming? The whole ship cries out for us to stop."

"I hear it," said Ondo quietly. His distaste at what they were doing was clear in his eyes.

"Perhaps they're locks put in place by Concordance to stop anyone using the ship to reach the Depository," she said. She knew she was saying it to make herself feel better. The ship's resistance went too deep; it felt *terrified*. "Are similar strictures built into the *Aether Dragon*?"

"In my experience, all vessels built by pre-Omnian War civilisations had such bars embedded into their navigational systems. Whatever the perceived danger is, it goes deep."

"It may have been a cultural response to revered sites. Like, sacred ground."

"I could have believed that if it was only a few cultures, but not all of them."

"This golden age of yours – perhaps this was one of their spiritual beliefs or their social taboos. Regions of space only the elect few could approach."

Ondo shook his head. "It seems so unlikely. We know little of the culture, of course, and all cultures are complex, conflicted melanges rather than a single, simple *thing*. But from all I've learned, I don't believe it. They seemed so enlightened, so advanced."

"But those are all subjective concepts, and you're defining what you consider to be *advanced*. Besides, they weren't so superior that they didn't crumble when Concordance burst out of the galactic centre."

Ondo was about to reply when a shock jolted through the ship, as if they'd struck something solid – impossible as that was in metaspace. A look of anxiety shot between them.

"This is going to get worse before it gets better," he said. "Even if the ship doesn't refuse to follow your instructions, it might tear itself to pieces before we get there."

"If we do get there, let's just hope it feels better about getting away afterwards. Flying like this is agony, it's tearing my head in two."

In the end, they stuttered rather than jumped into existence within visual range of the blue dwarf star. Selene detached her mind from the ship's navigational controls with a sense of huge relief. It was like some constant, nerve-shredding noise finally stopping, the absence of it glorious.

Ondo placed a reassuring hand on her shoulder. "No sign of any Concordance incursion at all. If they have scrambled to protect multiple locations, this doesn't appear to be one of them."

Her *eyes* ached from the effort of forcing the ship to move. "Or they left when we showed up at Coronade."

Ondo was examining telemetry while Selene stood and stretched. He said, "The nanosensors you left indicate no activity whatsoever. Either they're waiting beyond our light-speed horizon, or they're simply not here."

"Let's get in and out before they show up," she said. "The sooner we can leave here, the better."

This time they took a lander down to the alien planet, boiling under the harsh blue light of the raging star. The previous time, she'd only made it into the pyramidal structure by racing against the damage that the hard radiation was inflicting upon her suit, but she doubted Ondo would be strong enough for such an effort. She nestled the tiny ship down between two of the high, converging walls, thirty metres from the triangular entranceway.

The building was exactly as she'd left it, no sign that Concordance or anyone else had been there since her visit, no footprints in the dust other than her own. That was something. She hurried towards the centre of the vault where the door had appeared. Ondo lingered behind her, turning around, fascinated by every detail of the alien structure.

"The age of this place," he mused over the comms, but mostly speaking to himself. "Do I have this wrong? I thought it might predate the war by a few years, a few centuries, but now I see it properly, I don't know. It could be millennia older. But then, who built it? And why? This hard radiation … perhaps a spectroscopic analysis of the walls would tell me something."

"We have to hurry, remember," she called to him. "Galaxy under threat, enemies massing to defeat us, clock ticking."

"Of course. It's just … this structure. I could study it for decades."

"Please don't, not now anyway. Give me the bead."

He handed her the glass sphere he'd brought with him from the Refuge. Clutching it in her gauntlet, she strode confidently towards the point where the doorway had appeared. As before, she sensed the electromagnetic tickle of the mechanism before the oblong slid out of the floor. Clearly visible through it lay the gallery with its multitude of plinths, stretching impossibly away into an unknown distance.

"After you," she said.

"Did you have any feeling of translation last time, like a fall into metaspace?"

"Nothing. It's as easy as stepping through a door."

"You said there was atmosphere in there. How does it not escape when the entrance appears?"

"I have no idea; some mechanism prevents the inner vault from explosive decompression. None of this makes sense; the vault is clearly not directly *here*. Are we going to go in?"

"Yes. Of course."

She followed him as he stepped through.

As before, the doorway slid back into the floor as they strode into the cavernous vault that was either deep underground – or somewhere else entirely. So far as she could tell, the artefacts on the plinths were arranged in the same order as before. She'd dispersed nanosensors on her previous visit, but she couldn't detect a whisper from them. As before, she overrode the life-support alerts from her suit and slid back her visor.

"Are you sure that's wise?" asked Ondo.

"Not completely."

"What happens if you accidentally go near the doorway and it activates?"

"Whoever built this place knew what they were doing. There's no damage here despite the planetary bombardment the surface structures have been subjected to."

After a moment, Ondo slid back his own helmet. "This talk about metaspace tunnels … I can't help wondering if we're even on the same planet. We might be anywhere."

"None of my sensors can provide any kind of positioning lock. The gravity's the same as outside, that's all I know."

Ondo leaned in to examine each artefact closely, peering through his multiglasses to study each across a wide spectrum of electromagnetic radiation, walking around the plinths to see each object from every angle. He muttered to himself as he did so, "This is incredible. But how? I don't even… Oh, now *this*..."

The moving object, the X-shaped four-legged spider thing, especially fascinated him as it flicked to and fro inside its stasis containment.

"Do you see it move?" he asked.

His question puzzled her. "You don't?"

"I see it disappear and reappear, but I don't see it occupying the spatial points in between."

She looked closer. He was right; there were no intervening points in the object's movement that she could detect. "Some sort of drive mechanism? Or a prototype of one?" she suggested.

"I could spend lifetimes down here studying these objects," was his only answer.

They moved to the item they'd come for: the silvery totem whose arrangement of lines and rings resembled the structures on the surface of Coronade. Selene scanned the object more closely, looking for details she might have missed. There were no markings, but the higher-resolution images revealed an even greater fidelity to the layout of the planetary islands. Either the object had been made to accurately represent the land masses, or the islands had been constructed to replicate the object. Or both were based on some other, unknown design.

"How did you summon the Warden before?" asked Ondo. "It must know what these objects are, what their function is."

"Last time it turned up when I spoke out loud. Maybe it's broken completely now and can't materialize."

"What did you say last time?"

"You know me, I'm always polite. Just *hello*."

Ondo raised his voice to address the entire room. "Hello. Please, we need you."

The shimmering, slow-motion explosion flickered into existence. It had clearly been aware of their presence all along but was only manifesting when summoned. It seemed its original purpose was to be helpful rather than protective, but that didn't mean it couldn't be both.

"We'd like to take this object," she said. Always best to take the direct approach. "You said you kept them under your warding until the day they are needed. We need this one now."

The shards of light making up the entity's form swirled and glinted, as if it were giving her request due thought.

"The long night..." it began.

She held up her hand. "The long night must see a dawn, yes. This is us, trying to bring it about. You must release this object."

"The long night," it said again, then stopped. Its neural pathways were fritzed to fuck; reasoning with it wasn't going to get them very far. She drew the blaster held in her suit's thigh holster and pointed it at the next plinth, the statue of the bipedal being. Which, now that she thought about it, somewhat resembled the entity inside the *Radiant Dragon*'s core, with its elongated limbs and head. Was that significant?

"A night without a dawn isn't a night," she said. "It's just endless darkness. I will start destroying these artefacts, one by one. Give us this item, and we'll be on our way, no damage done."

The shifting planes of the entity glinted with different colours, purples flashing into reds that it was hard not to interpret as anger or a threat. A rising whine came from it as some energy store built up charge. Either it was going to blast her to pieces and was having trouble lining the components of its weapons systems up, or it was simply going to explode from the suppressed effort of it. She'd hoped it would sacrifice one of the artefacts to save the rest, but it didn't look like that was going to work out. It was planning to sacrifice her and Ondo instead.

She flicked her aim to the plinth containing the totem they wanted. Maybe she could blast out the stasis field and grab the object before the Warden pulled itself together. She was sending the fire commands to the gun when Ondo intervened, stepping forwards to stand between her and the plinth, hands held up in a clear attempt to placate the alien mechanism. Only her augmented reactions stopped her firing and punching a hole clean through his body.

"Please, there is no need for this," he said. "We need to activate the Gamma Spinwards Tunnel."

For one, two seconds, the entity stopped flashing, stopped swirling as it absorbed Ondo's words. It appeared to understand what he was talking about. She knew for a fact that Ondo did not.

"The Tunnel is dark," said the entity. "Sealed off. The risk is too great."

Selene caught the flash of delight on Ondo's features as he glanced back at her over the swelling of his helmet yoke. His guess had struck home.

"We wish to open the Tunnel again," said Ondo.

He held up his gauntlet and projected moving images from it into the air in front of the entity. They were the correlated telemetry streams she'd pulled from Coronade, rendered as a complete globe, the land masses of the continents and, clearly visible, the pattern of islands and lines in the ocean. Ondo had subtly emphasised them, marking them out for clarity.

Selene talked to him directly, brain-to-brain. She had to hope the Warden entity didn't have the technomagic required to decrypt what they were saying. "If this entity thinks we're going to try and use this tunnel, it might decide it's best to kill both of us."

"Perhaps," Ondo replied, "but it hasn't done so yet. I think it's confused about us. Whoever placed these objects under its care clearly assumed the time would come for them to be released, or else why go to so much trouble? The same may be true of the Coronade structures; they also haven't been wiped from the face of the galaxy. I think that's because, someday, it was thought they might be needed."

"You don't know they haven't been destroyed. You want to think there's something active on Coronade, I get it, but there may not be, not anymore."

The entity still hadn't responded. Ondo spoke out loud to it. "The Gamma Spinwards Tunnel is damaged and broken, but we believe it has survived. The risk of using it may be great, but so is the danger of doing nothing. You must be capable of weighing up the best course of action, to decide what is best for the objects in your care. The galaxy is reaching a turning point, and if we don't take the correct step, all could be lost. The dawn may never come."

Was any of that true? The Warden was certainly spending its time considering Ondo's words. The energy signature within it was a constant, jarring note in her head: not falling back, but not climbing either. She picked up stutters in it, hesitations, as if the entity were drawing on all its reserves to perform its computations.

Ondo pressed his point, a catch of emotion in his voice. "Please. I have followed this trail for many years, for most of my life. I have dug in the dust of dead planets only to find more dust, and I've been lost in the despair of dead-ends, feeling I would never uncover the secrets. I have been shown only glimpses and shadows. Now, here, you must let me take the next step."

The entity finally responded. It shimmered backwards, like it was getting a good angle to spray both of them with blaster fire. The constituent shards of its body pulsed and swirled, and then finally aligned into the shape of the body it had intended to have all along. Or, in fact, multiple forms: different arrangements and structures to suit the different needs it might have. It morphed into a squat tank-like entity bristling with kill-weaponry, then to a small, slight sliver of life little more than a shaft of light, then to a towering form with an elongated, animal head that had to be, from its jackhammer limbs, immensely strong. Maybe it had drawn greater energy from its surroundings and, for a moment, and quite literally, pulled itself together. Finally, it settled on a polished-smooth black body, like the blank of a person before all the features were added, a standardish bipedal form like, she thought, her artificial half before any features were added.

As the Warden's body and movements came together, so, apparently, did its thoughts. It began to speak in complete sentences rather than broken fragments. "In the darkness of your mind, you imagine what is not there, Ondo Lagan. I do not know what this dream-journey you describe is, nor where it may take you. But you may take a metakey. This one however, must remain under my guard. The gateway it controls is to remain sealed until the end of days."

With a sweep of one of its arms, it set the winding row of plinths into sudden motion. Selene flung herself back from them, pulling Ondo with her. The line of objects slid past at a greater and greater rate, as if the white floor were a conveyor belt, although she could see no join, no mechanism by which the meandering line could be moving.

The columns picked up speed, faster and faster until only her left eye could resolve each in the millisecond moment they were in front of her. More and more unfathomable objects, small and large, their nature mechanical, organic, unidentifiable. She caught Ondo's look: his senses were enhanced, too, but not as highly as hers. She could count the objects, image each, but to him they would be nothing more than a blur.

Through them, in staccato freeze-frames, the featureless black form of the Warden looked on.

Abruptly, the plinths stopped, seemingly untroubled by their former momentum. The plinth directly before them bore another silver totem like the one they were seeking. Stepping forwards, Selene could see that the single bead it contained occupied a different circle within its design. The good news was, the island it corresponded to on Coronade was another that had survived the planetary bombardment.

The Warden did something to the mechanism, sent instructions to it, and the stasis field around the object dissipated, exposing the totem to the air. The invitation was clear. Not waiting to be asked, Selene picked it from its pedestal.

It was surprisingly weighty, constructed from a dense metallic substance she couldn't identify. The Warden made no attempt to stop her removing the object.

"Can we take this?" she asked. "You'll let us walk out of here carrying it?"

"I will. The night must have a dawn."

"How do you know you can trust us to do the right thing?"

"The ship that carries you is weak, torn by the rigours of your journeys here. Still, in its broken state, it vouches for you, croaks to me who and what you are. It tells me you should take the metakey."

It took them both a moment to work out the meaning of the Warden's words.

"You've been in communication with the *Radiant Dragon*?" she asked.

"I hear him. He bleeds into the void, but still he fights for you."

"He? Who is *he*?"

The Warden ignored them, and the line of plinths began to move again, streaming in the opposite direction until, in a few moments, the originals were in their former place in front of them. In seven seconds, she counted 3,212 items flying past. The doorway they'd come through slid into existence. The meaning of that was clear, too. They were to leave.

But, before they did so, Ondo turned to address the Warden once more. "This long night you talk about, how long has it been precisely?"

Spiderweb lines appeared on the Warden's body, white, dividing its surface into a series of geometric shapes. Then its hard form fractured to return to the cloud of spinning mirrors and planes, its integrity apparently unsustainable. At the same time, it reverted to talking in its vague metaphors and half-sentences. "The long night."

Ondo tried again. "Please, the moving object, the four-legged spider. What is that?"

"The night without a morning. The eternal darkness."

"This whole place, all these artefacts. Who placed them here, and when? And why did they do so?"

This time, instead of answering, the shards of the Warden's form swirled and glinted blue for a moment, then blinked out of existence.

"I think we've had all the help it's going to give us," said Selene. "Do you think this *eternal darkness* is Concordance? A metaphor because it couldn't find the right words?"

Ondo was looking around, clearly longing to remain in

the hall of artefacts. Remain and maybe never leave. "Or it was describing the weapon Vulpis encountered, some technology capable of fearsome destruction."

"We should go."

"Yes."

Their visors resealed, they returned to the outer chamber and then out into the searing radiation of the blue sun. She carried the totem they'd retrieved, the *metakey*, in her gauntlet. Her breath rushed in her ears as they hustled back to the lander. Neither of them spoke. When they reached the safety of the *Radiant Dragon*, Selene placed her hand onto the airlock bulkhead for a moment, seeking the ship's core Mind. It was also, perhaps, a gesture of contact or gratitude. The entity remained locked away from her. Whatever the Warden had done to establish contact, she could not reproduce it.

But she did detect, as they rose from the planet and accelerated away from the star for metaspace translation, a sense of something like relief. Whether it was hers, or an emotion she was picking up from the ship, she couldn't say.

Ondo, meanwhile, was clearly having trouble tearing himself away from the system and its mysteries: his attention was now consumed by telemetry from the mesh that surrounded the star and its planet.

"You say you passed through the gap in the mesh last time?" he asked.

"Ten or twenty metres, no more. You see something?"

"Hard to be sure. Odd energy signatures. So far as I can tell, the gap is having a lensing effect, diffracting the radiation from outside in unusual ways. Either that or the radiation itself is unusual."

"We do not have time to go and investigate, you do know that, don't you?"

"Yes, yes. Did you detect anything beyond the gap? Anything anomalous?"

"You saw every datum of telemetry I recovered. Why

do you ask?"

"The readings are … odd."

"Every damned thing here is odd, but whatever's out there will have to wait; we're running up to metaspace translation now."

"We could…" But his objections were cut short as she activated the metaspace projectors, and the ship swoop-dropped out of normal space, the dizzying headlong rush of it stilling them both.

As before, the *Dragon* trembled and bucked as they followed the careful sequence of dance steps through the void, but it responded to her navigational inputs without deviation. Eventually, they dropped into normal space at the point where they'd left the *Aether Dragon*. Selene sent across her final instructions for their assault on Coronade to the other ship, then the two vessels accelerated into their translation run-ups together.

As she'd feared, Concordance activity had redoubled since her escape from the system. Beyond a certain range, it was impossible to know what was truly taking place, but they could see a bustle of activity around Coronade itself, as well as a cluster of Cathedral ships nearer the sun.

"What are they doing there?" Ondo mused as they stood within the three-dimensional model of the system. "What is this fascination with stars?"

"Who cares?" said Selene. "Some religious obsession we can't begin to understand. It's the ships near the planet we need to worry about. The question is, which will react when the *Aether Dragon* shows up."

"Assuming it holds together long enough to survive the translation."

"It has to. Without it, we have no chance of getting back to the planet."

They didn't have to wait long. The unmanned vessel had been instructed to materialise on the opposite side of the ecliptic disc from Selene and Ondo, two hundred million kilometres farther away from the star. The first indications they picked up was the sight of a number of closer Concordance vessels reacting, breaking orbit from the planet and accelerating onto vectors that matched the *Aether Dragon*'s assigned incursion point.

"It made it," said Selene.

"Yes. The ship's last act."

"Have you ever used multiple vessels before? Do Concordance know you have them?"

"I don't believe they do. They'll assume they've picked up the arrival of the *Radiant Dragon*. They'll realise soon enough their mistake."

Another two Cathedral ships manoeuvred to join the attack, surrounded by an insect cloud of Void Walker attack ships. Selene itched to flare the *Radiant Dragon*'s reaction drives, push into the system. She held back; once again the timing of it was critical. Move too soon, and the Concordance ships would return to intercept them. Move too late, and they'd be returning anyway, the *Aether Dragon* obliterated.

Finally, she could bear it no longer. They'd hit the earliest moment that their incursion was viable, but they didn't really know the optimal point. Always, there might be unknown Concordance ships arriving from outside their sphere of knowledge. At some point, they had to take a chance.

"Let's see how good this fogging technology of yours is," she said.

She fired the reaction drives, pushing the *Radiant Dragon* onto a maximum acceleration intercept course with Coronade. Once again, the plan depended upon achieving the highest possible velocity – which, once again, increased their chances of being able to flash through the ring of Concordance defences and flee back to metaspace at the expense of tactical manoeuvrability.

She felt the fogging system kick in. Ondo had explained it was a rapid series of partial and abandoned metaspace translations, too quick for any dangerous gravitational effect to pull them in. The sensation of it was disconcerting, like being shaken violently, although to her eyes the bulkheads around her remained solid and unmoving. The ship, too, reacted; she felt unease juddering through it as they sped forwards.

They finally picked up telemetry from the *Aether Dragon*, speeding in-system on its allotted trajectory. It was behaving precisely as intended, drawing Concordance vessels towards it. Once it was clear it had been spotted, it powered up its beam-weapon arrays. They were puny and would do little damage to a Cathedral ship, but Concordance would pick up the energy signature change and might be pulled a little deeper into the deception.

The battle, when it came, didn't last long. All but three of the Concordance vessels peeled away before they reached weapons' range as realisation of the deception struck. The remaining ships pressed on. Beam-weaponry and missile arrays blazed. The events unfolded twenty light-minutes away, meaning that the *Aether Dragon* was already long-gone by the time they saw its final destruction, but it was still a sobering moment.

Selene returned her attention to the Cathedral ships that had pulled out of the attack, watching as they arced onto return vectors for Coronade, studying how they intended to slot back into the shield around the world. Here was another critical moment when everything could go wrong: if the defensive shield was reconstructed quickly enough, there might be no way through.

It wasn't good. Accelerating at maximum g even as they were, it soon became clear that the bulk of the Cathedral ships would beat them to Coronade. The pretence with the *Aether Dragon* hadn't fooled Concordance for long enough. The only hope she and Ondo had lay in remaining undetected until the last moment. They stayed on course, powering towards the planet and its single surviving moon. Each passing instant increased their odds by a few points, even if their overall chances of success were, by Selene's projections, poor.

There came the moment when a Concordance sensor or vessel spotted them. She saw attack ships flare into action, breaking away onto intercept trajectories. The heavier, more momentum-bound Cathedral ships followed. Now was the critical moment of the action: the vectors they adopted; the intercept points picked. The dance of starships and planet and moon.

"There," she said, the trajectories in space and time filling her mind. "There is our window." It was tiny, much smaller than she would have liked, but it would have to do. Their velocity meant that the reacting Concordance ships had to scramble onto vectors beyond the planet. Were they confused by the *Radiant Dragon*'s trajectory? They had to know she couldn't possibly decelerate in time for atmospheric insertion. The hope was that Concordance would think she was skimming the planet to pick up more telemetry. It seemed they'd bought it. Which meant that, as the enemy ships manoeuvred and their spheres of awareness shifted, there was the briefest moment in the shadow of the moon when the *Dragon* would be unobserved. There was the chance. Free-floating nanosensors might still spot them, but they had to hope that the Cathedral ships' controlling Minds, or their convocation circles, ignored that telemetry for long enough.

Time, suddenly, was short. She and Ondo raced down the curving walkways of the *Dragon* to the lander bay. They strapped themselves into their seats while they checked systems were fully functional. Outside, their window of undetectability shrank even further as a Cathedral ship moved onto an unanticipated vector, but the shot was still there.

Her mind filled with the ballet of ships, she waited for the critical moment, the millisecond, when the lander could fling itself free of the *Dragon*.

There. She fired the commands, the brief lag of them built into her calculations. The lander fired itself out of the bay, the moon alarmingly near, and immediately flared its reaction drives, adding its own thrust to the acceleration the *Dragon* had given it. The high-g was gruelling, even for her. Next to her, Ondo blacked out. Her own organic brain was doing the same. As before, only her artificial self remained alert, controlling the trajectory as they grazed the surface of the moon at a speed that would mean instant annihilation if she misjudged things by a few centimetres.

Now the only question was whether Concordance would fall for this second feint. The *Radiant Dragon* was already light-seconds away, accelerating hard on its trajectory out-system. Once again, it would use the slight slingshot effect of the planet to move onto an unexpected vector, increasing its odds of escaping the system a little. It still didn't look to be enough. Multiple Concordance ships converged on it, from the planet and from the sun, aggressive trajectories that clearly indicated the intent to destroy the ship before it could jump.

The *Radiant Dragon* would escape or be obliterated. Whichever it was, half the surviving Concordance ships would return to the planet immediately afterwards. That was the window. She and Ondo had to attempt atmospheric insertion now, race for the planet in plain view and simply hope they could reach it in time.

The moon filled the lander's forwards view. She had to fight all her instincts to pull away. The ship, mercifully, was quiescent, obeying her commands. There was no high-powered Mind controlling it; it was simply a vehicle. Peeping over the limb of the moon, directly ahead, the grey smudge of Coronade was rising.

They grazed the grey, rocky surface of the moon. She nudged the lander into a valley between two hills and for a moment the outcrops of rocks were actually above them, the hard surfaces of the walls three metres from the voidhull of the lander. The slightest brushing contact would spell disaster.

Then they shot free, and the moon was behind them. The dash for the planet would take long minutes, longer because they'd have to decelerate hard as they neared. Now there was little she could do but hope. The Concordance fleet was still preoccupied with the *Radiant Dragon*. That much of the plan was succeeding. Two Cathedral ships had remained in orbit of Coronade, but they were over the horizon, eclipsed by the planet's bulk. Once again, each passing second improved her and Ondo's odds by a notch. A precious few percentage points, counting up impossibly slowly.

Once again, she saw the moment when Concordance became aware of them. Ondo, stirring, saw it too. "They are coming."

Selene ran the calculations through her brain, saw how it would go. "We'll make it, but barely. We'll have to hit the atmosphere a lot harder than I'd have liked."

She could hear the tension in his voice, his effort to remain calm. "The hull may not withstand the thermal shock."

He was right. Nothing to be done about it. It certainly wouldn't withstand an assault from multiple Cathedral ships and Void Walkers.

She left the deceleration as long she dared, then counted three more long seconds, before firing the forwards reaction drives and killing the aft. Judders shook through the lander as it flipped from high-g acceleration to deceleration. It felt like the tiny ship was going to rattle itself into its constituent components from the stresses running through it.

Their velocity was still high, dangerously high, as they hit the first wisps of the atmosphere. At the same moment, beam-weapon shots from the nearest attack ships flickered and flickered around them.

5. Dead Star

As they crashed through the atmosphere of Coronade, it was her two ascents from Maes Far in identical landers that came back to Selene. She saw again the blinding light of the Cathedral ship's beam-weapon strike from her first ascent, the gaping gulf of air beneath her as her fuselage was cut away and she spiralled out of control. She lived again the violence of the concussions shaking through the craft, the helplessness of her situation. The wanting it to end. She saw again, also, the blinding plume of the nuke blasts from her second ascent, moments after the murder of her father.

Perhaps Ondo guessed what she was going through. He spoke directly to her, brain-to-brain. "Are you okay?"

She nodded to him, forced herself to concentrate. "They'll struggle to target us as these winds throw us around. They'll be as blind as we are."

Their headlong plunge at least slowed them down, but they paid for the velocity they dumped in mounting thermal energy. Before jumping in-system, they'd amped-up the lander's energy hull as much as possible, routing energy from weapons-systems and anything else that could be considered non-essential.

The energy hull did what it was designed to do, shunting heat away from the planetward edges of the craft, but it simply couldn't do so rapidly enough. The shield reacted to the mounting thermal load of the raging heat by drawing more power, overdriving its propagation arrays and diminishing its ability to protect the craft. Selene watched the numbers coming from the hull as they ticked rapidly down. The degraded system went into a failure cascade, its protection levels falling from 100% to 0 in 27 seconds.

After that, it was the voidhull's bare metal against the thermal shock of their entry into the atmosphere. They'd had no time to enhance the lander's physical structure in any way. It was designed to withstand hot entries, steep insertion corridors, but they were flying well beyond its operational capabilities.

Fortunately, the extreme violence of Coronade's high atmosphere came to their aid. They hit supersonic winds, denser and denser as they fell, and the rapidly-moving air streamed the heat away far more effectively than the energy hull had been able to. They reached a point where the hull's temperature peaked, then began to slide back towards the outer edges of its ideal safety levels.

Once again, they were made to pay for it, this time by the increasing violence of the turbulent atmosphere. As they dropped through the raging air streams, they were hurled around like dried peas in an empty box, rattling Selene's brain until it hurt.

They left a trail of free-floating sensors behind them, in the hope that they could triangulate off them and maintain an approximate navigational lock on the circular oceanic islands they were aiming for. Their trajectory was going to be vague as the sensors were blasted in every direction and they lost lock with those higher up in the air. At least she and Ondo were cut off from outside surveillance. Sunlight faded rapidly as they sank, until it was utterly dark across the visible electromagnetic spectrum. Twice she saw a sunburst of blinding yellow light flare in the atmosphere some way in the distance and far above them – an atmospheric nuke detonation, she guessed – but none exploded nearby.

Ondo said, "They may not even attempt to enter the atmosphere. They can just wait in orbit for us to emerge."

"Or wait for these winds to do their work for them," she replied.

"Or that," agreed Ondo.

The small size of the lander was an advantage as they fell: they were swept along with the screaming wind-currents rather than being pulverized by them. Selene, piloting, put all her effort into simply staying upright as they were thrown around like a leaf in a hurricane. The main risk would be as they neared the ground; the last thing she wanted was to come so far only to be dashed into the side of a mountain or flung at the ground the wrong way up. She peered downwards using the lander's sensors, mainly in the radio wave spectrum, desperate for any indistinct detail. Atmospheric pressures suggested they were within ten kilometres of the surface, but the margin of error was wide given the air's extreme turbulence.

In the end it was a faint warble from a nanosensor dropped on her previous visit that gave her the ghost of the reading she needed. She caught a glimpse of a coastline beneath the sensor. She calculated her approximate distance from the device based on its signal strength, while pattern-matching the line of the landmass with what they knew of the geography of Coronade.

The approximate fix was encouraging: they were over the western edge of the ocean containing the circular islands, around a hundred kilometres from where they needed to be. Pretty good. She glanced across at Ondo as he saw the calculations. The look of anticipation in his eyes was bright. He was so near the answers he craved.

Battling the bucking lander, she pulled the nose up to some semblance of level and eased on the undercarriage thrusters to slow their descent. The winds were less extreme at the surface, but they were still violent, scouring the rugged terrain three hundred metres below. Going down any lower was dangerous: a sudden sidewind could flip them over and dash them to the rocks before she had chance to react. She turned the lander's nose south and edged on the thrusters. They passed in and out of the base of the streaming cloud layers, enough to give her an occasional radar glimpse of the surface terrain. She picked out structures that were clearly the ruins of buildings, lining the coast for hundreds of kilometres. There were, seemingly, the outlines of many different architectural styles: the embassies and enclaves of a thousand different cultures. They passed over the ruins of a city, arranged around three wide, spiralling roads running from its centre to its edges.

Two minutes later, she picked up the radial line of the oceanic structure that would lead them across the water to the gateway island corresponding to the Warden's metakey. On their images it had been a delicate spiderweb line, but on the ground the true scale of it was apparent: it was a thirty-metre-wide bridge, joining the continental landmass to the circular islands strung out through the ocean. Its foundations had to be firmly embedded in the ocean floor bedrock, even out in the depths: a pontoon would have been swept away long ago. She turned the lander onto a vector to follow it.

Another light flared in the high atmosphere, hundreds of kilometres away. In a way it was good. Their escape plan involved lurking in the atmosphere for as long as they could stand it – Ondo had suggested a week – then bursting out at a random spot to hook up with the *Radiant Dragon*. The more nukes Concordance dropped, the more they might speculate that she and Ondo were dead.

She slowed the lander to a halt as it neared the island. It was clearly artificial: the smooth walls plunging down through the tortured oceans could be the product of no natural process. It was small, a hundred metres in diameter, and its land surface was completely flat, forty metres above the surge of the mountainous waves.

Perhaps there had been more structures upon it once, buildings swept away by repeated tsunami devastation, but there was a single object extant upon the island: a pointed stone arch in the precise centre. Battling the vicious sidewinds that threw the lander around, she put the lander onto an approach vector.

When they passed over the lip of the island, the buffeting from the air immediately cut out. They were in clear air.

"The island is shielded." said Ondo.

She studied the lander's external environment. "Partially. We're still open to the atmosphere. Sunlight too, if there were any. But the winds have been cancelled out."

"Engineered to allow ships to land safely."

"Looks that way. How can that work? And how in the name of Omn's perfectly-formed balls is it still operating?"

Ondo didn't reply, but she could tell he was quietly delighted at the discovery. She put the ship down ten metres from the arch, pointing one battery of the lander's external lights upon it so they could study it in detail. They sat in a bubble of illumination, hundreds of kilometres of raging darkness around them, the arch eerie in the gloom. Selene and Ondo suited up and descended the lander's ramp to approach, their bodies casting long shadows on the ground before them. A faint blue light glowed from the arch as they neared. It was thirty metres tall, twenty wide, and numerous symbols she couldn't read were etched around its stonework. She'd seen their like before, though: around the star charts in the viewing orb at the Depository. The archway appeared to be the product of the same technological culture.

There was a space in the line of symbols two metres off the ground. A slot into which the metakey object would fit perfectly.

"Shall we put it in and see what it does?" she said to Ondo.

"We have to."

"What if it does nothing at all?"

"Then our journey has been wasted. We've taken the wrong road."

She pulled the metakey from the leg-pocket she carried it in. Disappointingly, it didn't glow or feel warmer to the touch. She'd been expecting – what – a clue that she held the key to open up this ancient lock? *Something.* She placed the metakey into the slot.

A quiver running through the ground was the first indication that the mechanism was active. She picked up a high-pitched whine, rapidly disappearing into the far supersonic, and then the archway turned into light. It glowed white, the symbols adorning it burning in blues and reds. The space between the uprights of the arch *moved* in a way she couldn't quite identify. It swirled, and the darkness she could see through it became, somehow, blacker still. Then there was an audible *crack*, like a small sonic boom, and the space through the arch flicked to a creamy white.

Selene's left eye adjusted near-instantly to the change in illumination. The archway now led to a tunnel, leading for two hundred metres, or three, to another archway. None of it, clearly, was physically there on Coronade. Like the doorway at the Depository, if she walked around the side of the archway, she could see the tunnel leading the other way, through where she'd been standing.

"It's here," said Ondo, the delight clear in his voice. "It's really here."

Another light flared then, somewhere above them, a ball of pearlescent white in the heavy gloom of the atmosphere. Another came, and then another. It took her a moment to grasp they were nothing to do with the archway.

They were more aerial nuke blasts, nearby. Concordance had seen the lights from the lander or the archway and reacted. She and Ondo had only moments before the blast wave slammed into them. Could the safe-landing shield around the island protect them? She didn't want to wait around to find out.

Ondo still hadn't moved, still hadn't worked it out, his brain running too slowly. She grasped him by the hand and threw herself through the archway, into the whiteness of the tunnel. Ondo sprawled onto the floor while she turned to the archway. The same symbols were on this side, too, and there was the metakey, somehow on the *inside* of the doorway. She plucked it from its slot. Outside, the light of an exploding sun boiled the air. Then it was gone as the doorway blinked back to darkness.

There was a moment of calm during which neither of them moved and nothing happened. She held out a hand to haul Ondo to his feet.

He spoke out loud. "We can't go back."

"No. Not now, anyway. Perhaps not ever. But you were right about this place, your golden age and your trail through the stars. Coronade and our forgotten history. It's all real."

"The question is, what lies at the other end of this tunnel?"

"Only one way to find out."

They walked slowly, warily. The portal behind them did not open again. Concordance, it seemed, did not possess a metakey of their own, did not know the secret of the archways.

Or, she thought, maybe they *did*, and were happy for her and Ondo to take the walk they were taking.

One hundred metres along, equidistant between the two archways, she paused. Part of her brain was scanning for threats but another part had bubbled up a question from nowhere. She might not get chance to ask him again. And perhaps she simply wanted to hear his voice in the still quiet of the alien structure. Speaking over the comms link, she said, "My father … how well did he know Marita and your daughter?"

Ondo took a moment to react to the conversational switch. He stopped to look at her. "Well enough. He took being Juma's folkfather very seriously."

"In a way she would have been my sister."

A sad smile spread across Ondo's features, visible through his visor. "In a way. Except, if she'd survived, I suspect none of this would have happened, at least not to me, and Seben, and therefore you. If I hadn't lost Juma and Marita, I'd still be on Sintorus and the universe wouldn't have you in it."

"I'm sorry."

"Don't be; it is pointless to attempt to tally these things, to weigh one possible timeline against another. The galaxy unfolds as it does and this is all we have: a past we have to live with and a future we can attempt to change. And, between them, the *now*, the fleeting moment where we can act, try to do the right thing. But, given what happened, you should know I'm very glad you came into my life. Little has made sense to me over the years, but your arrival at the Refuge felt like the pieces of a broken picture slotting into place. Like the Warden suddenly becoming coherent rather than a collection of shattered pieces. You are not my daughter, of course, but I have secretly thought of you as my folkdaughter. If you don't mind."

Perhaps he was taking the opportunity to say things he might not get chance to again, as well.

"No, I don't mind," she said. "What do you hope we'll find at the end of this tunnel?"

"Hope? I *hope* to find an enclave of an unknown pre-Omnian War culture, a survivor of the golden age that can give us the answers we crave — and also the tools we need to battle Concordance." He smiled to himself. "You see, it is easy to hope."

"I haven't always found it easy."

He conceded the point with a slight nod of his head. "But when it does come, it is easy to hope for the stars. Shall we go and see?"

"Yes. We should."

The metakey activated the archway at the far end of the tunnel, just as it had at the entranceway. The arrangement was interesting; it was apparently designed to ensure that both doors couldn't be open at the same time. Like an airlock, but not for air. She let Ondo step through first before following him.

They found themselves in a circle of three archways, the one they'd stepped through and two shorter ones. Towering over them stood the ruins of a city: domes and fallen towers, rank upon rank, all dark. Beyond them lay a sky that was a blazing arc of plasma stretching from one horizon to the other, bright enough to illuminate the scene around them. It was undeniably beautiful, glowing across a wide electromagnetic spectrum.

It was hard to pick out the background stars through the nebulous cloud, but from those she could discern, she got a rough fix on their galactic coordinates. "We're nowhere near Coronade. By the look of it, we're on the opposite side of the galactic wheel completely."

"The metaspace tunnels," Ondo replied.

"I guess." She ran some more calculations, triangulating off the magnitudes of the stars she could identify. "There's something else, too: I think we're bang in the middle of one of the dead zones."

"How sure are you?"

"Pretty sure. We're in another corner of the galaxy that someone does not want us to visit."

Scanning local space with her augmentations, Selene picked out the dead sun at the system's core by its intense magnetic field: the superdense neutron star that had ejected most of its mass in the cataclysmic convulsion of its end. A supernova. The star was tiny, now, a few kilometres in diameter, blasting out gamma rays but giving off no heat. A neutron sun around which there could be no life.

Ondo was silent for a moment. She'd given him access to the enhanced telemetry her left eye could gather.

"This close the blast wave should have obliterated everything," said Ondo. "The planet's atmosphere would have been stripped away, but these structures survive. That's remarkable."

"Protected by some unknown tech, like the archways. However that works, it's clear there's no life here. There's no biosphere left."

"The ruined structures are extensive. A lot of people must have lived here. Lived and died."

"We should try the other archways. Perhaps they lead where we need to go."

The smaller archways appeared to require no metakey to activate them. White tunnels, shorter than the one they'd arrived by, were visible down both.

They tried the first and emerged on another dead planet. This time they were upon a mountain peak, the devastated world spread out around them, buildings and structures stretching to the horizon in every direction. From her readings of the dead star, she calculated that she and Ondo were some fifty million kilometres farther out of the system. Still, the annihilation was total. Once again, miraculously, structures had survived, but the planet was utterly lifeless.

Neither of them speaking, they returned to their arrival point and took the third archway.

This time it was clear they were on a world much nearer the star. There was nothing of the planet left: the archway and the fragment of rock it stood upon tumbled alone through the void. A cloud of other fragments was smeared across local space, scraps of rock and ice that might, in time, coalesce to form a new world. The supernova had blasted the planet to pieces.

Selene finally spoke. "There is no one here. No golden age civilisation, no miraculous weapon. The trail has led us to a dead end."

Something in the spectrography of the dead star was engrossing Ondo. "Are you sure of that?" he asked.

"Of course I'm sure. *Look* at this place. There's nothing here but death and destruction. Whoever we were supposed to find, they're long-gone."

Even then, there was a note of hope in Ondo's voice. "Which means, perhaps, that someone wanted us to see the death and destruction, understand what has happened and what might happen again. Someone is giving us this warning. The trail has led us to this point, but it does not end here, I know it. See: this supernova has been engineered; from what I can calculate of the original star's mass, it shouldn't have exploded for a billion years. Someone *did* this."

"You can't know that. The corpse sun may have sucked in mass from a sister star."

"There's no sign of any second star, judging by the orbits of the surviving planets. They look too regular."

She looked at the readings, saw that he was probably right. Which meant that billions of lives across at least three planets, a significant interplanetary culture, had been wiped out in a single galactic moment. A sickening trickle of dread wormed through her. It was another technosignature of a highly-advanced stellar engineering capability: the Depository in Dead Space, its star altered to create an impossible blue dwarf. Now this. Was it possible *Morn* was a weapon for obliterating worlds? For annihilating entire star systems?

"You think Concordance did this?" she said. The horror of it was too large to fully grasp. So many lives ended, so much love and achievement and hope snuffed out. Did they know what was coming at the end, all those people?

"I don't think so," said Ondo. "This has to be an older atrocity. I think we are seeing another echo of events predating Vulpis."

"Which shows us your idea of a golden age of peace and civilisation centred on Coronade is completely wrong after all. The galaxy *was* riven by war and horror, before

Concordance arose to impose their order upon it."

Ondo shook his head, troubled. "The age of this; once again, I'm not sure it fits. I think this has to be much older. If I could make proper observations, study them from the Refuge, I'd be able to arrive at a more accurate date."

"Whatever the truth of it, we're trapped here," said Selene. "We've proven your theories, but we'll still run out of oxygen in a few hours and die. There's no way out."

"I don't believe it," said Ondo. "We were meant to travel here. Someone will come, I know it."

"Who? There's no one here. There can be no one here."

"Someone," said Ondo. "I'm sure of it."

"You're saying that without any evidence. You're saying you just *believe*, Ondo."

"I'm saying the trail is real, and that it wouldn't just stop. Someone will come."

She didn't respond. All she could think about, suddenly, were the Cathedral ships, one within each inhabited solar system. Perhaps she and Ondo *had* been brought here for a moment of realisation.

"Maybe this is their plan." she spoke quietly. "You were always puzzled by the Cathedral ships' fascination with the suns in their systems. Don't you see? They aren't watching the planets; they're studying the stars. Altering the stars. One ship in each system, ready to trigger stellar collapse when the moment comes. *This* is Godel's catastrophism, this is their design. This is what they found at the heart of the galaxy, the means to do this. The rest of it – suppressing superluminal travel, imposing their own history, the shrouds – they're keeping the galaxy in line while they prepare for the ultimate act of destruction."

Ondo opened his mouth, about to reply, but then didn't. He knew she was right. They were safe from Concordance for the moment, they'd walked the path, but they were out of weapons, without a ship, hundreds of light-years from the Refuge or any hope of rescue. The need to act was greater than ever, but suddenly there was nothing they could do.

A familiar rage coiled within Selene, raising its head: the need to strike out. But for the moment, she had nothing to strike with, and no one to strike at. She let out a cry of frustration. Somehow, she didn't know how, but somehow, she'd continue the fight. If the trail had led them nowhere, then she would force a path of her own. Ondo placed a hand upon her shoulder but didn't speak.

She sank to the ground, leaning back against the archway. A few stars were visible through the glow of the nova cloud. How many of those suns had a Cathedral ship in attendance? Were Concordance already acting, putting their plans for their galactic Final Day into effect? Perhaps people were already dying in their teeming trillions. The stars might be winking out of existence, the flare of their countless supernovae taking their years to reach her point in space. The end of days might already be unfolding around her, while Concordance and their divine Omn laughed in their madness.

She stared at the stars, and the stars, unblinking, stared back at her.

Selene's journey continues in *Red Star* and concludes in *God Star*.

The return of an ancient galactic threat

Selene and Ondo piece together the secrets of Concordance's ascension to galactic domination, and the truth of what it was Vulpis encountered at the heart of the galaxy three hundred years previously.

They uncover an ancient threat to all life – a threat that Concordance seems intent on reawakening to complete its genocidal aims. But they also follow another trail – one left for them by someone or something unknown, a hidden intelligence seemingly guiding them to hopes of a possible salvation.

But each time they unearth a new fragment of the puzzle, Concordance are waiting, its ships and miraculous technology unleashed against them…

The darkness at the heart of the galaxy

Following the clues given them by the Aetheral, the *Radiant Dragon* and Toruk, Selene and Ondo close in on the existential threat to galactic life unleashed by Vulpis.

They battle Concordance all the way, aided by unlikely allies and mysterious messages. The trail leads them to more artefacts left behind by the Tok, drawing them ever-closer to the secrets at the heart of the galaxy.

But what they find there, and the truth they uncover about galactic history, changes everything…

ABOUT THE AUTHOR

Simon Kewin was born on the misty Isle of Man but now lives deep in the English countryside. He writes fantasy, science fiction and some things that can't make their minds up. He is the author of over 100 published short stories as well as a growing number of novels.

To find out about his other books, go to:

www.simonkewin.co.uk

Sign up for his newsletter and you'll be the first to know when he has new books out. There are some fine sci/fi and fantasy books to download for free as thanks.

www.ingramcontent.com/pod-product-compliance
Lightning Source LLC
Chambersburg PA
CBHW061312190726

48288CB00002B/464